Warm, his mouth was warm in the coolness of the night, its touch exquisitely gentle, and yet the contact sent a tremor leaping along her nerves that she acknowledged in the deepest reaches of her body.

Desire flooded in upon her, swirling in her veins, heating her skin, settling with aching vulnerability in the lower part of her body. She spread her hand over René's back and was bemused by the ripple of the muscles under the skin and the scorch of his lips in the valley between her breasts.

Oh, he knew the curves and hollows of a woman's body, knew the careful and patient attention required to set them aflame. Powerless in the grasp of ecstasy, she could not deny the turbulent pressure building inside her, the urgent need that hovered, waiting. . . .

LOUISIANA DAWN

Jennifer Blake

FAWCETT GOLD MEDAL • NEW YORK

A Fawcett Gold Medal Book
Published by Ballantine Books
Copyright © 1987 by Patricia Maxwell

All rights reserved under International and Pan-American Copyright Conventions. Published in the United States by Ballantine Books, a division of Random House, Inc., New York, and simultaneously in Canada by Random House of Canada Limited, Toronto.

Library of Congress Catalog Card Number: 86-92112

ISBN 0-449-14820-3

Manufactured in the United States of America

First Trade Edition: October 1987
First Mass Market Edition: March 1993

I

THE MISSISSIPPI RIVER flowed wide and deep, rippling gently with its current, reflecting the pale light of the quarter moon with a dancing silver sheen. The water gurgled around the edges of the flatboat that rode high on its flood. It tugged at the heavy craft so that it strained against its mooring ropes, nudging the levee with a slow and regular rhythm. The motion lulled Cyrene Marie Estelle Nolté where she sat on a low stool with her back to the unpeeled logs of the flatboat's cabin. She yawned and settled deeper into the quilt she had wrapped around her against the damp chill of the night.

A low laugh sounded from somewhere on her right. The moonlight caught a faint golden gleam from the thick braid trailing over her shoulder as she turned her head. A quick grin tilted one corner of her mouth. Gaston was at it again. What a satyr he was becoming, forever chasing after women. Not that the one he was talking to there in the tree shadows minded being caught, for the right price. The question was, Did Gaston have the fee? Livres were not particularly plentiful just now.

It appeared that he had struck a bargain of some kind; he was leading his light-o'-love toward the rear of the pothouse where the woman had her accommodations, just down the muddy track beyond the levee. It was not unknown, of course, for Gaston to trade on ready compliments, his engaging smile, and the promise in his brawny shoulders to win a woman's favors. He was a charming rascal.

But he would be lucky indeed if he was able to charm his way out of the trouble he would be in if his father and his uncle were to catch him away from his post. It was Gaston's turn as her guard, and Pierre and Jean Breton did not brook dereliction or excuses. Not that the two older men were so far away themselves, any more than they ever were. They had gone to the pothouse for a drink or two and a few hands of faro.

From the flatboat, which was riding on the flood behind the embankment of the levee as if it were on a high road, Cyrene could just see the pothouse with the track of the river road like a pale ribbon before it. The bulk of the building was dark except for the stray gleams around the shuttered windows and the occasional long yellow shaft that was flung into the darkness as the door opened and closed with the coming and going of customers. Beyond it, through the trees to the left, the rooftops of New Orleans made a jumbled pattern of moonlit and shadowed squares and angles. To the right and behind the pothouse lay the swamp, a dark, far-reaching stretch of uncleared land with trees so big that it took four men to reach around them, strange and too-luxuriant plants, green-scummed water, and a singing silence in which lived vicious insects and slithering creatures.

The night was black, the hour late. Cyrene was alone, a fact she realized with dawning amazement. She was not afraid, any more than she feared the river or the swampland beyond. What she felt was sudden joy. Alone. She took a deep breath and let it out slowly, savoring the rare experience. She was alone.

It was not that Cyrene didn't appreciate the reasons for the close watch kept over her; she knew well enough the dangers of the riverfront, especially for an unattached female. Still, there were times when the constant surveillance kept on her made her want to do something desperate, to slip away and go sauntering through the streets in her lowest-cut bodice, to take the pirogue tied to the flatboat and paddle away down the river—anything to gain some sense of freedom. How long had it been since she had felt truly free, when she had been without one of the Bretons at her elbow? It must have been years. The best part of three years.

They had done their best, Pierre and Jean Breton and Jean's son Gaston. It had not been easy, having a young woman thrown among them. No one had thought, when the Bretons had taken Cyrene and her parents in after they had stumbled off the vessel from France shaking with ship's fever, that it would be so long. But first her mother had died of the illness, then her father had sought to lose his sorrow and shame for their exile because of his debts in drink and gambling. There never seemed to be enough money for other lodgings, or else the time was never right to shift their place of abode. Her father's evening hours were spent staggering from one gambling den to another with friends, if such they could be called; friends who were as indigent as he and as full of wild schemes for easy riches and a glorious return to France. His daylight hours were devoted to sleeping off the excesses of the night before.

Cyrene had seen little of him, hardly more than she had as a child in France when her days had been spent in the company of her nursemaid and governess. It mattered little; she and her father had never been close. She had hardly mourned at all when he had disappeared one night nearly a month before. It was assumed that he had missed his step and fallen overboard on his return to the flatboat, since his friends had seen him winding that way. His body had not been recovered, though that was not unusual. Few men were found once they vanished beneath the rippling surface of the river. The Mississippi had a habit of keeping its dead.

Cyrene had remained with the Bretons. She earned her way by helping with the cooking and laundry and by keeping the account books in which the trading transactions of the two brothers were set down. The latter was something she was good at, something she enjoyed nearly as much as the trading itself: the give and take of bargaining, the challenge of turning a profit. Her father had said that she had a bourgeois soul like her grandfather, her mother's father who had been a respected and wealthy merchant from Le Havre. She could not deny it.

Life on the river suited her also. She liked dressing as she pleased: going without a coif, or cap; wearing her hair braided down the back of her head; and rolling the sleeves of her chemise to her elbows like an Indian woman or a peasant. She loved the smell and the movement and the ever-changing face of the great waterway. She did not think she could sleep, now, without the rocking of the flatboat to lull her. Nor could she envision living without the convenience of a constant source of water flowing past the doorway, water that did not have to be drawn laboriously from a well, water that swiftly bore away even the worst accumulation of slop and garbage.

Cyrene allowed her gaze to drift over the river and along the levee toward the wide crescent bend that swept around the town. She stiffened, sitting erect. There was movement in that direction, in the shadows just beyond the pothouse. Two men were emerging from the trees. Though indistinct in the pale moonlight and distance, they appeared to be carrying a cumbersome burden. Portions of it flopped and dragged as they struggled up the slope of the levee. There could be little doubt that it was the body of a man, and even less of what the two men meant to do with it.

Cyrene got to her feet, shrugging the quilt from her shoulders so that it crumpled to the stool. She flung her long braid back over her shoulder and, with her hands on her hips, stepped to the front of the flatboat. The night wind caught the fullness of her rough skirt, flapping it about her bare ankles, and molded the sleeves of her chemise to her arms. She ignored the chill, narrowing her eyes as she stared into the glimmering darkness.

The pair wrestled the dead man over the top of the levee, slipping in the mud, then gave the body a slow swing back and forth. At the top of the final swing, they heaved. The

body arched out over the water, turning slowly. There was a
glint of silver, then it struck the surface with a great splash.
Water rose in a sparkling fountain, cascading, faintly splattering, closing over the long, lean shape. There was a quiet
moment, then the body rose, gently bobbing to the top as it
began to move downstream toward the flatboat. The two men
swung away from the river, then strode away, leaping back
down the levee in the direction from which they had come.

Cyrene did not hesitate. Her face alight with purpose, she
whirled and ran toward the pirogue at the flatboat's stern.
The flash of silver she had caught meant one of two things.
It had come either from a piece of jewelry or else from silver
lace, the ornamental braiding on a man's coat, probably a
gentleman's *justaucorps*. It was unusual in the extreme for a
body to be disposed of without having had the valuables and
clothing removed. She did not actually hope for jewels, but
she would be glad of the coat. Garments of any kind were
costly since they had to be imported from France—there was
a royal edict against spinning and weaving in the colonies of
New France and Louisiane—but anything with gold or silver
lace was dear indeed. A man's coat with such decoration was
worth well above a hundred livres even secondhand.

It would not be Cyrene's first experience with a "floater,"
as the bodies disposed of in the river were called. Pierre and
Jean Breton, as well as being traders, were good *voyageurs*
bred and trained in New France, which was located far to
the north. They hated waste and dearly loved to get something for nothing. They were forever pulling things from the
river, from logs and broken crates for use as firewood to kegs
of sour wine and wads of tangled rope. There had been at
least five bodies in the past three years that they had hauled
aboard the flatboat to strip, throwing Cyrene the clothing to
launder and also to mend where violence had been done to
it in dispatching the victim. But even they had never retrieved
a coat with silver lace.

Cyrene kept her eye on the floating body as she stepped
into the pirogue and pushed away from the flatboat. Taking

up the paddle that lay in the bottom, she pulled toward the long dark shape on the shining river's surface. The current was faster than she had thought it would be in its winter flood stage; the body was racing down toward her, rolling slightly in the swift current.

She dug in her paddle, sending the pirogue shooting forward to intercept that black form. Wavelets slapped against the sides of the small craft made from a hollowed-out tree trunk. It wallowed in the water with every dip of her strong young arms. Her paddle rose and fell, flinging a handful of water droplets forward like glittering jewels with every stroke, though the entry of the paddle into the water's surface made scarcely a sound.

The body was upon her. She dropped the paddle into the bottom of the boat and leaned forward, going to her knees. She stretched, reaching, straining. Her fingertips touched cloth, fine brocade. She grasped, pulled. The body shifted toward her. She saw the limp, wet spread of hair in the water. She released her uncertain grasp of the coat and sank her fingers into the thick strands, dragging the waterlogged shape of the dead man. He was surprisingly heavy; he must have been tall and broad or else his pockets were weighted with gold.

The body turned slowly. The pale angles and hollows of a face appeared. An arm came up with the fingers of the hand spread, reaching. It flailed toward the pirogue, striking the side, clutching, grasping.

The floater was alive!

Cyrene made a strangled, gasping sound. She released her hold, pulling her hand back. The man gave a soft groan. His head sank beneath the water. His fingers slipped from the rounded side of the pirogue.

Alive!

Cyrene dived forward once more, plunging her hand and arm into the river up to her shoulder. Her fingers touched hair. She twisted them into it, clenching tight as she surged back on her heels. Once more the pale, strained face, streaming with water, came into view. The arm floated in the water, without strength.

She could not let go of his hair or she might lose him under the water. She lacked the strength to haul him by main force into the pirogue, nor could she manage to paddle back to the flatboat with her one free hand, and her left one at that. For the first time she thought of Gaston and was incensed at his amorous tendencies. If he had been where he should, he would be out here in the pirogue instead of her. For him this rescue would have been simple.

But it was not, after all, so difficult. The line that had tied the pirogue to the flatboat was lying in the prow. She reached for it with her free hand and, leaning forward as far as possible, passed it around the man under his arms, then tied a slipknot near where the rope was fastened. The extra weight threatened to swamp the unstable craft; still, his face was more out of water than in it. With the man secured to the front of the pirogue like the war trophy of some ancient goddess, she paddled back toward the flatboat.

Gaston was still nowhere to be seen. Cyrene stepped from the pirogue as it glided alongside the bigger boat, then dropped at once to her knees to hold the smaller craft against the logs of the flatboat's deck. She reached to loosen the slipknot of the rope securing the man, making a grab for his cravat as he began to slip away. She made the pirogue fast by the simple expedient of wrapping the rope around the small post set in the deck for that purpose, then towed the man toward her until he was against the log decking.

He was going to be too heavy for her to lift on board; she knew that well enough, though for the moment the water buoyed his weight. The flatboat rose and fell with a gentle motion as she considered the problem. She thought of calling out for Gaston but had no faith in her ability to make him hear her, even if he would spare her the attention to recognize her need of him. There was only one thing to be done, though it would likely cause the man she had rescued a few bruises and aggravate whatever injuries he might have. He certainly could not stay where he was. His skin was already icy from the cold water, and she herself was beginning to shiver in spite of her exertions.

Cyrene grasped one of the man's arms, bringing it out of the water, then, releasing his cravat, took hold of the other, drawing both up and resting them on the big log of the flatboat's side. Holding on to one hand, she got to her feet, then took his wrists in a firm hold. Once, twice, she pressed him down into the river to his chin, testing his weight and her own strength, feeling the surge of the water thrusting him upward again. Then she caught a hard breath, set her teeth, and pulled with all her might.

The flatboat dipped. The man came out of the water to his armpits. Swiftly she bent and grasped him there, pulling with her muscles, heaving herself backward with straining arms and deep, panting breaths.

He was caught on something, a button or perhaps the bulge of a timepiece in his pocket. She made another tremendous effort. He was dragged forward over the end log. Again. He slid upward as slowly, grudgingly the river gave him up. She had him. His chest was free of the water. Quickly, before he could slide back again, she went to her knees once more and reached for one of his legs, dragging his knee up and onto the boat. Now it was easier. She stood, took his hands, and hauled backward. Her bare feet slipped on the logs made slippery by their splashing and his dripping clothes. She stumbled and fell.

The man was more on the deck than not. Cyrene let go and lay back. Her chest rose and fell with the rocking of the flatboat as she tried to catch her breath. She stared up at the stars swinging crazily above her. They danced, then slowed. Stopped. At last the boat was steady once more.

The man's head was between her legs, one of his hands resting at the juncture of her thighs. She rolled, scrambling out from under him, and cursed under her breath, using phrases she hardly knew the meaning of but had heard the Breton brothers use. They helped to relieve her feelings. She had not bargained for this much labor, especially when there was little hope now of a reward since a live man would require his coat. Nor was there any way of knowing if the man was worth her effort.

It was irritation that gave her the strength to drag him, bumping, across the logs and into the flatboat's small cabin. Leaving him in the middle of the floor, she moved to strike tinder and to light a tallow dip in an earthenware bowl. She stepped outside for the quilt she had abandoned earlier; then, inside once more, she added to it a length of linen toweling and a handful of clean rags. Dropping these things to the floor near the man she had rescued, she went down on her knees beside him.

Her hands were on his coat, tugging it open, when she looked at his face. Her movements stilled. A frown creased her brow. Reaching to catch his chin, she turned his head so that he faced the light. She drew in her breath.

René Lemonnier, the Sieur de Vouvray.

The community of New Orleans was a small one. There were fewer than two thousand people in and around the town, with half that number being soldiers of the king or African slaves. Everyone knew everyone else and most of their business. Any newcomer was an object of much curiosity and more speculation.

The attention paid to the man on the floor since his arrival a month before had been even greater than usual. A gentleman of noble family, he had been a favorite at the court of Louis XV, though with a far-reaching repute as a wastrel, gambler, and noted rake. The gossips would have it that he had somehow displeased the king's *maîtresse en titre*, La Pompadour. The result had been a *lettre de cachet* issued in his name. He had disappeared into the Bastille, Paris's prison for political prisoners, but there had been such a constant vigil of women, such wailing before the gate, that he had been deported instead to keep the peace.

His reception had not been that of a man in disgrace. Handsome of countenance, dark as a pirate, with the shoul-

ders of a swordsman and the grace of a courtier, he had found
favor with the Marquise de Vaudreuil-Cavagnal, wife of the
governor of the colony of Louisiane. Consequently, he had
been much fêted at the Government House in recent days.
The *bon mots* he had let fall from his lips had been repeated
everywhere. Boys had followed him as he swaggered along
the streets, and the young men of the town had taken to
wearing their wigs powdered and curled in the fashion he
preferred and their garters tied with the knots that he affected.

None of which mattered now.

The man was bleeding.

Cyrene was brought to a sense of what she should be doing
by the sight of red-tinged water trickling out of his hair. She
explored his scalp, gently pushing her fingers through the
wet and matted thickness of the dark waves that grew in such
luxuriance over it. He had a great knot above his ear. The
skin was broken, seeping blood, but the skull underneath
seemed undamaged. Still, his face was gray and there was a
white line around his mouth.

With more haste than care, she stripped off his coat, pausing for only a brief and regretful moment to touch the silver
braiding on the lapels before laying it aside. It made a dull,
clinking sound as she dropped it. The cause was quickly
found. It was a monogrammed leather purse filled with coins
as well as a large turnip watch in a chased gold case. That
Lemonnier had not been robbed was amazing, unbelievable.
She puzzled over it as she unbuttoned his waistcoat and
slipped it down first one arm and then the other, casting it
aside before dragging his shirt off over his head.

But either he had made enemies since his arrival in the
colony or else had strayed into the wrong lady's bedroom,
for he had been stabbed. The wound was ugly, the result of
a vicious blow. The blade had been inferior, however, for it
had broken off as it struck a rib and was still embedded in
the bone. The slash was oblique, a ragged tear that extended
from the back to the side, as if the assailant had stabbed from

behind just as Lemonnier turned to grapple with him. The court rake had been extremely lucky or else had the agility of a Parisian alley cat, for by all rights he should have been dead.

Cyrene made a pad of one of the rags. She shifted Lemonnier, pulling him toward her onto his side. With the pad in her hand, she grasped the broken and protruding upper half of the knife blade, settled her grip, then pulled. Lemonnier jerked convulsively and a sigh left his lips. Blood welled around the blade, but it remained stubbornly encased in the rib bone that held it. She reached for another of the rags, holding it firmly around the knife blade to staunch the flow. Pressing down hard, she pulled once more.

The knife came free. Cyrene rocked back on her feet, which were tucked under her, with the suddenness of it. She did not stop but went sprawling, twisting to the side, as Lemonnier wrenched himself up on one elbow and launched himself at her. Her breath left her in a rush as his weight pinned her to the rough planking. A hard hand caught her wrist, grinding the bones so that the reddened blade fell from her numb fingers and clanged onto the floor. Before she could cry out, before she could protest, the hard edge of a forearm was across her throat, cutting off her air and sending bright flashes of pain exploding behind her eyes.

"An assassin of uncommon beauty," Lemonnier said, his voice tight, his breathing too controlled, as if it had to be measured against the pain it caused. "Would you care to try again?"

Cyrene stared up at him with disbelief skittering across her mind. He had been unconscious, she knew it. How was it that he could, on the instant, be so lucid, so dangerous? The last was there in his face beyond mistaking, shining in the icy gray of his eyes, showing plainly in the hard set of his cleanly molded lips. It left her cold, wary, and furious.

"I wish," she said, her voice hoarse yet virulent in her constricted throat, "that I had let you drown."

Surprise registered in René's mind as he recognized the

anger that thickened her voice and burned in the heated color of her face, saw the pure indignation that set sparks of fire gleaming in the rich golden brown of her eyes. A peculiar fog seemed to fade from his mind, and he realized that he was not only half naked but wet to the skin. Water dripped from his hair, wetting the thin material of the chemise that the girl under him wore. It created a quite interesting effect on the mound of her breast, one he was in no condition to appreciate properly. And there was the hot glide of what he suspected was his own blood circling his rib cage, soaking into the waist of his breeches.

The clarity in his brain lasted no more than an instant. The fog began to spread, bringing with it desperate and confounding weakness. He lifted his arm from the girl's throat as best he could. His head was so heavy. He allowed it to droop until it rested on the wet yet soft and warm pillow of her breast. He closed his eyes. His tone calm yet immensely tired, he said, "I seem to have made a mistake. I tender you . . . my most abject . . ."

He did not finish, though Cyrene thought she felt his lips move against her in his apology. She was still a moment, floundering in a confusing morass of pity and rage, admiration, frustration, contempt, and something more that had to do with the sheer male force she had sensed inside this man during the brief instant he had held her at his mercy.

But there was warm blood seeping into her skirt where he had fallen against her. With an exclamation of mingled distress and disgust, she flung him from her. She found her folded pads once more and slapped them over his wound, holding them with firm pressure as she looked around for the linen toweling to tie them in place.

The flatboat rocked, a sure signal that someone had come aboard. Cyrene paused with an unaccountable surge of fear in her chest as a shadow fell across the deck outside the doorway. The thought of the two men who had tried to kill Lemonnier flitted across her mind.

A man stepped inside, then stopped and let fall a sharp curse.

"Gaston," she cried, "and about time, too."

"What in the name of all the saints have you been doing? A bit of butchering?"

The youngest of the Bretons came forward, a square-built youth of no more than medium height, with tightly curling brown hair tied back at the nape to show the gold hoop earring that he wore in his left ear only—the recoil of a musket when it was fired being likely to tear any such ornament out of a man's right ear. There was a copper cast to his skin, evidence of his Indian mother, and his eyes were fiercely blue. In the gaze he bent upon her, there was a hint of censure but also an irrepressible teasing glint.

"I was fishing for a coat," Cyrene said shortly before nodding at the pad under her hand. "Come and hold this while I tie the bandage."

"You went out on the river for him? Are you mad?"

"The coat had silver lace."

"Oh."

It was explanation enough. Gaston stepped toward her and went down on his knees to help. His tone was resigned as he spoke. "Papa and Uncle Pierre will have my skin in little strips."

"Serve you right for chasing after that skirt."

"You are a woman with no heart. You have not the least idea how a man feels when he sees a beautiful and willing female."

"Beautiful, huh?" Cyrene gave him a skeptical glance as she worked.

"Well, she was beautiful to me, at least until—"

"I don't want to hear it!"

"But, *chère*, I was only going to say until I saw her in the light!"

"Certainly you were. Move your hand."

He complied. "I would not sully your pure ears with the details of what transpired between me and this woman. Not only would it be no fun, since you no longer blush at such subjects as you used to, but it would be unmanly. Besides, Uncle Pierre would skin me like a squirrel if he should hear.''

''True,'' she said pointedly. ''Will you now leave off talking of your amours and look at this man?''

Gaston swung to do her bidding. His breath left him in an astonished grunt. ''*Sacré!* It's Lemonnier.''

''Precisely. Do you think that Madame la Marquise will give us a reward if we send to tell her he is saved?''

The younger Breton grinned. ''She very well might, though I'm not sure Lemonnier will thank you. They say he's avoided her invitations to a *tête-à-tête* with some success so far.''

The governor's wife was a woman with an eye for younger men. Her husband, the marquis, was himself fifteen years her junior. Their marriage seemed to be one based on mutual respect, mutual avarice, and mutual ambition. It was the goal of the couple to obtain for the marquis the governorship of New France, a post that had been held by his father. The colony was also the place where the marquis had been born. There were whispers that the office was his. He was an able administrator with a sound knowledge of the shifts required to govern a far colony inhabited by savages, an ill-assorted collection of displaced French subjects, and a set of *voyageurs* and *coureurs des bois* who had been in the wilderness so long they had taken on its wildness. But the appointment was not yet official, nor would it be until a man could be found to replace him in Louisiane. In the meantime, Madame was swift to reach out for what riches and comforts she could discover in the colony.

The thought of René Lemonnier with Madame de Vaudreuil was distasteful. Cyrene pushed it from her mind. Her tone sharp, she said, ''Hand me the quilt, and let's get it around him. Then you may remove his wet breeches.''

''Remove his—Cyrene!''

Gaston's expression of shock was, she saw, real, at least

in part. "Well, he can't stay in them, can he? He'll never get warm!"

"If Papa and Uncle Pierre come back and find you not only with a notorious womanizer like Lemonnier, but a naked womanizer—"

"He's half dead! Besides, he'll be decently covered."

"It won't matter. They'll kill me."

"In that case, you may as well help me get him into my room."

Gaston's tone of resignation abruptly left him. "Your room? Never!"

"He can't lie in the middle of the cabin floor forever. It's the only place where he'll be out of the way."

The room she called her own was little more than a lean-to the size of an armoire built onto the side of the flatboat. It held her sleeping hammock, which was slung from wall to wall, and in one corner the trunk containing her clothes. The other corner was stacked high with animal traps and cages and a few extra trading blankets and rolled furs, along with various other debris of questionable usefulness from which the Bretons could not be parted.

Gaston protested and grumbled and composed epitaphs for himself both comical and profane, but he could find no alternative to her suggestion. At last, he helped her make a pallet of a buffalo fur, blankets, and a bearskin coverlet on the floor under her hammock and shift Lemonnier onto it. Only when he had covered the unconscious man with the bearskin did he strip off Lemonnier's breeches and fling them at Cyrene.

They were of heavy brocade, like his coat. She stood, turning the garment right side out, smoothing the rich cloth with absent care as she stared down at Lemonnier. "I should have made him drink some brandy while he was awake."

"Why didn't you?" Gaston said in mock accusation, then gave a shout of laughter when she told him.

"It wasn't funny!"

"Poor little Cyrene, caught in the arms of the master of

rakes, and what takes place? Nothing. It isn't fair." His blue eyes danced with amusement that was only slightly lascivious, while the hoop swinging in his ear gleamed gold in the candlelight.

"Out," Cyrene said between her teeth.

"Where's your sense of humor?"

"Out!" She flailed at him with the breeches, following as he backed away into the main room and warded her off with his hands.

Then came the noise of a man clearing his throat that was half growl, half command for silence. Gaston and Cyrene swung to face Pierre Breton, who stood in the cabin doorway surveying the spilled blood and the ragged, bloodstained cloths scattered over the wet floor. "You will tell me, please," the older man drawled with mildness that was belied by the hard light in his eyes, "just what is going on here?"

2

I T WAS CYRENE WHO explained, for Gaston, as always when faced by his uncle, was not only bereft of his facile charm but very nearly his power of speech, too. Jean Breton, Gaston's father, walked in during the recital. When Cyrene was done, the two men looked at each other in a moment of steady and oddly significant communion.

The two men were alike and yet different. They both had eyes the clear blue color of the summer sky; both had the same rough-hewn features and brawny shoulders developed over years of paddling boats of every size and kind along the winding rivers from their birthplace in New France to the gulf. Their clothing, too, was similar, consisting of simple shirts of muslin tucked into loose woolen pantaloons reaching below the knees and Indian moccasins without stockings. But there the resemblance ended.

Pierre was the taller of the two, with a barrel chest, dark brown hair streaked with gray, and deep lines of past grief cut into his face. Jean was more blond than not and his hair curled in profusion over his head. His eyes often danced with merriment, and he was prone to wearing neckerchiefs brightened with huge polka dots in yellow and red that were paired with shirts striped in brilliant hues, and to covering his head with a knit toque that boasted a dangling tassel. Less serious than his older brother, he loved to dance and could sometimes be persuaded to play the concertina.

Regardless, the two men stood shoulder to shoulder against the world. To injure one was to injure both, to gain the friendship of either was to acquire a second ally. They were peaceable and law-abiding, so long as the laws were just, but had little respect for petty regulations. And they were always and without question fair.

"Let us see this gentleman," Pierre said when Cyrene was finished.

He picked up the tallow dip and, his steps heavy, walked to the cubicle Cyrene called her own. Holding the light high, he drew aside the drab curtain that was the sole concession to her privacy and looked down at the unconscious man. Cyrene moved in behind him, as did the others. There was a furtive movement at her side, and she turned to see Jean Breton cross himself as he stared at the long form on the pallet. She frowned in puzzlement at the expression, almost like some superstitious fear, that she saw mirrored on his face. Gaston's father, catching her glance, summoned a smile and a shrug before looking away from her.

"It's René Lemonnier, yes," Pierre said. Once more he exchanged a long look with his brother.

"Did you think it would not be?" There was something here that Cyrene did not understand. Suspicion made her tone sharp.

The older Breton turned away, his face stolid. "It was possible. But tell me, how does it come about that he is on the boat? Why was he not carried to the bank, and from there to his lodgings where he belongs?"

"It might have taken forever to find help, and he needed tending at once."

"But you had Gaston to do those things. Isn't this so?"

Gaston made a gasping noise, like a landed fish. Cyrene, with a quelling glance at the younger man, countered with a question. "Do you not want Lemonnier on the boat?"

"I want no man here, as you well know, especially not a roué like this man."

"He's hardly in any condition to be a threat!"

"They are always a threat, his kind, even in their graves. Now, Gaston, you helped Cyrene, yes? You let her bring this man aboard the boat?"

Gaston was incapable of lying; it was one of his most endearing traits. He might stretch the truth about the attributes of some women, of course, but it was not the same thing. In any case, it almost seemed that to him all women were indeed beautiful.

The young man hung his curly head. "I wasn't here all the time, Uncle Pierre."

"Ah."

"I was gone only the smallest half hour, no more! How could I know Lemonnier would be thrown into the river?"

"You would have seen, if you had been on guard."

There was in the quiet words the portent of a sentence. There would be punishment. Cyrene's patience snapped. "What does it matter? The man is here, and he is badly wounded! We have to do something; send for a doctor or at least let someone know what has happened to him."

"She's right," Jean said, watching his brother. "It would be wrong to let him die."

"I fear so," Pierre said with a sigh. "Gaston, the doctor."

The doctor, a man of doubtful competence and a strong addiction to brandy—but the only one who could be persuaded by the crown to take on what amounted to a post in exile—came finally at good daylight. He removed the bandaging Cyrene had applied and replaced it with more that was not a great deal different. He looked at the patient's eyeballs and tongue, announced that he was being invaded by a fever, bled him copiously, and went away.

He was right about the fever. It climbed steadily through the day. Cyrene wiped her patient's face and upper body with cool wet cloths to keep it at bay. His stillness and lack of response troubled her, and though she went about her usual chores of cooking and washing and scrubbing, she was drawn back to kneel beside his pallet again and again.

It was a strange thing, but she could not think of René

Lemonnier as a rake and a scoundrel as he lay there. There was such strength in his face, in the square shape of his jaw and the jut of his chin. The width of his forehead hinted at superior intelligence. His mouth was firm and marked by a half-moon-shaped line on one side, as if he found much to amuse him, but there was nothing of the sensualist about the generous curves. Nor was his body that of a man given to self-indulgence. His shoulders and chest were swathed in muscle and his abdomen was flat and iron-hard, without an ounce of fat.

She combed his hair when it was dry, hoping that it would make him look less drawn. It was not as difficult as she expected, for it was cut short, the better to fit under the gentleman's wig that he must wear as a habit—no doubt the same wig that had saved his skull from cracking, though he must have lost it when he fell or as he was thrown into the water. That he covered his hair was a pity, for it waved back from his face in a most entrancing fashion, the shining blue-black softness clinging to her fingers as she pushed it into place.

The Breton men did not leave the flatboat that day, but stayed close, mending traps, weaving nets, whittling out pegs and other useful bits and pieces. Gaston was subdued. What had been meted out to him for his dereliction of duty, no one said, but he had been taken out onto the levee by the two older men the night before and now moved with some stiffness and leaned back in his chair only with great care.

The doctor came again at dusk, entering with much more bustle than before. He had taken it upon himself, he said, to inform the governor and his lady of the whereabouts of M'sieur Lemonnier and had been instructed most particularly to use every skill at his command to make him well.

"I'm sure you meant to do that, anyway," Cyrene said, standing over the man as he knelt and began to take his bleeding bowl and scalpel from his bag.

"But yes, of course. Still, one would not wish to fail the governor."

"What about M'sieur Lemonnier?"

"Pardon?"

"He would be much more concerned at your failure."

"Yes, yes. Now, if you would kindly step outside?"

"Why?" She could not bring herself to leave Lemonnier to the doctor's mercy. She eyed the rust-stained blade of the scalpel he held and felt an odd frisson run through her, as if she must feel the bite of the blade in her own flesh.

"You are pale, mademoiselle. The sight of blood is objectionable to many, and I would prefer not to be forced to revive you."

"It isn't the blood, it's your scalpel," she answered. "Are you certain another bleeding is necessary? He has lost so much blood already."

The doctor, a small man with a bagwig of enormous size on his small head, drew himself up. "Are you questioning my treatment, mademoiselle?"

Cyrene held her ground. "If need be."

The doctor turned and cast his implements back into his bag. "I will not stand for this. Either you will depart, mademoiselle, or I shall."

Cyrene glanced into the other room, but the Breton men were bent over their tasks as if deaf to the conflict. She would receive no help from them. The man on the pallet was her responsibility. She turned back to the doctor and crossed her arms over her chest. "You will do as you must, as will I."

"Very well. Upon your head be it. I depart." The doctor picked up his bag and strode out, his shoulders back and his nose elevated. A moment later, the flatboat dipped and rocked as he left it for the bank.

Cyrene stared down at Lemonnier with a sinking sensation in her chest. She had tended the Breton men in their rare illnesses, such as the malaria that sometimes struck Pierre or when one of them smashed a finger or overindulged in wine, but she had no idea what to do for a more serious case. She had a few herbs she had bought from the Choctaw Indian women who came to market, though she had no great faith in their efficacy. René Lemonnier was a strong man and, barring festering in his wounds, would doubtless recover with or without her. Still, it was frightening to think that his life was in her hands.

The cubicle was growing dim with the advance of evening and also cooler. Cyrene knelt beside the pallet, drawing the quilted coverlet up over her patient's arms. She was leaning over him to tuck it under his shoulder when he spoke.

"I am in your debt, mademoiselle. I was lying here trying to decide whether to slit the pompous little man's throat with his dirty blade or to just break his arm—and wondering if I had the strength for either."

She sat back on her heels hurriedly. "You're awake!"

"Something near it," he agreed without opening his eyes.

She collected herself with an effort. "You must not waste your strength talking. I have some good broth on the fire. Wait, and I'll get it."

The ghost of a smile flitted across his features. "I can do no less, and certainly no . . . more."

Of course he could not. How had she come to say something so silly? She ladled the broth into a wooden bowl, slopping half of it over the sides in her haste. She could not find a spoon or a clean dishcloth to use as a napkin, and when she turned toward the cubicle, she nearly tripped over the heap of woven netting beside Jean's stool.

"Steady," Jean said, the word shaded with warning as well as wry amusement.

Cyrene brought herself up short. What was the matter with her? Lemonnier was not going to expire if she did not get broth into him on the instant. It was a great thing that he was going to live but hardly something to overset her usual calm.

"He's awake," she said as prosaically as possible.

Jean opened his eyes wide. "Who?"

"You know who! Lemonnier." She sent him a scathing glance.

"I'd never have guessed."

She stepped past him without another word or so much as a glance at the others, though she could feel their gazes upon her as she ducked around the curtain and into the small cubicle once more.

René lay with his head turned toward the doorway. He watched as she put down the bowl and took up a bolster to thrust under his head and shoulders for support. When she ladled a spoonful of steaming liquid and extended it toward him, he looked at it, then at her, and opened his mouth.

He had not been spoon-fed since he was a child of five abed with the measles. It was a strange sensation, but not disagreeable. He felt he should protest but could not find the energy. There was something about the woman who tipped broth into him with such ease that troubled him. She wore no coif, the cap that usually covered a woman's hair during the day, a sign of loose morals. Though she now had a striped bodice on over her chemise, he seemed to remember her without one, seemed to remember also the rose-peach gleam of a nipple through the cloth. She was with him here in this cubicle alone, while he was as naked under the covers as the day he was born, as if it was something she did every day of her life. She must, then, be some manner of harlot.

And yet there was not the slightest trace of paint on the smooth oval of her face, and her skin had the glow of health that spoke of wholesome food and drink and long, uninterrupted nights of sleep. Her gaze as she met his was without coquetry, and in her brisk, no-nonsense air there was more than a little reminder of a nursing sister of charity.

There was nothing of the nun about her, however. There was instead a little something of a Botticelli angel in her features and in the golden tendrils that escaped from her braided hair to lie against her cheeks. Or if not the master's angels, then his depiction of *Primavera*, the feminine essence of spring. René paused in his thoughts, startled. He was not usually given to such maudlin fancies. He must be more drained of blood than he had thought. Regardless, he was fully conscious enough to realize that this woman at his side was unusual.

The females of the Louisiane colony were sometimes dif-

ficult to place. Most kept to accepted behavior, but there was
now and then one who ventured to be independent. It came
from their relative rarity; there were not enough of their sex
to supply the demand, which tended to place a high value
upon those available. Since men would condone anything in
order to appease their desires, propriety was pushed to the
limit. It would be best to tread warily.

He waited until the broth was gone and she was preparing
to rise. His voice quiet, tentative, he said, "Who are you?"

Cyrene was well aware of his scrutiny and of the heat of
the flush rising to her cheeks. She gave him her full name,
then reached to blot a drop of broth from his chest before
meeting his gaze.

He stared at her for long moments, his expression blank.
At last he lowered his lashes and a soft sound escaped him
that might have been a laugh or a sigh. "Mademoiselle Nolté,
of course," he whispered. "Who else?"

For forty-eight hours, the wound in René Lemmonier's
back seeped blood and fluid, and for that length of time it
seemed dangerous to move him. On the third day, Cyrene
began to wonder if he would not be more comfortable in his
own lodgings than on the hard pallet beneath her hammock.
Certainly it would be more convenient for her if he were to
go; she could have her quarters to herself once more instead
of having to be so careful not to wake him when she went to
bed or when she dressed herself in the morning.

It could not be said that he was much trouble. The fever
made him inclined to sleep; he woke only to eat the rich
meat stews and bouillabaisse she cooked for them all. Gaston
bathed him and attended to his more private needs as further
penance for being absent from his post. And yet the man's
very presence put them all under constraint. There was no
word spoken that he could not hear if he cared to listen and,
since Pierre insisted that the curtain to the cubicle remain
draped to one side, few actions that he could not observe.

Cyrene was not surprised when on the morning of the fourth day Pierre called her out onto the levee.

"How long is this man going to stay with us? Is there no one else who can care for him, no place he can go to?"

In the bright winter sunlight, there were lines she had not noticed before on his weatherbeaten face. There was also in the blue depths of his eyes the shadow of the old pain that she had seen before but never quite dared to question. "I don't know, M'sieur Pierre," she said, giving him the courtesy name he had suggested when she first came. "I could ask."

He puffed on the reed stem of the pipe he held in his hand. "I don't begrudge him his place, but there must be an end to it."

"So many of the men who come to the colony have no one to help them when they are sick."

"That's what the hospital of the Ursuline nuns is for."

There was a note both dogged and hard in his voice that made Cyrene search his face. "What is it you are afraid of? Do you think whoever tried to kill him will track him here?"

"I think he needs to be among his own kind, and away from you, *chère*."

The term of affection coupled with that same stringent warning was convincing. Cyrene wrinkled her nose at him. "You are mad on that subject."

"With good reason."

"None that I can see!"

"Look in the mirror."

She shook her head with a smile. "Poor M'sieur Pierre! What a fate, to be saddled with the worry of someone else's chick like a cuckoo in your nest."

His eyes darkened, and he reached to put his hands on her shoulders. "You're no cuckoo. Who said such a thing? Gaston?"

"No one needed to say it; I feel it."

"Don't. To look after you is my pleasure. I promised your mother."

So he had. Her mother, ill not only with ship's fever but with the disgrace of her husband's exile, had died in Pierre's arms while her father was out getting uproariously drunk to celebrate their safe arrival in the colony.

Cyrene had never quite understood how it had come about that her father had been shipped out to Louisiane, but she did know that it was only the influence of her mother's family that had prevented him from going to debtors' prison. She remembered well the quarrel over whether she and her mother would accompany her father to the New World. Cyrene's grandfather, a merchant who had made his fortune in the fur trade in New France and retreated with it in middle age back to Le Havre, had wanted his daughter to abandon her husband, to let him go alone. The hardships of that rough land had killed his wife, he had said; he could not bear to think of his daughter returning to its dangers when he had thought her safe from them at last in France. Cyrene's mother would not be moved, nor would she let her husband go into exile without her support. She had made her choice years before, she had said, and would not repudiate it now. It had been a costly decision. They had all been disowned.

Cyrene looked at the man who had been more of a father to her for the past three years than her own had ever been. "You must let me make my own way some time."

"There is no way for you to do that here."

"I know, there are only whores, wives, and nuns in the colony. I am unsuited, so you say, to be the first or last, but you won't let a man near me so that I may become a wife."

"There is no man worthy enough to come near."

It was a familiar argument. She sighed and turned her head away without answering. She could run away from the Bretons at any time; they had no real hold on her except that of obligation and, perhaps, affection. But what else was there? She might take up with some officer, become his mistress; there were a number of women who held such positions in the town. No, even if such a course were not so distasteful to her personally, she could not. The Bretons would be so disappointed in her, would feel they had failed her. She could not do that to them when they were the only family she had.

"Especially unworthy is this Lemonnier," Pierre continued, his voice hard.

Cyrene gave a tired shrug. "Since I doubt he would even look at me, you have no worry."

"Oh, he will look. But no more than that, if there is breath in my body."

"You're impossible!"

"I know men as you do not, *petite*. Now go and ask Lemonnier when he leaves us."

René was awake when Cyrene returned to the cabin. Seeing him lying propped on the bolster, watching the door as she entered, she wondered if he could have heard her exchange with Pierre. It did not seem likely; still, she was uncomfortable under his gaze. She searched her mind for some way of bringing up the subject she had been instructed to broach, but nothing came. Moving to the cook table, she took up her task, which Pierre had interrupted, of crumbling bread for a bread pudding.

"How are you feeling?" she asked over her shoulder when the knowledge that her patient was watching her became too uncomfortable to bear in silence.

"Better. I have been trying to think. I seem to remember— was it you who pulled me from the river?"

His voice was quiet but strong enough, the words perfectly lucid. It was the first time he had spoken beyond simple and necessary requests. He was truly mending. A smile of triumph and gladness curved her lips, and she sent him a quick look before she answered. "Dragged might be a better word."

"I would have said you couldn't do it. You aren't a large woman."

"I'm stronger than I look, but I'm afraid you may have a few extra bruises."

"What of it, compared to what you did for me? The only thing I find unusual is how sore the top of my head is, almost more so than the hole in my back." He reached up to run his fingers through his hair, grimacing.

Cyrene paused. Her tone compressed, she said, "My fault, also, I'm afraid. It wasn't easy to find a handhold on you."

The puzzlement vanished from his face. "Forget I complained, then, if you please. It's been some time since I owed so much to another. It's difficult for me to find the words to thank you."

She was embarrassed, though why it should be so she did not know. She affected a careless air as she threw the breadcrumbs into a pan and reached for a handful of eggs from a bowl, cracking them into the pan one by one. "You need not let it trouble you. I did it for your coat, you know."

"For my coat?" His expression was completely blank.

"I saw the silver lace. I have no use for such things, but in exchange for a coat with such decoration I could have gotten cloth for three new shirts—one each for Pierre and Jean and Gaston—plus a Sunday bodice for myself, and maybe even a pair of real shoes."

A slow smile gathered in his eyes, edging their gray with silver like the sun behind a cloud. He gave a soft, amazed laugh as he repeated, "For my coat."

"I thought you were dead, you see."

"Yes, I think I do. I value the service you performed somewhat higher, I assure you, but the coat is yours."

She looked up, her eyes wide. "Oh, I couldn't take it now."

"Why not?"

"It wouldn't be right."

"I give it to you, a gift of gratitude, along with anything else you fancy that might have been on me. Though it would be nice if I could retain my breeches."

He was teasing her. She bent to her task once more, pursing her lips. "I suppose I could leave you that much."

"There is one condition."

She looked up again. "Yes?"

"You must not tell anyone why you came to my rescue. The blow to my consequence would be too great."

It was easy to see why he was such a favorite with the ladies. It was not only that he was tall and handsome, with a caressing note in his deep voice that seemed to reach far down inside a woman. Nor was it just his manner—though that was so compelling while he was lying with a hole in his side, wearing a shirt and breeches much wrinkled from where she had tried to wash away the bloodstains, and covered by a moth-eaten bearskin that it must be devastating when he was upright and hale and clothed in brocade and fine linen. His smile was warm, his concentration alarmingly intent, and there was in his eyes a glint of appreciation that could easily go to a female's head, but there was more still. He had the ultimate grace: the ability to laugh at himself.

Cyrene looked around at the crude flatboat cabin, at the rough log walls pierced by a single shuttered window; at the fireplace of mud plaster; at the beams of the open roof hung with smoked hams, strings of garlic bulbs, onions, peppers, and bunches of dried herbs; at the hooks for the sleeping hammocks preferred by the Bretons that were the result of a past brush with sailing ships. It was a temporary home, rescued by Pierre and Jean after it had served to bring a load of hogs and cattle downriver from the Illinois country. It was also the home of rootless men, men who did not care to be tied to the land with its back-breaking labor. She wondered what Lemonnier, who must be familiar with beautifully appointed townhouses and châteaux, must think of it. Not that it mattered, of course.

Cyrene wiped her fingertips free of egg on the apron at her waist and tilted her head to one side. "I can't promise not to tell," she said.

"Now, why?"

"It isn't to my advantage."

Wariness moved over his features and then was gone. "I begin to fear for mine."

"So you should. Only think how many bodices I can buy if I become a charge upon you for my silence?"

He stared at her, and his mood of bonhomie was slowly replaced by cold implacability. It was incredible, that transformation. Cyrene, watching it, felt the rise of anger. His sense of humor was not as broad as she had supposed. She lifted a small pitcher of wild honey and dumped half its contents into the pan of eggs and bread before her, then thumped it back down on the table before she spoke.

"You needn't look as if you mean to guard your purse. It was only a jest; I would not stoop to blackmail."

He lay staring at her. "What is there to keep you from it?"

"You have heard of principles, I suppose."

"The principles," he said with deliberation, "of a woman who serves as doxy to three men?"

She picked up the pan of bread and eggs and honey, drawing it back to throw. Just in time she remembered that he was an injured man. She set the pan down again and, taking a deep breath, gave him her sweetest smile. "Four."

"Four?"

"I have also been serving you."

"You're no doxy of mine!"

"Or any other man!" she snapped, hard on his words.

There was an interlude during which the only sound was the pouring of milk into the pan and the vicious beat of Cyrene's spoon stirring the ingredients of her pudding into mush.

"I apologize," René said.

He had not meant to speak of her circumstances. It was just that they had been exercising his mind in his brief moments of consciousness for what seemed like a long time, and so were in the forefront of his thoughts. His constitution, inherited from his soldier forebears, was not as weak as he pretended, nor had he always been asleep when his eyes were closed. He knew more about the situation around him than was suspected, more, in fact, than he understood. But he must not jeopardize what he had so unexpectedly gained by inconvenient curiosity. That would be more than foolhardy: it would be stupid.

Cyrene did not look at him. "Apologize? Well you may."

"I am not used to women who wear their hair uncovered or leave their arms exposed."

"Indeed? I have always thought that a man must be a perfect fool to be thrown into a fit of passion by the sight of a hank of hair or an elbow."

"Perhaps so. In any case, I beg your pardon abjectly. I have no right to question how you live, or with whom. Forgive me."

It was too smooth, that request for pardon; she would swear there was no sincerity in it. But there was an opening for the task M'sieur Pierre had set her.

"Since you disapprove of our arrangement here, you must be anxious to leave us. I will ask M'sieur Pierre to see about a litter to take you back to your quarters."

"I beg you won't trouble yourself. I can walk the distance if you wish to be rid of me."

"It isn't a question of—"

"I have offended you. That was not my intention, but it's understandable that you should be annoyed. I will, of course, remove myself from your presence." He raised himself onto his elbows as if he meant to rise.

"Stay where you are!" Cyrene came around the end of the table, then hesitated, confused by her own distress at the successfulness of her ploy.

"No, I insist." René pushed himself higher, then clamped an arm around his ribs, allowing a grimace of pain to cross his face. "I would not trespass upon your hospitality any longer."

Remorse assailed Cyrene. She went quickly to him and dropped to one knee, pressing him back down on the pallet. "You will injure yourself again, that's what you will do. Don't be so foolishly proud. Of course, you are welcome."

He lay back, gazing up at her, though he still held his ribs. "Are you certain?"

"Naturally, I'm certain."

"I am forgiven?"

"Yes, yes! Don't be ridiculous."

How had she come to be urging this man to stay when she should be waving him out the door? A vague uneasiness touched Cyrene, but she dismissed it. M'sieur Pierre would have to understand that it had been impossible to send away a man so ill. There was nothing Lemonnier could want from them, no reason for him to linger. And no reason at all to think that she had seen satisfaction flicker like lightning across his face.

She went back to her pudding, dusting the top with cinnamon, placing the pan in an open kettle filled a quarter full with water, swinging the kettle on its hook over the coals on the fire bricks lining the chimney that took up one side of the cabin. With that done, she poured a cup of water for René and carried it to him.

While he drank, she drew up a three-legged stool to the curtained doorway. Her voice abrupt, she asked, "Is there no one who will be concerned about you if you don't return? No servant brought with you from France, no—no companion?"

"No one." He paused a moment, glancing at the crude leather footwear on her neat and narrow feet. "Do you really have no shoes?"

"Only the moccasins made by Jean's Choctaw wife, and sabots, of course." The last were the wooden shoes of French peasants, worn in the mud and the wet.

"His wife?"

She nodded. "She lives with her people. She says New Orleans is too noisy and the fires with the big pipes in the rooftops don't give off enough smoke to keep away the mosquitoes. The truth is . . ."

"Yes?" he said when she did not continue.

"I was going to say, the truth is, she likes variety in men."

"And Jean, he doesn't mind?"

"He prefers variety in women."

"Then everything is all right."

"Yes, except—except it doesn't seem much of a way to live."

"There are a great many marriages in France that are exactly the same."

"Does that make it right?"

"It makes it human."

"As opposed to being inhuman, savage, in fact?"

He looked at her, his eyes dark. "You are so—"

"What?" she asked in constricted tones.

He could not tell her, for she would not understand. He was not sure he did himself. She looked like an angel, talked like a courtesan, and used the logic of a law clerk. She cooked, she cleaned, she handled a boat like a *voyageur* and could lift half again her own weight, yet she had the most gentle hands he had ever known. Moreover, if he closed his eyes and listened to nothing more than the clear cadences of her voice, he would swear he was hearing a princess of royal blood. She was an enigma, was Cyrene Nolté, one that intrigued him, even entranced him. And that would not do.

"You are so damnably reasonable," he answered in haste, "and right, of course."

Cyrene leaned her elbows on her knees and propped her chin in her hands. After a moment she said, "Is it true that you were at court?"

"Yes, for a time."

"Tell me about it."

"What do you want to know?"

"What was it like? What kind of man is the king? Is La Pompadour as beautiful as they say, and as cultured? Did you enjoy it?"

"Court is boring ceremony and decorum, but exciting for all that because there is the smell of power in every room. The king, like most monarchs, is totally self-centered, but he's a man of some ability, if he could be brought to use it.

La Pompadour is a lovely creature with exquisite taste in furniture and clothing, but poor judgment in men. As for enjoying being there, sometimes yes, sometimes no. It is not a place in which I would choose to spend all my life.''

The candor of his comments could be taken as a compliment or it could indicate how negligible he considered her. Cyrene frowned. ''This is treason, m'sieur, is it not? I thought one was obliged to be dazzled?''

''Treason is trafficking with the English, not scorning the glories of Versailles.''

''I thought we had been done with the English these four months, since this treaty of Aix-la-Chapelle everyone is discussing.''

''There may be peace in Europe, but not here.''

''Do you take time to consider what is happening in the colony? I had not expected it.''

He met her clear gaze, his own wry. ''I am not such a court fop that I don't know your problems here.''

''Apparently not, but I assure you there are many who have not the slightest idea or the least concern when they arrive.''

The major problem was the struggle for this vast new continent, though that struggle created a host of minor annoyances, such as constant warfare with the Indians. For years, the English, spreading westward from the Carolinas, had been arming and inciting the Chickasaws, portions of the Choctaw, and other minor southern tribes against the French. The French government, with great enthusiasm, retaliated in kind. During the previous autumn, the most famous of the Choctaw renegades in the pay of the English, Red Shoe, had been assassinated by his own tribesmen in an effort to settle the conflict. It had not helped.

There had been many casualties, most recently among the farmers of the German coast, the hard-working people of Aryan stock brought over by John Law, who kept New Orleans supplied with vegetables. New Orleans had also lost its dancing master, the much-lamented M'sieur Babi, in a skirmish with the savages. Still, the greatest effect of the difficulties was on trade.

Trading with the English was forbidden by letters patent of the king, and the practice was considered treason. On the other hand, due to the parsimony of the crown and the corruption of the French supply system, the goods sent to the colony were not only inferior to English goods but less than adequate in amount as well. There were times when the French in Louisiane would have been naked and starving without the traffic with the English. In addition, the Indians had learned discrimination. They preferred the red and blue limbourg cloth and the iron pots and clasp knives of the British, though French faïence wares and brandy found greater favor.

But if English goods were what the Indians wanted, then English goods they must have, for the furs harvested by the savages were far and away the most valuable commodity in the colony. The Indian allies of the French were sworn to kill any English traders who came among them, but the only thing that kept a wily French trader from passing out English goods was the difficulty in getting to English ships, ships prevented from ascending the Mississippi River. Louisiane indigo was far superior to that raised anywhere else in the world and was in great demand in England. If he could reach the English ships, a man could barter a few casks of the precious blue powder for goods that, when exchanged for pelts, could establish the base for a fortune or supply a family for a year. Such Frenchmen called themselves traders. A more accurate name for them would be smugglers. The Bretons were of that independent and intrepid breed.

Trading with the English under the circumstances was, of course, treason. The attempts to stop it were zealous, primarily because the post commandants usually enjoyed exclusive trading concessions for their areas, concessions obtained through favoritism or graft paid to the governor or his lady. But the soldiers sent to do the job were usually so undisciplined or incompetent that eluding them was hardly sport.

Born and bred in the New World, living most of their lives in the wilderness, the Bretons could take advantage of knowledge and skills undreamed of by the raw recruits, things they had taught Cyrene as a matter of survival when she went with them on their ventures.

"I am enough of the fop, however," René said, recapturing her attention, "to wish for my razor and a change of clothes, if there should be someone who might go to my lodging to fetch them. Or, failing that, I could send a note to Madame Vaudreuil asking that she arrange it."

"There should be no difficulty. I can do it myself."

There was a tread behind her. Gaston, striding into the cabin carrying a basket of fresh-cleaned fish, set it on the cook table. His voice was tight and his gaze shifted between the two of them as he said, "Do what?"

Cyrene repeated Lemonnier's civil request. Knowing she would not be allowed to walk into the city alone, she added, "You will go with me, won't you, Gaston?"

"Don't be an idiot. You can't go."

"Not alone, but there should be nothing wrong if you went with me."

"Nothing wrong? You want to visit the quarters of the most notorious libertine in Paris, stay long enough to bundle up his personal belongings, then walk out with them in your arms, and you see nothing wrong?"

"He won't be there!" Cyrene exclaimed, rising to her feet in her irritation. "And I can hardly be contaminated by carrying his clothes."

"That's exactly what you will be. A virginal girl has no business handling a man's personal belongings."

"I wash your breeches all the time!"

"That's different!"

"Explain to me how."

"Papa and Uncle Pierre are chaperons."

"I need a chaperon to wash your breeches?"

"You know what I mean!" Gaston shouted, his face hot under René Lemonnier's interested and ironic gaze.

"Yes, I know," Cyrene said, her eyes flashing. "Sometimes I think it would be better if I weren't virginal! Then maybe I wouldn't be treated like a prisoner."

"Cyrene!"

"Is that so shocking? How would you like it if your every move was watched from morning till night? If you could not come and go without permission and a guard?"

"We are concerned for you, for your safety."

"I don't doubt that, but it comes at a hard price."

"It can't be helped, except by a husband."

"What, another jailer? I'm not sure that's a solution."

"Then you must put up with it."

"Must I?"

Gaston gave her a grin that was not without sympathy. "In the meantime, I'll fetch the things required."

Cyrene nodded, but in her mind there beat a simple and daring refrain. *Must I, indeed?*

3

FROM THE TIME she was ten until her parents had left France, Cyrene had attended the convent of the Ursulines at Quimperle, an institution that dated back to 1652. There she had studied French, history, and the rudiments of science including sums; practical labors, such as the correct methods of cleaning, baking, preserving food, and gardening; and the social arts of music, dancing, and drawing. She had traveled to and from the convent with her mother, her grandfather, who was paying her expenses, and her governess. While she was there, she had been under the supervision not only of the nuns but also of her governess, who had stayed to look after her room and her toilette and to accompany her on excursions and holiday visits to her home.

There had never, in fact, been a time that Cyrene could remember when she had been entirely on her own, entirely unsupervised.

At the convent there had been girls who were envious of her for having her governess with her, a familiar companion, someone to see to her needs. But even then Cyrene had chafed at the restriction, at the constant admonitions that did not cease even in her bedchamber. She had been told that she was being readied for the time when she would have social position and the responsibility of managing her own household. There was mention of the dowry her grandfather would provide and the man of excellent family and fortune she would surely marry. She must learn deportment and a woman's proper place in order to enjoy such benefits.

The result had been a stubborn sort of rebellion. She had joined a group of girls who had delighted in taking risks, such as stealing plums and apples from the convent orchard, passing notes to the village boys over the walls, or flirting demurely with the virile gentleman who came to teach them drawing. The discipline when the misdemeanors were discovered was stern; the older nuns deplored such habits in the strongest of terms. However, there had been one young nun, Sister Delores, who had understood the urge behind them; Cyrene still wrote to her from time to time. The reckless feeling of those days had never quite left her, though the chance of a fine dowry and a brilliant marriage had come to nothing when she and her parents had left France.

Cyrene did not bewail her lost prospects. There was a time when she would have welcomed a husband chosen for her, if he had been young and not bad-looking and respectably placed. This was no longer true. As she had told Gaston, a husband represented nothing more to her now than another restraint. She sometimes thought of balls and routs and masquerade parties, but since she had never tasted these pleasures, she was able to relinquish them without much distress. Her greatest wish was for freedom, the freedom to get on with her life, to get out and make a place for herself. She could do that, she knew, by trading.

She was no stranger to the occupation. Pierre had never considered her father a reliable chaperon, and so had always taken her with him on his trading expeditions. After the second trip, she had assumed an active part, often helping to choose the goods for which the men bartered and keeping an accounting of values and quantities so that the Bretons would not be cheated. Pierre and Jean had a voluminous knowledge of furs and prices and could do complicated sums in their heads, but in common with many men raised in the wilds of New France, they could read little and write less. In token of their respect for her knowledge and her services with her pen, Pierre had the year before given Cyrene a few pounds of indigo, which she had traded to the English for glass beads, combs, polished steel mirrors, and small iron pots. She had then traded these things to the Indian women in the Choctaw villages for worked leather garments, woven baskets, and a few small furs. Finally, she had then bartered the Indian goods in the market in town for a tidy profit, enough to buy twice as much indigo as Pierre had given her.

Her activities had not gone unnoticed. Pierre's and Jean's friends among the smuggling fraternity, those with whom they drank and gambled at the pothouse down the road, laughed and teased the two men, swearing that they were led by a lady smuggler. Pierre and Jean merely smiled and shrugged and jingled the extra coins, which she had helped them acquire, in their purses.

But she had been handicapped in her business venture by the necessity of having one of the Bretons always at her shoulder while she bargained, whether it was in the English camp, the Indian villages, or the town. The Indian women in particular had thought it marvelously funny, asking what valuable commodity she had hidden about her or what crime she had committed that she must be so closely held. Cyrene had failed to see the humor. Nor did she see it now.

What she did see was a way to make the protection given her unnecessary. Gaston had provided the key. Virginal, that was what he had called her. In the end, what they were all protecting, or so it seemed, was her virginity. If she were no longer chaste, no longer untouched, there would be no need for such worry. How very simple it was.

Ridding herself of her inconvenient chastity could be difficult. If no man was allowed near her because she was a virgin, then it was also true that she must remain a virgin because no man was allowed near her.

The exception was the Bretons themselves. There was nothing to say that any one of them would allow themselves to be seduced, but she dismissed the thought almost before it occurred. Even if the two brothers had not been so much older, there was still something unnatural about it, most likely because she had been living with them for so long. Gaston might be of a convenient age, but she had squabbled and worked and played with him until he was more like a brother than a prospective lover.

The ideal prospect, of course, would be René Lemonnier. There were many reasons why that should be so—his age, his repute as a rake, his proximity—but unfortunately it was not possible. Even if she could find a way to be left alone with him for sufficient time, he was simply in no physical condition for the task.

Which was just as well. Despite the feeling of control over her life such an idea gave her, and regardless of the peculiar warmth that invaded her senses at the thought of petitioning Lemonnier for such a favor, she knew well enough that she would never dare. The solution might be practical, but it was just too drastic. There must be some other way to gain a measure of independence.

The idea could not be dismissed completely, however. It remained at the back of Cyrene's mind, a secret amusement, for the rest of the day. It surfaced when she happened to glance at her small room and the man who lay there, and when the Breton brothers left Gaston on guard while they went into town for a few hours. It was also in the forefront of her mind as she made ready for bed.

Ordinarily she would have heated water and bathed in the privacy of her cubicle. That being impossible since Lemonnier had gained consciousness, she made do with a few quick splashes on the darkened deck using water dipped up from the river. Returning to the cabin, she warmed herself before the dying fire while the Bretons hung their hammocks and unrolled their bedding. When Pierre dumped out his pipe, a sure sign that he was ready to go to bed, she moved to her sleeping quarters.

René Lemonnier lay watching her in the fireglow as she stepped inside and dropped the curtain. She sent him a quick look as she took the much-worn chemise that served as her nightgown from its hook. It was dim in the small space, but still she could see the faint gleam of his eyes.

"I must ask you to turn your head," she said, the words shaded with amusement as she considered the difference between her modest pose and the idea she had contemplated earlier.

"Certainly."

René complied. It seemed the wisest course, considering the closeness of her protectors just beyond the curtain. Watching her was a pleasure he was finding it increasingly difficult to forgo. She was conscious of him as a man, he knew; her request had proven it, if proof was needed. Still, there was none of the arch coquetry or nervous fluttering in her manner that his reputation usually elicited. The cause, he suspected, was simply that she was accustomed to men in a way that most young women never achieved. Or perhaps she did not perceive him as a threat while he lay flat on his back, dependent on her attentions. That he could be dismissed so easily piqued him, and also intrigued him.

Cyrene skimmed quickly out of her clothing and pulled the old chemise on over her head. Taking up her coverlet of buffalo fur lined with quilting, she wrapped herself in it, then stepped over Lemonnier to climb into her hammock and lie back.

Silence, broken only by the soft and steady lap of the river and the occasional creak of the mooring ropes, settled over the boat. Quiet snores began to issue from the cabin. At least two of the Bretons were asleep. Beneath her, Lemonnier shifted on his pallet.

"Are you all right?" she asked in a whisper. "Can I get you anything?"

It was sheer perversity that made René answer, his tone husky, provocative, "What manner of thing did you have in mind?"

"Another coverlet? Something to drink?"

He should have known better. "No, nothing. Thank you."

"I don't suppose you are used to the early nights that we keep?"

He thought of the many long evenings of yawning boredom he had spent waiting for the time when it would be the king's pleasure to leave an entertainment so that he might go also; of the endless round of balls and banquets where one saw the same vapid faces, heard the same inane complaints and scurrilous stories. "I have no objections."

"For the moment?"

"As you say."

Cyrene had forgotten to loop back the curtain before she got into her hammock. She had been doing that since Lemonnier came, though ordinarily she left it down for the illusion of privacy it gave. There was a strong sense of intimacy in whispering together, closed off in this tiny space. She was also aware of a secret stir of excitement along her veins, the result of doing something forbidden.

That it might also have something to do with the tentative part she had assigned René Lemonnier for securing her freedom she also knew. The strangeness of having him there on the floor beneath her had been with her from the first, but never before had it occurred to her that if she turned and reached down her hand she might touch him. She had never stopped to think that if he reached up he might trace the curving outline of her body through the canvas of her hammock. There was no point in thinking of it now, of course; still, the images conjured up in her mind had a curious fascination. It was difficult to be rid of them.

The carriage drew up in the road beyond the levee. A lackey in satin livery and a curled wig jumped down and hurried to open the door. A woman stepped down. No longer young, she wore her powdered hair swept well back from her forehead and covered by a small, lace-edged coif *à la Parisienne*. Her petticoats, or skirts, came to her ankles and were of green brocade. Over them she wore a shorter skirt that was open at the front and elaborately constructed of ruffles and poufs in gold brocade embroidered in green. The overskirt was topped by a bodice of the same material. Around her shoulders was a fichu of folded gauze held in place by a large emerald. Her ankles were covered by white silk stockings, and on her feet were green silk shoes with hourglass heels. Even if it had not been for the carriage—the first in the colony with four wheels and a conveyance that had caused every planter with any pretensions to gentility to write to Paris for something similar—the cut and extravagance of her clothing would have marked the woman as the governor's lady, the Marquise de Vaudreuil.

Cyrene, hastily searching out a clean apron and smoothing her braided hair, was on the front deck beside Pierre and Jean by the time the lackey handed Madame Vaudreuil across the gangplank that led to the flatboat. At a short order from his mistress, the lackey returned to the carriage. The lady turned to Pierre.

"You are, one supposes, M'sieur Breton?"

Pierre bowed in his best manner. "As you say, madame. And this is my brother Jean and my ward, Mademoiselle Nolté."

Cyrene, making her curtsy, could not prevent herself from sending Pierre a startled glance. There was more courtliness in his air than she had dreamed he could assume.

Madame Vaudreuil inclined her head in a gracious nod. "Charming. I believe it was you, mademoiselle, who intervened to protect the life of M'sieur Lemonnier. You have the gratitude of his friends."

"It was nothing. If you will step inside, I'm sure he will be happy to see you."

"How kind," the marquise murmured, though the dryness of her tone indicated that she had never intended anything else. She eyed Cyrene's uncovered hair with a lift of her brow as she swept past her into the cabin. Inside, the woman paused, and her brows rose higher at the spartan furnishings and the sight of René on his pallet.

What Cyrene had expected, she did not know; still, she

was puzzled at the look of annoyance she caught on Lemonnier's face as he watched the governor's lady advance. A moment later, she wondered if she had imagined it as he smiled and greeted his visitor with a sketchy pretense of a bow, raising himself on one elbow and begging to be excused for his inability to stand.

"René, *mon cher*, what a relief it is to see you well," the older woman declared. "I feared the worst when you sent word you would remain here."

The irritation returned, then was banished. He swept the black waves of his hair, free of any tie, back from his face. "I am devastated to have caused concern. Forgive me."

"Yes, indeed. Always, as you well know." Madame Vaudreuil looked around for a chair. When Cyrene pulled a stool forward, the woman seated herself upon it rather gingerly. It creaked under her weight. The marquise needed no bum roll of padding at the hips. She was decidedly plump, with dimples in her white hands and a second chin above her short neck. Her eyes were large and magnetic, but her mouth rather small, and it was pursed now with displeasure as she turned to look at Cyrene.

In compliance with the suggestive tilt of the other woman's head, Cyrene hurried into speech. "You will wish to speak to M'sieur Lemonnier alone, I'm sure, madame. Pray excuse us." Turning, she motioned to Pierre and Jean standing just inside the door to leave.

"Cyrene, wait," René called. "There is no need. It will please me if you stay."

She turned in surprise. It was the first time he had used her name instead of the more formal title of mademoiselle, the first time also that he had spoken to her with such rich warmth in his voice. She met his gaze, a question in her own. He appeared not to notice but waved in the direction of another stool.

"I begin to see what keeps you here," Madame Vaudreuil said.

"Do you?" René answered, his tone dulcet as he watched Cyrene.

"I should have known there was a woman involved. With you it could not be otherwise."

He looked at the older woman then. "How little you know me."

"Well enough!"

Cyrene, made intensely uncomfortable by the woman's implication as well as by René's odd behavior and hovering in uncertainty over whether to go with the Bretons or stay, roused herself to protest. "I assure you, he is here only because of his injuries."

"Oh, without doubt," the lady replied without a glance in Cyrene's direction. "Well, you rogue, we have missed you."

"You are too kind, but I would have been desolate to think otherwise."

"When do you return?"

"That depends on many things." His answer was glib, his expression bland.

"I am aware," Madame Vaudreuil said with another flickering glance in Cyrene's direction.

"I may decide to become a *voyageur*."

"Indeed?"

"I must do something now that I'm here in the colony."

"Surely your family—"

"No doubt, but living on a stipend has no appeal. Besides, I've never cared for idleness."

"There are few here who care for anything else. Why should you be different?"

"Perverse of me, isn't it? But I find in myself a desire to see more of this wilderness and what is happening in it, to seek out its possibilities."

Madame Vaudreuil sat in frowning silence for long moments. Finally she said, "I begin to see."

"And I have your blessing?"

"How can I withhold it? But you will be careful of yourself, for you are a valued addition to our company here."

"I'm always careful."

"That I beg leave to question! If you were, you would not be lying here on the floor at this moment."

"Unarguable," he admitted, his smile all rueful charm, "and cruel of you to remind me."

"I am never cruel, only candid. And I require the same from others."

He inclined his head. "You shall have it."

"I wonder." The governor's lady rose to her feet. "I must go. I have your portmanteau from your lodgings in the carriage, plus a few comforts, if you will accept them."

"With pleasure."

"Then I will hope to see you soon."

There were a few more words of farewell, a little more banter. The lackey delivered the portmanteau of clothing, also a basket of wine, cheese, and sweetmeats, and another filled with various comforts. Then at last the marquise was gone and the rattle of her carriage faded away back down the track into town.

Cyrene unpacked the baskets. She tossed René a fluffy down pillow, which he caught and tugged under his head. She then uncorked a bottle of wine and poured a few inches into a fine crystal wineglass that had been included in the basket. Her movements stiff, she carried the wine to him and set it on the floor beside his pallet.

"Won't you drink with me?" he asked.

"I wouldn't care for wine just now."

He picked up the glass and swirled the rich burgundy liquid, inhaling the bouquet as he watched her over the rim. "Are you angry with me?"

"I don't understand you enough to be angry."

"You are offended, then?"

She swung to face him. "Why did you do that? Why did you suggest that you are here because of me?"

"Can you deny that you are the cause?" The color across

her cheekbones was entrancing. To see if it would deepen was irresistible.

"I've seen nothing to suggest it."

Such self-possession was worthy of something nearer to the truth. He abandoned subterfuge. "You're right. It was an excuse the marquise would accept with little question, given my reprehensible past. Since I had no wish to be dragged into town and put up at the governor's house with the lady in constant attendance, I made use of you. If you were embarrassed, I'm sorry."

"It seems to me that your injuries should have been excuse enough not to move."

"They might have been, two days ago."

There was a silver flash of laughter in his eyes. Cyrene moved closer as he spoke, the better to see it. "You mean that you—you are recovered?"

"Not that, no, but I may be a little stronger than it appears." To illustrate his words, he set the wineglass aside and raised himself without discernible effort to sit braced on one arm with the other resting across his bent knee.

"Why?" she said abruptly. Because it seemed impolite to force him to look up at her, she dropped to one knee in front of him.

He shrugged. "A whim. Maybe I wanted to stay. Maybe I will be a *voyageur* after all."

A small smile curled her lips. "It isn't an easy life."

He matched her smile. "It could be I'm not an easy man."

She studied the hard, bronze planes of his face, the steady light in his gray eyes. At last she said, "It may well be that you aren't, at that."

"Now that is a concession." His voice soft, he reached with his free hand to take hers, carried it to his lips.

Behind them the cabin door crashed open. Pierre stood in the opening with Jean and Gaston behind him. "Madame Vaudreuil was right," he growled.

He charged across the cabin and lashed out with a hard kick. Cyrene cried out as the blow caught René on the shoul-

der, throwing him backward. His breath left him in a soft
sound of pain and surprise. The burly *voyageur*, with his
brother behind him, reached for the injured man. René
twisted out of the way, pulling himself to his feet by one
hand, which was tangled in the switching, swaying hammock. With his shoulders wedged into a back corner, he
crouched, waiting. Between his hands, stretched so tight that
the links sang, was a length of chain he had snatched up with
one of the animal traps dangling from it.

"Stop it! Stop it!" Cyrene's voice was high-pitched as she
threw herself at Pierre and Jean, dragging at them with handfuls of their shirts knotted in her fists, pushing in front of
them. They had stopped in midattack, their faces blank as
they saw René's defense. Relief flooded through Cyrene,
mounting to her head in a rush of blood. She felt hot with it,
and yet a shiver ran through her as she stepped to place herself between René Lemonnier and the two men.

She rounded on her would-be protectors. "What do you
think you're doing?"

"Teaching him manners, *petite*," Pierre said. "By Madame Vaudreuil's own admission, he has need of them."

"But what did she say?"

"That your smiles seemed the medicine he requires."

"And that's all?"

"It's enough."

"For murder? He may be bleeding again, even now."

Pierre Breton surveyed the man in the corner. "He seems
well enough to me."

So he did, though he had sunk to one knee and his face
was white. Cyrene said, "You would be served as you deserve if his recovery is half again as long."

It was plain the two men had not considered that possibility. Nor did they intend to consider it now. "A man who can
rise to fight, can rise to leave," Pierre said, his voice ringing
like struck iron.

"If he has opened the cut in his back again, he will need
at least another week of rest."

"Another day, *petite*, two at the most. No more."

She refused to acknowledge such an ultimatum. Swinging away from the older Breton in a whirl of petticoats, she gave her arm to René. He leaned on it hardly at all while the Breton men remained, but when they had gone—except for Gaston, who retreated no farther than a stool before the fire— he allowed her to seat him on the bearskin pallet, the better to see to his wounds.

She knelt in front of him, tugging his shirt from his breeches, gathering the folds in her hands as she lifted it upward. He raised his arms and she whipped it off over his head. As she freed his hands, she met his gaze. It was steady on her face, assessing, vital.

"I've been undressed by women before," he said, "but I've never had one defend and shield me."

Her hands were suddenly clumsy as she sought to turn the shirt right side out again. "A protective instinct only. I'm sorry it was necessary."

"I'm neither your chick nor child."

"You are injured."

"And that's enough?"

Golden fragments of light moved in her eyes and a corner of her mouth twitched. "I also have the promise of your coat."

"Yes," he said. "I was forgetting."

"I beg you won't. I depend on your word."

He was so very close. She could see the individual black hairs of his brows, like small curving wires, that made the strong, silken arches; the indentation of a faint scar above his eye; the chiseled molding of his mouth; and the dark sheen of his beard under the skin. The warmth of his body and the clean male scent of him crept in upon her senses. He was still and yet there was such strength in that stillness, such quiet confidence, that it was like an aura surrounding her.

He shifted to turn his back to her, waiting. It was difficult to force herself to touch him, to trace the wrapping of the bandaging around his chest, smoothing her fingers under the edges, testing for looseness caused by his violent movements. She leaned closer, delicately touching the thick pad that covered the jagged cut along his ribs.

She drew in her breath. The touch had caused a red stain on the cloth.

"Stupid idiots!" she exclaimed.

"Bleeding?" he asked over his shoulder.

"They might have killed you, had they got their hands on you!" She snatched up a cloth pad and untied the strip of bandaging to press it into place. "And for nothing. Nothing! They are mad, all three of them. They think every man who looks at me is going to take me by force unless they prevent it. They guard my chastity every waking minute as if it were purest gold. It's unbearable!"

"Your chastity." The words were tentative, as if he was uncertain of their meaning. They were also quiet, for Gaston was near and the voices of the brothers could be heard out on the levee.

She sent him a scathing look. "What did you think they were protecting? My favors?"

The idea had occurred to him, though it did not seem the time to say so. The only thing against it was the fact that she had been sleeping alone since he came.

"That's exactly what you thought, isn't it? I might have guessed as much from a man like you!"

"Like me?"

"Such a notorious libertine can hardly be expected to understand anything else."

The contempt in her tone stung. "You know nothing about it."

"I know enough. You are a man experienced in the ways of love and of women. To you it's all a game, a grand chase full of pretty gestures and clever stratagems, snatched kisses and daring caresses. But even such men as you have their uses. If you were not injured, and weak with it, I would let you teach—"

She stopped, aghast at what she had been about to say.

He swung his head to look at her over his shoulder, and the sudden tightness in his chest had nothing to do with the cloth wrapped around it. "You would what?"

Her wide gaze met his and fiery color swept upward to her hairline, burning in her cheeks. She bent her head to her task, though her fingers trembled. "Nothing."

"I don't think I can accept that."

"I . . . was annoyed and didn't stop to think. Let it pass."

"You were about to suggest some service I might perform for you, if I were able. Were you not?"

"No!" she cried, startled at his acuteness.

"I think you were. It would give me great satisfaction to repay you in some way for what you have done for me. Won't you tell me how I may do that?"

The bleeding was not dangerous; the pressure of the pad she had applied seemed to have stopped it. She tied the bandaging back again and tucked the ends under, then sat back, preparing to rise.

"There is no need for repayment," she said.

His fingers closed warm and firm over her wrist. "The need is mine. Tell me."

The timbre of his voice, low and seductive, seemed to vibrate somewhere deep inside her. The gray light in his eyes was hypnotic, compelling an answer. The firmness of his hold on her sent a flutter of apprehension edged with reluctant excitement along her veins. She wanted to confide in him, she discovered; it seemed important that she should.

She moistened her lips. "I only thought, that is, I am so confined, so endlessly guarded. I sometimes feel desperate to be free of it. It seems that there would be no need for such close watch if I were no longer . . . chaste."

To suspect her meaning was one thing, to hear it voiced quite another. For a long moment René could not breathe, could not think. The words compressed, he said finally, "Do you know what you're saying?"

"Very well. I also realize that it's not possible."

"An error. There is no obstacle, at least from my point of view."

Her heart fluttered in her chest. "You mean that you would be capable of it."

"It doesn't," he said softly, "require a great deal of strength."

She swallowed against the steel band that seemed to have become clamped about her throat. "I see."

"What it requires is desire and time and privacy, and also a certain resolve."

"But if there were those things, you would be willing?"

It was humiliating, this need to ask. Why had she not foreseen how it would be? The reason was because she had never really expected to broach the idea. She could withdraw it now, could say she had changed her mind. Something inside her refused to permit it. The need to know what he would do, what he would say, was too strong.

René watched her in hope and fear and with a faint edge of self-loathing. He could feel the swift and ragged throb of her pulse in the wrist he held, and the tumult of emotions it suggested disturbed him. It also excited him. To refuse this unexpected opportunity was unthinkable; it suited his needs too closely to be forgone, even if the prospect offered had not been tempting beyond belief. It would be the first time that he stood to gain some reward for the notoriety he had so laboriously attained. He was not so without compunction, however, that he could take advantage of his lovely benefactress without some attempt to bring her to a sense of what it might cost her.

"You are sure it's what you want?"

Irritation rose in her at the doubt she heard in his voice, especially since it mirrored what she felt. "Of course I'm not sure," she snapped. "What woman ever can be at a time like this? But the Bretons have gone too far. They can't attack every man who smiles at me. Something has to be done."

"So it would seem."

She forced conviction she did not feel into her voice. "I'm

not a simpering convent miss, ready to tease and run away; this is entirely different. But if you would rather have nothing to do with it, that is, of course, your privilege.''

He made a swift arresting gesture. ''I didn't say that.''

''If—if we should reach an agreement, there would be no obligation involved. I would require nothing more of you, I assure you. You need not fear I would hold you responsible for the consequences or attempt to constrain you in any way.''

''Would you not?'' The implication that she had no other use for him other than the one outlined gave him pause. Always before, it had been he who had made it plain that he would not be held by his actions. This reversal of roles might have been a blow to his ego if it had not been for the humor of it.

''This isn't funny,'' she said between her teeth as she saw the wry amusement rise in his eyes.

''No. No,'' he agreed, his voice rich with promise. ''It is altogether intriguing. I can't think when I have been so enthralled or so honored. I am, *chérie*, indisputably at your service. Use me as you will.''

It was a munificent offer; she was well aware of it, and not a little startled by the generosity. She stared at him, her eyes clouded with doubt. ''I . . . would not like to take advantage of your weakness.''

''I beg you to do so.''

''Nor would I like to think that I might hurt you.''

The gravity of his features was controlled by the hard, clamped muscles of his jaw. ''Be assured, I do not flinch from it.''

The timbre of her voice became softer, dropping even lower in tone. ''They say there is some pain for the woman.''

''There are also ways to make it less, and I will pledge myself to use them and to show you the way to joy.''

Inside the other room, Gaston stirred. ''What are you two whispering about?''

The intrusion of his call was a reminder. Cyrene lifted her

chin in sudden decision. "I will accept your pledge then, since I cannot think that I will ever be offered more."

René met her clear gaze with something like remorse lying deep in his gray eyes. All desire to laugh was gone. "It's little enough," he said, "less than you deserve. I would that it was more, indeed."

The problem that faced them was how to find a way to achieve their object in the time allowed. Two days. In two days René Lemonnier must be gone. It would be of no use to appeal to Pierre and Jean, to plead Lemonnier's desire to learn their trade, to become a *voyageur*, even if his mention of it was a true aim, something of which Cyrene was by no means certain. The Bretons' suspicions of him, uneasy from the start, had been brought to fever heat by the attentions they had seen. For the remainder of the day, there was always one or more of them moving in and out of the cabin, cleaning and oiling traps on the front deck or else congregating with their friends at the end of the gangplank.

Late in the afternoon, they also accepted delivery of twenty casks of indigo. The sight of the fat, blue-stained containers marked conspicuously with the word *flour* did much to explain the late hours the brothers had been keeping during the last week at the pothouse. They must have been meeting with the planter who had grown the crop, haggling over the price. Its value had increased of late. News had been received that there was to be a subsidy paid on the delivery of indigo to English ports, the purpose of which was to promote production of the dye in the English colony of Carolina. The result, however, would be to increase the value of that grown in Louisiane as well.

The reasons, or at least one of them, for the increased nervousness and irascibility of the Bretons that Cyrene had noticed in the past few days also became obvious. So long as Lemonnier remained with them, they could not plan the trading expedition the casks signaled, could not even speak of it, much less leave upon it. As a crowning irritation, due to Lemonnier's presence they were forced to smuggle the dye onto their own flatboat and conceal it under canvases.

The arrival of the indigo, on top of their distrust of Lemonnier, meant that when evening fell the brothers made no move toward the pothouse but instead lolled about the cabin, exchanging jokes and bits of news and gossip and getting in Cyrene's way as she stirred a dish of fish and shrimp and herbs in a brown sauce that would be served over the rice that steamed gently in its black iron pot.

When the meal was eaten and the men had brought their wooden bowls and spoons to her to be washed, Cyrene said to them, "Aren't you thirsty? I hear music, I think, from the pothouse."

"Water will suffice tonight, *chère*," Pierre answered.

Jean chuckled from where he lay on a bearskin before the fire, coaxing a tune from a concertina. "It always suffices when a man's pockets are empty."

She might have been able to send Gaston on some errand, but it was not possible to find excuses to be rid of all three without arousing suspicion. Cyrene, exchanging a glance with René Lemonnier where he lay propped on his elbow on his pallet, gave him a rueful smile and an infinitesimal shrug.

There would be no opportunity that night for her seduction. She did not know whether to be glad or sorry.

4

T HE FOLLOWING AFTERNOON, Cyrene walked into town to the market. Her reasons for going were many. She needed to replenish her supplies, yes, but she also felt on her mettle with her cooking now that René was able to appreciate her efforts. In addition, she needed to check the available foodstuffs and begin stocking up for the trading expedition the Bretons would make to the English. But more than these things, she needed to escape for an hour or so from the flatboat cabin.

She had hardly left it since she had fished René Lemonnier from the river and the confinement was becoming oppressive. That was not the main cause, however. Since her agreement with the rake, she had become self-conscious beyond belief around him. She could feel his gaze on her with every step she made; there was no way to avoid it in the small cabin. It might have been her overwrought imagination, but the look in his eyes seemed possessive, impatient, as if he were eager to claim her. Her movements under such surveillance had become increasingly clumsy as her usual smooth coordination deserted her. She was suddenly tongue-tied and stupid, with nothing to say. Moreover, since daybreak this morning she had developed a disconcerting tendency to flush when her eyes met his. She didn't like it. She didn't like it at all.

Gaston sauntered beside Cyrene, carrying her basket and

whistling between the small gap in his teeth. Their sabots made dull, slapping sounds in the mud of the track. The afternoon was overcast, with a cold wind that flipped the ends of Gaston's neckerchief and ruffled the edges of Cyrene's plain linen coif, which she had donned for the outing. The sound of the wind in the trees along the track they walked was like a weary sighing, while farther on the tree limbs were loaded with blackbirds that squawked and squabbled, dropping to the ground and rising back up again so that they looked like swirls of autumn leaves in glossy black. Overhead, a flight of ducks, too numerous to count, winged their way in a ragged vee. Watching from the forest's edge was a wildcat with a bobbed tail that hissed and fled at the approach of humans.

There was no danger in the cat so long as he was running away. Cyrene and Gaston hardly noticed it.

Cyrene glanced at the square young man beside her. "Do you ever think, Gaston, about leaving your father and your uncle, about going off on your own?"

He stopped whistling to give her an incredulous stare. "Why should I do that?"

"You're of age. You could be your own man, do what you wanted."

"I do what I want now."

That was certainly true. "But don't you ever think of building something for yourself, for your future?"

"You mean like a house?"

"A house, land, an estate."

"When I marry, maybe; I don't know. I like being a trader, living on the flatboat. Having land means you have to clear it and plant it and look after the crop, and that's hard work. Why do it when there are easier ways to make money?"

"Dangerous ways."

"You think planting isn't dangerous when there are storms and floods, snakes and wild beasts in the woods, not to mention Indian raids?" He lifted his shoulders, his tone taking on deliberate insouciance. "Just living is a danger. Our only choice is which chance we will take."

It was plain he did not feel her dissatisfaction, did not understand her discontent. Cyrene said no more on the subject but inquired instead about his latest conquest, a certain distraction.

New Orleans, built on the closest high ground to where the Mississippi River met the Gulf of Mexico, was carved out of the swamp and marsh well over a hundred miles distant from deep salt water. Occupying a narrow strip perhaps a league and a half long that followed a wide curve in the river, crowded at the rear by the dense forest, the town was growing again after years of stagnation and even decline. The cause was, in part, the influence of the brides sent out by the crown, but it was also the presence of the Marquis de Vaudreuil-Cavagnal, who made the colony seem less of a backwater, thereby arousing interest in investment.

The streets were laid out with military precision in blocks known as islets due to the ditches dug around them for drainage, each of which was bridged at the street crossings. The houses were constructed in different ways. Some were built of upright timbers covered by thatched roofs; others had rooftops of split cypress shingles covering walls made of crossed posts with *bousillage*, a plaster made of mud and deer hair, or the gray moss called Capuchin's beard, between them, or else with bricks in a construction technique known as *brique entre poteaux*, brick between posts. There were even a few dwellings, those of the more well-to-do, which had a lower floor of brick topped by an upper floor of planking. A few window glasses sparkled here and there, but most openings were covered by simple shutters, or with oiled paper or thinly scraped skins to admit light and keep out cold in winter and with loosely woven linen that let in the air but kept out most of the hordes of flies and mosquitoes, moths, and other flying insects in summer.

The heart of the town was the Place Royale, which was an open square that fronted on the river. On the back side of it, facing the water, was the Church of St. Louis, with the house of the Capuchin fathers on its left and the town prison and guardhouse on the right. On each side of the square was a row of soldiers' barracks. Not too far away was the Ursuline convent in a fine new building and a hospital operated for charity with funds provided by the estate of a sailor. To improve the flood problems of the town, always critical due to its low level, there was a moat outside the Palisade of the town which collected the runoff from the many drainage ditches, and the governor had issued strict regulations for extending and maintaining the levee.

Cyrene had no desire to live in the town, however. Compared to the flatboat, it was a place of incredible filth. The streets were seas of mud more often than not, making the blocks of houses islands, indeed, and when they were dry the gutters that cut down the middle of them were filled with garbage and the contents of the chamber pots emptied into them every morning. The sticky black mud that adhered to boots and shoes could not be kept from the lower floors of the houses; it made a solid layer that had to be removed with a spade. Dogs and cats, chickens and pigs wandered at will, scavenging in the gutters and fluttering and squawking out of doorways as they were waved away with brooms.

Along the riverfront, where the ships docked, there was the smell of spoiled grain, soured wine, and rancid salt beef and of rotting bananas off a ship just in from Saint-Domingue, as well as of the fresher odors of wood and pine tar and the tobacco and green myrtle wax for candles waiting in the king's warehouses to be shipped to France and the West Indies aboard the king's vessels, *La Pie* and *Le Parham*.

The riverfront was also where most of the taverns, cabarets, pothouses, and gambling dens were located. As a result, it was also where the soldiers who were off duty congregated, and where gathered the prostitutes, thieves, and vagabonds who preyed upon them. There, too, along the levee before the Place Royale, was where the market was held.

There was no formality about it. Sometimes a makeshift thatch shelter was erected to keep out the sun and rain, but when it blew down, as it generally did during the fall gales, there was no hurry to replace it. At this time of year, in midwinter, the farmers of the German coast brought their onions and cabbages and turnips to sell, while trappers supplied raccoons and squirrels, bear hides and rendered grease, and fishermen displayed their catches, from lake shrimp and fine fish to turtles for soup. Some good French housewives presented their extra chickens, geese, ducks, swans, and pigeons, and others offered baked goods for sale. There was a free woman of color who always sold confections made of boiled milk and sugar and chocolate or, when the last ingredient wasn't available, of the first two plus wild pecans. And often there were the chattering Choctaw Indian women with their baskets and worked leather goods and dried woodland plants for medicines and seasoning.

Vegetables were in scarce supply this winter due to the slave-stealing raids of the renegade Choctaw along the German coast below the city this past November. Due to the unrest, many of the Germans had abandoned their fields for a time, coming into town for the protection of the soldiers; others had deserted them entirely in order to start over on new, less isolated lands.

The Indian troubles were still quietly fomenting. It was not a good time to be going into the wilderness from the standpoint of safety; hardly a month passed without some tale reaching town of a hunting or trading party being attacked with loss of life. On the other hand, with things so unsettled, many traders were staying home, so the Indians would be eager for the goods brought to them. There were risks in any enterprise. They simply had to be weighed with care against the benefits.

So it was with the situation in which Cyrene found herself. She wanted to be free of the supervision of the Bretons. To achieve that goal, she must be intimate with René Lemonnier. If it was not possible to arrange matters to bring this about in solitude and privacy, then it must be done without. The inescapable conclusion then was that the necessary physical contact must be made in the flatboat cabin, while the Bretons slept. Not only was the time allowed by Pierre for René's recovery nearly gone, but her own strength of purpose was flagging; therefore the deed must be carried out tonight. It was amazing how clear everything was, once a person got far enough away from the problem to acquire detachment.

The people moving about the market were a motley assemblage. Housewives with baskets over their arms rubbed elbows with the African cooks from the more prosperous households and bewigged gentlemen who fancied themselves astute shoppers or else preferred to keep the purse strings in their own hands. A nun in a pure white wimple haggled with a woman in a gray and ragged coif over a bundle of fresh parsley. A half-naked Choctaw warrior stalked along, ignoring the commerce. Behind him came a pair of soldiers, one in uniform, the other still in his nightcap and dressing gown, a liberty in dress that marked him as a relative of Madame Vaudreuil, or so the jest went. Here and there was a woman ostentatiously gowned in silk who might have been taken for a great lady, but was more likely the mistress of one of the army officers. Such women were not only kept openly but were freely received, even at the Government House where, if their charms were sufficient, they might be placed above the more dowdy wives of colonists. The governor had an eye for an attractive woman.

The preferred method of doing business at the market was barter. Hard money was practically nonexistent, and the paper scrip issued by the crown fluctuated so widely in value that people accepted it with reluctance. Moreover, there had been a number of counterfeit notes floating about in the last year, making people even more leery. Many lived so close to the bone that the loss represented by even one counterfeit bill could be catastrophic.

Cyrene traded a beaded leather drawstring bag she had made herself for a pair of chickens, then swapped one of the chickens for a cabbage, a handful of scallions, and two long and crusty loaves of bread. Gaston took possession of the chicken, carrying it by its bound feet, while Cyrene swung the basket of vegetables and bread over her arm. They turned homeward.

They were nearing the flatboat when Gaston came to an abrupt stop in the road.

''What is this?'' he asked, his voice unnaturally hard.

She followed his gaze. There was a man on the flatboat. He had just crossed the gangplank and was moving toward the cabin door that faced the front of the craft. Short and wiry, he wore a stocking cap and striped pantaloons with a blue coat, and was barefoot. He did not walk with a normal stride but rather was creeping over the logs, staying close to the wall. He was no friend.

''Hey, you!'' Gaston shouted. He dropped the chicken in the road, where it flapped and squawked as he took off at a run. Cyrene started after Gaston, clutching her basket.

The man on the flatboat flung a wild look in their direction. He cursed, a sound that came faintly to Cyrene above the thud of her footfalls. From the waist of his pantaloons, the intruder pulled out a pistol and leaped for the cabin door. He shoved the door open and darted inside. There came the thunderous roar of a shot. Gray powder smoke billowed from the doorway. The man in striped pantaloons erupted through the smoke as if flung by a giant hand. He fell to his knees, then scrambled up again. Behind him, René appeared in the door with his hands clenched at his sides. The man in striped pantaloons gave a hoarse yell and took to his heels. He clattered over the gangplank and flung himself across the road into the swamp.

Gaston outdistanced Cyrene. Still, she ran on with her blood pounding in her ears and a suffocating knot in her chest. She saw the younger Breton bound onto the gangplank and grasp René's arm, then after a few words clap him on the back. She knew it was all right, but she could not slow down. The gangplank sprang up and down as she ran across it. The two men turned toward her. Before she reached them, she was calling out, "What is it? What happened?"

"That one tried to kill René!" Gaston said, outrage vying with excitement in his tone.

"Pierre? Jean? Where are they?"

It was René who answered. "There was a message. They had to go into town."

"Pierre would not do that." Pierre Breton disliked towns and crowds of strangers; he never went near them if it could be avoided.

"Possibly a ploy." Gaston made a fine gesture of contempt.

"At any rate, a note was delivered. They left. The man came." René gave a light shrug.

Cyrene ran her gaze up and down René's tall form. "You weren't injured?"

He shook his head. "It isn't easy to board a craft like this without some sign. I felt the boat rock, but there was no other sound, no footsteps, no hail. It seemed wrong."

"So he got up to see about it," Gaston supplied with satisfaction, "as who would not?"

"Exactly. I'm afraid you have a pistol ball in the roof."

"A bagatelle, a mere nothing," Gaston said expansively. "Tell us how you threw him out the door."

"That was a mistake, an elbow in the wrong place when I pushed the pistol up, else he might not have got away."

There was more, but Cyrene did not stay to hear it. She stepped into the cabin and put down her basket. For a moment she paused to stare up at the splintered place in the roof sheeting overhead where the ball had struck. It was not small; the charge behind the ball must have been enough to stop a bear. Cyrene poured water into a pan and washed her hands, then wrung out a cloth and pressed it to her hot face. Putting it down after a moment, she smoothed her hair. Only then did she go back out onto the deck.

"Why?" she asked into the first silence that occurred between the two men.

Gaston glanced at her over his shoulder with the light glinting on his earring and a good-natured grin on his face. "Why what, *chère*?"

"Why did the man try to kill M'sieur Lemonnier?"

"He was a thief who saw the two of us leave, then enticed Papa and Uncle Pierre away. He thought the boat was empty, ripe for plunder."

"He took out his pistol before he stepped inside."

"A precaution, and a most sensible one."

"That may be," Cyrene said, her eyes clear as she looked toward René. "Or it may have been that his sole purpose was murder, as someone tried to murder our guest before?"

As Gaston turned toward him also, René appeared to give the idea consideration. "It's possible, of course, but I can't think why."

"I tell you the man's a thief and a cutthroat, I'm almost sure of it," Gaston said in disgust.

Cyrene turned quickly in his direction. "You know him?"

"If he's the one I think, he used to work out of a tavern near the barracks in town, though I haven't seen him around lately."

"And I don't suppose he will be seen again soon."

"You can be sure of it."

There were many places a man on the run could go, into the woods with the Indians, to the outlying French posts stretching from Natchitoches and Mobile to the Illinois country, to New France far to the north, or even to English Carolina or Spanish Florida. To make it to safety was the trick. The number of men who had vanished into the wilderness never to be heard of again was vast.

René resumed his place on his pallet while Gaston trotted back down the road to retrieve the chicken before a fox or some two-legged varmint made off with it. He ended the days of the fowl with an ax but brought it to Cyrene to be plucked for the pot, a job he despised. She was still at that task when Pierre and Jean returned.

Their errand had been no ruse, though it had not taken

them all the way into town. It concerned a commission for an old friend who was bedridden, a Scotsman come to Louisiane by way of France and Culloden Moor who thought a pint or two of good Scots whiskey just might put him on his feet again if the Bretons could bring it to him—even if his coin did enrich the bloody English. Pierre was inclined to agree with Gaston that the intruder was a thief. The matter seemed to end there, though discussing it lasted them, off and on, until the evening meal of stewed chicken and dumplings had been consumed.

They sat for a time around the fire. Cyrene, knowing the Bretons now had money in their pockets since the Scotsman had paid them in advance for his commission, waited until a lull in the conversation. As artlessly as she was able, she said, "I've never tasted whiskey."

Jean pursed his lips as if he had just swallowed a dram. "It can't compare with good brandy."

"Is it perhaps stronger?" She looked to Pierre, as to the oldest and therefore the authority.

"More potent, you mean? That depends on where it's made, and how. But it has a bite, does whiskey, while brandy goes down as smooth as satin and lifts a man's spirits until he can touch the sky." He smacked his lips.

"But Scots whiskey must be powerful if it can cure your friend."

A tolerant smile rose in Pierre's eyes. "All spirits act on the mind, which is where most cures begin."

"I think," Jean said, "that I feel a sore throat coming on."

Cyrene clicked her tongue. "I suppose you feel it would be wise to nip it in the bud?"

"The thought had crossed my mind."

"You shouldn't encourage him," Pierre said to Cyrene.

"No," Jean said, "it's most unnecessary."

They left soon after for the pothouse, the two older men. Gaston, much to his disgust, was delegated as guard once more. He slammed from the cabin and threw himself down on the bench outside where he sat thumping his heels on one of the logs.

Cyrene sat listening to that regular thudding for long moments, then looked at René. He was watching her, and in his eyes were admiration and distrust.

His voice soft, he said, "That was a splendid bit of maneuvering, but I fail to see the point."

There was no use in pretending with him. "The point is, Gaston sleeps at all times like a bear who has been in the corn, but Pierre and Jean do not. Except when they drink."

Something bright and warm leaped into his eyes. "Ah."

He needed no detailed explanations but grasped the implications at once. It gave her a secure feeling to know that it was so. Most people had to be told, and plainly at that.

"There will still be a certain danger," she said.

"Did you not know," he said, his voice a rustle of sound, "that danger adds spice?"

Time passed with aching slowness. There was no way of knowing how long the two brothers would be gone or how long it would take for Gaston to get over his chagrin and become cold enough to seek the fire again. It was not a cold night, but neither was it warm. The clouds that had been hovering all day pressed down, and what little wind there was had rounded and was coming mostly from the south. There was a heavy feeling of moisture in the air, and also of anticipation, as if the heavens might open at any moment and the rain come pelting down.

That feeling, Cyrene thought, might just as well be coming from inside herself. She was on edge, her nerves leaping under the skin at the least noise, the slightest movement. She wanted the waiting to end and, at the same time, dreaded the moment when it would be over. Her heart beat high in her chest and her skin tingled. Never in her life had she been so aware of another human being as she was of René Lemonnier, of his presence, his size, the measured strength of his every movement, the rise and fall of his breathing, the shape of his face, his mouth, his hands.

She was mad to think she could go through with this, mad to question her lot. What was wrong with the way she lived? Didn't she have a roof over her head, plenty to eat, generous, reasonable, and concerned companions with whom she had been happy? So what if they kept her close? It was for her protection. To rail against it was the most ridiculous ingratitude. To risk it for a chimera, such as her freedom might prove to be, was stupid.

Oh, but she was tired of being an unpaid housekeeper to the Bretons, tired of being secluded like a nun. There was more to life than pots and pans and an occasional foray into trade. There were things she wanted to do, ideas she wanted to pursue. Inside her were feelings she yearned to have brought to fruition, to share. For everything there was a time, and for her the time was now.

Virginity. What a burden it was for women. Why could they not be like men, able to accomplish their initiation into the rites of passion without pain or proof? Why should a tiny, thin piece of flesh that served to protect a young and growing girl's organs of birth assume such importance? It mattered little, in all truth, except to allow men to establish their paternity by an obvious marking of a woman's first time with a male.

Not that any great value was attached to it in the colony. The first shipload of women sent out as wives, most of them from the prisons of Paris, had hardly had a maidenhead among them. There had been, in fact, a midwife sent with them on the voyage who attended three birthings before they reached their destination. So scarce were females other than Indian women in the early days and so desperate the need for them, that purity was the last thing a prospective bridegroom inquired about when these so-called correction girls stepped onto the muddy shore. The casket girls who came later, middle-class women without family sent by the king and provided with a box containing their dowry of a few pieces of clothing and other goods, were all assumed, rightly or wrongly, to be untouched. But their greatest value was that they were strong and hard-working and, most important of all, able to bear children—for so far from purity had the first group been that disease such as the Spanish pox had made many of them sterile.

The possibility that she might bear a child was not one that Cyrene cared to consider. Such things happened, yes, but it was not as if she was taking a husband, a man with whom she must be constantly intimate. The one physical experience would be enough for her purpose, and it was unlikely there would be such definite results. When it was over, that would be the end of her close acquaintance with René Lemonnier.

An additional advantage to choosing the Parisian rake, however, was that he was as unlikely to desire to be wed to her as he was to father a child upon her.

So many of the men in the colony seemed obsessed, after a few years' residence, with having a woman of their own, someone to cook and clean for them and to warm their beds. Cyrene had no urge whatever to become the helpmate of some *voyageur* or planter. From what she had observed of matrimony, in the union of her parents to the many between the women sent out by the crown and the men who took them as brides, a woman simply exchanged one set of constraints and tasks for another, and with little to compensate for the loss of freedom. There were those who thought that they could not live without a man or who did not care to try; most of the women who lost their husbands to the constant fevers and infections and accidents married a second or third or even a fourth time, especially those with small children and no way to support themselves. Still, the happiest women seemed to be the widows with property, women who controlled their own lives as well as their fortunes. As she meant to do.

No, the way she had chosen was best. It was only necessary now to embark upon it.

The Breton brothers, when they returned a few hours later, could be heard coming long before they reached the flatboat.

Their voices raised in song set the swamp to ringing and
echoed back from the trees across the river. They were as
drunk as musketeers, and mirthful with it, so that they
shouted with laughter as they staggered across the deck,
shoving and pushing as they each tried to open the door for
the other. Cyrene's one fear, as she came to their aid by
unbarring the door from the inside, was that they would fall
into the river. The plunge would have little danger for men
who swam like eels, but it would be entirely too sobering for
her purpose.

Gaston had come inside earlier but had taken to his swinging bed only a half hour before. Even so, he was already
asleep, nor did he rouse as his father and his uncle blundered
around in the darkness, knocking into him and kicking over
stools. Cyrene scolded a little, as she usually did, then retreated to her cubicle out of the men's way. There were a few
more minutes of banging, bumping, and creaking. Finally
quiet descended.

Cyrene waited a half hour. The breathing of the two brothers was deep and sonorous, bordering on snoring. She could
not hear Gaston, but from him she feared little. She had no
idea whether René was asleep or not; certainly he made no
sound. She was not disturbed, however. She had discovered
that, like the Breton brothers under normal circumstances,
he came awake at the slightest noise or movement. The difficulty, the few times that she had tried, was in getting out
of her hammock without awakening him.

This time was no different. The hook of her hammock
made the barest squeak as she eased to the floor and stepped
to drop the curtain between her cubicle and the cabin into
place. Still, when she turned, she heard the rustle of bed-
clothing as René raised himself on his pallet. Afraid he would
speak, she went at once to her knees and reached out in the
darkness, making a soft, silencing sound.

Her fingers came into contact with his shoulder. The skin
was warm and smooth, firm with the muscles that lay underneath, vibrant with life. Her breath caught in her throat

with a choking sensation. For an instant, she could not speak, could not move.

"Is it tonight, then, Cyrene?" he whispered, his voice a deep, rustling sigh.

The sound of it released her. "Yes, tonight."

"I thought you had changed your mind."

"No. No, I didn't do that."

"You're shivering. Are you cold?"

She hadn't been aware of the trembling in her fingers that also ran along her arms and into the core of her body. It had nothing to do with the chill of the air, though it was impossible to admit to it. "Perhaps I am, a little."

"Then let me warm you."

He took her wrist in his hand and drew her down beside him. There was resistance in her muscles at first, and an increase in her shivering, but after a moment of lying against the hard angles and hollows of his body, of being cradled in the circle of his arms, it began to subside. His hold was so warm, so sure. There was comfort there, and safety, but little sign of disturbing desire.

It took faith to lie there unmoving, yielding to whatever he might require. Faith and trust. Why had she not considered it? Women gave themselves to men every night all over the world in this same act of faith, and with how much justification? Men took the gift women gave without thought, as their right. How many ever realized that it should be a generous sharing, not something that must be given up as a duty or taken as a right?

Such thoughts were a distraction. She needed them to prevent the tensing of her nerves as René touched the braid of hair that lay over her shoulder, clasping its warm, silken weight in his hand. He found the thong that held the end and slipped it off, then pushed his fingers through the thick twining strands, spreading them over the curve of her shoulder and across her back.

The fragrance that was released was her own, a summery freshness like open meadowland. René inhaled it, slowly smoothing his hand over the rippling silk cape of hair as he pressed her against him. There was a swelling in his chest to match that in his loins. The incredible surrender of the woman he held was a boon he did not deserve. He knew it well, but he was powerless to refuse. The danger of accepting was acute—he was supremely conscious of the men sleeping on the other side of the curtain—but it was all the sweeter for that. No, he must not, could not, resist, but as God was his witness, she would not be the loser. His last few misspent months made it possible for him to see to that, and he would. There might be more than one purpose to the long hours spent in strange boudoirs and the tender lessons he had learned. Of what would come afterward, he did not want to think. It would have to take care of itself.

Cyrene was convent-educated, but there had been outings for shopping and for holidays. Her governess had been a rather worldly widow who did not believe in mincing words or ignoring facts. Moreover, there had been several pupils whose parents were on the fringes of the court at Versailles and who had heard more gossip and seen more irregular conduct of courtiers with servants girls and the like than their parents imagined. Even if it had not been for these things, Cyrene could hardly have lived with the Bretons along the riverfront and remained in ignorance of the physical nature of the union of men and women. She was ready, she thought, to suffer that indignity for the sake of what it would do for her. What she was unprepared for was the slow rise of curiosity concerning it that she felt inside her and the unmistakable unfurling of what must be anticipation.

Strange, but her breasts against René's chest were firm and tingling, and there was a slight tendency of the muscles of her abdomen to contract in a fluttering spasm as her body conformed to his. The blood in her veins quickened. The cloth of her chemise felt rough, an irritating impediment. With some sense she did not know she possessed, she recognized the restraint in which he held himself for her sake, and was gratified by it, while at the same time she was, in some peculiar way, freed from her own.

Cyrene looked up, trying to see the man who held her in the dark. She could make out no more than the dim outline of his head. It was as well that it was so. She lowered her eyelids and lifted her hand, trailing her fingers over his shoulder to the strong curve of his neck. She touched the square turn of his jaw and the faintly stubbled firmness of his cheek, then brushed her fingers across the chiseled curves of his lips, exploring their smooth yet firm surfaces.

It was almost involuntary, that slight lift of her own mouth in invitation. He needed no more but lowered his lips to hers.

Warm, his mouth was warm in the coolness of the night, its touch exquisitely gentle, and yet the contact sent a tremor leaping along her nerves that she acknowledged in the deepest reaches of her body. Her breath caught in her throat and she allowed her lips to mold to his, engulfed in purest sensation as the pressure increased. His lips parted infinitesimally and she felt the tip of his tongue in delicate play. Blindly she followed his lead, enticed by the sweetness, the fine-nubbed abrasiveness, the insidious invasion, and inside her burgeoned an odd constrained excitement.

Her pleasure would have been greater if it had not been for the men on the other side of the curtain. Regret that there could not have been found a time and place without their presence touched her, then was gone. It could not be helped.

Hurry, they should hurry before the others woke and they were interrupted. The thought tumbled inside Cyrene's brain, but René seemed to feel no such tense need. He probed the fragile lining of her mouth and ran the tip of his tongue along the edges of her teeth, he probed the corners of her lips and the sensitive molded outline. He kissed her chin and tasted the salt flavor of her eyelids and followed the intricate turning of her ear. So beguiling was the moist fire of his exploration that she scarcely knew when he slipped free the tie that held the neckline of her thin, much-washed chemise, when he slid the sleeve from her shoulder and put his hand on the gentle swell of her breast. She gave a soundless gasp and her breathing quickened as he trailed a moist and fiery path along the curve of her neck and downward over her collarbone. He drew the chemise lower and his breath wafted over the straining, tender peak of her bared breast, causing it to tighten before he took it into the heated adhesion of his mouth.

Desire flooded in upon her, swirling in her veins, heating her skin, settling with aching vulnerability in the lower part of her body. A soft cry gathered in her throat, and she barely suppressed it. Panic assaulted her. This was too magical, too cataclysmic. It might well be a binding thing, a necessity for which even happy widows remarried. She had been wrong to think it could be used so easily. She wanted to stop it, to go back to the way things had been before, but she knew in some corner of her mind that it was too late. Too late.

Her strength of will was gone, transmuted into rich and acquiescing languor. She spread her hand over René's back, avoiding his bandaging, and was bemused by the ripple of the muscles under the skin and the scorch of his lips in the valley between her breasts. She shifted, allowing him to draw the chemise slowly down the length of her body and to follow its retreat with delicate application of mouth and tongue.

Oh, he knew the curves and hollows of a woman's body, knew the careful and patient attention required to set them aflame. He was a tender invader, a bringer of rapture and joy. Cyrene lay, pulsing and entranced, lapped in beguiling waves of pleasure. Captivated by the splendor of it, and the wonder, she drifted in voluptuous acceptance that had yet a shivering edge of distress. Powerless in the grasp of ecstasy, she fretted at the soft sounds, the strained breathing, the soft rustling of the pallet, and the sense of fleeting time. And yet she could not deny the turbulent pressure building inside her, the urgent need that hovered, waiting.

The bright ravishment rushed in upon her so suddenly that she arched against him with a cry locked in her throat and her hands clutching his arms in a grip of ferocious power. Swiftly he stripped away the breeches he wore for sleeping and eased between her thighs. His entry, heated and stretching, brought an instant of burning anguish that eased, miraculously, as he pressed deeper. Her breath of relief and of glimpsed glory fanned his shoulder.

He moved upon her then with careful strength, and she thrust against him, rising to meet the tumult of his need that had been so long denied, so valiantly withheld, encompassing it with her own. Together in the darkness, fused yet shadowed and apart, they strained toward the ineffable grandeur that waited. It ignited around them, a brightness to meld or to destroy, to vanquish or to offer the rare gift of grace, and so brilliant was it that only time could reveal the difference.

5

THE FLATBOAT BEGAN to swing on its mooring ropes toward dawn. Thunder grumbled low overhead. The wind whistled around the cabin's roof, fluttering at the corners. Cyrene came awake in a rush. She stared into the darkness for a long moment, disoriented by the solidity of the floor under her and the odd confinement of her position on her side when she should be rocking in comfort in her hammock. Then she remembered.

René lay at her back with his long body curled around her. His arm was across her waist with his fingers curved at her breast. She could feel the ridges of muscles on his legs and the roughness of his body hair against her own nakedness. The comfort of his warmth surrounded her under the bearskin that covered them, though the air she breathed was cool.

She had not meant to fall asleep with him. It was unbelievable to her that she had spent most of the night lying so close in his arms. Even now she was reluctant to move, though cramped muscles urged her to stretch. It was not that she had any liking for how she was placed, not at all; it was only that she would rather not wake René at this moment. She first needed to collect herself, to repair her defenses and decide how she must behave toward him.

It was also necessary to decide what she must do now. If the purpose of losing her virginity was to convince the Bretons to give her more freedom, they must be informed, therefore, that she was no longer intact. The difficulties in doing that suddenly appeared enormous.

They would not be pleased. That was a major consideration, but not so great a one as how she was to find the words to convey her new status. She did not fear Pierre and Jean, not for herself; they had never attempted to impose discipline upon her, never raised a hand to her. It was, she realized, their disapproval and their disappointment with her that she dreaded.

What they would do to René was another matter entirely. That had always been at the back of her mind; still, an aspect of it that she had not considered was that she would be responsible for whatever was visited upon him. He was in no real condition to defend himself just now. Under normal circumstances there would be little cause for concern; when René was free of injury, he would doubtless be equal to most situations, particularly those of this nature. Past experience would probably aid him tremendously.

That last rather acid thought disturbed her. His experience was no concern of hers, had, in fact, been to her benefit. Not that she wished to think of the manner in which it had proven useful. Certainly not. Though on consideration she could recall little indication that René's injuries had affected his ability as a lover the night before. There had, perhaps, been a little more care and tenderness and less vigor in his treatment of her, but she did not think it had anything to do with his strength or lack of it. That was a bit puzzling, but also a relief. She was glad to know that he would not be defenseless against her protectors.

Nor would he be caught off guard. He was no more asleep than she was. How she knew, she was not certain; he had not moved or made a sound. Still, she would swear that he lay alert and intent. She considered it while thunder muttered once more over the wide river beyond the dipping, swaying flatboat.

Abruptly she knew what had given him away. It was the tension in his muscles. There was good cause for it. Beyond

the curtained doorway, there was a shifting sound and a slight
creak as one of the Bretons left his hammock, Pierre from
the position of the sound. An instant later, there came the
blossoming yellow glow as a tallow dip was lighted. It would
be the storm that had disturbed him, that and the wild swing
of the flatboat. The mooring ropes would need checking.

Cyrene made a small, convulsive movement, as if she
would spring up and leap for her hammock. René's arm tightened around her. She subsided. He was right, it would be
better to make no sudden sound, no violent moves that might
draw attention. On the other hand, the curtain closing off the
cubicle was almost always looped up at night after she had
dressed for bed. That it was down might arouse suspicion.

But if it did, what of it? Wasn't that what she wanted?
Wouldn't it be better to be discovered than to have to make
a stumbling explanation?

Cyrene relaxed, lying perfectly still. Her nakedness under
the bearskin brushed her mind with an instant of embarrassment, but she refused to regard it. If she and René were
found out, it would be because it was meant. Such fatalism
was soothing to her strained nerves, even if it was a sham.

The outer door of the cabin opened and closed. The sound
of footsteps moving about on the outside deck came clearly
through the walls. Overhead, the rain began to spatter on the
split cypress shingles. It fell harder, taking on a wet reso-
nance. Then the cabin door banged open, letting in a rush of
wind that flapped the door curtain, sucking it outward into
the cabin. Beneath it, Cyrene saw Pierre standing in the outer
doorway with the rainswept darkness behind him. He was
staring straight at her.

There was the thud of bare feet. The curtain was thrown
aside. Pierre stood over them, his face contorted with rage
and pained disbelief.

"Cyrene!"

She sat up, clutching the bearskin cover to her chest. A
heated flush mounted to her face. She had not expected the
guilt that pressed in upon her. It robbed her of speech and

made her feel as chastened as a wayward child. Beside her, René raised himself to a sitting position also and began with deliberate movements to put on his breeches.

"What does this mean?" It was Jean who spoke, moving to stand behind his brother. Gaston, rousing in his hammock, peered past them with his eyes widening with shock.

Cyrene could not answer. It was René who spoke. "I would think," he said, his tone dry, "that the meaning is obvious."

The remark drew Pierre's fire, as it was meant to do. "Name of a name! Is this the way you repay us?"

"Oddly enough—" René began.

As Pierre, his blue eyes murderous, started toward him, Cyrene threw up a hand to stop him. "The fault is mine, not his," she said, her voice tight. "He did nothing that I did not wish."

"How can you say such a thing?" Jean doubled his fists, putting them on his hips.

"Because it's true."

"Impossible! He seduced you, beguiled you with lies."

She shook back her hair; the action was also a denial. "No. I asked this of him."

"The way of a whore? Never. You seek to protect him, but it's no use." Jean made as if he would push past his older brother. Gaston, his face grim, was on his feet, moving toward the cubicle to join them.

"I need no protection." René's voice was armored in steel as he went to one knee. As he faced the Bretons his gaze was level and challenging and without fear. "I will give any one or all of you satisfaction, if you require it, but first you might ask yourselves what reason Cyrene would have for what has been done."

Jean spat out an epithet, lunging past his brother. Pierre shot out his hand and caught his shirtfront, dragging him to a halt. "Wait," he said, a dangerous edge to his words, "Lemonnier has a point. Let us hear Cyrene."

The rain was loud in the sudden quiet. Cyrene's heart jarred in her chest. She moistened her lips. "The reason is my freedom. I am so tired of being watched and guarded like some prize."

"You are a prize, one of great value," Pierre said roughly.

"I'm a person. I want to come and go without having a man always at my side. I want to do what I like, when I like. I want to be free."

"You don't know what you say." The elder Breton made a quick gesture with a hand much-callused in the palm from years of rowing. "Women must be protected."

"Why? To ensure their purity or their fidelity? There is a difference between protection and imprisonment."

Pierre stared at her, a frown drawing his brows together. "We never meant to imprison you, *chère*, or to make you unhappy."

Cyrene clenched her hands on the fur of the buffalo hide. "I haven't been unhappy, only maddened by the constant vigil held over me. I've tried to tell you, but you never listened. I will go mad if it doesn't stop."

"And you think this is the way to end it?"

"How better? There will no longer be a need now for your protection."

"You think not?"

"Why should there be? Unchaste women walk the streets alone day and night, especially at night."

"You mean to become a whore?" The older man's tone was dangerously soft.

"Of course not! But such women go unguarded simply because they no longer have anything to lose."

"You expect us to let you go about the streets now as you please, without escort?"

"Why not?"

"But you don't wish to be a whore?"

"I told you, no!"

"Who is going to save you from the wolves who will gather when they learn that you have known a man? Who is going to keep you from becoming their prey, their whore?"

Anger and humiliation sparkled in her brown eyes. Never had anyone said such a thing to her, certainly not Pierre Breton. Still, she refused to let him know how he had wounded her. With a lift of her chin, she said, "I'll protect myself. I have the knife you gave me, and I remember how to use it."

"You'll need more than that. You are far too choice a morsel to go unclaimed because of a puny blade or a few lessons from me in cut and thrust."

René, listening with intent purpose beside Cyrene, spoke suddenly. "I will be her protection."

Jean growled and would have stepped forward once more if Pierre had not held him back with an imperative gesture. Cyrene swung around to face René, her eyes startled. "There is no need," she said in an urgent undertone. "This isn't your quarrel."

"Let him speak," Pierre said, though an odd flicker of something like distress crossed his features.

René rose to his feet, facing the other men squarely. "Make no mistake, I do this out of neither fear nor gratitude. I have in the past few days discovered in myself a strong attachment to Cyrene. What she is to you, or you to her, I don't know, but this much I can promise you. No harm will come to her because of me, nor will anyone else be allowed to offer her insult or injury while she is under my guardianship."

Cyrene, listening in amazement, roused herself to remonstrate. "Will you be quiet? I need no help from you."

"Your guardianship," Pierre repeated. "And what would she be to you?"

"That is a matter between us."

Jean gave a soft grunt. "Your mistress, then. Or is it that your guardianship may not extend beyond a night or two?"

"I trust it will be longer. I had thought, even hoped, that it might be at least as long as your next expedition to meet the English will last."

Jean cursed and Gaston echoed his father, his face pale.

Pierre remained calm, though his eyes narrowed. "You mean to explain that, I hope."

"Forgive my abruptness," René said, inclining his head in acquiescence. "I realized what the indigo was shortly after you brought it aboard. It wasn't hard to know that it must be here since Jean, before he washed his hands, had a beautiful shade of blue under his fingernails. I have been lying here thinking of the adventure you were embarking on and the profits you stand to make, and I discovered within myself a great desire to join you in this enterprise."

"For the money, naturally?" Pierre said.

"I don't scorn it, though truthfully I have sufficient for my needs from my family, providing, of course, that I don't squander it at the gaming tables. You may not credit the real reason, but I can tell you. I am tired of civilization and its rules; I've had a surfeit. I long to explore the wilderness now that I'm here, to see the Indians and how they live, and perhaps to do something that carries a certain risk. I can't explain to you this need, I can only tell you it's there."

It was doubtful that he could have hit upon an explanation more likely to please the Bretons. Smuggling was not just their profession, it was their recreation and their joy. The profit to be gained was a consideration, but it was far outweighed by the sheer pleasure of gaining it while avoiding being caught by the king's soldiers, killed by renegade Indians, or lost in any of the other natural disasters to which the vast country was prone.

"You want to come with us?" Jean said. "A Parisian dandy like you? You wouldn't last ten minutes in the wilderness."

"That's possible," René agreed, a faint smile in his gray eyes. "It's also possible that I might surprise you."

Cyrene looked from Pierre to Jean. The two men gazed at each other, their faces grim. Something in their expressions, a wariness, an acceptance, told her that they were considering the suggestion. They were actually considering taking René Lemonnier with them.

''No,'' she said.

She was ignored.

''Can you paddle a boat?'' Pierre asked as he looked back at René.

''I've rowed on the Seine.''

''The Mississippi is not so tame, or so forgiving. Can you shoot?''

''That I can do.''

''No,'' Cyrene said again.

''But have you ever killed a man?'' Jean asked, his gaze steady on René.

René did not answer but neither did he look away.

''Of course, you may not consider a savage a man, but he is a deadly foe,'' the younger Breton went on with irony. ''But, saying you can defend yourself as well as our Cyrene, do you go for the outing or do you plan to invest?''

''I'll share the risk, if you will allow it.''

Cyrene got to her feet, wrapping the bearskin around her. ''What is this?'' she demanded, looking from one to the other. ''What are you doing?''

It was Pierre who answered. ''This is an agreement among men, *chère*. As for what we are doing, we are taking on a partner.''

''You can do as you like,'' she said, the words firm, well measured, ''but understand this, all of you. I'm no part of it.''

''That is a matter between you and the man you have chosen.''

''I've chosen no one!''

''Haven't you? It appears otherwise.''

Cyrene lifted her chin, her eyes fierce and dark with her distress. ''I don't care how it appears, I require no protector, nor do I want one!''

''That is unfortunate, *chère*, for it seems you have one whether you wish it or not.''

Pierre looked at her for a long moment, his face hard though the pain lingered in his eyes. He turned sharply as if in disdain and, motioning Jean and Gaston back, swept the curtain down into place. From the other side, he spoke again. "We leave within the week, Lemonnier. Be ready."

Why? That was what Cyrene could not understand. It wasn't that the Bretons had never taken a partner with them; it was not unusual for them to take on another man or even two. But these men were always fellow *voyageurs*, men born in this harsh new world and familiar with its ways; always men they had long known and trusted. It made no sense for them to accept a newcomer, a man who was not only strange to the wilderness but who was also on terms of friendship with the governor himself and therefore suspect.

It was the governor's duty, as supreme authority here so far from mother France, to stop the smuggling that was rife. Toward that end, rewards had been established for informing on the men engaged in such illegal and treasonous activities. Smuggling was seen, in fact, as stealing from the French state since it diverted revenues that would otherwise go into the royal treasury. The penalty was flogging, the number of lashes to be decided according to the degree of the offense, then branding with the fleur-de-lis and a sentence of life on the king's galleys.

Was it possible that she had brought an informer among them?

Cyrene turned slowly to look at René Lemonnier. "Why are you doing this?"

"I think you heard."

His gray gaze was clear, without guile, and yet there was something in it that disturbed her. "If this is just an impulse, I beg you will reconsider. A man who knows nothing of the swamps and woodlands can be a danger to everyone as well as to himself."

"I appreciate your concern, though I could wish for greater confidence."

"That's something you must earn, like all men newly come to Louisiane."

René watched her and was impressed by her close-held

composure that belied the fury that caused her breasts to rise and fall so quickly. She felt she had been betrayed, and she was right. For that fact, he did not like himself much. She would not lose by it, however. This he vowed again in silence as he allowed his gaze to touch the strong oval of her face, the rich warmth of her hair, the magnificence of her form that was gilded across the shoulders by the haze of wavering light through the curtain. One did not, of a certainty, marry a woman of such a lower class, but he would see that she lacked for nothing, not even a husband, before he returned to France.

Aloud, he said, "I will try to remember."

"There is something else you should understand beyond doubting, so hear me well. You may go on this expedition, you may call yourself my protector if it pleases you, but that is the end of it. You will not share my bed. You owe me nothing, nor do I owe you. Is that clear?"

A slow smile curved his mouth, rising in his eyes. "Your position is clear, and I would like to agree. It is only fair for me to warn you, however, that I can't."

"What does that mean?" She clenched her teeth together with the effort it took not to scream at him and bring the Bretons back down on them again.

"I consider that I still owe you a great deal—and I have found in myself a strong preference for your method of repayment."

"Touch me," she said in sibilant tones, "and I will kill you."

He tilted his head, surveying her through his lashes. "You have been free with your warnings; now, listen to me. I have never forced a woman, nor do I intend to start now. But that isn't to say that I won't woo you when the chance arises and bed you if I am allowed, or can create, the opportunity. So prime your defenses, *ma chérie*, I don't mind. In fact, I prefer it. Easy conquests are not nearly as interesting."

"I'm no conquest of yours!"

"Not yet."

"Out," she said, her voice trembling with suppressed rage. "Get out."

He gave a low laugh. "Put me out."

She could not struggle with him in her present state of undress; it would not be at all wise. She turned her back. "I wouldn't give you the pleasure!"

"Then I suppose I stay," he said, settling himself back down on the pallet, "at least until morning."

Cyrene disdained to answer. She climbed into her hammock and struggled to lie down without losing her bearskin wrapping. The bed suspended between hooks swayed and creaked until it finally fell silent.

René lay with his hands behind his head, staring up at the ceiling. He had not been able to resist baiting her, though if she had shown the least sign of real trepidation he would have put her mind to rest at once. It was not his intention to be tied to her day and night, though he must and would stay close. Nor did he need the annoyance of a woman making emotional scenes at the wrong moments. He would carry on a flirtation with her, press his attentions upon her just enough to fan the flames of her rage and keep her at odds with him, but he would not involve himself further.

Or would he? The taste and feel of her ran rich in his mind, and he would like to take her again now, pulling her down with him on this hard floor. It was not going to be easy to remain celibate with her always near at hand.

He would manage because he must. Honor required it. Honor could be a hard taskmaster.

It was cold without the curves of Cyrene's body against his and without his cover, which she had taken with her.

"Cyrene?" he called softly up to her. "Do I get a coverlet, a blanket, if not the bearskin?"

She made no reply.

He reached above him, running a fingertip along the curve of the hammock, down her back to her hips. She wriggled away from him. Muffled by the bearskin pulled over her head, her answer came.

"Freeze. It may cure your excessive ardor."

It certainly might. Muttering under his breath, René turned on his side and pulled part of his buffalo robe pallet over him. A moment later, he slept.

They left New Orleans five days later. The departure was triggered by a message from downriver that the English ship they had been expecting had been sighted off Biloxi. By the time they reached the coast, threading through the bayous, lakes, and streams that formed this clandestine passageway below New Orleans, the ship would be anchored in one of the smaller inlets or bays that indented the Louisiane shoreline. The time it could remain there was limited. It was necessary for the Breton party to travel fast and with few delays.

For transport they used a pair of large pirogues. Pierre, Cyrene, and René were in the lead boat, while Jean and Gaston pressed them from behind. The crafts, though sometimes treacherous to handle, were perfect for the meandering trip where occasionally there were stretches of marshlands that had to be crossed on little more than a heavy dew.

It was cold and damp on the water, but there was the labor of paddling to warm them. Cyrene wielded a paddle with the rest. To be idle was to become chilled, and besides, she preferred to do her part. She rested perhaps a little more often than the others, not so much because she could not keep up as from a fascination with the wet country around her, the swampland.

The bayous and other streams twisted and snaked toward the gulf, sometimes doubling back on themselves, so that it was often necessary to travel three leagues to make one of southward progress. The lakes were wide and placid, natural reservoirs. The water of the intricate network was muddy and dark, the result of its silt content and the acid in the tree leaves that sifted down into it. In some places there was a perceptible current, but in others the waterway lay still and quietly reflective, as if it were fathoms deep, though the bottom might be no more than a few inches under the pirogue's hull. Crisp water plants grew along its verge, and great cypress trees rose from a cluster of stumplike roots with smooth tops called cypress knees to soar skyward like the groin-topped columns of a cathedral. Gray swags of moss as wispy as old men's beards hung from the tree branches, swaying in the wind with somber grace. Here and there were flat, open stretches of floating vegetation, green and brown mats that looked solid enough to stand on but would not support anything much heavier than a dragonfly.

Now and then a fish roiled the water as it fed, a family of native ducks skated out of the way, or a great blue crane, a solitary fisherman, lifted into flight. Sometimes a covey of small birds rose out of the reeds like a swarm of gnats or a raccoon came waddling down to the water's edge to drink. There was little else to be seen. The frogs and turtles, snakes and alligators, and the myriad insect life, including the clouds of mosquitoes that gave these backwaters life and made them a misery during the warmer months, were taking their refuge from the brief weeks of chill, damp weather that marked the winter.

This time of year was not only best for traveling the waterways, but also best for trade for those who lived in and around New Orleans. The high water caused by the winter rains made travel easier, while the snows farther north would prevent the traders from the Illinois country, with their richer and deeper pelts, from coming downriver for a few more weeks. A man who got out and gathered furs from the southern Indians, even though they were not as good a grade as those from farther north, would be ahead of the market and could get a better price for his pelts now than he would later in the season.

Even without the plague of insect and reptile life, the task of paddling the pirogue was not an easy one. The constant bending, dipping, and pulling put a strain on the back and arm muscles that could quickly become a burning torture. The ease with which René Lemonnier fell into the way of it came close to being an annoyance to Cyrene. He not only found the particular rhythm that was the only remedy against the strain, but he soon learned the words to all the chants and songs that the Bretons used to hold the pace and temper the monotony. To make matters worse, his voice, a rich baritone, rang without a sign of breathlessness and with no concession whatever to the stiffness and pain she was sure he must feel in his injured back and side.

He was only putting a good face on it, she told herself at first; he would soon begin to flag. When he did not, she became convinced that it was because of her own efforts, the third paddle that lessened the work that must be done by the other two to remain ahead of the other boat. The only other possibility was that his wounds had not been as serious by far as they had appeared and he had pretended, though it made no sense for it to be so.

If such a thought occurred to Jean and Pierre, they gave no sign of it. They only watched René for the first few leagues to be certain he would not overturn the pirogue, then left him alone.

For René, the paddling was a chance to work some of the deeper soreness out of his back. The movements, once he had settled into them, were soothing in their repetition. They gave him the freedom to let his mind roam, to work on some deeper level on the problems that might lie ahead.

That was, of course, when his attention wasn't drawn to the woman in front of him. The smooth grace of her movements was engrossing, as was the way her skirts hugged her waist and lay across the outstretched leg she used to brace herself. The line of her back held such symmetry, and in her slender arms was such strength, that it was fascinating to watch the glide of her movements. She wore a scarf tied over her head against the chill, but the thick, shining rope of her braid hung down from under it, glinting in the light, curling with childlike softness at the end.

She had been his. It was odd how much pleasure the memory gave him. He had thought himself beyond such sentimentality concerning a woman. None of the scores of others he had flirted with and bedded had ever remained in his thoughts the way this one did. It was the novelty of it, he assured himself. No other female had ever made it so plain that she had no use for him beyond his services for a night. He was miffed, if the truth was known, but also intrigued.

Still, it wasn't her rejection he remembered. It was the feel of her against him, the sweet firmness of her lips as she responded to him, quickly learning the nuances of a kiss, the sweet clasp of her arms about him, the heated velvet depths of her.

The reason might be because she had been a virgin. It had been no surprise; she had set it before him plainly enough, but that was another thing that was new to him. The women to whom he had chosen to direct his attentions in the past had been lascivious widows, bored wives of perennially straying husbands, trollops in the guise of noble ladies, or else opera dancers who expected to have their bills paid by their patrons. It was not his practice to seduce innocents, not only because it would have added little to the building of his reputation but because it went against his nature. He might have to play the game, but he preferred to keep it fair.

That had not been possible with Cyrene. He regretted it, but could not help it. Nor was he certain that his regret was more than surface deep. By all the saints, he liked knowing that he alone had made love to her. It made her special to him, linked her to him in some nebulous way he did not understand. How long it would last, he had no way of knowing, but for now it gave him a perilous pleasure. She was his excuse, but she might also prove a danger, indeed. Perhaps even his greatest one.

To ease his back, he switched sides of the pirogue with his paddle. The blade slung droplets of water in an arch as he swung around. The water splattered the back of Cyrene's neck. She gasped at the cold wetness and slewed around in her seat to glare at him.

"Sorry," he murmured, though he could not prevent the grin that curved his mouth.

"I'll bet you are," she snapped, then turned forward once more. She absolved him of splashing her purposefully, but he need not have looked so impenitent about it or so pleased with himself.

They stopped for the noon meal on a grassy *chêniere*, a flattened ridge made of sand and ancient sea shells and dotted with the oak trees that gave it its name, one of many scattered throughout the marshland. Their morning's exercise had made their appetites sharp; there was high praise for the *sagamite* cakes Cyrene passed out, the mixture of cornmeal, fat, chopped pork, and beans that was shaped into flat cakes and baked in a skillet. They washed them down with water, but for stimulation during the afternoon ahead, they built a small fire of fallen oak limbs and boiled a pot of coffee.

They lounged here and there, most of them sitting with their backs against an oak tree or a log as relief from the long hours in the pirogue without back support. Cyrene had brought a blanket from the pirogue, and she lay back on it with her knees flexed and her hands behind her head, staring up at the pale winter sky.

She felt odd, unsettled in her mind. The few days before their departure had been disturbing. René had left them the morning after what she thought of as the night of the storm. She had not known what to expect of the Bretons. She had thought there might be further recriminations or perhaps a few jokes, a little crude banter. Instead, there had been nothing. It was almost as if they were content with the arrangement. It left her to wonder if they weren't just a little relieved to be free of the care of her. It was not a comfortable idea.

And yet it wasn't normal, their silence. They were gregarious men, given to talk and laughter and endless teasing. Thinking back, she realized they had been too quiet for some time, since the night René had come. She could recall nothing he had said or done to account for it, and yet it was so. Was there something about the man that held them subdued?

She turned her head, allowing her gaze to rest on René.

He had remained at his own lodgings for the short time before they left, though he had visited once or twice in the evening to discuss some detail about the procuring of his share of the indigo or outfitting himself for the expedition. He had made no move toward intimacy with her, though he had been pleasant enough, according her a bow and a smile. Once or twice she had caught him watching her, but no more. It was just as well; she had been ready with a blistering rejection if he had made any such attempt. She might yet have an opportunity to use it.

She had to admit that he looked different. A large part of it was his clothes; she had become used to seeing him either nearly naked or in the elegant attire of a gentleman. He was dressed now with commendable plainness in a coat of gray cloth with horn buttons and a pair of black wool breeches worn with plain stockings and shoes. His tricorn was well made but without ornamentation. Only his linen was fine, though it carried not a vestige of lace. Beside him rested a flintlock musket of the latest manufacture.

But the difference was more than the clothes or even the weapon. He seemed bigger beside the Breton men, with more latent strength held inside him. His face had lost its drawn look, filling out under the cheekbones, and his skin had regained its healthy color. His eyes held the penetration of intelligence, and the firmness around his mouth hinted at unsuspected reserves of strength. His hair, though short, had been drawn back in a small, neat queue tied with a black ribbon, as innocent of wig or powder as that of the Bretons themselves. He looked, in fact, like a determined gentleman planter out to survey his concession, one who would not hesitate to turn his hand to a task if it came along. And he did not look patient.

René felt Cyrene's gaze upon him and turned his head to meet it. He would give much to know what was passing through her mind behind the brooding darkness of her eyes. He would, indeed.

They were lounging about, sipping their coffee and talking

among themselves when Pierre suddenly raised his head and made a swift gesture for silence.

The older Breton slowly stood and walked from under the shelter of the cluster of oaks where they rested. He turned first this way and then that way, scanning with narrowed eyes the snaking waterway over which they had just come and the stretch of marsh that lay around them. He sniffed the wind.

The others stood also, looking this way and that, shifting to stare in every direction. It may have been no more than the communication of Pierre's alertness, but it seemed to Cyrene that there was a strained feeling in the air and it was unnaturally quiet. From the trees back the way they had just come, there was the sudden rise of a flock of blackbirds, twittering in alarm. Something was not right.

Jean downed the last of his coffee in a quick swallow and turned the empty wooden cup upside down to empty the grounds. He went to stand at his brother's side. "We go, yes?"

"Yes," Pierre said with decision. "We go."

It was the work of no more than a moment to gather up the water keg and cups, the coffee kettle, and the leather pouch that held the *sagamite* cakes. They piled them in the pirogues and shoved off.

Before they could pick up their paddles, another boat came sweeping from among the trees. It looked huge; it was a dugout filled with an army of Indian warriors. It was no friendly party. Their faces were painted and they held their muskets ready and their bows with arrows notched. A shout rose at the sight of the pirogues. Musket fire boomed out, thundering over the water.

The shot rattled around them, making geysers in the water. One ball thudded into the side of the pirogue, and Cyrene heard another whistle between René and herself. The dugout, manned by some nine or ten renegade Choctaw, was obscured for an instant by a roiling cloud of gray powder smoke; then, like fiends breaking from hell, the Indians tore through it and bore down upon them.

''Paddle, for the love of the Holy Mother! Dig deep!''

They bent to the task, sending the smaller, more light-weight pirogues surging over the water. It was possible they could outdistance their attackers, or at least put enough space between them so that the Indians might give up the chase as not worth the effort.

The Indians showed no sign of flagging. Their faces contorted with blood lust made fiercer by their paint, they bent their labors to the chase. Among them those with muskets could be seen reloading.

The pirogue Cyrène was in skimmed over the water, leaping forward with each concerted stroke of the paddles. There was no wasted movement, no wasted energy, just gut-wrenching effort. They were able to keep their distance but could not draw away. There was a small shift in the feel of the boat. She looked back and saw that René had put down his paddle and picked up his musket. He aimed, fired.

The concussion flung the pirogue forward, wildly rocking. Through the smoke, Cyrène saw a warrior throw up his arms and crash back among his fellows as if struck by a giant hand. She did not hesitate but leaned forward to snatch Pierre's musket and hand it back to René. Pierre grunted approval, taking all of the paddling upon himself, his shirt tightening over his brawny shoulders as he bent into it.

René took the musket from her and instantly passed her his own, at the same time stripping off his powder horn and bullet pouch and pitching them to her. She put down her paddle and began at once to reload for him. She heard him fire again, but there was no time to look. Her movements swift and sure, she primed the pan, poured powder, and rammed in patch and ball. They exchanged muskets. She began to reload once more. René fired again.

Cyrène spared a glance as they exchanged muskets yet again. The Indians were gaining. There was one less renegade than there had been before, however, and another had a red streak of blood down his arm.

Reload. Fire. Reload. An arrow hit the side of the pirogue

with a solid *thunk*. Cyrene could hear Gaston cursing and knew he had been hit. The sharp cries of the Indians were louder, closer. She looked up to hand the loaded musket to René. The dugout was so near her breath caught in her throat. She was staring into the eyes of a warrior with his teeth bared and his bow drawn with an arrow pointing straight at her. There was no time to aim. She pointed the musket at him, pulled the hammer back to full cock, and squeezed the trigger.

The warrior's eyes widened. His arrow was released as he began to topple backward. It flew high, arching, falling, falling. Cyrene watched helplessly as it curved over her head, wobbling in its descent, striking toward Pierre, slicing into his back. He let out his breath with a soft oath, but the rhythm of his paddling did not falter.

Fear and sickness made a hard knot in her stomach, but there was no time to acknowledge it, much less give in to it. Blindly, she turned from Pierre and began to reload the weapon in her hands. She reached to hand it to René. For an instant their eyes met, and in his she saw a hard flash of something that might have been admiration but could equally have been derision for her lack of sensibility.

The renegade Choctaw were closing in. They meant to strike between the two pirogues, engaging both, which was odd; their surest chance of booty was to concentrate on one. It might be a tactical error, but it could also mean they intended that no one should escape.

They reckoned without the Bretons' skill as boatmen. As the dugout drew even, Pierre in one pirogue and Gaston in the other dropped their paddles and grappled with the attackers, but Jean rose up with an axe and began to smash the prow of the Indian dugout near the waterline. The fighting took on a frenzied edge. A warrior slashed at René with a knife. René smashed his musket butt into the painted face, knocking the Indian over the side, then turned to face another one with a hand axe. That man was not after him. He was making toward Cyrene with the fanatical gleam of vengeance in his eyes.

Cyrene fended him off with the musket she had been reloading, stabbing at him with the ramrod that protruded from the end. He dodged aside. She drew back. The warrior rose up, preparing to leap across the few inches that divided the gliding span of boats. She scrambled to her knees, the better to face him.

"Fire, Cyrene, fire!" René yelled.

There was no other choice, though she knew it was wrong the moment she felt the musket explode with the shot. The ramrod flew like a spear, impaling the warrior, but the recoil from firing that heavy projectile threw her backward. The pirogue rolled. She flung the musket from her as she fought for balance. She could not gain it. She struck the water with a solid splash. It closed over her, taking her down. The sounds of the struggle, the yells and grunts and thuds, receded as the boats moved away with the current and their own impetus.

The shock of being catapulted into the ice-cold water held Cyrene immobile for drifting, slow-moving seconds, but then she felt the imperative need for air. She kicked out, shooting toward the surface. She broke free in time to see the three boats heading around a bend. They were apart, and the pirogues were in the lead once more.

Then beside her was a roiling splash in the water. She was caught by hard hands, dragged against a strong, lean body. Water dashed across her face. It caught in her nose, almost strangling her.

Her knife was in its sheath at her waist. She closed her hand around the hilt and dragged it free, then raised it to strike. The man lunged aside at the last moment. Her wrist was caught, twisted; the knife left her grasp. She lashed out with her fist and felt it land on solid flesh and bone, a square hit. They both went under. Pulled down, her legs entangled with those of the man who held her, and hampered by her skirts, she could not find the air she needed. When she came up again, she was coughing, blinded by the water.

"It's all right. I have you." The voice was rough with concern and all too familiar. René. He must have been thrown from the pirogue with her.

"Let me go, damn you!" She pushed at him, kicking.

"I'm trying to help you. Be still before we both drown."

"I don't need your help," she gasped in frustrated rage and mounting panic as she felt herself sinking once more. She thrust back from his hold, almost pushing him under in her frantic need to be free of him. "I can—"

She never finished the words. The blow came out of nowhere. She felt the pain of it on the point of her chin, then there was nothing but floating gray darkness.

6

"**Y**OU CAN SWIM. That's what you wanted to say."

Cyrene stared up at René as he hovered above her. His gray eyes were bleak yet narrowed with concern, and a lock of his hair, shining black with wet, dangled across his forehead. His words, ringing in her ears, had the sound of an accusation. Cyrene's jaw ached and her very bones felt limp. She was lying on the ground under the cover of a thicket of evergreen myrtle shrubs well back from the bayou. Her clothes were sodden and water oozed from her hair. She was cold but not freezing as she might have been. The reason was the close hold of René's arms around her and the weight of his wet coat that lay over them both.

She tried, abruptly, to sit up, but fell back with a gasp as sickness rushed in upon her. She closed her eyes tight. "You bastard," she said through gritted teeth. "You hit me."

"You were trying to kill me, and damned near succeeded."

"Why not? You were drowning me."

"I was trying to save you." His voice was grim.

"Thank you very much. I was perfectly capable of doing it myself."

"I realize that, now. Only a woman in a thousand knows how to swim, and you have to be that one."

She would have liked to berate him further, but she didn't feel like it. Besides, it would be best to keep their voices down until they knew where the Choctaw renegades were. After a moment, she said more quietly, "I really thought you were one of the Indians."

"I realize that, too," he said shortly. From the ground near her head, he picked up the knife he had taken from her and presented it with the hilt forward in a gesture of studied politeness. "Your weapon, if you are still determined to use it."

She brought her hand from under the coat and snatched the knife from him. "Don't be ridiculous!"

"There was always the possibility." When she gave him a dark look without answering, he went on abruptly, "I'm sorry I struck you. It seemed necessary, and I just . . . did it before I thought."

"Never mind." It was embarrassment that made her words so short. She tried again. "There's no harm done. What about—what about the others?"

"The last I saw of them, they were pulling ahead, going around the bend. The savages were having to bail."

"Pierre and Jean will come back for us."

"Yes, when they can."

And if they were able. Neither spoke the words, but both acknowledged them with a long glance. In the meantime, they did not dare light a fire to warm themselves and to dry their clothing. They had no weapon beyond Cyrene's knife, no shelter, nothing to eat. To move from where they were might be to run into the Indians, either in their retreat or, if they had been victorious, in their search for them. For the moment, there was nothing they could do but lie still and wait.

It was not a comfortable situation by any means. It was not just the wind that whispered through the leaves above them, chilling damp flesh and turning wet cloth icy cold, nor was it the uneven ground under them with its litter of leaves covering sticks that grew sharper as the minutes passed. It was the enforced closeness, the touch of thigh against thigh, breast against breast. As a reminder of things better forgotten, it was nearly intolerable.

"Are you all right?"

"Well enough," Cyrene answered, her eyes closed. She thought René was watching her as he lay with his head propped on his hand, but she did not care to make certain.

"Are you sure?"

She lifted her lashes, caught by something in his voice. "Yes, why?"

"I hardly expected you to take this part of it so calmly."

"You mean lying here with you?" She could feel heat in her face.

"In a word, yes."

"We are both cold, unless you are immune to the weather. It would be a ridiculous martyrdom to deny it or to try to keep you at a distance. We need each other, need the little warmth we can find between us."

"A very practical view."

"Here in the wilderness you learn to be practical, to cooperate with each other in spite of—of differences. Those who don't have a way of dying."

"I have no intention of dying." He meant it, he found, with a fervor he had applied to few things in his life. His intention was to discover in what other ways this woman was different from all others.

He could think of no other female of his acquaintance who would accept his presence after what he had done without screaming in rage or shrinking from him in abject fright, none who would be resigned to the discomfort of their position without complaints and demands that he do something, and certainly none with the courage and knowledge to lend her aid to the repulsion of the Indian attack in the first place. Such a paragon he had never seen, most particularly one who could appear delectable, in the fashion of a half-drowned mermaid, through it all.

Somewhere a bird called, a faint, plaintive sound. A limb fell from a tree behind them, clattering through the branches, snapping in two as it thudded to the ground. Cyrene became aware of the steady beat of René's heart against her shoulder and the rise and fall of his breathing. Her own pulse was ragged, throbbing against her ribs. A sense of emptiness began in the lower part of her body and slowly spread upward. As an added danger in their situation began to make itself known, she hurried into whispered speech.

"Why—why did you come after me? Why did you leave the boat?"

"I was the one who told you to fire, else you wouldn't have gone overboard. On top of that, if you will remember, I thought you needed saving."

"I would have fired, anyway."

"Would you? But the fault was still mine."

"Not at all," she insisted. "Anyway, I'm surprised Pierre, or Jean either, let you do it."

"Instead of one of them? They had no choice; their hands were full at the time."

"But you must have been quick to beat them to it."

He raised a brow. "Aren't you forgetting something?"

"What?"

"You are under my protection."

"Surely it doesn't extend to this?"

"Why would you think otherwise?"

"It isn't the same thing at all!" Her tone was cross, mainly because she suspected him of baiting her.

"What is it, then?"

"You have no obligation to save my life, for one thing."

"What about the right?"

"That either! You make it sound as if you think I belong to you."

"Don't you?"

"I do not!" She raised herself up on one elbow, her eyes hard with anger and her voice sibilant in its quietness. "I don't care what Pierre and Jean said, I belong to me. I'm grateful that you dived in after me, but that doesn't mean I accept any part of this bargain you made with them."

''What happened,'' he drawled, a smile rising in his gray eyes, ''to cooperation? To needing each other?''

Their faces were only inches apart. Cyrene's gaze dropped to his lips. She could feel the magnetic force of the attraction between them, sense its slow pull. It would take only a little, a slight swaying, the parting of her lips, and their mouths would be joined. She knew it.

She took a deep, slow breath and eased slowly back down to the ground.

She stared up into the myrtle branches. Her voice was flat as she spoke again. ''What is it you want?''

''You, of course.''

The answer was flippant, without thought, because René could not think. He felt as if he were standing on the edge of a precipice with the earth falling from under his feet. He must learn not to underestimate this woman. He would learn, or else.

''Oh, please,'' she said, the look in her brown eyes scathing. ''You don't care about me, and you don't care about trading. You're just like all the others. You'll stay in Louisiane as long as you have to, but the minute they give you leave, you'll take ship back to France and kiss the stony wharf there when you go ashore. You'll hie yourself to Paris and dine out for years on tales of what a barbarous land this is and what strange creatures and uncouth people live here.''

''You don't think much of such men, do you?''

''Why should I? They aren't suited to this new country, and so it's better they leave. We don't need them.''

''What makes you so sure I'm one of them?''

''Next you will tell me you intend to take up a concession of land here and make it your life's work.''

Something in her tone, as of judgment passed, stung René. ''Who knows? I might enjoy that. I just might like being far away from authority, might prefer carving my own estate out of virgin land.''

''Living in a house of logs, fighting the gales and floods and the scorching sun? The fevers and agues and fluxes? The mosquitoes and snakes, the chiggers and ticks and every kind of stinging, biting bug?''

''You think I couldn't?''

''Oh, you could, if you really wanted it. The trouble is, so few men do.''

It was an odd thing, but for an idea that had never crossed his mind until this moment, this one had a marvelously strong appeal. He knew beyond doubting that he could enjoy the challenge of this new land. He could take great pleasure in wresting a living, and perhaps a fortune, from it under the circumstances she had described. That was, of course, if the challenge was his to accept, if it were allowed. It was not.

''And what of you?'' he asked with considerable irony. ''Are you content as you are, trading with the Bretons? Do you never think of helping build an estate?''

She gave him a defiant look. ''I think of making money enough to buy land of my own.''

''And who will work it?''

''I will!'' she said fiercely. ''Or I will buy an African or two to help.''

''You should have no trouble finding a husband to do the labor or to oversee the slaves.''

''Yes, and to sell everything when my back is turned or to drink away the profits. I've seen it all before.''

''How does it come about that you have so little opinion of marriage? Or men?'' His curiosity was genuine, though the question had a purpose.

''Let's say the examples I've seen haven't been impressive.''

''Thank you,'' he said, his tone dry.

She slanted him a quick glance through her lashes, then looked away again. ''I didn't mean you.''

''I wish I could believe that. What of your parents' marriage? That couldn't have been so bad if it produced you.''

The implied compliment was disturbing; she decided to ignore it. ''My father managed to gamble away my mother's dowry, her inheritance, and a great deal more before being banished to the colony in disgrace. My mother died of the privations he brought upon her, and the shame.''

It occurred to Cyrene as she spoke that there was not so much difference between René Lemonnier and her father. Not only was René an outcast, but he had something of the same rakish manner. There were other similarities: their fine clothing, the taint of the fleshpots of Paris, the hint of less than saintly principles.

"What of the Bretons? Are they such paragons that you stay with them?"

"They took us in, my mother and father and I, when we had no place to go. They've been good to me, almost like family. If I left them, I'd have no one.''

"You could have me, if you would abandon yourself to my care." He put the suggestion, then waited in some trepidation.

"Indeed? And for how long? Until you grow tired of me? Until you go back to France? No, I thank you.''

"At least you're polite.''

It would be all right, his pose of the ardent lover intent on winning a further taste of her charms. As long as she remained adamant, he would be safe in using his pursuit of her—the constant besieging of the citadel—as the excuse for his sudden interest in trade. What he would do if she capitulated, he did not know. A woman at close quarters would be a major hindrance. Not that he thought there was cause for worry. He obviously had little attraction for Cyrene. There were those, he did not doubt, who would rejoice if they ever learned of the constant rejection he was enduring. No doubt it was a suitable penance, one good for his soul regardless of the effect on his vanity.

Cyrene studied his face from under her lashes. Was he like her father, in truth? There was no outward sign; it was only in the repute both men had gained for themselves, in the faint swagger about them, and in the penalty imposed upon them by their government that the similarity lay.

Or did it? What, actually, did she know about René? The answer was next to nothing other than the whispers of the gossips. During his time on the flatboat he had said little about himself, and the conventions operating in the colony concerning a person's past had prevented too many questions. Was it possible that the distrust she felt toward René was rooted in her memory of the failings of her father? She did not like to think that she had been so unfair.

But had she? The way to discover the right of the matter lay open. By inquiring into her affairs he had given her the opportunity to do the same.

She shifted a little, drawing back to better see his face. "What about you? It seems that if I care for men too little, you like women far too much."

"Impossible," he declared with a flamboyant gesture of one hand as he lay with his head propped on the other.

"Even if it makes you an exile?"

"An inconvenience that is beginning to reveal compensations."

She held his glinting gaze for a long moment. "I take it you don't mean to give a straight answer."

"I have yet to hear a straight question."

"Is that what's required?" she inquired with astringency. "Straight out, then: Are you here because you could not forebear to set up a flirtation with La Pompadour?"

"Alas, I was the soul of discretion."

"But you were caught in spite of it?"

"I played the part of loyal subject to my king and left the lady's favors unsought and unsavored. I should have at least worshiped from afar."

He might have changed his style of coat and hair, but he was still the courtier, using ten words to say what one would do. "I wish you would not speak in that affected way."

"How would you have me speak?"

"Plainly."

"Plainly, then, the lady was incensed at my lack of attention. In common with some other women, she craved the pleasure of refusing it."

She narrowed her eyes. "If you are suggesting that I am one of those women—"

"You wrong me," he said with a wounded air.

"I doubt it."

He leaned forward until his mouth just brushed her cheek. "What did you say? I didn't quite catch it."

"Never mind. Are you sure that was all?"

"All? Do you realize I was very nearly left to rot in the darkest corner of the Bastille? The *lettre de cachet* was signed, the cell door firmly closed. Only the intervention of my friend Maurepas saved me."

"The minister? But I thought he and La Pompadour were sworn enemies?"

"They are. It needed only for Maurepas to say in the presence of Louis's mistress that he was sure I preferred the Bastille, where my disappearance was providing the final stroke to a legend to equal that of Don Juan himself, to being banished to Louisiane where all the women were either old or ugly. The deed was done in an instant."

"Old? Ugly?"

"An error for which Maurepas must be forgiven. But one concocted in a good cause, or so I thought."

"I can see how you might." She didn't believe him. There was something he was hiding behind his glib pose of the sensualist. What it was, she didn't know, but she meant to find out.

"An error," he added, "that gives me great pleasure."

René could see that she was not convinced. He wished that he could tell her the truth, but he knew with grim certainty that it would not make her think better of him.

"Tell me," she said, her tone brittle. "What did you do in France? Besides seduce susceptible females, of course."

"Do? Why I paid my court at Versailles. I also hunted, attended levees, routs, and balls, gambled a little—the usual things." There was no harm in admitting to that much of the truth.

"You have estates?"

"It would be more proper to say that my father has them, though I have an income produced by a portion of them."

"What does he think of your banishment, your father?"

"I had no time to ask before I was hustled onto a ship and locked in my cabin. I'm sure he would say, if asked, that he hoped it would be the making of me, though he would wager little on the chance."

There was an edge to his tone that told her she had struck a nerve. "He is making an effort to have you pardoned and recalled, I suppose?"

"Now, why should you suppose any such thing? I'm not his only son or even the eldest. There were five of us, but one died in infancy and another is an invalid." He watched her closely as he spoke. "Still, there are sufficient to carry on the line without me."

"The only consideration to move him?"

It was a moment before René could bring his attention to bear on what she had said. The possibility of a reaction had been remote. The lack of one proved nothing.

He said, "You are thinking, maybe, of parental affection? But I have besmirched the family honor and so have forfeited such sentiment. Would you care to replace the loss?"

He moved his hand at her waist in a caressing motion, sliding it upward as if to cup the fullness of her breast.

"I would not!" Cyrene caught his hand and flung it from her body as if it were a bothersome insect. "Does everything lead to this with you?"

"Most everything," he admitted, his gaze hooded as he watched the quick rise and fall of her bodice. The cheap cloth had dried to semidampness as they talked. It no longer clung with such distracting fidelity, molding every feature. That was a blessing, for in his last answer, at least as it pertained to Cyrene Nolté, he had not lied.

Before Cyrene could speak, there came a faint splash from the bayou. The sound was repeated, drawing nearer; it was the steady dipping of paddles. René threw back his coat, which covered them, and raised himself into a sitting position with the careful contraction of hard muscles. He nudged aside the crisp green foliage of the myrtle with one finger, then peered out. He went still.

"The renegades?" she whispered, a breath of sound.

He gave a brief nod in answer. "Only three left. No prisoners."

Cyrene released a trembling breath. The Bretons had not been taken prisoner.

The renegade Choctaw did not pause, gave no sign they remembered where she and René had entered the water. Either they had wounded among them who needed attention that could only be provided at their camp, wherever that might be, or else they had lost their enthusiasm for harassing *voyageurs*. Within minutes they were out of sight and the quiet sounds of their passage had died away among the trees and waving marsh grass.

When it was safe, René rose to his feet. "Can you walk if you lean on me?"

"I could, yes," she said doubtfully, "but if you mean to move from here, I don't think we should do that."

"It will help to warm us, besides shortening the time before we meet with the others."

"Pierre and Jean will have taken careful note of the place where they left us and will expect to find us here if . . . when they return. If we move downstream, we may not be able to follow the bayou for the undergrowth and dead water sloughs. We could miss them."

The compulsion to be doing something to better their position warred inside René with recognition of the wisdom of what Cyrene said. To sit still, tamely waiting for rescue, went against his every instinct. He might be able to overcome her objections, though it would make little difference. There was not a great deal from which to choose between dying of exposure somewhere downstream while trying to reach the English ship and doing it under the myrtle where they had been lying. Though he did not like to say so, the renegades could just as easily have failed to search them out because they had succeeded in what they were trying to do, rob the trading *voyageurs* of their indigo. On the other hand, though he had been here a month, this was not his territory. He did not fully understand its dangers. Cyrene did.

Cyrene, sensing his ambivalence, said with emphasis, "Pierre and Jean will come."

"Ah, well," he answered as he sank down beside her once more, "we'll wait then if it means so much to you to stay a little longer in my arms."

It seemed like a long time before the Breton men returned, though it could have been no more than an hour. As it was, Cyrene and René nearly missed their arrival, so quietly were they moving. By the time they disentangled themselves and stood, the pirogues were already grounded on the bank.

A pair of buffalo robes were unwrapped from the bedrolls for the wet pair, but all shoved off again without tarrying. It was miles deeper in the maze of marsh and bayou before Pierre gave the signal to land once more. They built a fire, though their exertions at the paddles had warmed them by that time and their clothing was so nearly dry that changing was a needless effort.

One thing Cyrene insisted on doing at once was tending the wounds of Gaston and Pierre. She had been worried about them for what seemed like hours, despite their unimpaired ability to send the pirogues skimming over the water.

The younger man's arm had a jagged cut that would need to have the edges sewn together for proper healing. In common with most of the *voyageurs* of Cyrene's acquaintance, Gaston made a great deal of noise under her ministrations with a needle, groaning and breathing curses as if he were being tortured, but held his arm out as steady as a cross beam without so much as a single flinch.

The arrow in Pierre's back was more serious. Jean had broken off the protruding shaft, leaving a stub of some four inches as well as the flint head of the arrow embedded in the muscle just under the shoulder blade. The angle at which it had entered had prevented it from going deep, but had caused it to burrow under the skin at a long angle, encasing itself in a tight pocket. It was a freak occurrence. The arrow should have plunged straight in, burying itself in Pierre's lungs. What had deflected the penetration of the arrow was the toughness of the skin of Pierre's back, which was a leatherlike matting of scars, hundreds of them crisscrossing one upon the other, that covered the upper part of his body.

Cyrene had seen the scars before, but never so close or at such length. The older Breton permitted few to view his back, nor did he talk about it. The reason was not difficult to understand. There was only one thing that could bring about such massive scarring and that was a sentence of life on the king's galley, endless years of daily, even hourly, whippings. The men who carried that particular badge of penal servitude were few. Most men died after a year or two in the galleys; to escape was rare, indeed. Even then, the danger was not at an end. For an escaped galley slave to be taken up by the authorities meant hanging, and that after the imposition of such torture as the judge could devise, from breaking on the rack to drawing and quartering to the slow crushing of the head. The scars were more than a mark of servitude; they were a sentence of death.

Gaston and Jean were used to the sight and paid scant attention. If René found it unusual, it appeared he had the intelligence to deduce the cause and consequences, for he asked no questions.

Due to the barbed sides of the arrowhead, the only way to remove it was to cut it out. That would not be easy to do without inflicting more damage than had already been done.

Cyrene cleaned her knife in the sand, then buried the blade in the glowing red coals of the fire. She gave Pierre a beaker of brandy, then rinsed the blood from his back with more of the distilled liquor. There were some who recommended setting the brandy aflame to cauterize wounds, but she had never seen the necessity. Anything that burned so badly on its way down the throat need not depend on flame for its powers to stop putrefaction.

Gaston had lain down and promptly dropped off to sleep, exhausted from his labors and his endurance of her aid, no matter how careful. That left Jean to help with his brother. Cyrene had no thought of entrusting the knife to him, however, and was not certain of his usefulness otherwise. Jean might gut and skin a deer in less time than it took most to find the tail or scalp a renegade Indian for the bounty on his hair without a qualm, but the sight of the blood of those close to him, and more especially his own, turned him parsley green.

Watching her stitch up Gaston had already taxed his stomach. She noted a slight palsy in his hands as she beckoned him to come and pull the skin of Pierre's back taut over the deep-burrowed arrow.

Jean did as he was instructed, but swallowed hard and turned his head away as she picked up the white-hot knife and waved it in the air to cool. She could not say that she blamed him; she didn't exactly relish the task herself. She took a firm grip on the handle of the knife, shifting her index finger along the top of the blade for control.

Jean made the mistake of looking just as the first drop of bright red blood welled up around the tip of the knife. He swayed, giving a small grunt. His hands dropped to his sides. Cyrene's free hand shot out, trying to grab him.

There was a swift movement and then René was there. He supported Jean to a seat on a tree trunk, then returned to stand beside Cyrene.

"Would you allow me to do it?" he asked, his gaze on her white face as he put out his hand for the knife.

"Can you?"

"I can try. I've seen a few wounds treated."

Where could that have been, on a dueling field? It hardly mattered. She spoke to the injured man with only the barest glance over her shoulder before her gaze returned to René's. "Pierre?"

The older Breton brother was watching them, his expression intent despite the grooves etched by pain on either side of his mouth. "Whatever you please, *chère*, so long as it is done quickly."

Cyrene weighed the problem an instant longer. It may have been some surety she saw in the gray depths of René's eyes, or else her own reluctance for the task that persuaded her. Whatever it was, it was decisive.

She passed the knife to him and took Jean's place. They seemed to need no words. Together they exposed the arrow, making an opening for its removal, then plucked it from its bed. Cyrene cleaned the wound with more brandy, tacked it together with a few stitches, and bandaged it tightly.

When they were done, René moved to the brandy keg and refilled Pierre's beaker, then splashed generous tots of the liquor into two more. He handed one to Cyrene, then raised his own in salute.

"Thank you," Cyrene said.

"Don't thank me, you earned it."

"So did you." She took a sip of the liquid heat, and as it burned its way down, it occurred to her where else René might have learned his skill with a knife blade and his stomach for wounds. Some men were born with such talents, but they were more often gained in use, such as on a battlefield or in prison.

The ship, the *Half Moon*, rode at anchor on the brown-tinted blue waters of the bay. It did not look particularly furtive. A merchantman with sails of utilitarian brown, it was English made and as rounded and thick-waisted as a burgher's wife. It flew no flag, however, and stood in readiness for a swift retreat should a French patrol appear.

The Bretons did not approach at once; that would have been to appear too eager. Nor did they depend on the usual invitation to sleep on board the merchantman, which, Pierre contended, only gave the other man the advantage of doing business on his home ground. Their first task when they arrived at the bay, therefore, was to set up camp on the beach. What remained unacknowledged among them was that the true cause of the rough bivouac was Pierre. He hated any floating craft larger than a keelboat. He could stay aboard a ship for only a matter of hours before his hands began to shake, and to sleep on one he had to be dead drunk. Even then he was haunted by terrifying nightmares of his days at the oar of a galley.

The beach stretched empty, edged with its ragged tide line of sea-blackened driftwood. There was no sign of other traders; they were the first. They unloaded the pirogues and built a fire, then set about building a pair of temporary shelters. The structures were far from elaborate, being little more than a pair of peeled poles for uprights and two more slanting to the ground to make a framework for a covering of brush and palmetto thatch. Still, they would turn the wind and protect them from any rain that might blow up at this season, though in milder weather a blanket roll would have sufficed.

As she tied palmetto fronds to the shelter pointed out as her own, Cyrene cast a critical eye over the other. It was a little bigger, but not that much. Pierre and Jean must have forgotten that René would have to share it, or else they expected him to sleep on the ship whether they did or not. If he decided on the beach, the four men were going to be crowded. Or perhaps not, since the Bretons usually took turns standing guard at night on these expeditions.

In anticipation of a meal on the ship, if not more, Cyrene had brought her best bodice and skirt and nicest coif. Not that they were a great deal different from her others. Luxury in clothing was not one of her preoccupations, though it sometimes seemed a passion in the colony. Possessing the most fashionable items that could be obtained, even if they were two years or more behind the styles of Paris and Versailles, seemed to make people feel less isolated, less condemned to eternal provincialism. When Cyrene and her parents had first come, she had been well supplied with clothing. Most of it had been outgrown during the first year. She had patched and pieced the rest—using one skirt to add a flounce to another, turning a too-tight coat into a bodice and a pair of pockets, making a coif and fichu from the good parts of a chemise, and other such necessities—but the constant wearing and washing in the river had turned much of what was left into near rags. Pierre and Jean sometimes bought a few ells of cloth for her, but for the most part it was coarse, rough stuff, traders' goods in harsh colors and bold patterns.

It was seldom that Cyrene took much notice of what she wore beyond the fact that it was clean and reasonably modest. This evening, however, she discovered within herself an odd dissatisfaction with her appearance. She would like, just once, to see how she looked in a *grande toilette*, in powdered hair and panniers, in the silk and satin and lace-lavished costume required at court and at the governor's house. René must be used to seeing women in such finery. Not that she cared for that. Her discontent was fleeting. She was actually happy as she was, without the bother of keeping such long skirts from trailing in the mud or the difficulty of breathing against the tight squeeze of a corset. As for panniers so wide that women had to turn sideways to get through doors and to take up the place of two people at a dinner table, wouldn't she look funny in them on the flatboat or climbing the side of a ship?

Despite her derision, she took special pains with her appearance once the expected invitation from the ship's captain arrived. She loosened her hair from the braid and brushed it until it shone with a soft golden sheen, then let it hang free down her back with a few tendrils escaping from her coif around her face in the style of young women who advertised their eligibility for marriage. She also borrowed their trick of loosening the tie at the gathered neckline of her chemise, exposing the smooth upper curves of her breasts. The purpose, she told herself, had nothing to do with fashion or with René's expectations about women's attire. Rather, it was another tactic for sharp trading. Anything that might serve to distract the English captain must be to the good.

The early dark of late January had closed in when they finally paddled out to the merchant vessel. Cyrene was first up the swaying ship's ladder. She climbed with easy agility, though she was glad for the concealing darkness as the off-shore wind billowed her skirts up around her waist.

The captain stood ready on deck to hand her aboard. He was a Rhode Islander and also the ship's owner. Captain Dodsworth was tall and freckled, with carrot-colored hair and a ready laugh. His hospitality was generous, and he always listened to news of the events in the French colony as if they took place on the moon itself. Still, he was a sharp trader. The Bretons had dealt with him before, not always to advantage. Jean called him a cold-water pirate.

"Mademoiselle Nolté," he said, bowing over her hand, "it's always a pleasure to welcome you on the *Half Moon*."

A smile of pleasure rose in her eyes. "Captain Dodsworth, as gallant as ever, I see."

"If so, it's because you bring it out in me."

"The question is, do I bring out your generosity?"

He threw back his head to laugh. "Always!"

From the dimness beyond the captain, a man stepped forward. "If it isn't the beauteous lady smuggler. There are few men, mademoiselle, who wouldn't be generous to someone of your charms for the desired return."

Behind her, Cyrene heard Gaston board, then René's light leap down to the deck. There was no time to turn back, no time for a warning.

The newcomer, the man already entrenched on the ship like a wood worm in the planking, was one Touchet, though it was doubtful he had been baptized under the name. Short and thin, with the sinuous body of a hungry cat and a flat, avid face, he was known as a former cutpurse, petty thief, and peddler of forbidden brandy to slaves and Indians. He was also, according to most persistent rumor, the trading agent for the marquise, Madame Vaudreuil. And her paid informer.

7

IT WAS A wary gathering that sat down to partake of Captain Dodsworth's table fare. The meal was a plain one of bean soup and fish pan-broiled in butter followed by a main course of boiled beef seasoned with onion and thyme and served with boiled potatoes and cabbage. The *Half Moon* had come directly from the Bahamas where they had traded salted cod and ship's timbers for the trade goods brought out from England on the deep-water frigates; they had also picked up the oranges they had for dessert and the rum they drank, along with the less alcoholic brew of sugarcane juice known as tafia.

They were eight in number. Cyrene, as the only woman present, had the place of honor at the captain's right, with Jean beside her and Gaston on his other side. Across from her was Pierre, with René on his left and Touchet beside him, while the seat at the foot of the table was taken by the ship's first mate.

The main occupation of the evening, if not the main purpose, was introduced early. Captain Dodsworth, raising his cup of rum to Cyrene, proclaimed, ''To the blackest eyes and sweetest smile afloat tonight on the waters of the world!''

It was to be a drinking match. The winner of the contest would be the man with the strongest head and the prize would be the trading edge gained by the least-befuddled man. But there was more to it than that. Cyrene had the feeling, as she watched the captain, that he might also be playing the Breton party against the marquise's agent, hoping to encourage a competition. Two could, perhaps, play such a game. The compliment to her being no more than a ploy, it could be accepted and used. Moreover, though she had no intention of entering the drinking bout, she could throw her weight to the side of the Bretons. She inclined her head with a smile of appreciation and lifted her cup of tafia. "To all seamen who risk so much in search of . . . smiles."

The toasts came thick and fast, growing increasingly outrageous. They toasted George of England and Louis of France, the queens of both countries and the mistresses of both men. They drank to the damnation of excise men of any nationality and paid homage to the beauty of the color indigo blue; to La Pompadour's favorite peach shade that might or might not be the color of her nipples; and to the noble and supposedly rejuvenating, if not aphrodisiacal, qualities of the codfish and the catfish.

Cyrene gave the bantering and the deep drinking only a minor portion of her attention. The tale of their escape from the renegades was told with only a small comment from her thrown in now and again. The mulling over of the economic and political situation in Europe now that the war was at an end could not hold her interest for long. She watched instead the marquise's agent, Touchet.

He was a small man with a hollow chest and the sharp, chinless features of a weasel. His skin was sallow and pockmarked, and his fingernails were as long and curving and yellow as cow's horns, or like the nails of the Choctaw bonepickers who removed the decayed flesh of the dead before burial. His expression was secretive and supercilious, and though he tossed off the contents of his glass with each toast there was no discernible effect. He joined in the general discussion, but there was an edge to his remarks that was as sharp and jagged as broken glass.

What troubled Cyrene's mind was exactly why Touchet was on the ship. The worry was not hers alone. During a lull, Jean spoke across the table to the marquise's man. "Are you setting up as a trader, Touchet, or do you act as an agent?"

The question that hung unspoken in the air was whether the man was acting for the marquise. It was not impossible, and the knowledge that it was so would considerably lessen their danger. If Touchet was representing the marquise in a deal with the Rhode Islander, it was unlikely, though not impossible, that he would inform on them for *their* dealings.

But Touchet was not so easily drawn out. "It depends," he said with a small smile, "on the money."

Jean sent Pierre a brief glance. Touchet's answer could be taken to mean that he was open to a bribe to suppress his knowledge of their activities or simply that the decision to use that knowledge or engage in trade would depend on the amount to be made either way.

"The prospects for trade have never looked better," Jean said, his manner offhand.

"Or the chances for success against the smuggling patrols worse."

"A body would think they would be more lax, now that the war is over," Captain Dodsworth complained.

Pierre swirled the rum in his glass. "The war won't be over between our countries here until one of them is supreme in the New World."

"It will be us, my friend. We work harder and we don't give up."

"You will wear yourselves out," Pierre said with a laugh, "or else the Indians will kill you for pushing them from their lands. We take life easier, we French, as a gift instead of a task, and so we will endure in peace beside the savages when you English are long back on your little island."

Touchet gave a short laugh. "Ah, you *voyageurs*, you talk big but you never build anything, will never have anything."

"Nor do we destroy anything," Pierre said with dignity. "What more do we need except a boat, food and drink, maybe a little tobacco or a bit of gambling to liven the days?"

"Riches? A fine home? Servants to work so you may take your ease?"

"Bah! Such things can be torn away overnight. What matters is people, family and friends."

"You won't mind, then, if you are bested in trade or if some man comes along and takes Mademoiselle Cyrene from you with an offer of better things?"

Pierre's blue eyes took on a sparkle. "Trade is a gamble and I'll not be beaten at it if I can help it. As for Cyrene, we do not hold her. She can go if she wishes, but she has too much good sense, I think, to be fooled by fine talk and fancy show."

Cyrene, meeting Pierre's gaze as he finished speaking, thought there was a message in his words for her. Not for the first time, she wondered if she had been a fool. But no, she had known well enough that she was not a prisoner of the Bretons. It was their affection, and their fears for her, that caused them to guard her. What Pierre meant her to understand was that they trusted her judgment and had transferred the right to protect her to René because of it. She wished that she could feel so certain.

Captain Dodsworth reached out to cover Cyrene's hand where it rested on the table edge. "Mademoiselle Cyrene is one of those rare creatures, a handsome woman with a mind under her hair. She will not be fooled."

Since she knew very well that the captain not only had sharp business instincts but a wife and three children as well, Cyrene was less than overwhelmed by the compliment. She gave him a slight smile while wondering if Madame Dodsworth was considered a rare creature by her husband. She somehow doubted it.

René, watching Dodsworth fondle Cyrene's hand, was surprised to feel the steady rise of irritation. He should be paying attention to the men, listening to them talk, feeling out their intentions, but again and again his attention strayed to the only female at the table. Her poise there in the midst of that all-male gathering was remarkable. She did not put herself forward, but neither did she withdraw into silence. She did not join in the risqué comments, but gave no sign of being offended by them, not even for the sake of convention. Her hair shone like molten gold in the light of the whale oil lamps, and her skin had the sheen of pearls. The black depths of her eyes held quick thought and a secret, ellusive amusement that was fascinating, that he would give much to be able to share.

René wanted, suddenly, to stand up and knock the fatuous, grinning Rhode Islander flat on his backside, then scoop up Cyrene, throw her over his shoulder, and carry her from the ship back to the bay shore. There he would make love to her until they were both breathless and intoxicated with the richness of it. They would lie together in splendid nakedness among the furs that made up Cyrene's pallet, and he would press his lips to every delectable inch . . .

Madness. He sat still, breathing deep, willing composure. He could not remember ever having such a vivid and nearly uncontrollable flash of desire before, not even when he was young and callow. He didn't quite know what to make of it, as he did not know with certainty what to make of the woman who had caused it. He only knew that he was going to have to be on his guard. He could not afford such impulses.

"Our lady smuggler is unusual," Touchet was saying, "but is still a woman for all that. She must know she would be superb in silk and lace. The man who can give them to her will be amply rewarded, I have no doubt."

The man's tone was oily. René gave him a sharp glance. A frown appeared on Pierre's face. Cyrene turned to stare at him, her gaze cold though a flush of annoyance and dislike for being placed so squarely at the center of attention mounted to her forehead.

"Are you suggesting that I can be bought for a few lengths of cloth?" she asked.

"An expression only, Mademoiselle Cyrene. I refer to a certain way of life, to luxury and ease. Don't tell me they have no appeal?" The lips of the marquise's agent were twisted with cynicism though his gaze, resting on the soft white curves of her breasts above her bodice, was avid.

"I can't say that it does, if I have to sell my soul for it."

"Your soul? I doubt that's what the buyer will want in return."

Jean came to his feet with Pierre not far behind him. "That's enough, Touchet," the younger brother said.

The weasel-faced man looked at Jean. "The watchdogs awake. How very affecting."

René could remember no conscious decision to intervene. One moment he was watching Touchet, the next he was on his feet. He divided a level look between the Bretons before turning to Touchet in the chair next to him. He leaned over the smaller man, bracing his knuckles on the table. "The duty for this watch is mine," he said, "and I am indeed awake. Cyrene is not a subject for discussion at this table or elsewhere, nor are her wants and needs."

Touchet looked him up and down slowly. "You, I assume, will be looking after them as well as her good name and her . . . soul?"

"Precisely. Whatever she wishes can be hers; she has only to ask."

There was no need to add the last, but saying the words gave him real satisfaction. The arrested look in Cyrene's eyes also pleased him. If she had thought he would remain strictly confined to the place she had assigned to him, she was in for even more of a surprise. He had stayed at court too long, he knew that now; he had nearly forgotten how good it felt to speak plainly and to take simple direct action. He could not remember when he had felt more reckless or more determined. Or more guilty.

Cyrene heard René's declaration with disbelief. Almost as disturbing was the fact that the Bretons made no objection; in fact, they merely settled back in their seats as if the situation were well in hand. She felt marked, singled out as the possession of René Lemonnier. It was enraging. That she had brought it upon herself made no difference. Before the night was out, she would set M'sieur Lemonnier straight. Whatever she wished, indeed! She would tell him what her wishes were, and then they would see how well he complied.

Captain Dodsworth filled the breach by beginning to talk of the trade goods he had brought, particularly some fine faïence ware bowls and pitchers he thought might be of interest to Cyrene. He was on the point of turning to give the order to have the items displayed when there was a stir in the doorway.

The ship's officer on duty stepped inside. "Your pardon, Captain," he said, his tone carefully neutral. "There are Indians on the beach. Seems they want to parley."

Cyrene's first thought was that it was the renegades, that the savages had followed them and had come to demand that their prey be turned over to them. The same thought occurred at once to the Bretons, for they shoved back their chairs and sprang to their feet, heading out on deck. Captain Dodsworth, calling for his spyglass, followed, with the others behind him.

The Indians had built a fire. It was a leaping fountain of light on the dark shore. Figures moved around it, apparently without aim, black silhouettes against the flames. Overhead, the stars pricked the chill night sky with points of diamond brightness. The ship moved slowly up and down on the swells, with the water lapping at the hull. Somewhere from the bow came the low voices of men talking.

The spyglass was brought. Captain Dodsworth trained it on the Indians around the fire. Long seconds passed as he stared at them. Finally he brought the glass down and rubbed his eye.

"Choctaw," he said. "Old Drowned Oak's band."

Pierre grunted. Cyrene let out a sigh. Jean gave a low, mirthless laugh. Drowned Oak was the chief of a small Choctaw tribe allied to the French; he was also the father of the Indian woman known as Little Foot who had spent two winters with Jean some twenty years before, the woman who was Gaston's mother. Little Foot was not a doting parent, but she did tend to keep watch over the child she had borne and the man who had fathered him. If Drowned Oak was here now, it was because Little Foot had discovered that the Bretons had left the flatboat and knew enough about them and their business to guess at why and where to find them. Her purpose in bringing her father and his people would be simple. She would want first choice of the trade goods. And would expect special terms.

The atmosphere and inclination for close trading had been shattered. It was decided by mutual consent to postpone the matter. Captain Dodsworth, as a gesture of goodwill and for the sake of a closer look at the savages, ordered his longboat let down and had himself rowed ashore with the Bretons.

The Indians were waiting when the pirogues grounded on the beach. Some of the younger men pulled the prows of the crafts farther up on the sand so that the passengers would not have to get their feet wet, but the elders held back in dignified stances, ready to give their formal greetings. Once these were done, there were smiles all around as the captain brought out kegs of tafia and rum. It was a crime to sell liquor to the Indians, but there was none in giving it to them, and its power to impart goodwill was great, if short-lived.

Everyone settled around the main fire with cups and beakers in their hands. The talk began. Orange sparks spiraled skyward, dancing in the gray columns of smoke. The fragrance of the burning wood blended with the salt-and-mud smell of the marshlands, the freshness of the night, and the warm, wild odor of human bodies dressed in leather and wool. Some of the older Indian women sat on the outskirts of the circle about the main fire, while the younger ones moved here and there, laying out bedding, feeding babies, and bedding down toddlers. Older children scampered in circles, playing tag, running races.

Cyrene sank down at the fire beside the Bretons. For a time she enjoyed the exchange of solemn compliments and the round of tales. She had picked up enough of the Choctaw language so that she could follow the stories and boasts, each more fantastic than the last. Soon, however, the drone of voices, the warmth of the flames, and her exertions of the day lulled her to near somnolence. She yawned and blinked and yawned again. When the urge to put her head down on her knees and shut her eyes became nearly irresistible, she knew it was no use fighting any longer.

She was just ready to get up and go quietly to her shelter when she felt Jean stiffen beside her. She glanced at him, then followed his gaze to where an Indian woman had approached the fire. It was Little Foot. A woman of majestic stature, she had thick black hair, which she wore in a single braid, and bold features. She waited until she was sure she had Jean's notice, then she beckoned with an abrupt movement.

Cyrene could sense Jean's reluctance to answer the summons. Beyond the fact that it had been something less than courteous, she could see no reason for it. There was no enmity between the two of them so far as Cyrene knew. Little Foot, her value among the men of her own tribe much enhanced by her sojourn in a white man's bed, had long ago taken an Indian husband and given birth to other children. After being widowed, she had occupied herself with a series of affairs, each more short-lived than the last. Jean visited her from time to time and sent her gifts, and Gaston spent a few months every summer with her among the Choctaw, hunting with them, learning their woods lore, being made much of by their women.

Little Foot beckoned again. Jean sighed, then got to his feet and threaded his way to the outer edge of the circle. Little Foot joined him, and together they moved away into the darkness. Taking advantage of the disturbance Jean had already made, Cyrene followed after him for her own escape.

She did not mean to eavesdrop. Her sole intention was to reach her pallet and crawl into it. It was not her fault that Jean and Little Foot's quarrel caused them to stop not three paces from where her shelter had been set up on the edge of the encampment. Even then she did not stand listening but swerved around them and continued on to duck under the piece of leather that closed off the end of her shelter. She had dropped down on her bear fur in the darkness scented with resin from the peeled poles and was taking off her shoes when Little Foot's clear, hard tones reached her.

"How can you say I have no right after what I have done for you? Do you think it's so easy? Do you think I like it? If so, you are one mad Frenchman. You said I would be repaid. Now I ask this small thing, and you say I want too much? This I cannot bear!"

"Be reasonable, Little Foot. We are not rich men, my brother and I."

"Do I ask for riches? No! It may be I should talk to Gaston. He would be very interested in what I have to say. Or perhaps the other one would pay in gold to hear me. If that should happen, you could use your trade goods to—"

Cyrene had to grin at Little Foot's ribald suggestion as to what Jean might do with his trade goods. Her amusement receded as quickly as it had come as Jean issued a sharp command and their voices died away out of hearing. She had never known Little Foot to be importunate before, much less threatening. She was usually rather merry and placid, though dignified with it. Something had upset the Indian woman and Cyrene wanted to know what it was. She would make a point of asking Jean about it in the morning.

Cyrene had been asleep an hour, perhaps two, when the soft scuff of a footstep woke her. She lay for a moment, listening. The sound had come from directly outside her shelter, she knew, but it was not repeated. Then came a soft rustling as the leather flap was lifted and someone bent to enter.

"Who's there?" she said sharply.

"Your protector."

René. His words were dry and precise. Too precise. He was either angry or drunk, and Cyrene could not make up her mind which would be most disturbing. She sat up, pulling the bearskin with her. "What do you want?"

"Why, to share your pallet. What else?"

Her heart leaped inside her chest. "That isn't funny."

"It wasn't meant to be."

"We have an agreement. I expect you to follow it."

There was a quiet noise and a heavy piece of clothing like a coat landed on the foot of her pallet. "Willingly," he said, his voice low, "only the Breton brothers seem to expect me to be with you. I offered to stand guard duty with Gaston but was all but escorted here."

"Escort yourself elsewhere."

"There is nowhere else."

"I don't care!" she said, leaning forward in her urgency. "You can't stay here."

"Why not? Are you afraid of me?"

"Certainly not, but I don't want you in here. I don't want your protection. Can't you understand that?"

"I am not deficient in intelligence—or understanding, which is not always the same thing. You have made yourself abundantly clear. Now can you understand that I have no intention of shivering on the damp ground for the sake of our agreement? Can you bring yourself to believe that I don't lust after your magnificent body, at least at this moment, and have no intention of pressing unwanted attentions upon you?"

"Don't you?" She had meant the words to be scathing. Instead, they had a disconcerted ring.

"No. Unless you request it, in which case I will be happy to oblige, as I said earlier this evening."

"Never!"

"Then you're safe."

"Oh, yes," she cried, "while everyone assumes I'm your woman."

"That seems to be unavoidable."

"Not to me, not if you get out and stay out!"

He made no answer. His waistcoat plopped down onto the pallet followed by something lighter, which must be his shirt.

"Stop this," she said, her voice tight, "or I will scream

so loudly you'll have every man, woman, child, and dog in here.''

''It's going to be a little crowded, isn't it? And public?''

''I mean it!''

''Then again, preventing such a racket might make a fine excuse for me to kiss you thoroughly. I was thinking about how much I would like to do that earlier this evening while you flirted with Captain Dodsworth.''

''You were—I was not flirting with the captain!''

''It was a fine imitation.''

She knew she was allowing herself to be distracted. It was only while she reviewed her position. Screaming did not seem likely to be of much use, particularly if the Bretons were aware of where René was at this moment.

''I was only being friendly for the sake of trade.''

''Using your charms for commerce? There are words for women who do that.''

''You know very well I meant no such thing!''

He sat down to remove his boots. ''I do know, none better. But not everyone has my knowledge of your cool nature. You should be careful of what you say.''

''Cool nature? Because I don't fall into your arms again after having had a sample of your practiced lovemaking? What conceit!''

''Isn't it?'' he agreed, his voice even. ''Of course you could always prove me wrong.''

''Hah! You may gull some poor chambermaid or silly nobleman's wife with such a ploy, but not me. I don't have to prove anything to you.''

He removed his breeches and lifted the bearskin, sliding under it. ''No, you don't. All you have to do to put me firmly in my place is to go to sleep.''

Her muscles went rigid as she felt the waft of cool air and slide of the bearskin across her shoulders as he pulled it up over him. What she disliked most was his confidence. It was not, apparently, misplaced. She could see no way out of this predicament in which she found herself. As he shifted, searching for a comfortable position, his knee brushed the calf of her leg.

Abruptly, something snapped inside her. She flung herself at him, pushing, pummeling. "Get out," she hissed. "Get out! Leave me alone."

In an instant she was hurtled to her back. The air left her lungs as his weight came down upon her chest and the lower part of her body. Her wrists were caught in hard hands and wrenched above her head. She lay still with every muscle in her body clenched into a knot and a black and burning core of resentment in her brain.

"That wasn't very smart," he said.

Her breasts rose and fell against him with her short, hard breathing. The firm press of his taut-muscled thighs on her, his controlled strength, and the wrenching power of his hold were like a threat, though one held in careful abeyance. He was not hurting her, but she had never in her life felt more vulnerable or more certain that to try to fight would be painful.

"Maybe not, but it helped my feelings."

"Did it? You want to hit me?"

The impulse was rapidly fading. She grasped at it as a defense. "Are you surprised?"

"Why? Because I struck you, back there in the water?"

"That has nothing to do with it!"

"Doesn't it?" He released her, lifting his weight, moving back to rest on one elbow. "All right, then. Go ahead, hit me."

The temptation was strong. She clenched her hands into fists, still feeling the imprint of his hold on her like a brand. She did not like feeling that she could be rendered so helpless so easily.

She couldn't hit him. Why she couldn't, she did not know. She just couldn't do it.

"No?"

He was waiting for an answer. She shook her head, whispering, "No."

"Then let me tell you something. That is the last chance I will give you to be revenged. Don't attack me again, or you won't like the consequences, I promise. You won't like them at all."

He settled back, shifting to pull the bearskin that had been dislodged back up over him. He lay staring up into the darkness, and it was long moments before he realized that he was holding himself stiff and straight. By degrees, he relaxed his taut muscles, subduing by sheer strength of will the race of the blood in his veins and the need that fueled it. The feel of Cyrene's soft curves, the natural fragrance of her body lingered in his mind, taunting him. He had not realized what a torment it would be to lie beside her and yet be unable to touch her. But it was not the discomfort of inconvenient desire alone that troubled him. He felt a need to hold her, to make amends, perhaps for hitting her, perhaps for the way he was using her, or perhaps for the crime of involving her in his own need for vengeance. It did not help that the strongest prohibition against it, as well as against the appeasing of his other needs, was his own.

Cyrene lay unmoving for long moments, until the cool air brought the rise of gooseflesh. A shiver rippled through her, and in its aftermath she burrowed under the bearskin, her instinct being as much to hide as for the warmth. But there was heat under the thick fur. It radiated from the man beside her, inviting, enticing. She closed her eyes tightly, aware of him with every prickling nerve of her body. She hated this effect he had upon her, hated his assurance and his strength, hated the damnable coil in which she had become entangled with him. It was humiliating, then, that the thing she craved the most at that moment was the contentment, elusive and incredible, that she had found once in his arms.

8

RENÉ CAME AWAKE as he always did, in abrupt, total clarity. He opened his eyes and went rigid. Despite his reputation, despite the beds he had passed through, it was not his habit to wake up with a woman. He had always preferred to take his leave after a suitable interval, seeking his own bed before he slept.

Cyrene lay in his arms. At some time in the night his will had slipped his control and he must have reached for her, perhaps as she turned against him. Her warm breath caressed the hollow of his throat, her legs entwined with his, and his arm lay across the slender turn of her waist. In the gray and pellucid light of dawn filtering into the shelter, he could see the fine texture of her skin, the pure and meltingly sweet lines of her mouth, and the thick, black fans of her lashes. There was such strength in her face and such beauty that he felt a tightening around his heart, as if it were caught in a net that was slowly closing.

Dear God, he was an idiot.

What had made him think he could take this woman for the basest of reasons and emerge unscathed? This woman of all others? He should have known from the beginning how it would be. He had not been the same since he had come to his senses, lying waterlogged and bleeding on the rough boards of the flatboat floor, to see her hovering in annoyed concern over him. When he was a very old man, he would remember the simplicity with which she had offered herself to him and the mind-stopping joy of possessing her. It was likely that was all he would have to console him. It could hardly be otherwise.

He wished it was not so. He wished with sudden fervor that he could start all over, could put things back the way they had been. He would come to Cyrene openly, court her, reveal himself to her, and take his chances.

No. That way, he would have less of her than he did now. There was no way to change what had happened. He would have to endure the role he had assigned himself and accept the consequences.

The first of these, and the worst so far, was to lie there with Cyrene in his arms and desire throbbing in his veins and do nothing. He longed to kiss the soft curves of her lips, to run his hands over the gentle undulations of her body under the thin chemise and draw her closer against him, to set himself to give her pleasure in all the small ways he could discover by diligent searching and consummate, tender care. He wanted to lose himself in her, to forget who and what he was and why he was lying there beside her. He wanted to forge a bond between them that was so strong nothing else could, or would, matter.

It was impossible. He knew it, and so lay unmoving, inhaling the warm, clean scent of her, imprinting the feel of her upon some innermost part of his being, protecting her from all harm, as he had sworn, but most of all from himself.

There were limits to all endurance. It was some time later when he eased from the pallet with soft stealth, picked up his clothes, and ducked out of the shelter.

Cyrene watched him go through slitted eyes. She had awakened as she felt the removal of his warm hold, though she had been conscious in a vague, drifting manner of his regard for some time. Now she lay listening to his retreating footsteps. When he was far enough away, she sat up and got to her knees to push aside the leather curtain.

He had gone down to the beach. The tall shape of him was

indistinct in the early-morning light, yet it was still magnificent as he dropped his clothing in a pile and plunged into
the water. Cyrene shivered as she imagined that sudden chilling submersion. How he could bear it, she did not know; the
cold wind off the water that filtered into the shelter was
enough to raise the gooseflesh until she felt as scaly as an
alligator. Still, she stayed where she was, watching the strong
lift and stretch of René's arms and the dark, moving blot of
his head as he pulled toward deep water. Only when he was
lost to sight in the dimness did she let the curtain fall and
dive back under the bearskin.

She had escaped more lightly than she had expected. She
was glad, of course, but also puzzled. Why had René insisted
on sharing her shelter if he had not meant to press his attentions on her? Such restraint was at odds with what she knew
of him. Where was the practiced art of seduction in which
he was supposed to excel, the delicate assault upon her defenses, the charming siege of her fastness? It was possible
that he had been put off temporarily by her protests, her
resistance, but she had expected to have to defend herself
with a great deal more vigor.

It was possible that he had spoken no more than the truth,
that he had been in search of only a bed for the night. It was
also possible that after having had a sample of her lovemaking he was not anxious for more. She must have seemed
woefully inexperienced compared to the women he had
known. No doubt he was used to a great deal more finesse,
to say nothing of more cooperation, more enthusiasm.

Not that she cared. He was insufferable with his talk of
protecting her. He wanted something, she would swear it,
something more than a close look at the wilderness of this
vast land and insight into trading with the Indians. She only
wished she knew what it was.

She did not see René again until breakfast. The Bretons
were invited to partake of the meal around Drowned Oak's
fire. To refuse that hospitality would have been a grievous
insult, and so they dutifully sat while Little Foot and her

daughter, a nubile young girl who was a half sister to Gaston, brought their meal and set it in front of them. Cyrene looked to see if René meant to taste everything in his wooden bowl, from the venison to the turtle eggs and *sagamite*, for to fail to do so would also be an insult. He seemed to have some of the Choctaw's instinctive good manners, however, for he was carefully following Pierre's lead, eating with his fingers, chewing slowly. He seemed to have a bit of difficulty swallowing now and then, but he was sampling a little of everything in turn. He would not embarrass them.

René seemed to have the approval of Little Foot's daughter also. The girl known as Quick Squirrel lingered near him, brushing against his shoulder as she leaned to offer special tidbits of food, smiling at him with sparkling dark eyes. She was quite attractive, with rather exotic features in the eyes of a Frenchman, and a lithe, wild grace that was typical of the females of her race. That René appreciated the girl's charms was readily apparent from the way he returned her smiles.

Quick Squirrel had to be much as Little Foot had been when Jean had bedded with her to produce Gaston. It was easy to see why the younger Breton brother had succumbed; what man could be expected to resist such a natural and unrestrained approach? Certainly not men starved for women as those in Louisiana had been in the early days. Certainly not a hardened roué who had sampled so many others.

Well, let René respond to Quick Squirrel's blatant lures then. What did she care? That should allow him to expend his male urges without striking out into the cold waters of the bay. She only hoped that no other man had been there before him and left the girl diseased. It would be such a pity if his career as a rake was cut off in midstride.

The waspishness of her thoughts startled Cyrene. She had nothing against Quick Squirrel, had always liked her, if the truth were known. She had from time to time been envious of the Indian girl's freedom and her untrammeled behavior, but she had no cause to think her promiscuous. The strain of the past weeks was telling on her nerves, that was all.

It was going to be a mild day. There was warmth in the sun that climbed into the sky. It tempered the wind from the south, softening it, bringing out its smell of salt and sweet grasses and far distant island flowers, as it took away the chill of the night. It made fishing poles appear and set the Indian children running and playing in headlong glee.

The warmth also brought Captain Dodsworth from his ship to the beach for the trading negotiations. He knew he could depend on the Bretons to save his scalp, he said, and it would be nicer on shore than in his stuffy and cramped quarters. No one was fooled by the excuse. What the captain obviously thought was that the presence of the Choctaw band anxious for English goods would bring the Bretons speedily to terms.

He soon learned different. The Choctaw were quick to see what he was after, and it was not their way to aid an enemy or discomfit a friend. They went about their business, scarcely acknowledging the Rhode Islander and pretending they did not see the knives he laid out so that the blades flashed in the sun, the bolts of cloth he unrolled, or the beads he swung so that they danced with vivid rainbow colors. Their assumed indifference, in fact, soon became an advantage on the side of the Frenchmen.

The goods were spread, the indigo tested and weighed, and true bargaining began. The two older Bretons and the captain sat haranguing each other in more or less good nature, making offer and counteroffer, thinking, figuring in the sand with a pointed stick. Gaston and Cyrene watched and made an occasional comment, though now and then the younger man, losing patience, got up and strolled away to dally with the younger Indian women before returning. The day advanced. The Indian women brought food and drink. Captain Dodsworth talked and pulled off his wig to rake his fingers through his hair, then talked some more. He sent to his ship for a keg of rum, then, as the Bretons remained stubbornly sober, threatened in high dudgeon to go back in the longboat himself. Still the haggling went on.

René had taken a place beside Pierre and Jean, watching

closely. Now and then he asked a question. At first the answers were merely distracted. The Bretons were serious about their trading, however, and as the stakes grew higher, their tempers became short and their replies less amiable. After a time, René, afraid he might be jeopardizing their position, rose and took his leave, sauntering in the direction of the beach.

Cyrene watched him go but sat on herself, now and then supplying amounts and totals when called upon by Jean or Pierre, or pointing out deficiencies in craftsmanship in the articles displayed. After so long a time, however, the trading became a test of wills and stamina that was little aided by facts and figures, with little to entertain those who watched. When it began to look as if it were all over except for the ship captain's final capitulation, she got to her feet and eased away.

Cyrene had seen Little Foot only in passing that morning, and there had really been no time for a proper exchange of greetings and news the evening before. Such courtesies being extremely important to the Choctaw, she turned in the direction of the round shelter constructed of bent limbs, bark, and palmetto that she had seen Little Foot and her daughter enter.

Outside the Indian woman's hut, she called for Little Foot in quiet tones. Immediately, there was a rustling inside, added to what sounded like a whisper and a scuffle. A few seconds later, Little Foot emerged from the small opening of the hut. Her color was high, but her face was stolid as she greeted Cyrene. "Daughter of the house of my son's father, it gives me pleasure to see you."

In the Choctaw manner, Little Foot would not say the name of her lover any more than she would have her husband. This Cyrene accepted, just as she had accepted the fact that Little Foot considered her an adopted daughter of the Bretons since she was staying with them. She had tried patiently to explain that she was no relation to Jean and Pierre, but Little Foot would not have it. If Cyrene was not a wife or a lover of the Bretons, then she must be a daughter; there was no other category.

"I hope I see you well," Cyrene said.

Little Foot replied in the affirmative and there was a general exchange of other such compliments. A silence fell. Cyrene waited, expecting to be invited into the hut for refreshment. Such an expression of hospitality was a courtesy with the strength of a law. Only a hated foe would be denied.

Little Foot did not speak. She looked miserable, her face flushing with shame as she twisted her hands together. Still, she remained silent.

For Cyrene to demand to know why she was not offered hospitality would be as terrible a breach of manners as Little Foot's failure to extend it. One did not demand that which was always given freely, nor did one hint at the lack. Still, there was a formula for getting at the root of the problem.

"Tell me how I have offended you, Little Foot, and I will discover a way to repair the damage."

"Oh, Cyrene, there is no damage," the woman said, the words a near wail.

A possible explanation presented itself. "Do you have sickness in your house?"

"Yes, that's it." Relief spread over Little Foot's features and she tried to smile. "Come, walk with me and we will visit my sister."

The Indian woman moved away from the hut a step, pausing for Cyrene to join her. Cyrene moved to fall into step at her side.

The Choctaw did not lie well. Their consciousness of an untruth was so acute that they could not speak it with any naturalness. Little Foot was lying, there could be no doubt of it. More, she wanted Cyrene away from her hut.

Cyrene searched her mind for what she had done wrong. She could think of nothing. She had not trespassed upon Little Foot's conversation the night before with Jean. There was nothing in her life that was different except that she had become involved with René. It hardly seemed likely that Little Foot could have anything against the man; she could not know him. As for the moral question of Cyrene's intimacy with him, Little Foot was unlikely to consider it a matter for concern.

The only reason important enough for Little Foot to lie would be to protect Cyrene's feelings. Added to that was the intimation she had had that there was someone else in the woman's hut. The most likely person was her daughter, but that would have been no reason to keep Cyrene out. But what if there had been another person? A man? If Little Foot knew that Cyrene had spent the night before in a shelter with René Lemonnier, she would be reluctant to permit her to see him closeted in her hut with Quick Squirrel this afternoon.

"Your sickness—I hope it isn't serious?" Cyrene said as she walked beside the other woman. She did not listen to Little Foot's attempt to reassure her, however, but searched the encampment with her gaze. There was no sign of René or Quick Squirrel among the people milling here and there or sitting about in groups. That did not of itself mean anything, but it gave her a sinking sensation inside.

They reached the hut of Little Foot's sister. The woman invited Cyrene and Little Foot inside and brought out coffee from a precious hoard kept for special occasions, boiling a little over the fire. This was offered with a few corn cakes sweetened with berries. The two Indian women and Cyrene sat talking of this and that in a mixture of French, Choctaw, and the Chickasaw that was the lingua franca of the southeastern Indian tribes. As Little Foot relaxed enough to laugh and tell a salacious story or two about her aging father, Cyrene began to feel that her suspicions were ridiculous. In any case, it was no affair of hers what René chose to do or with whom; there was certainly no reason for her to be upset.

She had no sooner come to that conclusion when a flicker of movement drew her attention to Little Foot's hut. Quick Squirrel was just leaving it, whipping through the opening as if pursued. She straightened and moved away a few steps, then stopped to twist the wrapped leather of her skirt back into place and to smooth the braid of her hair. With a toss of her head, the girl moved on, swinging her hips as she made toward her grandfather's fire. Cyrene looked after her, and there was a hot ache in the center of her being. It was some time before she could return her attention to the other two women.

The arrangement between the Bretons and Captain Dodsworth was concluded perhaps an hour later. The remainder of the goods owed the Bretons were brought to shore in the longboat, after which the captain retreated to his ship. Pierre and Jean spread their new wares on their trading blankets and invited the people of Drowned Oak to gather close. Business was brisk and a great many of the furs brought in were of fine quality. Before Captain Dodsworth sailed there would be more trading, though in furs instead of indigo. Other Choctaw villages above New Orleans were just as hungry for items of English manufacture.

The sun shone down, glittering with winter brightness. The air grew more balmy. It was one of the wonders of the colony's climate, this change from winter to something like spring in a matter of hours, one of the things that most endeared the land to Cyrene. She left what had become an Indian village in miniature and wandered down to the beach. The water came rolling in onto the golden sand, gently lapping. Somewhere beyond the barrier islands was the tumbling turquoise gulf, but it did not intrude here. Overhead a shore bird called, a piercing cry. A pelican stood at the water's edge, as motionless and brown and silent as a half-rotted stump. The wind in her face was pleasant, soft with moisture, scented with salt. A fly hummed around her and winged away again. She began to walk away from the bustle and noise behind her, following the shoreline.

She did not consciously intend to be alone; still, the solitude of the far-stretching water's edge reached out to her, drawing her onward. The packed sand under her feet made walking easy, like an endless path. There was enjoyment in the movement of her body, the free swing of her stride. Now and then she bent to pick up a piece of driftwood, a curious bit of shell or fish bone. Always she moved on again.

She saw them in the distance, two men who stood talking with their heads bent and their shoulders almost touching as they faced the bay. The nearest one, alert to her approach, turned toward her, then said something to his companion. The other man seemed to make some answer before moving farther down the beach. The first man turned and began to walk toward her with a long, swift stride.

Cyrene's eyes had grown sharp in the past three years, as had her ability to see more when she looked and to remember what she saw. The man moving in her direction she would have known anywhere, any time. It was René. The other one just vanishing among the trees that edged the shore was the marquise's henchman, Touchet.

What had the two been doing together? Was it an accidental meeting, here away from everyone else, or was there some purpose behind it? René had been the marquise's favorite, and Touchet was her hireling. René had not been in New Orleans long; still, it would not be surprising if he knew the other man. It was unlikely that they were friends, however; certainly they had not greeted each other as such the night before. If they had business together, it must concern the wife of the governor. Madame Vaudreuil had many and varied interests, but one of her main ones was to stop the smuggling that cut into her profits. If René and Touchet were involved in that, it did not bode well for the Bretons.

"You're a long way from the camp," he greeted her as he drew near.

Cyrene looked at him as he stood before her with smiling ease, the light from the water giving his eyes a silver-gray sheen and the breeze lifting soft strands of his dark hair. She thought of Madame Vaudreuil's visit aboard the flatboat and also of Little Foot emerging from her hut, and her voice was cold. "I might say the same about you."

He lifted a brow at her tone though his comment was light. "Yes, but I don't require a guardian."

"No, you are one, or so I was given to understand."

"A post with little reward, though I would not have deserted it if I hadn't thought Pierre and Jean, not to mention Gaston, were on duty. Did you miss me?"

"I didn't come looking for you, if that's what you think."

"I should have known," he mourned.

"So you should. The question is, did you come looking for Touchet?"

The amusement faded from his face as he stared at her. "What is that supposed to mean?"

"Oh, come, I know he's the marquise's man."

"Which means that I may be also?"

She lifted her chin. "The thought naturally occurs."

"Naturally. And if I said that I had never met the man before last night?"

"Then," she said a shade less certainly, "I would have to warn you against him. It's known that he killed a man in Paris, if not more than one. He makes himself useful to Madame Vaudreuil, including purchasing opium and hashish for her, not for her use but for her steward to dispense, though she doesn't scruple to measure them out herself when he isn't available. They also say he is a spy, gathering information wherever he can and concocting out of whole cloth what he can't discover."

"A thoroughly disreputable character, one who must be avoided at all costs."

"I don't speak lightly."

His face hardened at her sharp tone and there was a hint of swift thought in his eyes. "I can see that, though why you presume to advise me at all is less plain. I may be at a disadvantage in the wilderness, but it's been some years since I needed to be coached in the ways of the world."

She would not back down. "Am I now supposed to retire, defeated by your sophistication? It doesn't explain why you were meeting Touchet."

René hesitated. There were two options available to him as he saw it. He could either stalk away in a fine rage, which would remove him from her company, the wisest course, or he could mollify her with a show of surrender. Why was it she was always where she might be least expected? She was fast becoming his nemesis, albeit a lovely one, with the wind molding her clothing to her gentle curves and fine tendrils of hair blowing about her face.

"Forgive me," he said, inclining his head in a bow of polished grace. "It's been some years also since I have been asked to give an accounting of myself. It goes against the grain. The truth is, I met the man in passing, returning from my walk."

Was it the truth? She would give much to know. She did not like the suspicions that jostled in her mind. Nor did she like the feeling that she was being humored, though there seemed little she could do about it.

When she made no reply, René spoke again. "Shall we walk on? Or would you prefer to return? I promise I will not neglect my duties again but will stick like a burr to your side."

"That will, I fear, prove most inconvenient," she said in stringent tones, and wished a moment later she had not spoken as she saw where the comment would lead her.

"For me or for you?"

Cyrene turned and began to walk so that she need not look at him as she answered over her shoulder, "For you, of course."

René had no trouble in catching up with her, though he made no effort to bring her to a halt as he would like but merely kept pace. He watched her closely, however, as he asked, "How is this?"

"It will most certainly get in the way of your conquests."

His brows drew together over his nose. "My what?"

"I speak of Quick Squirrel. It was hardly sporting of you to bed her with such haste."

"Quick Squirrel?"

"Little Foot's daughter, the granddaughter of Drowned Oak. You might at least have discovered her name."

"I have not," he said distinctly, "had the pleasure of either her acquaintance or her bed."

It was ridiculous of her to be relieved, but that was how she felt. She turned her face toward the water to hide it. "No?"

"No. Is it too much to ask what made you think I had?"

She told him, though with some reluctance.

"Because an Indian girl is caught dallying in a hut, I am immediately suspect? You give me too much credit. Or too little."

His words were dry, carrying scant expression. Cyrene could not tell if he was amused or annoyed, or perhaps both. "Too little?"

"By assuming that I make no distinction between women."

"And do you?"

"I have a reputation, I believe, for being selective."

She sent him a flashing glance. "Am I supposed to be flattered?"

"Now what," he said softly, "made you think I was referring to you? If I remember correctly, I was chosen, not the other way around."

"That's very true," she said through the tightness of mortification in her throat. She would have given anything to take back her words. They had the sound of pique entirely too much, and that was too close to jealousy for comfort.

"I have to tell you, however, that if I had been free to pursue you, without the restrictions of gratitude and hospitality, I would have done so from the moment you dragged me aboard the flatboat."

She stopped and turned to him, the look in the depths of her eyes suspended, vulnerable yet skeptical. "Would you?"

"I give you my word."

She wanted to believe René; that was her problem. Her female vanity required that sop. It didn't matter that she had little respect for him or liking for the kind of man he was so long as she could think he found her desirable, so long as she could think he had not agreed to her wanton request of him out of mere gratitude or excessive courtesy. It was a sad failing in her as a person, one she must set about remedying.

"It makes no difference," she said, keeping her gaze level with an effort as she summoned a smile, "but it's nice to know."

It made a great deal of difference to René, how much he was only beginning to understand. But he was in no position to say so. He inclined his head, and together they moved on again, back toward the encampment.

The feasting and dancing began as darkness fell. Drums beat and the drummers hummed in accompaniment while the Indians sang, now in wild harmony, now in determined discord. Cane flutes shrilled and gourds rattled in a mind-numbing, spirit-raising rhythm. Children ran and yelled, and dogs barked. The smell of roasting meat rose with the wood-smoke that hung in blue and gray layers in the air. Pipes filled with tobacco passed from hand to hand, as no Choctaw would think of smoking without offering every man within sight a puff. Kegs of tafia were broached and cups made the rounds, each man drinking according to his need but with respect for those who were still thirsty. The food was parceled out in much the same manner, with each serving himself from the common pots.

Only the men danced on this occasion, which was one of celebration for the conclusion of fine trading, plus a farewell to the Bretons and the English bringer of goods. The Choctaw would be returning to their village when daylight came the next morning. They had enjoyed their brief time away but had to return to their log lodges before others claimed them.

The Indian women ate and laughed and chattered and showed off their new finery: their cloth chemises or their beads, which they had sewn upon their bosoms or strung into necklaces, and the small mirrors of polished steel that hung on chains around their necks. Little Foot in particular seemed unusually bedecked, wearing not only a new silk skirt but a fine hat with a feather plume and a silver chatelaine from which was suspended a thimble, a tinder box, and a pair of scissors as well as a mirror.

The night was clear and just cool enough after the warmth of the day to make a fire feel good. The flames leaped high, reaching with licking tongues for the stars that hung low and bright above them. The faces of those sitting around it reflected the flickering red and yellow light. Joyous and somber, they gave back its glow while the fire danced in miniature in the pupils of their eyes. It drew them to its comfort, emphasizing the vast reach of the marshy land and untenanted waters around them, holding them in a warm circle of brotherhood.

Cyrene sat among the Indian women while she ate and afterwards for a time as they all watched the dancing displays of the men. There was much comment on the strength and endurance, the muscle development and the agility of the various dancers, along with approving or disparaging remarks about the music. It was as if the women considered the exhibition for their benefit, and perhaps it was.

After a time, the younger women with babies strapped to their backs or children at their skirts began to slip away to make the younger ones ready for bed. Cyrene got to her feet in order to help up a heavily pregnant girl with a two-year-old slung in a blanket on her back, then changed her own position, moving to the edge of the woods, which lay on the outer perimeter of the women's circle. She leaned her back against a tree with her hands behind her. The smells of food and smoke and warm human bodies were less here, and the fresh night wind in the branches of the tree overhead made a softer, more soothing music.

From where she stood, she could see René. He sat between Pierre and Captain Dodsworth, near the place of honor held by Drowned Oak. She wondered how he was enjoying the savage banquet and if he compared it in his mind with the more sumptuous occasions he had partaken of at Versailles. He certainly appeared to be in fine fettle as he leaned back, braced on one arm with his wrist on an upraised knee, drinking, listening to the jokes around him. Now and then he laughed with his head thrown back and his teeth gleaming white in his face. But then his kind was infinitely adaptable.

There was the soft sound of footsteps in the sand. Cyrene turned her head to see the man Touchet coming toward her. He made her a small bow as he drew near. "A fine night, is it not, mademoiselle, and a fine celebration?"

"Fine, indeed." She could not be rude without direct cause, but there was no encouragement in the words.

The dark and supercilious little man needed none. "The good Bretons have had a most profitable journey from New Orleans."

"And you also, I trust." It was a reminder that he was apparently on the same errand, if it was needed.

He shrugged away her comment. "But what of yourself? One hopes such a devastating creature has gained from the venture also."

"You needn't worry about me." In fact she had not yet spoken to Captain Dodsworth about her own trading transaction. She was waiting for the right time and somehow it had not yet seemed appropriate. Perhaps she would go out to the ship with Pierre and Jean in the morning when they traded the furs they had gained this afternoon for more goods.

"No? But some men are so unreasonable; they do not like to share their gain. Now if you were allied with me, I would see you decked in pearls and gold baubles, in silk and satin and perfumed lace."

Cyrene turned her head sharply to look at him. The expression she saw in his eyes made the skin on the back of her neck creep. Her voice was cold as she answered. "I assure you, I have no need of those things."

"Don't you? But they would suit you so well. You are like a rose in a dung heap with Pierre and Jean Breton. You deserve a much sweeter and more luxurious setting. I could give it to you."

"I don't desire any more than I have."

She would have moved away then, but he put out his hand to catch her arm. "Take care. There may come a time when you will regret refusing my offer. For it is an offer, you know. I would enjoy very much having you as my woman."

There was something in the intensity of the man's black gaze and the fierce bite of his fingers into her arm that disturbed her more than she wanted to admit. She sought in her mind for something that would deter him, and the words rose unbidden to her lips. "I already have a protector."

He released her arm, a smile twisting his thin lips. "Lemonnier? The interest of that one will not last long."

"That may be, but I hold it for now, and I doubt he would wish me to accept your gifts."

"A pity. I do hope he is generous?"

"That is none of your affair."

"Unfortunately. When he is through with you, you might come to me, to see if I'm still interested."

The arrogance of the man grated on her nerves. "I would advise you not to wait. Hired lackeys have no appeal to me."

He gave her a thin smile for the pleasantry. "What of gold? A great deal of it, enough to make you a fine lady with a fine and independent future?"

She had already started to move away when he spoke. Now she turned back, her attention caught not by his extravagant promise but by something like a threat she heard in his voice.

"What are you talking about?" she said sharply.

"The subject was gold."

"For what?"

"For becoming my . . . ally."

"Your ally," she repeated.

"You could be very helpful to me, as well as most dear. The reward for bringing in your former companions, the Bretons, on charges of smuggling could be high."

He was watching her closely, and there was a message in his eyes that was also the answer to the innuendo in his words. She saw it clearly, and cold anger settled in her stomach.

"You expect me to inform against Pierre and Jean, to join with you in handing them over to the authorities?"

"Why not? What are they to you?"

"My friends, something you would not understand."

"I understand a great deal more than you know, mademoiselle."

"Then understand this: I won't do it. Not now. Not ever."

"That is a decision you may live to regret, my fair one." But he called the words after her retreating back, for she left him in a whirl of skirts, striding away with clenched fists and clamped lips.

She did not stop until she reached the shelter she shared with René. There she halted abruptly with the leather curtain of the low doorway crumpled in her hand. She was shaking with sick rage and at the same time she felt unclean, as if she had been touched by something loathsome.

What exactly did Touchet want of her? Why should he need her to inform against the Bretons when he himself knew what they were doing? The answer seemed to be that she would provide proof of their activities, would be a witness to their guilt.

Never. She wanted security, but not at that price. If Pierre and Jean and Gaston were utter strangers she would not be able to betray them; how much less could she do it when she owed them everything. Her friends, she had called them, but they were so much more, as she had come to know in the last days. They were the nearest she might ever come to a family.

She drew in a deep breath and turned to look out over the bay with the shimmering glow of starlight dancing on its dark surface. Regardless of everything else, there was one good thing about the offer Touchet had made her. If the little man was looking for an ally in her, then it followed that he did not have one in René. She had not known how strong that fear was until it was removed or how much pain it had caused.

9

THE FEAST CONTINUED, increasing in noise and frenzy as the cups of tafia made their third and fourth rounds. There was no hope of sleep until the last drummer and dancer had sought his bed of branches. Despairing of rest while the drums throbbed in the night, Cyrene returned to the fire.

Pierre had moved away from the inner circle around the flames. He was watching as she approached. As she caught his eye, he motioned to her and indicated a seat beside him on the sand. She made her way toward him, threading among the men and women who lay about on their blankets.

"Are you well?" he asked, peering into her face with a frown drawing his thick brows together as she dropped down beside him. "You look a little pale."

"Yes, fine." His concern was like balm, soothing the nerves that leaped under her skin. He did not seem inclined to accept her assurances, for his expression remained grave.

"Tell me, *chère*, are you happy? Is this with Lemonnier what you want?"

She held his gaze with difficulty. "Why do you ask?"

"I don't like the way you act, the way you look since we made this bargain. There is nothing that holds you to it, neither law nor church, nor any other obligation. If you don't like it, walk away. Now."

"You would not mind?"

"Mind? Why should I mind?"

"I thought perhaps—" She paused, looking toward the glowing red coals at the heart of the fire before she went on. "I thought you and Jean and Gaston might be relieved that I'm off your hands."

"*Sacré*, but what a thing to say! You are our angel, our luck. We will be desolated without you. The only thing that makes us let you go is that we want you to have what you desire. If Lemonnier is the one, good. We are happy. If not, then something must be done."

"Oh, Pierre," she said, tears rising in an ache behind her eyes.

He reached out to clasp her shoulders in an awkward hold, clearing his throat with a rough sound. "*Bien*, that is settled. But are you happy, *chère*?"

Her chest rose and fell in a deep sigh. "I don't know. I suppose so."

"This thing of love, it is difficult, no?"

"It is difficult, yes." There was no love, but she could not hurt him by explaining why she had gone to René without it, especially now.

"Ah, yes. I remember—but you don't want to hear that. Tell me, does Lemonnier mistreat you?"

"Oh, no," she said quickly.

"I saw Quick Squirrel and one or two of the other Choctaw girls making eyes at him. Is he running after them?"

"I— No, I don't think so." She did not know it for a certainty.

"Does he not please you in bed?"

"Pierre!"

"Do I shock you, *petite*? But you have no mother to ask these things. If he does not please you, you must tell him, or show him, what he is doing wrong. A man cannot know it otherwise. Women are different, one from the other, in their needs."

"You speak from vast experience, of course?" she said in a pretense of teasing composure.

He lifted a massive shoulder. "Enough."

She looked at him there in the flickering firelight, at his weathered face cut with deep lines and his laughing blue eyes that always seemed to hold some incalculable sorrow in their depths. "You were married once, I think. What happened?"

"My wife . . . died."

"And you never thought of taking another?"

"Never. There was no other woman who could take her place."

"You had no children, I suppose." She could not imagine him not having a child of his with him, just as Jean had Gaston.

He turned his gaze from her to the night. "These things are as God wills."

They were silent for a few moments. The drums had taken on a deeper note. Red sparks spiraled upward, crackling, as more wood was added to the fire. The skin of the dancers glistened with the sweat of their efforts. The others watched them as if mesmerized or else stupefied with tafia. A few couples had disappeared, giggling, into the darkness at the edge of the woods or farther along the shore.

Cyrene ran her gaze around the circle about the fire. René was not there. Where had he gone, and when? He had been at his place when she came to sit with Pierre, for she had walked past him. Unconsciously, she looked toward Little Foot's hut some distance away. It huddled dark and still. It might be empty, then again it might not. But perhaps it was. Both Little Foot and her daughter were among the women at the edge of the firelight.

Cyrene spoke without looking at Pierre. "You are a judge of men. What do you think of René?"

"He is a good one to have at your back or on your side," he said with the deliberation that indicated previous thought, "but a bad one to cross. A man who goes his own way in most things, though he can pull with others if need be. One who sees a great deal, more than he makes known, but keeps his mouth shut."

"But what of his notoriety with women? Can he ever be trusted?"

"He will settle down when he finds the right one. There's truth in the saying that there's no husband so faithful as a reformed rake."

"But can I reform him?"

"Do you wish it?"

That was, of course, the question. It was not one she could answer at the moment, even if she wanted to. Instead, she said, "There is something I should tell you."

"About Lemonnier?"

"No, about Touchet." She outlined her talk with Madame Vaudreuil's toady in a few brief sentences.

"Name of a name, what a piece of filth that one is!"

"You aren't afraid of what he may do?"

Pierre snapped his fingers. "He has been trying to catch us with the goods for years and has not succeeded."

"This is different. He's never been so bold before."

"Perhaps, *chère*, it's you who are different."

She turned on him, her tone sharp. "What do you mean?"

"You are more—more . . ." He waved his hand in a comprehensive gesture.

"You think I invite men?"

"No, no, only that you . . . know yourself a woman, and so oblige a man to take notice of it also. It's no bad thing, nor should you try to stop it, for to do that goes against nature. It's meant to be this way."

He was right, she knew. She had felt what he was trying to say herself, though without putting it into words. She supposed she had René to thank for this awareness, though it might also have begun before. The source of her discontent these last few months might be that she was a woman in need of a place of her own, a future of her own, a man of her own.

"As for Touchet," Pierre went on, "I don't think he'll give you any more trouble soon. He has gone back to the ship for tonight, and I heard him tell Dodsworth that he leaves for New Orleans early in the morning. But if he troubles you again, you must tell René at once or else come to me. Touchet is used to taking what he wants, when he wants, with no one to stop him since he has the governor's wife in his pocket."

Cyrene narrowed her dark brown eyes. "If he tries to take me, he will find he has more on his hands than he bargained for."

"Have a care," Pierre said with a slow shake of his head. "If he ever had any good in him, it was snuffed out long ago. He would take the greatest pleasure in forcing you to his will for his own sake, to repay you for refusing him, but it will be doubled if he can also revenge himself on Jean and me for the way we have made him look the fool in the past."

It was good advice and she would follow it. But it was beginning to seem that in giving herself to René she had acted to lessen her freedom instead of adding to it.

Pierre's attention was claimed by an old man who had a lump of blue stone that he wanted to trade for a keg of the Englishman's tafia, a stone taken many years before from an Indian who had come from far away to the west where the earth rose to meet the sky, or so he said. Cyrene left Pierre trying to persuade the man to keep his treasure and made her way out of the circle once more.

She had no particular destination. She was just too restless to sit still, she told herself, but her footsteps took her to the shelter again. The leather curtain flapped in the wind. Inside, the bearskin lay straight and flat. René was not there.

"If you are looking for Lemonnier, he's aboard the *Half Moon*."

Cyrene whipped around with a gasp, her eyes wide. Captain Dodsworth was so close her skirts brushed his legs and she could smell the rum on his breath. She took a hasty step backward and saw the concern rise in his eyes.

"You startled me," she said.

"I'm sorry. I didn't mean to walk up on you like that, but it's infernally dark."

"You said something about M'sieur Lemonnier?"

"Right, that I did. I thought you might be wondering where

he was. He paddled out to my ship a few minutes ago, something about a few short and pointed words with Touchet. I'm going now myself, but Pierre mentioned in passing this morning that you had a few items in my stock you wanted to see. Thought I'd offer you a place in my boat for the trip out if you care to go now. You can come back with Lemonnier.''

Was it possible that René meant to quarrel with Touchet over her? She could not think how he knew that the little man had offered her an insult, nor did it matter; there was no need for his interference and she would tell him so. The arrangement the captain proposed sounded good enough and would be an admirable excuse for her presence on the ship. It was even possible that now might be the best time to do her own trading if the situation allowed.

The decision was made almost before Captain Dodsworth finished speaking. Her voice firm with purpose, she said, ''Let us go, then.''

The *Half Moon* rode the swells in the bay like a ghost ship, without lights, without sound, and with gray wisps of fog clinging to its sheets and tall masts. The officer of the watch materialized out of the darkness to help Cyrene aboard, then stood aside respectfully as the captain jumped to the deck. Captain Dodsworth gave the man a curt nod and an order to bring aboard the two casks of indigo that Cyrene had brought out with her, then took her arm.

''This way, mademoiselle. I'll send to tell Lemonnier that you are here and in the meantime I'll just lay out the special stock I have that you might be interested in seeing.''

Cyrene hung back a little. ''I would really prefer to go to Touchet's cabin or wherever you think he and René may be.''

''Most unwise, I should think,'' he said with a laugh. ''There's no telling what state of dress, or undress, the fellow may be in, and you wouldn't want to embarrass him.''

He meant that she would not want to be embarrassed. ''I don't care,'' she said. ''Suppose they are fighting? I have to stop them.''

''Must you? It seems a hare-brained thing to do when

Touchet has been needing a good hiding for these many years. But if you insist, I'll send the watch to break it up. Come along.''

His good humor and easy manners were hard to resist. She went with him, though not without a doubtful look around the quiet ship from over her shoulder.

The captain's cabin was by no means large; it contained a bunk, a basin recessed in the top of a small cabinet, and a table set under a lamp that hung, constantly swaying, from the ceiling. Cyrene sat down on the single chair at the table. Captain Dodsworth stepped around to drag a small chest forward until it sat at her side, then straightened.

"Would you care for a glass of wine?'' he asked, his eyes bright. "I have an excellent madeira.''

It appeared as if he might easily be offended if she refused and that would be a bad way to start their trading session. In any case, she did not like rum and had drunk next to nothing all evening. "That would be very nice.''

"Good,'' he said, his smile widening. "I'll be right back with it when I've seen about your friend. In the meantime, you can be taking a look at the things in the trunk.''

He departed so quickly that he left the door swinging on its hinges behind him. His pleasure seemed all out of proportion, as if she had granted him a favor. Cyrene stared after him with a frown between her eyes. She had never spoken to the man before without Pierre or Jean being present. She liked what she knew of him, but that was little. Surely a man who spoke so openly of his wife and children would not misconstrue her acceptance of the invitation to go with him to his ship. No, she was being foolish. René was about somewhere and would be arriving at any moment. She was safe enough. And confident enough of her safety to be wryly amused at her dependence at this moment on René's much-despised protection.

She pushed back her chair a bit and leaned to look at the latch of the chest. It was simple and yielded easily to her manipulation. She lifted the lid and laid it back on its hinges. Then she stopped, bemused.

There in the trunk before her lay a sparkling, glittering array of pearls, sapphires, aquamarines, and topazes in brooches, rings, hair ornaments, and buttons; delicate Venetian glassware in jewel colors; silver-backed mirrors set in china and painted with roses and cherubs; tiny colored glass vials of perfume with silver caps; cobweb lace edged with gold and silver thread; and coils of shimmering ribbons in rainbow shades. There was nothing there that was not beautiful and rare and incredibly expensive. If they were trade goods, they were to suit the taste of a marquise or a courtesan.

Cyrene reached to close the lid, letting it fall shut with a thud. These things bore no resemblance to what she needed, and Captain Dodsworth must realize that well enough. What his purpose was in showing them to her, she did not know, but she sat back in her chair with her hands on its arms and her eyes narrowed as she watched the door, waiting for his return.

He was not long in coming. He carried in his hands a pair of glasses and an open and dusty bottle. He stepped forward to set them on the table and began to pour the ruby liquid. "Well," he said with a quick, smiling glance, "what do you think?"

"About the goods in the trunk? I think they are too dear for my purse."

"Nonsense! They are nothing out of the ordinary."

"Not for some, perhaps, but as much as the Indian women might enjoy them, there's hardly enough woven baskets and powdered herbs among them all to equal a tenth of the value."

"Have you no ambitions beyond the Indian women?"

"What do you mean?"

"Suppose you could present these things to the ladies about the governor? Would they not be able to afford them?"

"Possibly. But you must realize that I could not pay you for them."

He handed her a glass and sipped his own wine before he answered. "It's possible we might form a partnership."

"Of what kind?" Cyrene's question carried swift suspicion.

"One, shall we say, of mutual benefit?"

It was possible that he meant nothing more or less than what he said. Or was it? "I don't think I understand."

"I will provide the goods, you'll sell them. We'll divide the profit equally between us."

"That's a very generous offer."

"One that promises an excellent return. The French ladies are extremely fond of their fripperies. Take this perfume, for instance." He reached into the trunk and picked up a vial, removing the top so that the rich and heady fragrance of damask roses filled the room.

She made a swift, dismissing gesture. "Perfume is something they are quite able to purchase from France."

"Yes, sight unseen. I believe they will leap at the chance to buy what they can put their hands on, particularly if they see the items suitable for dress occasions being worn by someone such as you."

"Me? I couldn't do that; it would be too ridiculous with my rough clothes."

"I could give you a dress allowance. In fact, it would be my pleasure to do so."

"For the sake of business, of course."

He smiled at her dry tone, confident that she understood the implication of his words, certain the two of them would reach an understanding. "Not entirely."

"I see." She got to her feet and moved around the table. "I fear I must refuse your offer."

He reached out to catch her arm. "Why, may I ask?"

"That must be obvious." She looked pointedly at his fingers wrapped around her forearm, but he did not remove them.

"Not to me it isn't. You are friendly enough, apparently, with Lemonnier, not to mention the Bretons. I've kept my distance until this year because I didn't relish tangling with Pierre and Jean, but if they are loaning you out—"

Cyrene wrenched her arm from his grasp and stepped back. "That's a vile thing to say!"

"I meant no insult," he said, moving after her. He was daunting in his size and confidence. "I'm grateful to the Bretons for finding you and bringing you here. It seems as if it was supposed to be this way. You are so very much as I always dreamed a woman should be; I've waited, wanting you, for what seems like an age. I admire you, and I think we could work well together, but most of all I want you."

"I had no idea, but it doesn't matter. I'm not for sale!"

"I don't want to buy you. I want to love you." He put out his hands to take her shoulders.

She ducked underneath his arms. Her shoulder caught the perfume vial he still held and knocked it from his hand. The liquid cascaded down the front of her bodice, inundating her with the overpowering smell of roses before the tiny glass bottle clattered to the floor and spun away toward the opposite side of the room. She whirled after it, backing away once more from Dodsworth's slow advance.

"I don't want to be loved!" she declared with a vigorous shake of her head.

"You are just saying that. Don't be so skittish. Sit down and let's talk this over."

"There's nothing to talk about."

She made a dive for the door and pulled it open. He was right behind her. He caught the door panel with the flat of his hand and slammed it shut again. His spread arms were braced on either side of her, hemming her in.

"Let's talk," he said, his voice threaded with triumphant amusement, "about what you're going to do now."

"Try this," she said, and doubling her fist as she stood with her back to him, she spun around, bringing it up from below her waist and smashing it against the point of his chin.

Her knuckles stung, but she had the pleasure of feeling his skin part under her blow.

He staggered back, stunned. Cyrene did not wait for his reaction but jerked open the door and stumbled into the ship's dark companionway. Behind her, there came a roar of anger. She plunged into the blackness. The thud of her footsteps was loud in her ears, as was the pounding of her heart. Then drowning them out was the heavy, booted footfalls of the captain. She scurried up the short ladder and pushed out on deck. Looking neither left nor right, she ran to the side and pulled herself up, ready to drop down the ladder to the boat that rose and fell below.

"Wait, damn you, Cyrene!"

The captain's voice was loud with bluster though threaded with rasping need. She did not answer.

René did.

"Wait for what?" he asked, and the syllables were frosted with such shards of icy danger that Cyrene went still and Captain Dodsworth halted in his tracks.

The faint glow of lamplight from below shown through the doorway. It cast the shadows of the two men, long, dark, and threatening, across the deck. The only sounds for long seconds were the creaking of the ship and the faint slap of a rope waving in the wind somewhere forward.

"I thought you had gone," the Rhode Islander said, the words like the bleat of a startled sheep as he stared at René.

"You tried hard enough to be rid of me. It's easy now to see why."

The exchange made it evident that Dodsworth had not expected to see René and therefore could not have told him that Cyrene was on the ship. The perfidy of it was breathtaking, especially since she had thought the captain to be so upstanding a family man and a straightforward trading associate. He was no better than Touchet; worse, in fact. Touchet did not hide behind a front of respectability.

The red-haired man licked his lips. "It—it isn't what you think."

"No? Tell me what it is," René invited.

"Cyrene misunderstood a little joke."

"Joke?" she said in fiery disgust. "If I were a man I'd knock your teeth down your throat."

René looked from Dodsworth's bloodied mouth to Cyrene. "Somebody seems to have made a start. You, I presume?"

"Me."

"Do you require that I finish it?"

"Require?" She sent him a startled look.

"Some women do."

Would he fight Dodsworth at her behest? Would he set himself as her champion? He stood there on the gently tilting deck, his shoulders square and his face hard with purpose and darkened by a shadow of what might have been self-blame, and offered her that favor as if it were no more than the picking up of a dropped handkerchief. But he showed no sign of having fought Touchet, the task he was supposed to have been engaged in here on the ship.

"I am not some women," she said.

A short laugh left him. "Shall we go, then?"

"Cyrene, don't," Captain Dodsworth protested. "Your indigo, it's still here."

"Send it in the morning."

"But our business—"

"Or send fair value for it."

"Please, I wish you would let me make amends."

She sent him an unsmiling glance. "Make it in merchandise. I will know then that you mean it."

Cyrene went over the side and dropped with ease into the boat. René followed. They pulled for shore in silence, nor did they speak until they stood outside the shelter they shared.

René stepped in front of her, putting out his hand to bar her entrance. "Would you mind telling me what that was about? I thought you had more sense than to go out there alone, and at night at that."

The accusation in his tone acted as pitch to the fire of her temper, which was strained by the fright Dodsworth had given her. She faced him with scorn in her eyes. "You were wrong, then, weren't you? Fancy that!"

"I could well be, about more things than one. What was all that about amends in merchandise? Was it payment in kind?"

"How dare you!"

She doubled her fist and brought it up as the shock of what he had said struck her. Before she had time to use it, or even to be sure she meant to, his hand shot out to close his fingers around her wrist, dragging her toward him.

"I wouldn't try that. I'm not Dodsworth."

She refused to flinch from the force of his grip. "Oh, I know that well enough. What I don't know is what makes you think you have the right to question me. And if you mention the word protector I may show you a trick or two I didn't have to use with the English captain!"

"Whore's tricks?" he asked softly.

She drew in her breath. "Why is it," she said in bitter, flashing rage, "that all men take an unattached woman for a whore?"

René was brought up short. He stared down at her pale, proud face and her bright hair, disheveled by the wind and her struggles aboard the ship and haloed by the fire somewhere behind her. He looked at her and recognized the black emotions that ate at him as jealousy and fear. Jealousy of even the glances of other men that fell on this woman. Fear of her vulnerability to other men and their base desires, which he had caused. Jealousy because some other man might reap the richness of her favors that he had denied himself. Fear that he might never recover from the denial. The rich scent of roses, mingled with her own unique and sweet fragrance, enveloped him like a haunting memory, one of vivid and scarifying pain.

At the fire a lone Indian chanted to himself, beating the drum with a quick and hard rhythm that matched René's heartbeat. And the song was a lament.

He released her. His voice controlled, barely, he asked, "Dodsworth?"

"And Touchet," she said, her voice laden with scorn. "I was told you had gone to the ship to chastise the little man. Isn't that funny?"

"For molesting you?"

"For trying. It seems to be all that men think of."

"Including me."

The strained words hovered between them. He had not meant to say them. They seemed to spring from some innermost recess of his being. And he waited to see what their effect would be in a confusion of longing and dread.

She lifted her chin and there was the lash of disdain in her voice. "Especially you! Maybe you would like repayment for your protection just now? Maybe that's the gratitude you require for such a grand gesture! Could that be it, my gallant protector?"

"And would you pay?" he inquired, the look in his eyes that of one who tests the limits of his own control.

"Who knows? My appreciation is great, I assure you. A few more threats and I might even hang on your neck, all trembling and pleading. Like this." She moved toward him as she finished speaking and lifted her hands to clasp them behind his head, pressing against him. Her eyes were bright with malice and something more that gathered inside her, spreading, tingling along her nerves.

René did not move, not so much as the twitch of a muscle. Neither did he look away from her provocative gaze. "That would, of course, gratify me."

"I thought it might."

Her eyelids were heavy with a languor that was not entirely a pretense as she watched him through her lashes. What she had expected, she was not sure, but it had not been this frozen lack of response. Impatience shifted in her mind, taking hold. When he did not reply, she spoke again.

"But perhaps you only want what you can't have? There

are men like that, I've heard it said; they don't value what is given too freely.''

A laugh totally lacking in amusement left his chest and he lifted his hands to catch her wrists, pulling them away from his neck. ''If I thought you would not draw yourself up in a knot like a cat who has seen a snake, I would take you inside there and strip away every stitch you are wearing before pressing my lips to your soft skin from your forehead to your toes. I would taste your mouth and your breasts and drink the very essence of you. I would take you with me into worlds of joy and explore you to the very core, if I thought you would let me. I don't think it. And so I won't.''

Annoyance flooded through her along with a strange, aching regret. She tightened her lips into a thin line and pushed away from him to stand alone. She pulled her wrists and he let them go with an instant, open-handed gesture that emphasized his utter detachment.

''If you had tried,'' she said in soft venom, ''I would have had your eyeballs for my bodice buttons.''

''I don't doubt it,'' he answered. He made her a short bow, then swept aside the leather curtain of the shelter and ducked inside. Then, in the concealing darkness, he went to one knee with his fists pressed against each other at his thighs, crushing his knuckles together until the pain became an antidote for the torment of desire. And on his hands lingered the smell of roses.

Outside, Cyrene stood irresolute. She could not meekly follow him into the shelter now, could not lie beside him in the night trying to hold this wild need inside her without letting it show, without permitting him to know if they should touch in the night by accident. But neither could she bear to return to the fire and pretend that nothing had happened, that everything was still the same. Slowly she sank down onto the sand, turning so that her back was to the shelter. She stared out over the dark, heaving surface of the water, shaking with the hard beat of her heart.

After a time it seemed that if only the beat of the drum

and the lament of the Indian warrior that echoed her disturbance would cease, then she could return to the way she had
been before she had pulled a half-drowned man from the
river, before the expedition had left New Orleans, before this
night when she discovered she had fallen in love with a rake
and ne'er-do-well known as René Lemonnier. The wild and
mournful song did not stop. It still assaulted the night when,
stiff with the increasing cold and exhausted by her distress,
she crawled into the shelter and settled beside René. It was
throbbing yet, mingling with her fevered dreams, when she
slept.

A pile of trade goods was found on the beach when the
camp began to stir. Pinned to them was an invoice in Captain
Dodsworth's hand made out to Cyrene and carefully totaled.
Of the *Half Moon* there was no sign anywhere on the calm
face of the bay. The ship had sailed on the morning tide.

Pierre and Jean broke camp early. They wanted to move
out ahead of the Choctaw, they said. That did not appear to
be a problem of moment. After the feasting of the night
before and the many rounds of rum and tafia, the Indians
were barely stirring. The only thing that might move them
before the middle of the day would be the appearance of a
Chickasaw raiding party.

There were farewells to be made and listened to, gifts to
be exchanged, and a future rendezvous to be arranged. It was
closer to midmorning than to daybreak when at last the Breton
party was allowed to depart. They gave a final wave and then
nosed their pirogues out into the marshy waterway leading
north. The pirogues were loaded to the rough-hewn gun-
wales. Each dip of the paddle, each surge forward seemed
certain to make it necessary to bail. Somehow the lap of the
water was always an eyelash too low. They stayed dry, if
more than a little crowded. They settled down, with Pierre,
Cyrene, and René in the lead boat as before and Gaston and
Jean following.

The current, as sluggish as it was here in these lowlands

below sea level, was still against them. There was not much breath left for talking or singing as they pulled into the ceaseless flow. Their paddles rose and fell in unison, digging into the muddy brown water, flinging bright droplets forward. The swing became monotonous, untiring. The miles began to drop behind them.

They stopped for the noon meal on another *chêniere*, but they did not linger. The trip upstream would take longer than it had coming down. They were soon back on the water again. The hours moved on. The bubbles of their wake flowed ever backward, the water rippling slowly outward behind them in a giant inverted vee that eventually lapped the shore. They left the marshlands and entered the more narrow and winding course of the bayou. The short winter day began to wane.

It was at that hour when the sun is just disappearing and the light takes on a melancholy blue shading tinted with the dying gold rays that a man appeared on the bank. He stepped from a thicket of evergreen myrtles that grew down to the water and called out, waving. Just in front of him at the bayou's edge could be seen the prow of his pirogue thrusting up, as if it had sunk stern first. A stroke more of the paddles and the face of the man became plain. It was Touchet.

René sat in the prow of the pirogue, where he had been since their last stop. He glanced over his shoulder at Pierre, his brow raised in query. There could be little doubt of the answer. A *voyageur* did not leave a man stranded on land in the wilderness any more than a ship at sea failed to stop for a shipwrecked mariner at sea, no matter how great a rogue he might be.

The two boats swept as one toward the bank. Touchet called out to them, saying how glad he was to see them and how much he had depended on them to be behind him, cursing his luck, thanking his saints. His voice rang across the water, a thin, almost shrill sound that seemed to frighten every other creature into silence. The steady and quiet dip of their paddles seemed loud. Nothing moved in the blue afterglow as the sun sank behind the trees and the shadows along the bank deepened. Nothing except Touchet as he stood with one hand on his hip and the other waving them in toward him.

"I don't like it," Cyrene murmured, almost to herself. She stopped paddling, resting her paddle against her knee as she searched the shoreline with narrowed eyes.

There was nothing to be seen. Closer the boats came. Closer. The prow of the first pirogue, that of Cyrene with René and Pierre, grounded on sand. René leaped out, splashing in the shallow water as he leaned over to pull the boat higher onto the bank. The other pirogue glided nearer under its own momentum, Jean and Gaston holding their paddles at rest.

It was at that moment that the French soldiers rose one by one from the myrtle thicket. Their uniforms were nondescript, faded by the semitropical sun until they were more gray than blue where they were not tattered or replaced in part by bits and pieces from the armies of a half-dozen other countries. They were small in stature and lacking in discipline, as evidenced by their ragged advance, but the muskets they held were primed and steady.

Touchet made a sweeping theatrical gesture. "Behold my friends the welcoming party! You are under arrest, all, for the crime of smuggling. Be so good as to come ashore and give yourselves up. Even the lovely Cyrene. Especially the lovely Cyrene!"

10

I T WAS A trap.

If it closed upon them, they would be taken as smugglers with the evidence against them almost in their laps. The penalty was too terrible to be faced.

In immediate, unthinking reaction, Cyrene thrust her paddle deep, pushing it into the mud of the stream's bottom. The forward motion of the pirogue slowed, stopped. It reversed. She felt Pierre's strong back paddle surging also, felt the craft respond, floating free of the shore once more.

René was standing ankle-deep in water, poised between the pirogue and the soldiers with indecision on his face. Cyrene shouted at him with fear cracking her voice, "Get in! Get in the boat!"

"Come back," he called. "It will be all right, I promise."

Behind him, Touchet turned to the soldiers. "On my order you will commence firing."

"No!" René whirled on him. "No, you bungling fool!"

His words carried the hard edge of command. Amazingly, they were obeyed, though Touchet muttered something that did not reach them.

René swung back toward the pirogue, lunging after the prow. He did not mean to get in but to catch it, to pull them back to land. Cyrene saw him lay hands on the pirogue, saw his purpose. For a brief, confused instant, her brain refused to function as she saw the soldiers lower their muskets.

Abruptly she cried out, a sound of rage and acknowledged betrayal, ''Traitor!''

She plunged to her knees, thrusting out with the muddy blade of her paddle and pushing it into his chest. She shoved with all her strength. He let go of the pirogue, catching at the paddle to keep his balance. Once more she rammed the paddle at him, then she let it go as the pirogue shot backward.

René staggered, off balance. Pierre dug deep, and the long, narrow craft leaped out into the stream. A boatman above all others, he swirled his paddle and the pirogue spun around, heading back the way they had come.

''Downstream,'' the older Breton called to his brother Jean. ''Their longboat will be waiting around the bend the other way.''

On the bank of the bayou, René was snapping out an order. The soldiers broke formation at a run. Touchet, cursing, snatched a musket from a man lagging behind. The marquise's agent raised the weapon. He fired.

The booming report rolled over the water. Before the sound reached the racing pirogues, there was a high-pitched whine overhead. Cyrene flinched but did not stop paddling. Risking a glance behind her, she saw a gray cloud of powder smoke floating out over the water and Touchet lying on the ground, nursing his jaw with one hand. Of the soldiers and René, the only sign was their retreating backs as they raced toward their concealed boat.

Bend, dip, pull. With aching muscles and back-wrenching effort, they sent the pirogues speeding over the water. The distance separating them from the place of attack lengthened. Ahead of them lay a winding curve. They began to take it, cutting across it to save precious time.

Behind them, there was a yell. They looked back to see a longboat just bursting through the pall of smoke. It was crowded with soldiers plying the long, sweeping oars that jutted out along the sides. They worked in unison, sending the laden craft skimming over the surface of the bayou like a waterbug skating down a drainage ditch. The soldiers yelled as they caught sight of their prey. The speed of the boat increased.

The two pirogues leaped ahead as fear pumped new strength into the veins of the Bretons. Cyrene scrambled forward to snatch up the paddle René had put down, then took her place once more, bending, dipping, pulling. They swept around the lower bend. They were lost to sight behind the trees.

Cyrene snatched a quick look at Pierre. He was scanning the bank, his gaze anxious. Before she could speak, Jean called out across the space of water that separated the racing pirogues.

"We leave the bayou?" he shouted.

Pierre gave a short nod. "Around the next bend, it may be."

"If we make it! Touchet will go after the pirogues with the goods if we turn them loose."

"So he would, but Lemonnier is in charge," Pierre returned.

Jean shrugged, his dark gaze never losing its bright light. "We can only hope."

The chance, or so it seemed to Cyrene, was a paltry one. The bigger boat with its superior crew was moving so fast it might well overtake them before they could put whatever plan it was that Pierre had into action. The trade goods were important as evidence and must be retrieved by the governor's soldiers, but it could be done at their leisure after they had taken their prisoners. Even if they managed to make land, there was nothing to keep their pursuers from giving chase and running them down. Nor was there anything to prevent them from shooting them on sight. René had held the soldiers back from firing before, perhaps for her sake, but he could not be expected to do that again, not if he expected what was apparently his mission to stop the smugglers to be a success.

Why? Why was René on such a mission? The question battered at Cyrene's mind. The answer was clear, no matter how much she might seek to avoid it. René, like Touchet, was the marquise's man, her spy and lackey. Madame Vaudreuil did not care for competition in her trade with the English; moreover, it was important that her husband give at least the appearance of trying to comply with the order to stop such commerce. Therefore, René, having been so fortunate as to gain a foothold on the flatboat of the Bretons, had been ordered to attach himself to them and draw them into the marquise's trap. He had, with Touchet's aid, done just that. And she had helped him also. Dear God, she had helped him.

From some deep reserve, Pierre brought forth added effort. Jean, not to be outdone, kept pace, and Gaston and Cyrene did what they could. The pirogues flew over the water, barely touching the surface. They swept into the next turn, scudded around it. A few more gasping pulls of the paddles, then they turned the prows of the two pirogues toward the bank and, with straining shoulders and vibrating sinews, sent them plowing into the overhanging willows.

At any moment the others would round the bend, would be upon them. There was no time to lament the rich goods left behind, only time to grab a food sack and leap ashore. The pirogues were shoved back out into the stream with mighty thrusts that sent them pitching and heaving away from the landing where they would mark the exact place too well. The two small crafts, lighter now, floated, still rocking a little, easing away with the slow creep of the current.

The three Bretons and Cyrene did not wait to see them go. They plunged at once into the wooded swampland that edged the bayou. Swift and silent as the Indians from whom they had learned their forest skills, they melted away out of sight.

It was the swift descent of darkness that saved them, something Pierre had held in account as he had made his plan. They heard the soldiers land, heard the shouted orders of René and the yells back and forth as the floundering search began. It did not last long. A half hour of tramping to and fro with torches, plunging into knee-deep muck where it had appeared there was firm ground, shooting at imaginary animals and each other in the growing dimness and increasing cold, and then the signal for recall was given. The pursuit retreated, died away, moving back to the bank where a fire was lit for reassurance and to boil coffee and beans. It leaped high, a distant beacon.

The darkness and damp of the winter night closed in. Cyrene, Pierre, Jean, and Gaston turned into the vastness of the swamp and put the beacon fire as far behind them as possible.

It was two days later when Cyrene and the Bretons emerged from the wetlands. Footsore, insect-bitten, they approached the outskirts of a plantation house. With no way of knowing what kind of search had been mounted for them, they could not make themselves known or ask for help. They waited until night fell once more, quieting their hunger pangs with their last few handfuls of dried *sagamite*. Under the cover of darkness, they searched out and borrowed a small sailboat that was beached on the bank of the bayou. By the time the sun rose, they were asleep in their hammocks on the flatboat.

There was no hue and cry. The Bretons could only assume that it was because they had not been captured with the trade goods that would have proven their guilt. The governor could have had them arrested on the strength of René's word and tortured until they confessed, but he made no move to do so. Pierre, ever the cynic, said the governor was waiting until he had evidence so that he could make an example of them. Jean declared that they need not worry, then; they would never be caught because they no longer had the means to venture out as traders.

The truth in the jest was slight comfort. Without the money brought in by trading, the next year would be hard. With the English goods now in the hands of the French government, the Bretons would have to hire themselves out as laborers, working for a pittance compared to what they could have earned trading. It wasn't fair that their activities could be so restricted, that they could be told who they could buy from and sell to and when, not when the food in the mouths of a man's family and the clothes on their backs depended on it. Let the government go and meddle somewhere else. Let the king and his ministers see to something a good deal more important, such as the pirates in the gulf or the steady western encroachment of the English farmers from the Carolinas.

If Cyrene and the Bretons wondered what René would do now, they were not left long in doubt. He took up his occupation of dancing attendance on Madame Vaudreuil and was seen riding out with his sponsor in her carriage, escorting her to various entertainments, standing up with her at the balls, and acting as her chamberlain at the absinthe socials that it was her delight to arrange at Government House. A sycophant was the least of the names he was beginning to be called for catering to a woman old enough to be his mother, but there could be no denying that he was in the midst of everything of interest that was happening in New Orleans.

Cyrene despised the man. She could not bear to hear his name spoken. The thought of the way he had used and betrayed both the Bretons and herself burned like a red-hot coal in her brain. To remember how she had given herself to him once, and come so near to offering herself again, gave her such shamed pain that she felt murderous with loathing for him. It had been that rage, and the images of the things she would do to him given the opportunity for revenge, that had kept her spirits alive in the swamp.

They haunted her, those images of vengeance, but she was also haunted by memories of René: the things he had said, how he had looked, the taste of his kiss, the feel of his caresses. She missed him, something that was as disturbing as it was unexpected. At odd times she looked up suddenly from what she was doing, expecting, wanting to see him on the floor of her sleeping cubicle, though knowing full well it was impossible.

She wondered if he thought of her at all, if he had regrets or if he was merely annoyed that his ploy had not been suc-

cessful. She imagined him speaking to Madame Vaudreuil
of her, laughing at how gullible she had been, how awkward
and inexperienced, how eager. She imagined him with other
women, smiling at them, flattering them, taking them into
his bed. And she pictured him with the aging wife of the
governor, bowing to her demands whether in the drawing
room or in the boudoir, bending his handsome head in smiling acquiescence.

The torment of her thoughts made her temper so uncertain
that she snapped at Pierre and Jean and Gaston and filled her
days with a constant round of tasks that exhausted her in body
and mind so she could sleep at night. Still, she sometimes
thought she would not be able to know peace until she had
found a way to make René pay for the damage he had done.
She wanted to make him suffer. The problem was finding the
means.

It was a week after their return when Cyrene saw René.
She had gone to the market, walking there without escort in
a concession that gave her much less satisfaction than she
would have expected a few short weeks before. She had bartered the braided coat René had given her for a gratifying
amount of food and clothing, then turned homeward, walking back across the Place Royale. René came from the barracks building that faced her across the square. He was
striding along beside a uniformed officer, the two of them in
close conversation. They stepped from under the barracks
gallery, angling toward the church.

Cyrene came to an abrupt stop. It was, perhaps, that sudden lack of movement that caught René's attention. He looked
up, said something to the officer, then, as the man moved
away, came slowly toward Cyrene.

His coat was of ultramarine velvet, a deep purple-tinted
blue, with silver basket-weave buttons. Under it he wore a
waistcoat of satin in the same color, which was embroidered
in black, and black breeches. His powdered wig, topped by
a tricorne with a small black plume, was tied back with a
black bow, and on his shoes were silver buckles. He carried

a long ebony cane and a handkerchief edged with lace, which he transferred to his left hand as he swept off the tricorne and made his bow in front of her.

Cyrene did not wait for him to straighten before she turned sharply to step around him. He moved with swift ease to forestall her.

"A moment of your time only, Cyrene. I heard you had returned. I can't tell you how glad I was to have the news."

"Yes, I'm sure," she said, the words scathing in their fury. "Your concern for us was, of course, the reason you searched the river so diligently."

"I can see you wouldn't believe me if I said it was."

"How astute of you."

René was silent as he gazed at her. She was magnificent with her hatred of him glinting in the dark brown of her eyes and the high color of rage burning across her cheekbones. She held herself like an empress, with her head up and her breasts straining against the material of her bodice with every deep and angry breath. He wanted to sweep her up in his arms and take her away to someplace where he could make her understand, where he could banish her fury and try to bring back that lovely light of surrender to her face, a light he had begun to think he had only imagined. But it was impossible.

"Smuggling is a crime against the crown," he said abruptly. "Did you think you would never be stopped?"

"Not by a man I had pulled from the river."

"I see. You think I should have been more grateful."

"I think—"

She stopped as her throat closed with pain and the onslaught of emotions too confused to express. It seemed suddenly that he was too near, that his shoulders were too broad and the gray of his eyes too intense. She did not want to be affected by him. She wanted to be cold and vindictive, not feel as if she needed to walk into the comfort of his arms.

She steeled herself, looking away over his shoulder. Her gaze fell on the flogging post that stood at the foot of the gallows before the church. The sight of both post and gallows was an effective reminder of what she and the Bretons had so narrowly escaped. When she returned her gaze to his, her expression was blank. Her tone almost casual, she asked, "What did you do with our trade goods?"

"They were confiscated, the property of the king."

"Were they, indeed?"

His face darkened. "You needn't sound as if you think I took them for myself."

"How am I to know where you draw the line? There's so much you will do, from conniving with scum like Touchet to dupe and betray those who saved your life to prostituting yourself for a rich woman of—shall we say—uncertain age and unlimited influence, that it's difficult to tell."

"You forget," he said softly, "the prostitution for the sake of a *young* woman."

"You mean what you did for me? No, I haven't forgotten. How can I forget something I will regret to my last breath?"

"You may regret it now, but you didn't then."

Her eyes flashed at the ungentlemanly reminder. "You flatter yourself. I did what was necessary for my purpose. The regret I have is that I did not choose a worthier man."

"A worthier man," he said, his smile bleak, "might have expected more in return."

"In return? I owed you nothing. The debt, I believe you said, was yours."

"Then if it was paid, you can't accuse me of ingratitude."

It was odd how much pain the thought gave her, that he had made love to her for no other reason than to repay her for saving his life. It was not as if she had any reason to believe he had desired her. She had only wanted to think so.

Her voice trembling, she said, "It was repaid, all right, repaid with deception and treachery, repaid by taking from us our means to make a living. Too bad it brought you no gain. Only think what a feather it would have been in your cap if you could have brought us all back in irons!"

She saw the leap of anger in his eyes before he inclined

his head in a bow. "It may happen yet," he said, and turned on his heel, walking away from her.

So great was her rage and chagrin, so many were the things she thought of that she could have said, that the walk back to the flatboat was as nothing. Gaston was alone on the front deck, whittling shavings from a limb to form a peg, as she strode down the gangplank. He watched her, his hands falling idle.

"Let me guess," he said in a pretense of frowning concentration. "You saw Lemonnier."

"I did, and I advise you not to tease me about it."

She moved past him into the flatboat where she thumped her basket down on the kitchen table. Gaston came into the room behind her and stood watching as she took off her coif and put it away, then took down an apron that she tied around her waist. Only then did he speak again.

"What did he say?"

"Nothing of interest."

"I see, and that's what has you in a lather?"

"I'm not in a lather."

"You could have fooled me."

"I don't want to talk about it," she said, a shading of desperation in her voice. "Where are Pierre and Jean?"

"Gone to see if M'sieur Claude will let us have more indigo and permit us to pay him when the trading is done."

"He won't."

The young man shrugged. "It doesn't hurt to ask."

There might be something salvaged of the trading season if they could get more indigo, though it would be dangerous, involving a long trek through Chickasaw country to meet with the English traders from Carolina since they could not wait for another ship. Even then, the profit would be small. She went to the table and began to unload her basket. She stopped.

With her hands clenched on a pair of nutmegs, she said in low tones, "It's all my fault."

"No, *chère*, there is no fault. These things happen."

She was grateful for the understanding in Gaston's voice, even as it surprised her. "If I had not brought Lemonnier on board—"

"And if I had not helped you? Don't blame yourself, I beg, because if you do I'll have to share it!"

There was wry humor in his gaze, which was so like Jean's. He meant what he said, but there was more to it than that. He meant also to cheer her.

"Did I ever tell you, Gaston, what a nice person you are and how much I like you?"

He heaved a sigh of mock gratification, though the glint in his eyes was as bright as the gold ring in his ear. "I thought you hadn't noticed. Do you think I'm nice-looking?"

"Excessively."

"And charming?"

"In the extreme."

"I like you, too," he said as if confessing some dark secret, and loped into the room to gather her in a bear hug and swing her around.

Cyrene laughed, hugging him in return, and felt a lightening sensation in her chest. It was horseplay, nothing more, but there was comfort in his impulsive embrace and an odd sense of belonging. As he set her down, she brushed a quick kiss along his neck.

His gaze was warm and there was a flush under his skin as he stepped back. He smiled down at her for an instant, then his gaze strayed to her basket. His tone casual, he asked, "What are you cooking?"

Pierre and Jean returned. They had had no luck with M'sieur Claude. It was well known about town now that the Bretons were under the governor's eye for their smuggling. As much as M'sieur Claude commiserated with them for their bad luck, he could not risk their losing his indigo to the soldiers; he had his own family to think of.

For once, Jean was dejected. Pierre was angry. He sat frowning into his coffee made with the last of the beans that they were likely to have for some time, and there was a smoldering look in his eyes. Gaston strode up and down. He alternately damned the governor and the policies of the French crown and flung out farfetched suggestions of places he might find a job. He was not afraid of work and could set his hand to anything. On the whole, he would rather fish or trap or trade with the Indians than resort to physical labor, but if he must, then he was ready. Of course the best position in New Orleans, the one with the best prospects and the least work, might be held by René, as the gallant friend of Madame la Marquise. What did they think of his chances of dislodging that gentleman?

Pierre only looked at him. Jean shook his head. "You'd have about as much luck as you would asking to be taken on as a guard at the king's warehouse."

"Now, why would I want to do that?"

"Because," said his father deliberately, "that's where our goods are stored."

Cyrene paused in the act of stirring the fish stew she was cooking. "If he could become a guard—"

"Yes, we just might steal back our belongings," Jean finished for her. "But they would no more hire one of us to be a guard than they would set a mouse to look after cheese."

"No," she said, her shoulders drooping.

The subject was allowed to languish. Cyrene set the meal she had prepared on the table and they ate. The Bretons, as they were wont to do, got up to help her with the dishes, scraping their plates over the side of the boat and rinsing them in the river before bringing them to be washed, scrubbing out the big kettle she had used, wiping the table, and sweeping the floor. Cyrene was preoccupied. She handed the last handful of wooden spoons to Gaston to be dried before she finally spoke.

"Suppose," she said, her voice grim, "suppose we were to steal our goods back, anyway?"

"You don't know what you're saying," Pierre objected. "It would be too dangerous."

"Theft of crown property? I can feel the whip now. And Pierre was not meant to hang." Jean gave a mock shudder.

"It isn't crown property," she reminded them stubbornly. "It's ours, taken from us by trickery."

"The governor wouldn't agree." Pierre's voice had a bitter edge.

"Then bedamned to him!" she burst out. "Are we going to let him deprive us of our livelihood, our only means of bettering ourselves?"

"Are you sure it's the governor you are talking about?"

"Who else?" She turned on Gaston, who had entered the fray with his comment.

"Lemonnier, for instance?"

She recognized the truth in the suggestion but refused to let it make a difference, just as she declined to admit that no small part of her rage was because her own personal goods had been taken, too, and with them her prospects for the future.

"What of it?" she demanded. "You call it theft to take it back, but we were robbed. We all know what will happen to our goods, if it hasn't already. They'll find their way into the coffers of the governor's wife or else those of the intendant commissary or some army officer. This fine colony is a nest of thieves of one sort or another, official or otherwise. The only rule for name calling is whether you get caught at what you do."

The men exchanged glances among themselves. It was Pierre who spoke at last. "The guards have been known to be lax after midnight."

"And before," Jean agreed, "especially if strong drink is offered."

"We couldn't take just what was ours; that would be like pointing a finger at ourselves." This bit of wisdom came from Gaston, who had an avid look in his eye.

"We are not common thieves," Jean told him with an assumption of dignity that was tarnished somewhat as he went on. "We could take only a few casks of indigo and maybe a bale or two of blankets, just to throw them off the track.''

"Bribing the guards is too risky," Pierre mused. "Maybe a diversion, now, a nice fire or a fight?"

"Or a naked woman running down the street?" Gaston suggested.

His father looked at him with pity. "There's nothing new about that."

"Maybe not, but it would get my attention."

"I don't doubt it would," Jean said sadly.

And so they bantered and tossed suggestions back and forth, and, within the span of twenty-four hours, had not only decided that it could be done but how it should be arranged and when was the best time. Regardless, they might not have decided once and for all to brave the consequences if it had not been for the note from René.

It was brought by a young boy who said the gentleman known as Lemonnier, the Sieur de Vouvray, had given him a piastre to deliver it. Brief and to the point, it said that Madame Vaudreuil desired to hire a number of boatmen for a trip upriver to supply merchandise to a post commandant. The lady would be happy to give employment to the Bretons if they cared to accept it.

"Our goods, do you think?" Gaston asked when the note had passed from hand to hand.

"It's possible," Pierre said.

Jean snorted. "Possible! I'd say it was certain."

"Are we going, then?" Gaston looked from his uncle to his father and back again.

Pierre's expression was dark as he said, "It's money, something we need."

"A paltry sum for breaking our backs in the service of the governor's wife when we could have had our rightful proceeds." Jean smiled. "Of course, the merchandise could disappear before it arrived."

"It could if we wanted to take to the woods forever," Pierre agreed.

They were quiet a moment. Cyrene spoke into that momentary silence. "Does it strike you that this offer is an insult?"

Pierre looked at her from under his brows. "In what way?"

"René, and the marquise, must know that we will understand we are being asked to transport our own property. It's like salt in a wound, something meant to sting."

Pierre gave a short laugh. "So it is. We'll hire ourselves out."

"What?"

"We will show ourselves willing, even happy, to earn our bread as the marquise's men. We will hire on to transport this merchandise as far up the Mississippi as a boat can go this time of year. We will bow and scrape, pull our forelocks and show our muscles. But we will never leave the levee."

"How is this?" Jean demanded, his gaze suspicious.

"The goods now in the warehouse, you understand, will be gone."

A smile began to glow in his brother's eyes. "Spirited away in the night?"

"A miraculous disappearance."

"Shall we moan about the loss of our hire?"

"We will cry until it would wring pity from a stone."

"And will we go trading again, blessed by, perhaps, a run of lady luck at the gaming table?"

"Another miracle."

Cyrene, her lips curving in a smile at their nonsense, said, "You don't want to place too much dependence on miracles."

"Why should we not," Pierre said, "when we have our lady luck still with us? Our Cyrene?"

II

T HE NIGHT WAS moonless and dull with overhanging clouds. The wind that had been out of the south all day had died, leaving the air thick with moisture and clammily cool. Gray fog rose off the river, drifting through the streets of New Orleans. It clung to rooftops and curled about the flagpole and the gallows in the Place Royale. It muffled sound so that the barking of a dog two streets over sounded flat and faraway. In its thickness were the smells of mud and the smoke of dying embers in banked fires.

The hour was late. Most of the town was sunk in sleep, though one or two pothouses still showed a light. The only movements in the streets were a drunk winding his way homeward and a cat stalking along with its fur glistening with damp and the limp body of a huge wharf rat hanging from its mouth.

It was even quieter and darker along the river levee that lay just beyond the square, where the ships docked and their cargoes were unloaded. The king's warehouses, repositories of the wares that poured from the ships' holds, were long buildings crudely constructed of logs and planking and lying at right angles to the river. Before the main warehouse a lantern of pierced tin gleamed, hanging from a crosspiece above the door. In its glow a pair of soldiers with muskets at the ready paraded slowly back and forth.

Cyrene, with Pierre, Jean, and Gaston, stood in the shadows of another warehouse belonging to a group of merchants and watched the guards. The two men were neither the best nor the worst of the crown's soldiers; they were only men carrying out the duty assigned to them. They kept moving because that was their orders and because it was the best way to ward off sleep. Their minds could not have been further from what they were doing. They exchanged a quip or two as they passed back and forth, but for the most part their eyes were glazed with boredom, with sleep denied, and with the contemplation of their own concerns.

It occurred to Cyrene to wonder what would happen to these two men if goods were stolen from the warehouse during their watch. It was almost certain they would be disciplined for allowing the loss. As regrettable as that might be, it could not be permitted to influence what they meant to do.

The plan was Pierre's. It had been carefully worked out to the last detail, but, as he had told them, there were always problems, errors of judgment, or circumstances that could not be controlled. They should be ready to improvise. Thinking of the things she must do, Cyrene felt sickness in the pit of her stomach. It had seemed so easy to take their things back from the king's warehouse and spirit them away when they first spoke of it on the flatboat. Right was on their side; why should it not prevail? But now, looking at the solid bulk of the warehouse, the military precision and lethal weapons of the guards, the whole idea appeared foolhardy in the extreme. It was she who had urged this course, inciting the Breton men to it out of her own anger and chagrin. If anything went wrong, if anything happened to these men who had become her family, she would not be able to forgive herself.

She had started this. It was possible she could stop it. She opened her mouth, but before she could make a sound, Pierre spoke.

"Ready?"

"Ready," Jean and Gaston echoed.

"Good, good. Remember, if there is a difficulty, we separate and fly. *En avant, mes enfants.* We go."

Pierre and Jean eased away, merging into the darkness. Gaston took Cyrene's arm, smiling down at her. Her feet were leaden as she began to move. Then the two of them were stepping into the muddy track that ran between the levee and the warehouses, moving into the searching beam of the lantern, staggering along as if they were supporting each other in drunkenness. They weaved their way toward the guards on duty.

Cyrene had pushed her hair under a coif so that it was completely covered. She had used flour to make her skin dead white and had stained her lips and cheeks with berry juice. A liberal sprinkling of black patches from a box of them that had belonged to her mother served to give her a dissipated look, as if she were covering blemishes or pox sores. It was the best she could do in the way of a disguise without appearing suspicious; she only hoped it would give her the anonymity required for success.

Gaston had also made an attempt to conceal his identity. His stocking cap was pulled down to his eyebrows and a couple of twists of bear fur had been turned into bristling mustaches. He walked with a gangling, bent-kneed stride and wore Pierre's oversized coat in an effort to appear older and shorter than he was in fact. It was possible that neither looked as grotesque as they felt; the guards gave them only the most cursory glance.

Onward they lurched, with Cyrene swinging her hips and Gaston clutching at her. When they were just so close and no closer, Cyrene gave a shrill cry and pushed Gaston so that he staggered back. He cursed in loud, slurred tones and rounded on her, grappling with her. The shawl Cyrene wore slipped, revealing a bare shoulder where the tie of her chemise was loosened. She slapped Gaston and he grasped her bodice, tearing the buttons. The lantern light over the warehouse door caught the gleam of firm white flesh. The soldiers paused, staring lasciviously.

Cyrene dragged herself from Gaston's hold, wailing, pleading. With one hand grasping the edges of her torn clothing without much benefit to her modesty, she ran toward the guards. They were frankly staring, perhaps out of concern, perhaps in enjoyment of the show. She spread her hands wide toward them in a gesture of supplication that allowed her chemise to spill open halfway to her waist. She felt the rush of cold night air on her naked skin, saw the eyes of the guards widen.

A pair of shadows, swift-moving and silent, detached themselves from the darkness at the sides of the warehouse, moving from the back. They closed in on the guards from behind. There came soft grunts, the thud of blows, and the two soldiers collapsed at the knees. They were dragged quickly out of sight around the building where they were bound and gagged. Cyrene, her lips thin with distaste, quickly did up her bodice.

The Bretons did not bother to force the lock on the front double doors of the long building. As with most wood structures in the damp climate, the foundation of the warehouse was half eaten away by rot and termites. It was the work of only a few minutes with a prize bar to lift off a section of the planking on the darker side of the warehouse wall near where the trussed soldiers lay. When the opening was wide enough, Cyrene took the lantern they had removed from its hook and slipped inside while Pierre and Gaston made the hole wide enough for the passage of the merchandise. Jean had already left at a run to bring the pirogues beached farther along the levee closer.

The interior of the warehouse smelled of leather and wool and rusting iron, of wheat, spices, and dried fruit, of salt beef and beans—all overlaid with the odors of mice and soured wine. The long space was divided down the middle by a raised platform, while more platforms to hold the merchandise above the damp earth floor were built against the wall, forming a double aisle. The wide, shelflike platforms were by no means full. It seemed the governor's complaints about the lack of tribute and trade goods for the Indians were valid.

There were a few barrels of coarsely ground flour, bundles of blankets, some kegs holding brandy and wine, and piles of long boxes that might have contained arms and ammunition or could just as easily have held the walking sticks decreed by fashion. Crates held iron pots and knives and hatchets. Bales of rough cloth in crude colors were stacked to the ceiling. A motley assortment of barrels, bundles, trunks, and cases in various sizes holding unknown contents were piled here and there. As a show of the might of France, it was not impressive.

The items that had been taken from the Bretons were easy enough to find. They were collected in one place on the central platform and neatly tagged with a lot number. In a gesture that came near to affectionate, Cyrene patted the top of a cask before she turned and gave a wave of triumph to the Bretons.

With the four of them working, the pile of goods rapidly dwindled as it was transferred to the pirogues. Despite the jokes they had made about taking extra casks of indigo or bales of blankets, they scrupulously left behind everything except what was theirs. Even so, the piles in the pirogues grew high as the boxes and bundles and bales of furs were moved with little concern for close packing.

The first indication of trouble was the sound a whistle from Jean outside. Gaston was just hefting a box of English steel knives. He looked at Cyrene. She straightened from where she had been stacking together her collection of pots that had for some reason been taken apart. Her gaze met that of the younger man, which was wide with anxiety. From Gaston she looked at Pierre, who had been making toward the opening in the wall with a sack holding glass beads in each hand. The older man's face was grim as he stood still, listening.

Almost immediately, there came the sound of a shouted order from somewhere down the street. Pierre dropped the sacks of beads and leaped to the wall opening. He ducked back inside again.

"It's a patrol! Douse the lantern. Jean's away to the pirogues. I'll take the other direction and divide the pursuit." He gave Cyrene and Gaston a hard, straight look. "You two get out when you can. And remember, separate."

He was gone in an instant. Cyrene whirled in the direction of the lantern, which sat on the platform. Gaston tucked the box of knives under his arm but did not move as he waited for her.

"Go on," she cried as she reached the lantern and picked it up. "I'm coming!"

The youngest of the Bretons hesitated, then turned to the opening in the wall. He took a long stride, then another, though he looked back at her over his shoulder. He rounded the end of the center section.

It was too late. There was a rasping noise and the great end door swung open directly in front of Gaston. Four soldiers, muskets at the ready, plunged inside. They came to a halt. There was a shouted order and the men dropped to one knee, raising their muskets.

Cyrene used the only weapon she had, the lantern. She flung it with all the strength of terror and tempered muscles at the soldier in the lead. He brought up the butt of his musket to bat it away. The tin buckled and hot oil spewed in a spreading stream as the lantern was struck and sent flying toward a pile of baled blankets. It landed against them, and fire exploded in a yellow rush of heat and fury. The blankets were engulfed. The air was filled with the smell of hot oil and the acrid stench of burning wool. Yelling in panic, the soldiers dropped their guns and began to pull off their coats to beat at the flames.

Fire was the most dreaded enemy of this isolated town. It was a more devastating foe than the wind storms that whirled in from the gulf flattening homes and shops. The threat of it would hold back the soldiers for precious seconds.

Gaston had already thrown down his knives and was gone.

Cyrene could not follow behind him because of the heat of the flames. She whirled instead, running back down the aisle to circle the far end, making for the hole in the wall by way of the second aisle. Like one of the flickering shadows cast by the leaping flames, she darted among the bales and barrels, keeping close to the wall as more men, soldiers and civilians, poured in through the main doorway.

She was ignored for the moment, or else forgotten in the greater emergency. She felt the draft of fresh air from the wall opening. It yawned before her, a dark square in the side of the warehouse. A moment later, she was slipping through.

"Hold on there, my pretty!"

The officer loomed up before Cyrene, his hands outspread as if cornering a nervous fowl in a hen yard. He was a veteran, for his eyes bulged in a face that was marked by battle and a thousand barracks-room brawls. His loose mouth was twisted by a taut grin of anticipation and cocky self-assurance that showed the blackened stumps of his teeth.

Cyrene sidestepped, whirling away from him to run. He looped out a long arm, grabbing a fistful of skirt. She pitched forward as she was thrown off balance. The man was on her at once, slamming her to the ground. The hilt of his sword gouged into her hip as he fell on top of her. He sank his fingers into her upper arms, wrestling her over onto her back. She wrenched at her arms, striking at him. Her coif worked loose as she was thrown from side to side, and her hair spilled from it, flailing like a silken banner in a high wind. The veteran twisted one hand into the fine warm mass, wrapping it around his wrist as he dragged her toward him and rose to one knee, pulling her upright as she caught at his arm to relieve the tearing pressure.

"Now," he said, giving her a hard shake that sent pain in a red and black rush to her head and threatened to snap her neck. "Let's see what we have here."

"Attention!"

The command rang out cold and clear, hard and imperious in its authority.

The officer stiffened, swinging around to something near a respectful stance, though he retained the hold of one hand on Cyrene's arm. "Sir?"

"Release that woman at once, Lieutenant."

Shock rippled over Cyrene at that all-too-familiar voice. And yet she knew a despairing inevitability at hearing it here, at this moment. The officer's grasp fell away. She was able to turn in slow anguish to face René Lemonnier as he strode toward them.

The lieutenant rushed into speech. "I caught this woman escaping, m'sieur. She is with the others."

"She may be and she may not. You can go about your duties. I'll take charge of the prisoner."

"But, sir—"

René's voice grated with soft menace. "You are allowing the culprits to escape while you dally with a woman. That will not make good hearing for the governor."

"Yes, sir. No, sir."

There was irony in the man's tone, but it was only a pose, a cover for the unwilling fear that shone in his eyes. He stepped back from Cyrene and made a jerky bow, then walked away as fast as his stiff back would allow.

René turned to Cyrene. He took her elbow, his fingers closing in warm support around it. "Are you hurt?"

She shook her head.

"Let's get you out of here, then."

What she had expected, she was not sure. Surprise took away her power of movement. For a long instant she stared, bemused by the concern and angry purpose she saw in the face of the man she had come to think of as an enemy. Behind her were shouts and the crackling of the flames. Somewhere a bell was ringing out an alarm, and not far away there was the clatter of wooden buckets as men hurried to form a line to bring water from the river.

Before she could find words for the questions that swarmed in her brain, René clamped a hard arm behind her back, sweeping her toward the rear of the warehouse, half leading, half flinging her into the darkness away from the noise and confusion and the gathering crowd.

Lights were beginning to blossom behind shutters. Men were peering out their doors or darting out into the street in their nightcaps and nightshirts to stare at the smoke and fire-glow. Questions were shouted at René, but he made vague answers, shielding Cyrene's disheveled state from view with his body as much as he could. In a caricature of the pose of lovers, they made their way through the streets. Their passage was swift but not so headlong as to be remembered, cautious but without panic. They did not stop until they reached the house where René was lodged.

It was a dwelling like thousands of others in hundreds of small towns across France, neither a hovel nor a mansion. There were a few differences, however. The lower floor was used for storage only since it was subject to flooding, and there was a porch, or gallery, from the word for a long room, *galerie*, on the front and rear of the upper floor to protect the inside rooms from the hot summer sun. The roof was of split cypress shingles instead of slate, and the walls between the crossed timbers were of soft bricks sealed with a plaster made of mud mixed with lime and deer hair instead of the stone of the old country. The entrance was through a door in the lower floor, then up an inside stair to the upper gallery.

Cyrene moved ahead of René up the narrow treads, feeling her way in the dark. On the gallery, she stood aside as he opened the door. At his gesture, which indicated that she was to pass before him into the house, she drew back, assailed by an accumulation of distrust.

"Why are you doing this?" she asked, her voice low.

"Oh, the purest self-interest. You would hardly expect anything else, would you? Of course, if you prefer the lieutenant's company, you are free to go."

He was a tall, broad shadow looming above her there in the dimness. She could not see his face, but the derision in his tone seemed directed indiscriminately at both her and himself. She would not let it or the threat she sensed in his presence sway her. "What do you expect to gain?"

"A few hours of your time."

"My time?"

René heard the suspicion in her tone with resignation. She could not be blamed for it, heaven knew. He wished that he could think she had no cause. It wasn't so. He had betrayed her, and he knew it. More, his most virulent impulse at this moment was to do the same again, to take advantage of the situation in which he had found her. He had not realized he had fallen so far. If she was not so independent, and so beautiful even with her painted face and wildly tangled hair, if the sight of her did not clutch at his insides and twist his soul with longing, then he might have been able to let her go or to give her up to the justice she doubtless deserved. Neither course was possible. Neither could be borne. There only remained the indelicate and debasing use of force. And the question of how far his elastic conscience would permit him to go to achieve what he wanted.

He inclined his head in a bow he was not certain she could see. His voice deep, he repeated, "Your time. If you please?"

There came from down the street the clatter of drums and the sound of a fife as the barracks was emptied of soldiers to fight the fire and search out those who had despoiled the king's warehouse. It struck Cyrene as less than prudent to stand debating René's purpose in spiriting her away there in full view while she was still in her disguise. With a pugnacious tilt to her chin, she went before him through the doorway. She stopped in the middle of the inside room, waiting as he closed and locked the panel door and moved to strike tinder to light a branch of candles.

The room was revealed to be a small salon. It was pleasantly livable, with a touch of luxury here and there. The furniture was of native cypress carved and fitted by hand here in Louisiane and was therefore simple in style. The chandelier, however, was of bronze dore and Baccarat crystal, and a series of Brussels tapestries depicting the hunt hung on the whitewashed walls, while the carpet had been made in Brussels also and the pair of vases on each end of the central fireplace was of superior faïence. The plan of the house was typical, with three large rooms across the front and three smaller ones at the back, and with each room opening out of the other without passageways. To the rear of the salon was a dining room where silver gleamed in the dimness. Through the doorway on the right could be seen the bedchamber with the bed of cypress wood swathed in velvet hangings. The other doors were closed.

Cyrene spoke out of bravado, to fill the silence. "You are lucky in your accommodations. Not many new arrivals here are so well placed."

"I had help in finding them."

"Madame Vaudreuil, I suppose."

"As you say. The house belongs to a woman recently widowed who wanted to return to France."

"You bought it?" There was sharp curiosity in her tone.

He shook his head. "Not yet."

What did he mean? Was he thinking of staying in the country? It was so unlikely, on second thought, that the possibility did not seem worth pursuing. Outside in the street could be heard the tramp of booted feet. She went still, listening. The soldiers passed on by, their regular treads fading.

Cyrene moistened her lips. "What will happen if—if they find me here with you? If they learn you took me away? Will there be trouble?"

"Nothing of moment, though it's kind of you to be concerned."

"I am not—" she began sharply, then stopped. She was concerned, though she did not want to be. She tried for a shrug. "I was thinking of myself, of course, and of just how beneficial your protection is likely to be now. But I would not have you think me ungrateful. I do thank you for the rescue; it was most . . . timely."

"It was my pleasure."

She sent him a quick glance, aware of an undertone to the

words she was not sure he intended. He had moved to a bellpull beside the fireplace. He gave it a tug. As he turned back to her, his expression was bland and yet the light in his gray eyes was clear and intent.

"It must be nice to have such highly placed friends to smooth your way, no matter what happens."

"Yes," he agreed, though the word was without inflection as an African serving woman appeared in the door and he gave her his attention, ordering that wine and glasses be brought. When the woman had slipped away to do his bidding, he turned toward Cyrene once more. "Tell me something: Did the escapade this evening have a purpose or was it merely to even the score between us?"

"It had a very good purpose," she said, the words sharp. "We wanted our property, which was taken from us. And we got it!"

"I see. The rest was an accident."

"The rest you and the soldiers brought on yourselves."

Her eyes caught the reflection of the fire that leaped and crackled under the mantel of the fireplace, giving her the wild look of some cornered animal that was heightened by the blue shadows of exhaustion under the fine skin beneath them. The hastily fastened tie of her chemise had come loose in their flight. Her torn bodice spilled open halfway to her waist, revealing the softly rounded curves of her breasts with their pale pink blush like the skin of perfect peaches. The combination of unbridled spirit and innocent vulnerability was maddening. René had been trying not to look, but now he allowed his gaze to rest on her like a pilgrim approaching a distant shrine. When he spoke his voice was abrupt.

"You risk a great deal for the sake of a few beads and pots. It would be a shame to have to watch the fleur-de-lis burned into such fine skin as yours or to see it scarred by the whip."

A flush rose to her cheeks as she looked down to see what he found so compelling and realized her exposed state. She clutched the edges of her bodice together, swinging away from him in a swirl of crumpled and stained skirts.

"It's more than pots and beads," she said over her shoulder. "It's our way of life."

He gave a mirthless laugh. "The lady smuggler. It will be a miracle if you escape hanging."

The color left her face as she faced him once more with her hand clutching her bodice. "But you said—I thought—"

The black rage that had been hovering in his mind closed in around him: anger that the Bretons would allow her to run the risk she had tonight, anger that she was so bound to them that she would do it for their sake, anger that he had no right to prevent it, but most of all, anger that she could think he would harm her. It became a shield, that anger, and a weapon.

"You thought," he said, "that I meant to keep you safe now that I have you?"

The coldness of his tone was like a blow. She would not let him see that she felt it, but neither could she pretend indifference. There was not only her safety involved but that of the Bretons, who would be implicated with her if she were brought up before the Superior Council on smuggling charges. Baldly she asked, "Don't you?"

"I might, if the reward equaled the risk."

"I have no way to repay you."

He shook his head, his smile pitying. "Except the traditional coin of an attractive woman."

"You expect me to—"

"I have need of a mistress."

The denial leaped like flame into the rich brown of her eyes before she answered. "Never!"

"Think carefully. You were alone when I saw you, but if you were questioned there are those who would wonder where Pierre and Jean Breton were last night, as well as Gaston."

A shiver ran through her. She wanted to speak, to marshal excuses for the Bretons, to exonerate them, but the words would not come. There was no excuse that anyone would accept, least of all this man. Long seconds passed. The light died from her gaze, leaving it desolate.

"I rather thought you might see reason," he said softly.

"Reason?" she said, her voice trembling with suppressed pain and an odd weakness. "Reason? When you are threatening my life?"

"A harsh accusation. I prefer to think of it as simple coercion."

She stared at him, at the taut planes of his face and the shadow of something like distaste in his eyes. She said slowly, "I have come to think there is nothing simple about you."

"You would be wrong. There is one thing. I want you, and whatever it may take, I will have you. If you mean to sacrifice yourself for the Bretons, it might as well be now as later."

His words scarcely penetrated. Suddenly there broke from her a single question. "Why?"

"I thought I had made that clear."

"I can't believe there isn't something more. There are plenty of other women who would be happy to accommodate you."

"You gratify me," he said, the comment acid with irony.

"What is it? What have I done to you?"

"You suspect revenge? Don't be ridiculous."

"There must be something." She stepped nearer as if to press home her point.

"Perhaps," he said slowly, "it's something I've done to you."

She blinked. "What?"

"You would not be in danger if I had not used you, had not been the cause of you losing your goods so that you felt the need to retrieve them. The fault is mine. I am in a position now to protect you, as I promised. And that's what I intend to do."

"Out of guilt? I absolve you of it. Now let me go."

"I can't do that."

"Of course you can!" she cried in desperation. "This

whole business is farcical. For all we know, Pierre and Jean and Gaston may be under arrest at this moment.''

"They appeared to be well away to me. Strange, isn't it, when you were caught?''

"We agreed to separate.''

"Ah. Of course.''

"It's true!''

"I'm sure it is. Will they come after you, do you think, if you don't return?''

"They certainly will. Is that what you are afraid of?''

"Only if they try to do something foolish. I think it will be best if you send a message explaining that you have taken refuge with me and decided to stay, for the time being.''

"I haven't agreed,'' she snapped.

"Haven't you?'' he asked, his voice as steady as his gaze. "Haven't you, indeed?''

Try as she might, Cyrene could discover no weakness in his stand, no relenting in his manner. There was nothing to be done except to write the letter to the Bretons detailing her whereabouts and urging caution. René gave her privacy for the task, going away to speak to the serving woman somewhere in the back of the house. Cyrene sat for long moments, bending the quill pen in her fingers and frowning into the fire, then dipped the point into the inkwell provided for her and began with slow reluctance to force it across the page.

René took charge of the message. It would be best to have it in the hands of the Bretons as soon as possible to prevent them from doing anything foolhardy, he said. He would find someone to deliver it at once while she made herself more comfortable. His serving woman, whose name was Martha, would see to her needs; she had only to ask for whatever she required.

Cyrene sat staring at the door when he had left her alone once more. Events had moved so quickly. Only a few short hours ago she had been at the flatboat, going about her usual tasks; now she was the mistress of René Lemonnier. It did not seem possible.

Soon he would return and what would happen then? What would he expect of her? She knew, of course, but could not bring herself to accept the reality. One thing was certain. If he thought to have a complaisant, smiling woman in his bed, eager to please him or satisfy his decadent whims learned at the court at Versailles, he was much mistaken. She had been compelled to this position by circumstances, but that did not mean she was prepared to submit abjectly to his demands. He thought he had won, but he would discover that the battle had just begun.

12

RENÉ WAS SLOW in returning. By the time Cyrene heard his tread on the stairs, she had bathed in the small porcelain tub that Martha had filled with hot water and washed the smell of smoke from her hair. She had also had time to brush her waist-length tresses dry before the fire, using René's silver-backed hairbrush and wearing his silk nightshirt, which had been laid out for her.

At the measured sound of his footsteps, she leaped up in sudden panic. Throwing down the brush, she fled to the darkened bedchamber. The ropes that supported the moss-filled mattress creaked and jounced as she flung herself onto the high bed and jerked up the linen sheet and down coverlet. Twisting to her side so that her back was to the door, she closed her eyes and concentrated on pretending that she was in the deepest sleep. He was, she knew, a considerate man. If he thought she was too tired to remain awake, he might leave her to rest alone. As a defense against his male ardor, it was not much, but it was the only one she had.

The main door of the house was locked, at René's express command. Cyrene heard him knock, then knock again. She lay undecided, wondering if she should not abandon her pose and let him in, worrying that it would be best not to anger him by keeping him locked outside. The questions were settled for her as Martha came from somewhere in the back of the house in answer to his summons.

The footsteps of the serving woman padded away again, fading from hearing. René moved about the salon. There came the rattle of the latch as he secured the door once more and the shifting of ashes and crackle of sparks as he banked the fire. His boots thudded one after the other to the floor. Then all was silent. She opened her eyes a slit and saw the flaring light of a candelabra being moved, approaching the bedchamber. She closed them tightly once more, forcing herself to relax, to breathe deeply and evenly.

Through her eyelids, she could see the glow as René neared the bed. She heard him place the branch of candles on the walnut table that stood beside the headboard. He set down his boots, and then came the rustle and slide of clothing as he removed his coat. It landed on the foot of the bed. A moment later, he stripped his shirt from his breeches and drew it off over his head.

He moved away then, through the connecting door into the small dressing room beyond the bedchamber. A vigorous splashing sounded as he took advantage of her cooling bath water. The splashing stopped.

Cyrene's mind presented her with the image, one entirely too vivid, of him standing naked in the semidarkness of the dressing room as he dried himself with the length of linen toweling, sweeping it quickly over his chest and shoulders, down his belly and along his thighs. The thought of it and of his leisurely preparations for bed were a severe strain on her temper. If his actions had not been so prosaic, and if she had not been pretending sleep, she might have suspected him of delaying his bedtime for the purpose of trying her nerve.

She had given a great deal of thought to where she would sleep. Since there was only one bedchamber, the choice had not been wide. She had thought of searching out Martha's room and asking to share a corner of it or else demanding the means to make a pallet before the fire in the salon. Either course would have risked René removing her bodily to his bed and might have required from him a display of the purpose for her being in it. No, it had seemed best to appear to accept his decree and depend temporarily on his better nature, saving her strength for more devious measures.

It was odd how sure she was that he had a better nature. Or perhaps it wasn't; she had benefited from it more than once. Except for the fact that he had led the soldiers in the attack on the pirogues and the attempt to jail her and the Bretons for smuggling, he had treated her with exquisite consideration.

It didn't make sense. It had not from the beginning, but particularly not now that he had done a volte-face and saved her from arrest on what was hardly a less serious charge. She didn't understand him, and it troubled her.

He moved so quietly on his bare feet that the first she knew of his presence beside the bed was the sag of the ropes under the mattress. She controlled a start and tensed her muscles as the bed sloped toward his greater weight.

He did not lie down at once, she thought, but propped himself on an elbow. Her every sense acutely alert, she knew that he was looking down at her in the candlelight. Her heart throbbed against her ribs and her lungs felt constricted so that it was nearly impossible to continue her even breathing. The nerves under her skin fluttered. The need to yawn came from somewhere in her chest to torment her.

René watched the throb of the pulse under the smooth skin of Cyrene's throat and the slow deepening of the wild rose color across her cheekbones, and his lips twitched in a smile. Asleep or awake, she was his. She was wearing his nightshirt, even if its neckline was half off her shoulder, and she was in his bed. Her hair spilled over his pillow as well as her own, the strands shimmering with the color of old gold, faintly damp where they were thickest, redolent of his sandalwood soap. He wanted her with a sweet and nearly intolerable ache, but he did not have to make love to her to possess her. Not at this moment.

It crossed his mind to give her the satisfaction of refusing him. It was little enough, after the way he had forced her capitulation. But it would not be right to let her take a stand that she could not hold. And she would not continue to refuse him, not if he could prevent it.

There was the shadow of a bruise on her wrist, a memento of her struggle with the lieutenant. The sight of it sickened him. He had come so close to killing the man who had inflicted it. The soldiers in Louisiane were the dregs of the French army; hardly a day passed that one wasn't flogged for some crime from drunkenness and petty thievery to insubordination. Some were worse than others, less open with their vices, more cunning. The lieutenant would bear watching.

René picked up a tress and let it drift like warm silk through his fingers. Lifting it, he pressed it to his lips, then carefully brushed it aside with the rest of the shining swath before he lay down and reached to blow out the candles. For long moments afterward he stared up into the darkness with his hands clasped behind his head, thinking of what it would be like if he stretched out his arms and drew Cyrene to him. The desire grew, suffusing him until his stomach muscles grew as hard as steel with the effort of self-abnegation. He closed his eyes and clenched his jaw tight. Control came. The need slowly subsided. He drew a deep, healing breath and slept.

Cyrene was elated, if a little surprised, as the moments passed and her escape became certain. She had depended on René not to force her, but she had expected some attempt to persuade her. For him to give up so easily was not much of a compliment.

The contradiction of her own thoughts was briefly amusing. She had not wanted him to try to make love to her, far from it. Still, he might have at least acknowledged her presence in his bed.

He was used to sleeping with women, of course. No doubt he required more animation; a man of such experience and sophistication would think it beneath him to pay his addresses to a woman who lay like a log. He would expect coy glances and scintillating banter, oblique enticements and elegantly lascivious caresses—all the stately advances and retreates that passed for flirtation at court. He could not be overly familiar with disappointment; she trusted it would not sour his disposition too much.

Long minutes passed. Cyrene grew cramped from lying so still. Apprehension had chilled her hands and feet until they were like ice, preventing the comfort that would permit her to sleep. She eased a little more to her back. There was no reaction from the man beside her. She turned more fully. He slept on. She had felt a current of warm air as the coverlet shifted. The heat was radiating from René's body. Inch by careful inch, she pushed one foot over the mattress toward him. The nearer she moved, the more the cold receded. She must take care not to touch him, she reminded herself; he was a light sleeper. She moved her other foot closer to the first.

René shifted uneasily in his sleep, turning to his side. The bed ropes tipped toward him. Cyrene slid and felt her cold foot touch his warm calf. An instant later, there came a soft expletive and strong hands reached out for her. She was drawn against René, fitted to the curve of his body, cradled in his warmth.

"You have the coldest feet I ever came across," he said against her ear, his voice rich with amused exasperation. "I don't mind warming them, but just don't sneak up on me."

"I didn't sneak—" she began, pushing at his arm.

"Oh, go to sleep, for the love of God," he growled, clamping her to him in a hold that could not be broken. "We can argue about it in the morning."

Did he mean her cold feet, his embrace, or their situation? There was no way of knowing, and it did not seem prudent at the moment to ask.

"I didn't send your message last night; I took it to the flatboat myself."

They were at the breakfast table when René spoke. Cyrene had been drinking her chocolate and pulling her brioche into sections and wondering if Pierre and Jean, and especially

Gaston, had got away the evening before. She looked up, certain for an instant that René had read her thoughts. But he was looking at the pile of crumbs on her plate, his gaze all too knowing for her liking.

"You saw the Bretons, spoke to them?"

He inclined his head in an assent. "They were all safe, but out of their minds with worry over you."

She could easily imagine it. "What did you tell them?"

"That you were safe with me but had nearly been captured and needed my protection. That it would be best if they left quietly on an expedition to the Choctaw for trade and did not hurry back. That they could depend on me to keep you safe until their return."

"And did they go?" she demanded.

"They did."

"Just like that?"

"It was time and they had the goods to make it profitable."

She could not believe she had been left behind. It was as if the Bretons had deserted her. The pain of it rose in her throat, pressing behind her eyes with the bitter sting of tears.

"Besides," René added, "they thought it best, for you."

She swallowed hard. "Best? It will look as if they are running away, as if they are guilty!"

"There are those who will swear they have been gone for days. You, it seems, decided to stay with me, and I'm prepared to explain to anyone who asks that you have been living secluded here since they left."

"And that will suffice?" She allowed her doubt to show openly.

"My word has never been questioned before."

There was steel in his voice, just as there would be a steel sword in his hand should any man choose to take issue with his explanation. For the first time his protection began to assume solid proportions. It was consoling but also disturbing. What kept her safe could also make her a prisoner once more.

She looked away from him, a fluttery sensation in her stomach. He was distractingly handsome in a saturnine fashion this morning as he lounged at the table in the dining room without his coat. His shirt was finely pleated at the shoulders for fullness. He had not yet put on his cravat and the neck slash flared open, revealing the strong column of his neck and the curling hair at his throat and upper chest.

It was difficult to believe that she had spent the night in his arms. When she awakened this morning, there had been only a spot of warmth in the bed to show that he had occupied it, that she had not dreamed his presence. He had shaved and donned his clothes in the dressing room. When he had emerged, he had tossed her his dressing gown and waited in the dining room for her to join him for breakfast. The show of tact had been unexpected and disarming.

Cyrene would have given much to avoid the intimacy of this midmorning meal. It had seemed cowardly to huddle in bed waiting for him to depart, however, and so she had trailed in to breakfast with his long velvet dressing gown wrapped around her and her hair spilling in an untidy curtain down her back. It was not easy to meet his eyes and pretend that she was unaffected by the events of the night. It was almost worse than if he had forced himself upon her.

She had meant to fight him, to refuse to be touched. Where had her resolve gone? Was she so trusting, so easily mollified or intimidated that he had only to tell her he meant her no harm and she believed him? Or was it that she was too susceptible to him, to his touch, to resist?

René sat watching the woman beside him with his gaze hooded and his hand idly toying with his chocolate cup. It was fascinating the way the color came and went across her cheekbones, not all of it the reflection of the ruby velvet of his dressing gown. She was totally charming in her naturalness as she sat with that oversized garment wrapped around her, the sleeves folded back to show her blue-veined wrists, and the fine, curling strands of her hair caught on the thick nap. He wanted to reach for her, to take her on his lap and part the lapels of the dressing gown, exploring the warm curves and hollows underneath. He restrained the impulse. He had the feeling that if he moved so much as a millimeter in her direction, she might jump up and lash out at him.

His gaze rested on the dressing gown once more. He said abruptly, "You will need new clothing. I'll send a seamstress to you this afernoon."

"You'll do nothing of the kind!" Her stare was militant. Here was something she could refuse in order to wipe out her weakness of the night.

"There will be functions to be attended at Government House."

"As your mistress? No, I thank you."

"You would not be the only woman not a wife by any means. There are many—"

"Officers' doxies. I don't care to join their number."

He lifted a brow. "If you prefer to remain shut up here like some concubine in a seraglio, that is, of course, your choice. The festivities of the Mardi Gras season are under way, however. There will be several masked balls."

"A Parisian conceit introduced by Madame Vaudreuil. What use do we have for such mummery? It's ridiculous."

"What use is music and dancing at all except to lighten our woes. You must admit that the masquerades are excellent diversions."

"I wouldn't know," she said baldly, "I've never been to one."

"A situation easily remedied. You will attend, at my side. I'll have the seamstress also construct a costume for you."

She glared at him in defiance. "I think not. I won't see this seamstress of yours, so you may as well save yourself the trouble of sending her."

"I see. Then perhaps I had better hie myself to a tailor."

"What?"

"If you will not have clothing made, then I must, if you intend to share my wardrobe."

Cyrene glanced down at his dressing gown, which he was

studying with such a pensive expression. "You gave this to me to wear! But I will naturally go to the flatboat for my own clothes." It was comforting to know that though the Bretons had gone, the flatboat still rocked at its mooring, a refuge in case of need.

"Wearing what you have on? I'm sure the officers' doxies will be titillated, not to mention the officers."

"Of course not in this! In my own things I was wearing last night."

He raised his brows in surprise. "You wanted them? But they were so torn and stained. I told Martha she could dispose of them."

"You what?" The exclamation was involuntary. She did not doubt him for a moment.

An apologetic expression came into his eyes, one so false it set her teeth on edge. "Well, how was I to know you had an affection for them?"

"You did that on purpose." Her eyes were narrow as she accused him.

"How can you say so?"

"Easily, not that it matters. Martha can go for my things."

He shook his head regretfully. "I fear I can't permit it."

"You won't, rather."

"Exactly," he said, his gaze direct as he smiled at her.

She abandoned her outrage since it appeared to have little effect on him and less chance of changing matters. Seconds passed while she stared at him, then she said, "Why do you want to humiliate me?"

A dark tide of color rose under the bronze of his skin. He said shortly, "I have no such desire. Is it so wrong to wish to see you gowned in a way that will best display your face and form, to want you beside me, to desire to see you enjoy the pleasures that are to be had?"

"I have no use for these things."

"I do," he said softly.

"I won't go."

"I believe you will."

Since neither could or would abandon their stand, the contest must inevitably go to the one in the strongest position.

René got to his feet. "I will not send the seamstress," he said in cool tones, "I'll bring her myself. You will permit the necessary measurements or I'll also take those myself."

"You will not find it easy," she said through clenched teeth.

"Maybe not, but it should be a distinct pleasure."

The trace of returning humor in his words, with its indication of his supreme confidence, galled her. "Even if you succeed, I'll never wear these gowns."

"You'll wear them or I'll be your maid as well as your seamstress."

"You can force me to stay here, even force me to wear what you will, but I will never be paraded as your kept woman!"

It was unwise to defy him so openly. She knew it but could not stop herself. It had to come some time, but not now, not so soon.

He leaned toward her, bracing his hands on the table. His voice as he spoke was hard, yet it carried a rough edge. "You are indeed my kept woman. Until I choose to let you go, you will grace my table, warm my bed, and be a public ornament for my person as surely as my lace handkerchief or the nosegay in my buttonhole. There is no alternative. There will be none. The sooner you accept that, the better it will be for you."

He pushed away from her, moving toward the door. She stopped him with a cold and clear question.

"And why should I stay to enjoy this grand position you have for me? You sent the Bretons away, arranged to have them cleared of any charge. What threat will you hold over me now?"

He turned slowly to face her. "I could say no threat, only the requirements of honor, of a bargain struck, but I doubt you would see it that way. That being so, I'm left with the alternative of explaining to the governor that I was deluded, temporarily deceived by you; blinded by your beauty, lulled and gulled by your charms. Do you think,'' he added gently, ''that he will believe me?''

The governor would believe him. Cyrene, surveying with despair the look of dark remorse and regret René had summoned at will, knew she was defeated. There were always terms of surrender, however, and those terms would be her own. They would.

Surrender. She did not like that word. A shiver ran through her that had nothing to do with the chill of the day. She pulled the heavy velvet of the dressing gown closer around her.

René watched that gesture of futile protection and was touched to the quick. For the thousandth time, he wished that things could have been different. That was equally futile he knew, but it could not be helped.

With abrupt decision, he moved toward her. He put his fingers under her chin, tilting her head, then bent to press his lips to hers. Her mouth under his was smooth and cool, fragile and incredibly sweet. It was all he could do not to increase the pressure, to draw her up into his arms and take her to his bed. Not yet. Not yet.

With the all-too-familiar ache in his chest driving into his loins, he released her, straightened, and walked away.

Cyrene watched him go, watched the swing of his broad shoulders, which tapered into the line of his hips, the muscular grace of his long legs. Passive denial was better than none, she told herself; she had not returned his kiss. The effort it had taken to gain that small victory frightened her. She must marshal her strength, prepare herself for the clashes between them, or she would wind up warming his bed, indeed.

The thought that came to her then brought a tight smile to her face. She had not warmed his bed the night before. Rather, he had, in a manner of speaking, warmed hers.

The seamstress came. She was a brash woman known as Madame Adèle, with red hair coarse with henna, a large, raw-boned frame, a strong scent of patchouli, and a faint air of disreputability. Regardless, her voice was surprisingly soft and her movements competent. Though she was escorted by René, once she was introduced to Cyrene and took out her length of ribbon to begin measuring, she paid him little attention. Her attitude toward Cyrene, unspoken but evident, was one of fellow feeling. It was not hard to imagine that once, before she had become a seamstress, she might have been a mistress.

Cyrene allowed herself to be divested of René's dressing gown. In his silk nightshirt, standing before the warmth of the sitting-room fire, she turned this way and that, lifting her arms on instruction, bending her neck or holding her head straight as required. While René had been out, she had come to the painful decision that defiance on the matter of clothing was without purpose. She was at enough of a disadvantage living in his house, subject to his will, without being half-naked at the same time. It worried her, the compromises she was making. It was as if she were being forced to retreat step by step. What would become of it, she did not care to guess, but for the moment she could see no alternative.

In spite of herself, she began to be interested in the subject at hand as Madame Adèle asked her preference in colors and styles and materials and discussed the latest variations in the formal dress of the court, the *robe à la française*.

"I'm afraid I know little of fashion," Cyrene said finally, her voice stiff.

"What is to know except what becomes you?" Madame Adèle said with a shrug of broad shoulders. "Madame Pompadour now has such a fondness for pink and peach, blue and gray; everything must be in these pale, so delicate shades. They are not for you, I think, *chère*; on you they would fade to nothing. Deeper colors, yes, bright and clear. These are what you need with your hair like the pale syrup of the sugarcane. And the fabrics from Lyon, the reembroidered brocades, yes! I see you in a deep blue-green embroidered in gold. What say you? Or perhaps a rich cream. Not with Pompadour's silver, but also with the gold?"

Cyrene frowned. "Aren't such fabrics very dear?"

"What of it? M'sieur Lemonnier has said you are to have the best that can be procured." The woman sent René a roguish glance that was also slightly feline and named a price that made Cyrene gasp.

"To spend so much on something to cover the body—it isn't right."

"Everyone does it, *chère*. Besides, it isn't just to cover the body but to lift the spirit, to make one think that we are not so removed from the grand affairs of France here in this provincial outpost."

"I like Louisiane."

"So do I, but you must admit it isn't *la belle France!*"

René sat in an armchair to one side of the fireplace with his legs stretched out before him, his feet crossed at the ankle, and his hands folded across his waist. He watched Cyrene turn back and forth, quietly enjoying the view of her slender form under the silk of his nightshirt outlined in a glowing red-orange nimbus by the fire behind her. Her cooperation was unexpected. It was also troubling. For some reason he did not care to analyze, it made him feel guilty, like a debauched roué. It did not help to realize that she probably saw him in that selfsame light. He had given her every reason to hold that opinion; still, it galled him to have his intentions so misread. And it chafed him even more to recognize that he would like nothing more than to play the roué, indeed.

Cyrene sent René a glance from under her lashes, wondering that he should be ready to dig so deep into his pocket to dress her, wondering just how far he would plunge to satisfy his whim to see her in finery. The burning expression she saw in his eyes stopped her breath for an instant. She had seen that look before. He wanted her.

She had known that her attraction for him was based on lust; even if she had not sensed it, he had told her so in plain words. And yet she had not until this moment discerned the depths of his desire. It had been masked by his self-control, she thought, carefully kept from her. The reason was not hard to find. It could be used as a weapon. A weapon against him.

"Cream brocade embroidered in gold, I like the sound of that," she mused aloud in answer to the seamstress, at the same time glancing down at herself, following the direction of René's gaze, which seemed to be directed at her lower body. She stiffened as she saw the exposure of her shape with the fire behind her. With an effort of will, she refrained from instantly moving away from in front of the fireplace. Anger touched her and she searched her mind for the most expensive material she could name. "But I also like the darker peach colors. I am thinking of satin with drapings of alençon lace, a veil of it with only a hint of the peach showing through. What of that?"

"Magnificent, chère," Madame Adèle said, dropping to her knees and spreading her arms wide to measure from Cyrene's waist to the floor.

"And can it be had also embroidered in gold?" Cyrene lifted her arms in the gesture of an embrace that allowed René an unimpeded view, turning slightly so that her body was in profile, and taking a deep breath so that her breasts lifted like proud globes.

"Of a certainty. It will be a toilette fit for a queen."

"Very well," she said with a seraphic smile directly into René's eyes. "That is what I want."

The revenge of the kept woman, to be kept as grandly as the keeper's resources would allow. René watched Cyrene take it with a tight feeling in his chest that had nothing to do with the ache in his loins. He had brought her to this, she who had been warm and open and straightforward, and without the need for such petty retaliation. He had not meant it to happen that way, but that was no excuse. He would have to repair the damage, somehow, some way. It might very well be a pleasurable occupation.

There was more discussion of fabrics, ribbons, and lace; of types of sleeves, skirt widths and lengths, and bodice trims; of coifs and cloaks; of hair powder and pins; and of a hundred other things. René endured it all. Cyrene kept the seamstress talking as long as possible. She ordered gowns and petticoats and shawls and cloaks and delicate lace coifs with abandon, taking intense pleasure in the idea of spending René's money, expecting at any moment to be told she had gone too far.

He said nothing, but neither did he take his gray gaze from her. In it there was a promise, if not of retribution then at least of a reckoning. She both dreaded and anticipated the moment when Madame Adèle would leave. She wanted to see what he would do, but at the same time there was something in the hooded depths of his eyes that made her wary.

Finally, the seamstress gathered up the tools of her trade and departed with promises ringing in the air of prodigies of labor and speed in producing something for Cyrene to wear. The door closed after her. Quiet gathered in the room so that the soft bursting of a coal in the fireplace was loud.

Cyrene looked around for the velvet dressing gown in an instinctive bid for protection. Before she could find it, René got to his feet and moved toward her. He reached to close his hands upon her shoulders, turning her to face him. Beneath the silk of the nightshirt, her skin was smooth and soft, but the bones of her shoulders felt fragile, easily breakable. Her lips were moist and parted, her breath sweet. She stared up at him in defiance, though her eyes were shadowed, concealing.

Cyrene felt the throb of the pulse in her throat. Inside her, the fear subsided, to be replaced by a curious waiting stillness. His hold was warm and firm, the grip of his hands and the slight caressing movements of his thumbs on her shoulders disturbing. His face was absorbed, the hard planes burnished to a copper glow by the firelight. Cyrene knew an odd mingling of triumph and fear, denial and desire. If she closed her eyes, swayed toward him . . .

Her power over him would be greater, her revenge more devastating if he was committed to physical intimacy with her. She knew that with some ancient instinct that had nothing to do with what had passed between them. The temptation to ensure that commitment mounted to her head like the fumes of fine brandy, potent, enticing.

No. It was too dangerous, too dishonorable.

But there was no gain without a gamble. And if he had no use for honor, why should she?

What, then, of her determination to resist him, her fine defiance? What guarantee was there that she would not succumb to his practiced seduction, that she would not abandon her quest for vengeance just as she was in danger of discarding her resistance?

What, indeed?

He bent his head to press his lips to hers with infinite care, with boundless and disarming tenderness. Her mouth was cool, tremulous at the corners, slowly warming, slowly firming. He brushed its smoothness with his own, engrossed in the silken sensation, in the honeyed taste of her, mindlessly rejoicing in her lack of withdrawal. He crossed his arms behind her back, bringing her closer, molding the curves of her body to the hard flatness of his chest and thighs, absorbing her soft resilience that was the perfect complement to his angular form as if he could possess her through the pores of his skin. The warm, womanly fragrance of her filled his senses. He felt the lift of her arms about him, the trembling of her fingers as she clasped her hands behind his neck.

Cyrene's mind was on fire. The blood raced in her veins, tumbling, hectic, molten with need and distress. The touch of his tongue upon hers was tantalizing yet jolting, frightening in its presage of a more intimate invasion. She could feel her defenses slipping away, receding with the hot rise of her own desire. There was enthrallment in the delicate probing of his kiss, which sought out the most sensitive and responsive areas of her mouth. He shifted with a whispering rustle of clothing, and she felt the touch of his hand at her breast, encircling, gently rubbing the exquisitely responsive peak. With a soft sound deep in her throat, she pressed against him.

There was despair in her sigh. René heard it and felt his heart constrict. The fervency of his need began to ebb. In a moment of vivid clarity, he saw what he was doing, and why, and a spasm of self-disgust gripped him. The muscles of his body went taut, then relaxed. By slow degrees, he compelled himself to release Cyrene's lips, to remove his hand from her breast, to draw back from her.

Cyrene stared up at him in confusion. She could no more comprehend what he was doing than she could her own dismayed reaction to it. Her only recourse was pride and pretense.

She swung away from him, her eyes bright and her voice husky with unshed tears. "I will thank you not to do that again!"

"I would give you my word if I thought I could keep it. At the moment, it seems unlikely."

"The next time you will regret it."

"And then again, I may not. It's a chance I'll have to take, won't I?"

She turned slowly to face him once more with her hands knotted into fists in front of her. "I can give you my word."

He was ninety-nine kinds of fool. What he could have of her, he did not want; what he wanted, he could not have. Or could he?

"Don't," he said. "Don't give me your word. But make ready to annihilate me if you must, and if you can. There will be a next time."

13

SELF-KNOWLEDGE COULD BE a bitter thing. Cyrene sat thinking long after René had finished dressing and left the house. She could not get over the fact that it was not she who had called a halt to their embrace. The thought was mortifying, but more dismaying still was the convoluted thinking that had allowed her to consider surrender. Had it been generated by a passion for revenge or by the powerful attraction René exerted as a man? That was the question that haunted her.

She had a much better appreciation now for the force of that attraction. There were men like that, men who stood out in a crowd, who seemed to draw people to them without conscious effort, without realizing their unique appeal.

But, of course, René knew his attraction well. As much as she hated admitting it, she had given him all too much reason to know his effect upon her. Her only consolation was that she seemed to have some degree of attraction for him also, else she would not be where she was. Not that she felt any inclination to preen herself over the fact. Many women had apparently appealed to him in the past for brief periods. He was a man of strong desires, one used to getting what he wanted. Which made it all the more unbelievable that he had not taken her when he had had the chance.

Was it possible that he was toying with her? Could he be taking some perverted pleasure in seeing how wide a breach he could make in her defenses? Or was it that he required not just a physical surrender but one of the spirit as well?

That, at least, he would not get. Whatever else she might do, she would not surrender her innermost self.

Whatever else.

Desire, she had discovered, could be a weapon. It was one she could use, one she would use. There was danger involved, yes, but it was a risk she could take.

She had thought once, for a mercifully brief time, that she loved René. Whatever she had felt had died with his betrayal and was unlikely to be resurrected. As for giving herself to him in physical union, she had done that once already of her own will. There was no great sacrifice in doing so again, not if it had a purpose. She had been foolish to place so much importance on the act or to be so afraid. Foolish, indeed.

The first of the gowns from Madame Adèle was ready to be fitted the following morning and was delivered by late afternoon, a little more than twenty-four hours after the order was placed. It was not some practical day costume as might be expected; with true French appreciation for what was important, it was one of the three formal court dresses, the ubiquitous *robe à la française* that had been commissioned. It arrived, not by coincidence, just in time for a musical soirée being given that evening by Madame Vaudreuil; Madame Adèle and her helpers had worked far into the midnight hours to be sure that it was ready. The seamstress stayed to help Cyrene into the gown in case there was a need for further minor fitting. She fussed around Cyrene, adjusting the bodice and twitching at the draped sides of the skirt front, then stood back.

"Magnifique!" she exclaimed, clasping her hands. "No one will be able to believe you haven't just this moment stepped off the ship from France. First the silk stockings and the slippers from the cobbler, then, if you will permit that I contrive with your hair, they will think you have come straight from Versailles itself!"

Cyrene submitted to having her hair dressed and powdered, though she was doubtful of the back combing that seemed necessary. When at last she was permitted to view the result in the mirror, she could only sit and stare. The person she knew was gone and in her place was a stranger. The hairstyle and revealing neckline of the formal gown made her look older, more sophisticated, and, at the same time, more frivolous. The gown itself was of azure-blue brocade with a square bodice inset with a pleated lace border known as a *tatez-y*, which meant, most slyly, touch here. The close-fitting sleeves reached to the elbow and were adorned with more pleated lace and bunches of ribbon, while the top skirt, held out at the sides over panniers, was open in front over an underskirt composed of tiers of ribbon-trimmed lace.

"You see? The essence of fashion!" the seamstress rattled on. "All that is needed is a touch of rouge applied with the hare's foot, perhaps a patch or two, and *voilà!* Hearts will be broken, perhaps even that of M'sieur René Lemonnier, yes?"

"Perhaps," Cyrene said with a faint, ironic smile.

"You permit, then?" The woman took out a hare's foot and a pot of rouge.

"I permit."

They were finishing with the rouge pot when René's footsteps were heard on the outside stairs. The seamstress paused in her ministrations and urged Cyrene to her feet. Standing back a few paces, she waited, her face alive with expectation. René opened the door and stepped inside. There was a faint murmur of voices as the serving woman met him and took his hat. A moment later he appeared in the bedchamber doorway.

René stopped short just inside the room. The woman who faced him was exquisite, with elegance of form combined with an ethereal air, but there was little to connect her with Cyrene. He had thought that having her gowned and powdered like the other women of his circle would make her seem more commonplace, less unusual. Instead, it lent her the remote quality not unlike that cultivated by the noble class. Her normal bearing with its straight, proud stance, when coupled with the correct formal clothing, marked her as a natural aristocrat. It was disconcerting and also disturbing.

He moved slowly into the room. His voice soft, he said, "Well, well."

"We are just down to the patches, m'sieur," Madame Adèle declared. "What say you? Shall it be a small heart at the corner of the mouth to draw the eye to its shape or perhaps a rose beneath the eye to direct attention there?"

"Nothing."

"Nothing? But, m'sieur, it is the fashion!"

"There are no blemishes to be covered. Why embellish perfection?" He stopped in front of Cyrene, his gaze direct, searching.

"There is that, of course," the seamstress allowed.

"You may leave us, madame."

"Certainly. Yes. At once." Smiling hugely to herself, Madame Adèle whisked up her various implements, brushes, and containers and took herself away.

When the woman had gone, Cyrene moistened her lips. "You—you are pleased?" she asked.

"I am pleased, in part."

She sent him a startled glance. "Only in part?"

"I think I preferred the nightshirt."

"You must learn to know your mind."

His lips curved slightly. "So I must. I bought you a gift, but now I'm not so sure I should give it to you."

"Because you think I am too fine already?" she asked, her eyes dark.

"Because you have no need of it and will undoubtedly find some way to make me feel a knave."

"That seems unlikely," she said, her tone tart, "unless of course you are—"

"Unless I am a knave? Thank you, I now have nothing to fear."

He removed a small velvet bag from the pocket of his

waistcoat. Reaching to take her hand, he placed the bag in it. Her fingers were not quite steady as she took it and drew it open. She caught the glitter and glimmer of jewels, then tipped the bag with one hand to pour a pair of eardrops made of pear-shaped baroque pearls attached to flower rosettes set with diamonds into the other.

It was a long moment before she could speak. Finally she said, "You are too generous."

"Not at all."

The politeness of his tone was a goad. "I see. You will expect payment in return."

Did he? René could not tell. "Are you offering it?" he said.

"You know I'm not!" she snapped, her eyes suddenly glittering as brightly as the diamonds. "I cannot be so easily bought."

"There was always the possibility."

"Your mistake, an expensive one."

When she was angry, she was much more like the Cyrene he knew, as tempestuous and without artifice as the elements. "Perhaps not. Will you wear them?"

"Why not?" She would show him she had no intention of being made to feel indebted by so underhanded a means. Reaching up, she removed from her ears the small gold hoops that had been her confirmation gift when she was twelve.

"Allow me," he said, and, taking one of the eardrops, began to screw it carefully into her ear. She could feel the hard metal pressing into the softness of her lobe, thrusting relentlessly into the opening pierced in her ear. It sank into the hole, the shaft, larger than that of her hoops, stretching the delicate skin. He fastened on the cunning back that held the shaft in place, then began on the other eardrop. As if compelled, she lifted her gaze to his. He smiled down at her as he inserted the second earring gently into her ear, and the feel of his knuckles against her cheek was like a caress.

He was not done. From his other pocket he took a small

vial. "Humor me in this also, if you will. You need it not at all, but it's something no lady of fashion should be without."

It was perfume. Cyrene took the beautifully wrought cut-glass bottle in her hand, feeling its ridges in her palm. She removed the tiny stopper wedged into the top. The scent of damask roses wafted on the air, bringing memories of a beach and a night she would just as soon forget. In defiance of them, she wet the stopper and touched it to the pulse point in her neck and the bends of her arms, and also to the gentle valley between her breasts.

René said nothing, but the look in his eyes as he inclined his head was disturbing, compounded of gratification and promise.

While René dressed for the evening's entertainment, Cyrene spent the time shaping her nails, buffing away the rough spots on her fingers with a piece of pumice stone and rubbing goose fat provided by the serving woman into her hands. The ministrations were inadequate to give her skin the smoothness required in a lady of idle pleasures, but might save her from total disgrace. Her nails, kept short by cooking and scrubbing, would doubtless grow if she remained in her present position. If.

René, when he emerged, was splendid in a purple velvet coat so deep in color that it was nearly black and lavender satin breeches. There was lace at his throat and wrists, and amethyst buttons on his coat. His wig was neat, tied with a black bow and powdered to a blinding white, and in his hand he carried an ebony cane. He was every inch the courtier, aloof, watchful. As he took Cyrene's hand and placed it on his arm before leading her from the house, a small frisson ran through her.

It was no more than a short walk from René's lodgings to the governor's residence where the soirée would be held. The marquis's house was located on the corner of the street that ran before the Place Royale and the second street up from it, with Government House itself, where the affairs of the colony were conducted, being just beyond, also fronting on the same street as the Place Royale. The streets of the town, laid out with military precision in a grid of neat squares, had names on maps that collected dust in the government's bins, but they were not posted and few used them. The thoroughfares were, for the most part, known by the surnames of the most important men who dwelled on them.

The official Government House, a two-story building with dormer windows let into the roof and walls of plaster over brick, was falling into such disrepair that already there was talk of building a new one farther up the river. Regardless, it was here that most of the larger functions were held, in the upstairs meeting chamber that also served as a ballroom. For more intimate gatherings, however, the governor's wife preferred to welcome her guests into the rarefied air of the home she shared with her husband. Such was the case for the evening.

It was impossible to tell who was responsible for the furnishing of the governor's house, whether it was the marquis himself or his wife, but to all appearances their aim had been to duplicate in so far as they were able the luxury of Versailles. One wall of the main salon was lined with windows, while opposite them was a row of reflecting mirrors. The wood interstices were painted to appear marblelike in shades of green and rose. Chandeliers gleamed icy with crystal luster and ropes of crystal medallions. Beside the entrance doors were a pair of massive six-feet-tall candelabra of bronze holding branches of tall, guttering candles, all of which, both in chandeliers and candelabra, were of the purest beeswax. The floor was of parquet polished to a high gloss that reflected the dancing flames in the great fireplaces of *faux marbre* at either end of the room. Overhead, the ceiling was painted with voluptuous goddesses and fat cherubs, while on either side of the fireplaces were wall panels of painted silk from Tours. Both the harpsichord on which the singer was to accompany herself and the chairs standing ready for the audience were carved and gilded and inset with sections of scenic tapestry.

The rococo splendor was overwhelming, not the least reason being the thought of how much care and thought and money had been expended on transporting it to the colony. It might have been more impressive, however, if Cyrene had not also known, through the grumblings of Jean and Pierre, of how much food and clothing for the colonial army and how much valuable merchandise consigned to Louisiane merchants had been left rotting on the wharves while space in ships' holds were filled with these items, which the governor and his wife felt were necessary for them to sustain what their friends in Paris no doubt considered their exile at the end of the world.

Cyrene and René were formally received by the governor and his lady just inside the salon. If the marquise, resplendent in gold lace over black velvet, remembered seeing Cyrene on her visit to the flatboat, she gave no sign. Pierre de Rigaud de Vaudreuil, equally grand in gray satin decorated by the order of a Knight of Saint Louis, declared himself enchanted. A man of grace and exquisite manners, he was not only much younger than his wife but more attractive, with a broad forehead, firm features, and compelling eyes. Fully aware of his exalted position, pleasure-loving, he was yet a fine administrator with a firm grasp of the problems of the far-flung colony and total confidence in his ability to solve them given time.

The smile he gave Cyrene as she made her curtsy was appreciative, his grasp upon her fingers warm and lingering. The marquise, noticing from the corner of her eye, waved a languid signal to a lackey in livery and a white wig, one of a dozen or more standing at intervals along the walls. The man leaped to place chairs for Cyrene and René. The governor released Cyrene with a faint air of regret nicely calculated as a tribute to her beauty, allowing them to move on into the room.

"Take care," René said, leaning to speak in soft tones near her ear as they strolled away, "the governor's wife is most unfashionably jealous."

"I thought she had a fondness for younger men?"

"One thing does not preclude the other. She is sometimes forced to console herself, like most wives."

Women had been so scarce in the colony for so long that marriage due to mutual attraction and mutual sentiments had become the common thing. There were arranged marriages among those with property, a trend that was increasing as more large concessions of land changed hands and more people arrived, but it was sometimes difficult to remember that things were very different in France. There, particularly among the landed nobility, marriages were contracted in the cradle with no pretense of anything more than a careful alliance of family and fortune. Adultery on the part of the husband was not only condoned but expected, and following the birth of an heir, wives could with proper discretion enjoy the company and embraces of lovers. To Cyrene, used to marriages where husband and wife worked side by side to feed and clothe themselves and supported each other through illness and pain and misfortune, the aristocratic idea of married union seemed cold and barren.

Not that she troubled to say so to René. Rather, she smiled and made pleasant remarks to the men and women to whom he presented her, then took her place for the musical evening.

The young woman who entertained them, the daughter of a planter, had a clear, sweet voice but made no pretension to professionalism. Supported by the meltingly approving looks of a plump woman who was obviously her mother, she was spritely and vivacious as she gave them light country airs with delicately risqué allusions to shepherds and milkmaids or else trilled her way through the pieces that had been popular the winter before at the Opéra-Comique.

It soon became obvious, however, that music was simply an excuse for the gathering. When the singer was done, a trio of musicians came forward and the chairs were pushed back against the wall to clear the floor for dancing. Those who were not inclined to take part in such strenuous activity were directed to a small connecting room where tables for cards were arranged. To sustain everyone in these proposed exertions, there was a supper laid out, with each of the various courses served in a different room, from seafood to fowl, meat to dessert.

Everyone who was anyone was there: the planters from their concessions along the Mississippi and the Bayou St. John; the town merchants, lawyers, notaries, and physicians; the officers of the king's army; and the town officials, from the guardian of the king's stores, the contractor of buildings and fortifications, and the attorney general to the intendant commissary Michel la Rouvilliere himself, who was the most influential man in the colony after the governor. With their wives and sons and daughters, they ate, they drank, they struck poses in their finery and indulged in flirtations and general merriment, but most of all they talked.

The sound of voices was a constant flow, rising and falling in repartee, in quick quips and droll asides, in superficial gossip but also in learned discourse and passionate dispute. Those who wanted to make their opinions known had to be swift in order to find an opening, and to the point if they hoped to hold the attention of their audience; the laggard of wit or tongue was soon left behind.

Some dozen guests had gathered at one end of the long main room, grouped around a settee placed before the fireplace. Madame Vaudreuil held court on the settee, skillfully directing the current of conversation, drawing out those who were shy, curbing those who would monopolize the floor. Cyrene, with René standing behind her, sat to one side enjoying the swift ebb and flow of ideas. She was greatly taken with a young man named Armand Moulin. This gentleman, with softly curling wig, sensitive features, and diamonds among the lace at his throat, appeared to be a firm supporter of the fair sex. He had much to say that made excellent sense as he paced up and down before the fire, declaiming in impassioned tones and with extravagant gestures about the place of women in current society.

"We live in a glorious age, an age of beauty and refinement. And why is this so? It's because in *la belle France* we have the felicity to worship women! Their grace, their charm, their love of the pure and delicate; their tender emotions pervade our art, our music, even the ordinary furnishings of our lives. Never before has there been such an attempt to make common objects things of beauty. To whom do we owe this influence? To women! They make us more sensitive and persuade us to greater tact so that manners and customs are closely observed. They teach us the rudiments of courtship and the tenderness of the boudoir. If we find triumph on the battlefield, are we satisfied? No, we must be rewarded by the appreciation of the women in the salons. Our greatest feats on the field of honor are carried out for the sake of a fair woman's name. Our poetry and philosophy are as nothing if there is not some feminine soul to applaud, to discuss, to encourage. Lacking clear power, their influence reaches everywhere, even into the innermost councils of the king. How very dull it would be without them, how drab and how brutish.''

"Ah, but would you be ruled, in truth, by a woman?''

The question was asked by a richly dressed lady, with an arch smile and the fine lines of approaching middle age about her eyes, who had been introduced as Madame Pradel. Younger by some years than her husband, she was alone. The Chevalier de Pradel did not care for society, preferring to spend his time and energy on his plans for a grand residence to be built across the river from New Orleans. Like Madame Vaudreuil, Madame Pradel was known for having a well-developed appreciation for younger men, particularly if they were idealistic as well as handsome.

Armand Moulin said with a sweeping gesture, "Why not, if she is educated to her position?''

"So speaks enraptured youth. Older men are more chary of sharing their honors.''

Several men protested, and Armand ran a hand over his soft wig curls before saying in earnest perplexity, "But women are seldom educated toward high estate or position.''

"Why should they bother with such things," a man said sotto voce, "when there are easier ways to achieve them, as with La Pompadour?"

Madame Pradel ignored the comment, smiling at Armand with a bright, warm look in her fine eyes. "What you say is true, but whose fault is it that we are so ill-prepared, I pray you? First we are put away with governesses or in convents for the early years of our lives, then blamed for our unworldliness. Then once we taste society, we are accused of being far too worldly for our own good."

"It's a mistake to think that because women are taught only a little reading and writing and embroidery that they are uneducated," Cyrene said.

The words fell into a brief pause and so were plainly heard. She had not meant to make so definite a statement. She felt the slow rise of embarrassment as her voice overrode the distant hum of conversation.

"What do you mean?" Madame Pradel asked, diverted.

"Education is a matter of pursuing learning. Learning is to be had from books. A woman who can read, like a man who is apprenticed to read law or medicine, can grasp the important ideas of our time."

"Very true," Armand declared. "Only look at women such as Madame Tencin and Madame du Deffand. People flock to their salons in Paris because they are women of wit and intellect and immense understanding."

The older woman stared at Cyrene, a shrewd look in her eyes. "What of you, *chère*? You were not educated in the colony, I think. Where did you come upon such a novel approach to learning?"

"I was sent to the convent of the Ursulines at Quimperle, but the idea of learning by reading came from a man I know."

"A man," the other woman said, as if that explained all.

"My—my guardian," Cyrene said, for want of another word. She spoke of Pierre, who read with difficulty but had strong ideas on the subject, though it would not be wise to mention his name here.

"I see. I will keep this place you mention in mind for my daughters. My oldest must go to be educated soon or marry, and her father doesn't wish to see her wed so young. And after her we have two others who will have to be placed."

The whispers had come even to Cyrene's ears that it was Madame Pradel who was encouraging the eldest Pradel girl toward a vocation as a nun because she could not face the thought of her marrying and almost certainly making a grandmother of her within a year. It might be true. Cyrene said only, "I'm sure your daughters will enjoy it."

"It's a great distance to send a young girl," the marquise said to the other woman. "Of course, you have Pradel connections, I believe, who can look after her interests, make profitable introductions."

"Indeed."

Armand Moulin spoke again. "We must hope that the seas will be safe from the English privateers since the signing of the treaty."

"We must hope we will all be safe," Madame Pradel said with a shudder. "I have never been so relieved in my life. Since the attack last winter and the death of poor Babi, I must have leaped from my bed in terror at least twice per night for every week since."

She spoke of the attack of the renegade Choctaw under the leadership of their chief Red Shoe. Rumors had run wild then of casualties in the hundreds, and the army had rallied to fight off a full-scale attack on the city before it was discovered that the band had numbered no more than thirteen or fourteen. Red Shoe had been executed by the Choctaw allies of the French the autumn before in a minor betrayal that had been expected to calm the general anxiety. The effect, so far, had been minimal. The death of the dancing master Babi, a dapper man of indeterminate age who was a general favorite of the ladies and a fixture at the governor's house, was, in typical New Orleans fashion, thought to be a greater loss than most. It had been Babi as much as the marquise who had brought the Parisian touch to the town and encouraged the formation of what was becoming its *haute société*.

"There are always these alarms," Madame Vaudreuil said, "though the firing of the warehouse the other night was more terrifying than most. Of all things to be dreaded, fire to me is the worst."

Armand clasped his hands together behind his back under the skirt of his coat, his gaze alight. "To think of these men breaking into the king's warehouse and making off with the stores. It was an intrepid deed, or else a desperate one. I am all admiration."

"You would be less so if your house had burned down around your ears because of the flames," the governor's wife said with asperity. "Fortunately, the building was isolated and the blaze discovered early."

"There was a great loss of commodities?"

The question came from the back of the group. It was the governor, strolling up to join them, who answered.

"We will not starve," he said, his smile genial, imparting easy confidence.

"The men responsible should be dealt with harshly when they are caught," another man commented.

"Of a certainty," the governor answered, and took out his snuffbox with languid grace.

Armand said, "Rumors say the men were smugglers after their confiscated goods. Most elusive characters, these smugglers."

"Indeed." The governor took a pinch of snuff, then sneezed delicately into the lace-edged handkerchief he pulled from his left sleeve. "The only person who seems able to— shall we say?—lay one by the heels is Lemonnier here. He has captured our only lady smuggler, Mademoiselle Cyrene, readily enough. We must be grateful to him, I suppose, though seeing her loveliness we are inclined to think that he has been rewarded enough."

The observation was gentle, even humorous, but the glance that went with it was neither. Governor Vaudreuil might be married to a woman who dabbled at will in commerce and the affairs of the colony, but he was not a fool. It was apparent, also, that he always knew more than he revealed. Cyrene felt a shiver of fear for the Bretons. She should have known that her part in their activities had not passed unnoticed. It had simply not occurred to her that someone as insignificant as herself could be of interest to the governor, the Marquis de Vaudreuil.

René, behind her, reached to put his hand on her shoulder. It rested there, a warm and intimate weight. It may have been meant to be reassuring, but it seemed to be oppressive to Cyrene, obvious in its possessiveness. Above her, he answered the governor in rich tones, "Amply rewarded."

The heat of angry chagrin that fear had held at bay swept in upon Cyrene now. She felt branded, and it seemed that every gaze turned upon René and herself with lascivious speculation. More, it was as if René had invited that intrusion upon their privacy.

She lifted her hand to cover his, clasping it lightly before turning her fingers to dig her nails into his palm. She felt his hand twitch slightly as he flinched, but he did not attempt to withdraw from her hold. She could continue to fondle his hand in a parody of affection or let it go and suffer being claimed by his touch. She released him.

At the first opportunity, however, she escaped, rising from her chair and moving away to watch the dancing before strolling into one of the refreshment rooms for a glass of wine. When she turned with it in her hand, Armand Moulin was at her side. He took wine also, then inclined his head in a bow as he introduced himself.

His smile was disarming and his rich brown eyes vivid with interest as they exchanged compliments and comments on the evening. He said then, "Is it true you were a lady smuggler?"

He was, Cyrene realized, some two or three years older than she was herself, but somehow she felt immeasurably more mature. He had a minor repute in the town. He was the only son of a family with three older sisters, the hope of a doting mother and proud father. He had been educated in Paris and was now expected to take up his position as the young seigneur of the Louisiane estates. No doubt there was a marriage being planned for him at that moment, an alliance with some girl barely beginning to blossom, one with a fine dowry of land and excellent family connections. In Paris, he had probably dallied with some pretty *grisette* or been taken under the wing of an older woman for an introduction to the delights of the flesh, but he had managed somehow to retain his look of idealistic and honorable youth. It sat well with his soft curls and guileless smile.

Cyrene was inclined to be gracious for a number of reasons: because she liked him, because he reminded her of Gaston, because he made her feel less conspicuous there in that gathering, and not least because René was watching their exchange with a faint frown between his brows. She made light of her experience with smuggling, pretending to Armand that it was in the distant past, leading him to talk of himself instead. Soon she forgot that René or anyone else was observing them.

Emboldened by Armand's example, a pair of his friends joined him as he stood with Cyrene. That pair drew others until gradually she acquired a circle of jostling, bantering admirers. The glances they gave her were bold, assessing, yet respectful and even rather diffident. Cyrene could not decide if the cause was their youth, her status under René's protection, or her connection with such a daring occupation as smuggling.

It was the governor who rescued her just as she was beginning to feel hemmed in, the center of too much close attention.

"I have been sent," he said with great amiability as he looked around the group, "to represent to you gentlemen that you are monopolizing the lady, and to the lady that you are detaining too many gentlemen from the dance. It is one of my more enjoyable duties as appointed leader of this colony to correct such inequities. Will you, mademoiselle, favor me with your hand for this musical measure?''

One did not refuse the governor while in Louisiane any more than one would the king in France. Cyrene expressed her pleasure and was paraded ceremoniously out onto the floor and bowed into her place in the forefront of the line of dancers forming for a minuet.

The music began. They moved to its stately cadence. The governor praised the lightness of her dancing. Cyrene thanked him for the politeness, according it little more importance. His next words were surprising, however.

''Do you care for theatricals?''

''Theatricals, Your Excellency?''

He smiled. ''It isn't a common thing here, is it, theaters being rather scarce?''

''Nonexistent, in fact.''

''Just so. But I speak of amateur theatricals. Do you enjoy performing?''

''I hardly know,'' she said. ''I haven't tried since convent school.''

''The mother superior permitted such diversions?''

''She was a worldly woman, and in any case we girls entertained only ourselves, out in the open air.''

''The location of the earliest theaters, the open air. Ours is held inside, but we would be delighted to have you take a part. We are in need of fresh faces.''

''You are very kind,'' she murmured. This was moving too fast. She could not help wondering how accepted she would be in the governor's circle if she wore her old clothes and was without the backing of a man like René, someone touched with the glitter of the court. She wondered, too, whether anyone in the that room full of people would acknowledge her on the street tomorrow if she were to run away and return to the flatboat. Cynicism was not an attractive trait; still, it was sometimes hard to avoid.

''And then, of course,'' the governor went on, ''there is

our *bal masqué* on Mardi Gras evening. Madame Vaudreuil and I will be vastly disappointed if you do not come.''

"It sounds fascinating, but I'm afraid I am . . . dependent on M'sieur Lemonnier, and I don't know his wishes in this.''

''Ah? Then I shall have to let him know mine. If he attends to me, you will be very much present, I assure you.''

The minuet came to an end. It was not long afterward that René came for Cyrene. He was perfectly pleasant as he made his adieus to his host and hostess, but his grip on her arm was a little tighter than need be, and his voice as he spoke to her was far too even, too polite. She looked at him carefully in the light of the torches beside the front doors of the governor's house as she passed between them. Very well. If he was annoyed, then so was she. Let him say something, just let him attempt to take her to task. He would regret it. He would, indeed.

14

THE AFRICAN SERVING woman was waiting up for them. She let them into the house, took René's tricorne and cane, and removed the shawl that Cyrene wore around her shoulders. She followed them into the bedchamber to put the items away in the great armoire, then turned, waiting expectantly.

"That will be all, Martha," René said.

The woman bobbed a curtsy and left them. A few minutes later, there came the sound of her footsteps on the back pantry stairs and the distant thud of the door closing to her small room beside the kitchen in the raised basement.

Cyrene, holding on to one of the bedposts, had stepped out of one shoe. She slipped off the other also before she spoke with a shading of acerbity. "I don't like to complain, but you might have asked if I needed Martha's help."

"You don't," René answered.

"No? This costume isn't easy to get out of."

"I'm aware. Helping you is my privilege."

His words were too smooth, as well as suggestive. She eyed him with suspicion. "I didn't say I couldn't undress myself, only that it was more difficult now."

"I wouldn't dream of letting you do it alone." He shrugged out of his coat as he spoke and tossed it onto a chair. The look in his gray eyes as he began to remove the diamond from his cravat held both anticipation and purpose.

"You really need not trouble yourself." She turned from him with a bell-like swing of her skirts as she fumbled at the ribbon bows that trimmed her stomacher, covering the fasteners.

"It will be no trouble to me but rather my pleasure."

He had threatened once before to play the part of her maid. It appeared that he intended to put the threat into action.

"It's odd to me that you have only just now decided to take this task on yourself," she said.

His voice was nearer, close behind her as he answered. "My dressing gown, as charming as it was on you, did not present much of an excuse."

"Nevertheless, I can manage."

Alarm coursed along her veins. She wanted to face him like an animal who senses danger. She would not give him that satisfaction, however. Instead, she drifted away with a movement as casual as she could make it. Her stomacher finally loosened under her fingers and she placed the handful of detachable ribbons she held on a table. There was a small chair beside it and she sat down, lifting her skirts to reach the garters that held her stockings. Her manner carefully distracted, she went on, "But what of the evening? Did you enjoy it?"

"It was much as expected. I was gratified by the success of my new mistress, of course." He moved to stand in front of her, then went down on one knee with easy grace. He put his hands on hers at her garter, taking the small embroidered strap from her fingers and unhooking it. He tossed it to one side before he slowly drew the silk of her stocking down the calf of her leg.

The touch of his fingers at the sensitive bend of her knee, the glide of them along her leg through the silk, was disturbing. More disquieting still was his calm assumption of the right to perform this service and the practiced ease with which he did it.

"I—I rather thought you were displeased at the attention paid me," she said. As he dropped her stocking to one side and reached for the other one, she hastened to catch and hold his hand.

René carried the hand that clasped his to his lips, pressing a kiss to its smooth back. The fragrance of damask roses, warmed by Cyrene's skin and fusing with her own delicate essence, assailed his senses with incalcuable pleasure. She wore his perfume. The gift of it had been a gesture of purest sentiment, a token of another moment of intolerable desire. He was a fool, but at this moment he was an uncaring one, a glad one.

He set her hand aside firmly and returned to her garter and her question disguised as a comment. He smiled into her eyes. "It was a momentary twinge of jealousy."

"Momentary."

"A small breach of manners, one permitted under the circumstances. I should have known you would attract men like flies to a sugarloaf. They are so starved for a fresh and attractive face."

"I'm not your mistress."

"Aren't you?"

The deep timbre of his voice was caressing. His touch was the same. She watched him, her eyes wide and dark as he loosened her other garter and slowly eased the tube of silk down the slender turning of her leg. There was a curious, aching stillness inside her. She searched for the resentment and pugnacious desire for a confrontation with him she had felt earlier, but it was gone. She grasped, in rising dismay, for a counterfeit as she caught and held his hand once more.

"What," she said evenly, "do you think you are doing?"

The silver gleam of laughter sprang into René's eyes. There was no one quite like Cyrene. "I thought it must be obvious," he said. "I'm seducing you."

"Are you, now? You might have warned me."

"That isn't a part of the game."

"Forgive me, I don't seem to know the rules. What am I supposed to do now that I've spoiled it? Scream and slap you or swoon with ecstasy?"

He released himself with a quick turn of his wrist and placed the palms of his hands on her knees, sliding them upward over the taut muscles of her upper thighs, spreading his fingers as he reached around to cup her hips. "Whichever you wish. But you might wait to see if anything happens that gives you pleasure."

"And if it doesn't?" His grasp seemed to burn her flesh. She kept her voice steady only with the greatest effort.

"If it doesn't, then you have a choice."

"Which is?"

"You can be cruel and tell me so or be kind and pretend."

She swallowed hard as his grasp tightened, pulling her toward him. "Tell me what reason there is for me to be kind."

"I would be grateful," he said, and removed one hand from under her skirts to touch her neck, pushing his fingers into her hair. He loosened the pins so that the thick tresses were released in a shower of white hair powder that sifted down upon her shoulders, sliding softly over her breasts. He closed his hand upon the tumbling waves, drawing her toward him until their mouths were inches apart. "I will also be as generous in return as you can bear. And more than that, pretending can sometimes make it so."

"I won't pretend," she said.

His mouth curved in a faint smile. "I thought not. I prefer it that way."

He was going to have her; she knew that. The decision had been made and he would not ask her permission. There would be no drawing back this time, no retreat from the final intimacy. What made it different, this occasion, she could not begin to guess. Unless it was something within René, some change, some new resolution that had more to do with his image of her as his kept woman than with what lay between them.

It did not matter. She could not remove her gaze from the firm curves of his lips, not even as his hold tightened and the softness of her breasts were against his chest, not until the instant before he took her mouth with his own.

Such incredible sweetness, honeyed, beguiling. How could she have forgotten? Or had she? Her mind might have set it aside, but her body had not. Careless of her will, her lips parted, taking, offering.

His jaw was firm under her questing fingers, the line where their lips joined exquisitely sensitive as she touched it. Against her cheek, the thick length of his lashes tickled, tangling in a loose wave of her hair. She placed the fingers of her other hand upon his shoulder, gently holding, sensing the controlled strength of the muscles beneath his loose shirt, feeling them glide as he smoothed her hip in slow circles.

Desire welled within her, a slow rise of consummate need. It spread, tingling in her veins, creeping over the surface of her skin, invading her heart in a red tide to quicken its beat. A soft, despairing sigh left her. She moved closer to him, molding the firm resilience of her breasts to the hard planes of his chest.

His kiss grew more insistent, deeper. With his tongue, he explored the lush moistness of the inner surfaces of her mouth and the fine edges of her teeth. He twined her tongue with his in sinuous play, encroaching, retreating, inviting her to venture in return. He slid his fingers over the intricate turnings of her ear to the curve of her neck, brushing the sensitive skin with a feather-light stroke of his thumb so that she shivered with reaction. He traced the fragile hollow of her collarbone, easing lower to the swell of her breast. He encircled it, clasping the perfect globe, filling his hand before he sought and found the delicately grained peak. The soft brushing of his fingers there sent a heated sensation spiraling through her to lodge in the lower portion of her body.

Cyrene wanted him. Nothing else mattered beyond that one fact. She had known for some time that he could have this effect on her, but she had refused to acknowledge it. She did so now without restraint. Circumstances had united to bring her to this point, against her will, against her every defense. Then let it be so. Since submit she must, she would wring from it every possible pleasure, every joy, every painful memory.

She pushed his wig from his head and threaded her fingers through the thick waves of his hair, loosening them, clasping her hands in their crispness. Parting her lips, she bent her head to brush his temple, touching the top curve of one brow with her tongue, giving herself to the wonder of the moment. She felt the swell of his chest in triumph before she was caught closer still, then came the warm slide of his hand as he released her hip and pressed it between her thighs under her chemise, which was drawn forward between them also and fastened in front at the waist as protection for the vulnerable and most secret recess of her being. He touched her there in gentle exploration.

Her heart leaped, thudding against her ribs. She could feel the hot race of her blood, feel its glow under her skin. She was light-headed with longing and incredulous at the swift ascension of it. His warm caress, so delicate, so relentless, took her breath and sent a rippling shudder through the muscles of her abdomen. Suffused with wild longing, she clenched her hands on his shoulders.

With a soft exclamation, he lifted his head, breaking her hold as he came erect. He caught her in his arms and surged upward with her close against him as he swung around toward the bed. He placed his knee on the springing softness of the moss-filled mattress and then eased her down upon its surface. The bed ropes creaked as he pushed away, moving to blow out the candles. There came in the darkness lit only by the fire the rustle of linen and broadcloth as he removed his clothing and flung it on a chair. As her eyes adjusted to the dimness, she could see the sculptured grace of his form made copper and bronze by firelight, the burning promise in his eyes. Then with the taut control of well-used muscles, he joined her on the bed, settling beside her.

He began at once to undress her. His movements were

unhurried but sure, as if her garments were an impediment but not an unusual one. Her open bodice, heavy with embroidery, was stripped away. Her skirts and panniers, under his ministrations, were eased from her hips with quiet, satin whispers. The chemise of finely woven silk wafted cool air over her body as it was drawn upward and off over her head. Naked, gloriously so, she stretched, turning at the same time until her breasts touched René's chest in delicate enticement.

None was needed. He drew her to him, molding her to his body so that the hardened peaks of her breasts burrowed into the curling growth of hair on his chest and the hard length of him pressed against the softness at the juncture of her legs. He spread his fingers over her back, testing the satin texture of the skin and the vital structure of bone and tendons, following the slim curve of her waist and the flare of her hips as if the discoveries to be made were beyond value. His chest rose and fell in a difficult sigh. He drew away and, with a hand on her shoulder, gently turned her onto her back.

For a feverish instant, she thought he meant to leave her and a cry rose in her throat. It was stifled in a gasp as a moment later he nuzzled the hollow between her breasts, his breath ticklish and warm upon the swollen curves of first one then the other. As he gave them closer attention with the warm adhesion of his mouth, the fingertips of one hand settled on her lower abdomen, circling, massaging, trailing downward. His touch was firmly marauding, demanding access to every curve and moist hollow and bringing vivid bliss. And slowly, with warm mouth and abrading tongue, he followed upon the advantage gained.

The blood in her veins was molten, pounding with the muffled throb of thunder in her ears. Her breath rasped with the quick rise and fall of her chest. The muscles of her thighs and hips were taut, quivering. Inside her, there was a liquid ache of suspended need. With a soft sound of distress, she clutched his shoulder.

He raised himself, hovering above her. A soft cry left her as he filled her tightness with his sure, sliding entry. He eased deeper, lowering himself upon her. She drew him close, holding him as her being contracted in slow pleasure around him. Long moments later, he entwined his legs with hers and, with the contraction of powerful muscles, turned her with him so that she mounted him with her hair swinging in a powdered curtain around them. With his hands upon her hips, he set the rhythm of their movements, then urged her to take it and make it her own. She assented in swelling joy, plunging upon him, taking him unimaginably deep inside until he was part of her, inseparable. Again and again she surged above him until she was spent and gasping. She paused then, resting her forehead on his. He took her face in his hands and kissed her parted lips, then heaved over, placing her on her back, rising above her to press into her once more.

She took the driven pressure of his thrusts, letting them send her soaring, higher and higher still. Together they strove, sharing the effort with inflamed senses and intoxicating ardor. Delight burst within her, a tumultuous thing, wondrous and rich with gratification that expanded, spreading, bringing heated glory.

It was the ultimate freedom, the unguarded secret of deliverance. Lost in its magic, they could not be held, they answered to nothing but the consuming demands of the joining. Snared in rigorous splendor they rode, separate beings bound by the moment yet without fetters, transfigured into one yet whole in themselves, transcending restraint. And the ecstasy that was their portion was likewise free, beyond price though not without cost.

Afterward, Cyrene lay staring into the darkness. She was human and therefore weak, and the matter of men and women had been arranged so that she and René might find pleasure in each other. Still, it no longer seemed strange that she had been used by René and then betrayed, for she had also betrayed herself.

Dawn came, rising behind the shutters in streaks of gray light. With it came a pounding on the outside door. René came awake with a soft curse. Flinging back the covers, he rolled from the bed and reached for his breeches. He stepped into them, then moved with swift strides to the armoire where he jerked his dressing gown from its hook. Whipping the velvet garment around him, he glanced at the bed where Cyrene lay.

"What is it?" She was surprised at how husky her voice sounded, and she cleared her throat, embarrassed by it for some reason.

"It's nothing," he said, his smile brief. "Go back to sleep."

When the door closed behind him, Cyrene raised herself to one elbow, listening. There came the sound of the bar being lifted from the door, then the low rumble of a masculine voice. A moment later, the outside door closed again. René did not return, however. A light appeared under the door as he used a tinder box and transferred the flame to a branch of candles. A few moments later Cyrene smelled the smoke and heard the spit and crackle of a newly made fire.

She lay back down and closed her eyes, but sleep was impossible. She had dozed off and on throughout the night but had not really rested, and now was no better. She had been, if she were truthful with herself, René's kept woman for some few days, but she had not felt the force of it until now. She tried to think what was going to become of her. He would grow tired of her eventually and set her free, or else he would go back to France and leave her behind. What then? The Bretons would take her back, she supposed. Or there would be another man. But what, then, of her hope to have land and a home, something secure of her own?

It was quiet in the other room. What was René doing? He had not slept a great deal better than she or perhaps she had disturbed him with her tossing, for he had changed positions each time she had and finally pulled her to him with a request that she be still or suffer the consequences. It had not been such a terrible threat, but the discovery that it was not had held her immobile long enough for sleep to overtake her for a while.

The memory was so disturbing that it brought her upright. She threw back the covers, combing her hair with her fingers, grimacing at the fall of powder as she pushed the tangled mass out of the way behind her shoulders. Moving to the armoire, she took down the nightshirt she had been wearing and slipped it on over her head. She hesitated for a moment, oddly reluctant to face René in the light of day. The bed-chamber was cool, the fire in its fireplace burned away to a heap of cold gray ash. There was no point in her hiding away, and none whatever in catching a chill. Neither would help. She stepped to the door of the salon and pulled it open.

René glanced up from where he sat at a long, narrow table set at a right angle to the fireplace on the opposite side of the room. Upon its surface was a sheaf of parchment sheets, while before him was an ornate inkwell and sand cellar made of twisted vermeil leaves and a selection of quill pens. A black lacquer box with a hasp from which a stout lock hung sat beside his chair with the lid laid open.

"What is it?" Cyrene asked.

"A messenger with papers from France. *Le Parham* made port this morning."

The king's vessel, *Le Parham*, with its sister ship, *La Pie*, made regular runs between France and its colonies in the New World, taking some six months, sometimes more, to make the voyage and return.

Cyrene gave a nod of understanding and a small smile. His lips curved in response. "One moment only," he said, then returned to his writing, finishing the sentence he had begun.

Cyrene went to stand with her back to the fire and her hands behind her to warm them. There was a faint frown between her eyes as she watched René send the quill slashing across the parchment. She did not think he was penning some simple missive or courtesy note. It was possible that he was addressing himself to his family in France, perhaps to his father, but there was something about the concentration that he brought to the task at hand that seemed to preclude that. She had never seen him employed in such grave industry before. It was as if she were suddenly seeing a side of him that had been kept hidden. It was this aspect, rather than what he was doing, that was most puzzling.

He came to the end of the page and signed it without any appearance of a flourish. He sat for a moment glancing over it, then sanded it. As he reached to set the sand cellar back in place, his dressing-gown sleeve caught the curling edge of one of the parchment sheets in front of him. The sheet dislodged, shifting. For an instant there was revealed a flash of gold and the dangling ribbons of seals on the sheet underneath. René dropped the sanded sheet on top of the others, then gathered them together in a pile. Only then did he tip the sand from the top sheet into a waiting tray. Without haste, he aligned the edges of the sheets more perfectly, then leaned to place them in the box at his side and close the lid.

He got to his feet, moving toward her around the end of the table. He lifted a brow as he let his gaze drift down her nightshirt-clad form, resting on the image cast by the fire-glow that shone through the white silk.

"I seem to recall another time when I saw you like this," he said, his voice rich with desire. "I wanted nothing so much then as to take you to bed and see if you were as rosy and warm underneath as you looked. I couldn't do it then. Isn't it a wonder how things change?"

As a distraction, the ploy was most effective. All interest in René's correspondence fled from Cyrene's mind, nor did it return for some time.

Armand Moulin came to call the following afternoon. The young man was charming and handsome in a fresh, untried fashion. He was dressed in the latest style, with a finely curled wig and a tall cane with a carved head of gold. In his hand he carried a poem to Cyrene's eyes. He presented what he insisted on calling his poor effort with a modest bow and such mischief lurking in his eyes that she was warned not to take him too seriously. Not that there was the least danger she might do so. Armand was an entertaining companion with a great deal of sense and an active sense of humor, but after her close acquaintance with René he also seemed rather immature.

Still, it was nice to have an admirer, to be treated to the gestures and graces of mild flirtation without the need to be constantly on guard. It was interesting, too, as day followed day and Armand's visits became more frequent, to have someone to question about various happenings: the details of which officer was keeping which woman; who among the upstanding members of the town society was sleeping with who's wife; who really had the important relatives in France that most claimed; and who had been cast off without a piastre. Many of the more flagrant cases Cyrene know about, but there were pitfalls in plenty left in those she did not. It was best to be prepared if she was to move among these people instead of watching them from a distance, as she had the past three years on the flatboat.

There was a rather pathetic example of an outcast of the political type, an elderly woman known to most simply as Madame H. She had been exiled by a *lettre de cachet* more than twenty years ago and had come out to the colony to live with a brother. Now the brother was dead, and she had been left a charge on the government. No one seemed to remember the reason for her exile; some said she had displeased the queen, others that her husband had simply desired her absence. Whatever the cause, she was an embarrassment, one which had the governor writing to the king's minister to know what he must do about her.

Such a tale held no interest for René when she related it to him. The reason could be that it was too close to his own case, or it may have been just that he had no time and less inclination to mull over the peccadilloes of his fellow men.

He spent more and more of his time at the writing table in the salon. Since the papers he had received on that first occasion had been delivered to him from the *Le Parham*, it was to be supposed that those René worked on so assiduously must go with the ship when it sailed again. Cyrene had come to the conclusion that his labors could only be in behalf of his return to France. There was nothing else so certain to engage his attention or to require so much diligence with a pen.

Armand, on the other hand, simply liked people and was interested in their quirks and foibles as well as their clandestine activities. He stored them up and brought them out to amuse Cyrene during his visits. Not even the governor and his lady were held sacrosanct from his impish humor. He had a tale to tell of them also.

It seemed that Madame la Marquise had brought before her husband one of their own servants as the marquis sat at the dining table. The man had been discovered stealing wine. The lady of the house accused the servant in no uncertain terms while the poor man stood with bowed head and trembling hands, moaning in fear of being sent to the flogging post or some other horrendous punishment for his crime. The marquis stared at the man with a measuring gaze during Madame Vaudreuil's diatribe. When it was over, he waved a negligent hand. "You have put the poor man in such a quake, my dear," he said, "that he deserves a bottle of wine to quiet his fears. Give it to him."

"And Madame Vaudreuil, what did she think of that?" Cyrene asked.

"No one knows. She makes no comments and no one dares ask if the story is even true. To me, it has the right ring, as a rebuke for the lady for making such a to-do over a bottle of wine like some merchant's wife. However, the governor is a man of great good humor who might also have seen it as a joke on the marquise."

"Do you think so?"

"One never knows; he is most adept at hiding his feelings. Only look at the way he received Rouvilliere at the musicale."

"The intendant commissary?"

"The same. I don't know why Rouvilliere puts in an appearance at the governor's house, except perhaps out of defiance and because he considers such affairs public gatherings. Nor do I understand why Madame Vaudreuil invites him, unless it is to pretend that she knows nothing of his complaints."

"That's much too unlikely, isn't it? Everyone knows the governor and the intendant commissary are always at odds, whoever they may be."

It was a weakness of the administration of the colony that the areas of authority of the governor and the intendant commissary, the man responsible for supplying the colony and its soldiers, overlapped. It had caused friction in the past and would do so as long as the situation lasted.

"Ah, but this is different. Rouvilliere attacks Vaudreuil through his wife, writing to the king's minister to accuse her of every crime imaginable, with the possible exception of prostitution. Vaudreuil, not to be outdone, files official dispatches charging Rouvilliere with selling the goods destined for Louisiane for his own profit and substituting inferior merchandise and then raising the price of the little that is delivered to astronomical heights."

"It's a feud, in fact."

"You might say so, one arising in no small part from the fact that both Madame Vaudreuil and Rouvilliere claim the right to sell the trading concessions and licenses for drinking establishments for the benefit of their own purses."

It was the cost in bribes of such trading concessions, as much as for the excitement of smuggling, that had prevented the Bretons from applying for legal trading status in the past.

"That is the way business is done, I suppose."

"Unfortunately."

"And how does the thought of a lady being involved in such transactions strike you after your praise the other night of the effect my sex has had on the shaping of our society?"

He smiled, his soft brown eyes sparkling. "You think you

have me, don't you? But I will admit that though I find the lady's arrangements less than delicate, I admire her acumen and her hardihood.''

''You admire strength in a woman?''

''To a degree only!'' he said in haste.

Cyrene's lips curved in a smile. She made no reply, however, allowing a small silence to fall as she stared at Armand, trying to decide whether to ask the question that hovered in her mind.

''What is it, mademoiselle? Do I have snuff on my cravat? The remains of my breakfast on my lapel? Tell me quickly!''

''No, no, I was only wondering if you know anything about Madame Vaudreuil's other activities in—in the realm of commerce.''

''How discreet you are, *chère*. If you mean her smuggling, it was an open secret in the past, though I believe she has not been so active since the war with the English. If you refer to her traffic in hashish among the soldiery, that isn't so well known but is still a rumor with great currency.''

Cyrene was not so sure the marquise's smuggling had declined, but she said nothing. ''You think the governor is aware of these things?''

''So I should imagine. How could it be otherwise? To be a royal governor is a most expensive undertaking. Vaudreuil may dispense lavish hospitality and make a grand gesture now and then with a bottle of wine, but he has a fine concern for his coffers.''

''He is concerned still about the traffic with the English.''

''Indeed. It's said that *Le Parham* brought a strong demand from the king for Vaudreuil to put an end to it. No excuses for failure to be accepted. Rumors also say, however, that the governor had advance warning of the strict new edict some months ago, brought by Lemonnier.''

''By René? How odd.'' Did it, perhaps, explain his part in the attempt to capture the Bretons?

''Just so, a friendly hint from the king's minister, Maurepas, from one politician to another.''

"Then the governor must surely stop the smuggling."

"So he must, or see his chances at the governorship of New France fade to nothing. And no doubt he will be successful. That will make it all the more lucrative for Madame la Marquise later when the competition is driven away and she is able to resume her activities."

Cyrene shook her head. "What a cynic you are."

"Am I?" He looked immensely pleased with himself. "Now there's a pose I must develop."

"I beg you will do no such thing!"

"You like me the way I am?"

"Very much so."

"Ah, a declaration at last. I was beginning to think you were immune to my charm."

"I would have complimented you earlier," she said with gentle irony, "had I known your ego was in such need of it."

"Cruel, cruel," he mourned. "Perhaps I should go straight from here to the marquise. She may be an avaricious lady who has forgotten how to count her years, but at least she knows how to appreciate fine form in a man, whether mental or physical."

Cyrene could not help laughing at his histrionics, though, an instant later, she sobered. "It's true, then, that the lady has young lovers?"

"As to lovers, I couldn't say, but she has a good eye for a manly leg and is not above testing with her own fingers to see if the shape is natural or has been helped with padding."

The loose breeches worn by most laborers, including the Bretons, were decent enough, but the tightly fitted garments made of silk and satin worn by gentlemen, designed to show that they could not possibly stoop, in the most literal meaning of the word, to manual labor made a fine display of manly attributes. "You mean she—"

"Frequently. If one is so unwise as to pay a visit to her alone or venture into a dark corner when she is near."

"There were rumors, but I can hardly credit such behavior. She has so much dignity."

"A useful thing, dignity, also honors and position," he said, his tone suggestive.

"Yes, I see what you mean." Cyrene paused a moment, then went on. "Had you heard—that is, do you know anything of her and René?"

"When Lemonnier first came he was as catnip to the cat; she practically purred when she saw him. Not only was he a fresh face but also wildly attractive, and with just that air of danger about him that some women enjoy. The pursuit was quite diverting, since he was more wily than most or perhaps more used to being hunted. His reputation had preceded him, naturally."

"Naturally," she echoed. Poor René, chased by Madame la Marquise, attacked, injured and half drowned in the river. Then what had happened when he was safe and dry and on the mend again? She had thrown herself at him.

Cyrene allowed her gaze to be caught and held by the flickering flames in the fireplace as she went on. "One might say he had brought it on himself with his past conduct."

"They might, of course," Armand said, tipping his head to one side with a judicious air.

"But you don't think so?"

"These things are always difficult. Who is to say why people do what they do, what drives them to their vices?"

"Must there be something?"

"Not always, but in the case of Lemonnier it would seem likely."

"What makes you say so?" she challenged him.

"I have the story from a great-aunt in Paris who knows the family and sometimes writes my mother, you understand, so you may judge how accurate it may be. It seems Lemonnier was not always as he is now, but was rather a dutiful youth, the second-born son. He was put to reading law and studying the management of large estates so that he might serve as custodian to his older brother, who would inherit the family lands and titles. Then the brother became embroiled in an unsavory scandal having to do with counterfeit bank notes. There was a great deal of money lost. The older Lemonnier son returned from Paris where the misfortune had taken place. One day he rode out to a lonely wooded spot where he shot himself in the head with his dueling pistol.''

Cyrene uttered a sound of shocked horror. Armand gave a nod. "Even so. The valued first son was no more. Overnight, Lemonnier fell heir to the responsibilities and duties of his brother, and also the debts and the scandal. He set off for Paris to discover what had brought his brother to ruin. He was made so welcome there that he soon forgot his purpose. He had been a provincial moldering on his father's lands too long; the pleasures of the city and the glories of Versailles went to his head, as it has to many others. He offended someone of importance, and *voilà*! Here he is in Louisiane, an exile—''

Armand broke off as footsteps sounded on the stairs and René appeared in the doorway. Smiling, making ready to greet his host, he went on smoothly. "But then we are all exiles, in one way or another.''

"Armand, so pleasant to see you again,'' René said, the irony of his tone a comment on the frequency of the younger man's visits.

Armand, not to be outdone in civility, sketched a slight bow. "I realize I trespass, but Mademoiselle Cyrene is that rare creature, a women of both physical charms and brain. One must have inspiration for one's literary efforts, after all, and how refreshing it is to find here also a true appreciation.''

"Ah,'' René said with an air of great affability, "you have brought her another poem. May I see it?''

He picked up the sheet of foolscap that lay on the settee beside Cyrene and began to peruse it as he moved to stand with his back to the fire.

Armand looked decidedly ill at ease, though he tried to be

nonchalant about it. "It's another of my poor efforts, I fear, one that comes nowhere near to doing Mademoiselle Cyrene justice. I'm sure that in your career you have written many that were much better."

"I've penned one or two. One can hardly escape, so mad has the world become over scribbling," René said without looking up. "However, I don't recall ever comparing a lady's eye to a swamp."

"Oh, but I only meant dark and deep and mysterious!"

"So I apprehend. And what of muddy and shifting and stagnant?"

"I never said that!"

"Didn't you? How odd? I thought you did." René turned to Cyrene, extending the poem to her between two fingers with an air that was indescribably negligent. "Would you ring for a pot of chocolate, *chérie*? I'm sure we all need it."

"To remove the taste of my poem?" Armand said, his sigh glum.

"Did I suggest such a thing?" René looked surprised.

"There was no need. I know it well. Spare me the chocolate, mademoiselle, if you please. I must go and commune with my muse."

"I thought," René said in polite puzzlement, "that she was here." He indicated Cyrene.

Armand was not to be drawn. With a look of great melancholy and many excuses, he took himself away.

When he had gone, Cyrene said to René, "Did you have to be so disagreeable?"

"Did you expect me to encourage him? You do enough of that."

"There's not the least harm in it. Every lady has her admirers."

"I know that well enough, but he admires you a bit too extravagantly, and too often, for comfort. His admiration is leaning toward an excess of affection that you will find embarrassing."

"Does that trouble you?"

"The question is, Does it appeal to you? Armand Moulin is young and idealistic and with a comfortable fortune behind him; he's everything, in fact, that you have a right to expect in a prospective husband."

Cyrene got to her feet, moving away from him. "Is that your way of saying that you think I should accept a proposal if it is made?"

"By no means. I'm only—only pointing out his suitability."

What he was doing, René saw well enough, was indulging his jealousy. It was, as Cyrene said, quite the thing for married women and those in the keeping of other men to have admirers, men who worshiped from afar and found in the forbidden object of their affection some outlet for their suppressed passions and a subject on which to perfect their techniques of amorous dalliance. Knowing these things did not make it easier for the man in possession of a beautiful woman to bear with the lovelorn.

"I see," Cyrene said. "Yes, I suppose he is suitable." What she also saw was that, whether he wished to admit it or not, he was telling her that she might wish to look around her, that her arrangement with him would not be permanent.

"What was he telling you when I came in just now?" René asked.

"Nothing of importance."

"That I have trouble believing. He has a glib tongue, but he has not yet learned to control his blushes."

Cyrene, standing with her hand on the back of the settee, could not help smiling a little; Armand had indeed been perfectly crimson. "It was nothing salacious at all. We were merely speaking of your brother."

"My brother?" René's tone was sharp.

"I had not known of his death. I'm sorry."

"He isn't dead."

The words were cold, their lack of expression more disturbing than a shout would have been. "But I understood—"

"He shot himself, but he did not die. He destroyed his

mind; his body lives and breathes, eats and sleeps and ages and will, when my father dies, carry the titles and honors of the eldest son.''

René watched her closely, but there was no reaction on her lovely face except pity and distress. They were useless emotions. He should know since he had expended so much of the same.

"Titles and honors that would have come to you if he had died?" she said, her tone tentative.

He made a quick gesture of repugnance. "No. Never that. For those things I have no use, none at all.''

15

GOVERNOR VAUDREUIL DID not forget the amateur theatricals that he had mentioned when Cyrene had first met him. The play they would do was a comedy by Marivaux, a shortened version of his *Le Jeu de l'amour et du hasard*, or *Game of Love and Chance*. With Mardi Gras, or Fat Tuesday, the day of final, frantic merriment before the forty days of abstention required by the Lenten season leading up to Easter, so close upon them, it would be some time before it could be presented. That was all to the good, however; they would need the time for rehearsal.

The story involved a gentleman and a lady promised to each other, sight unseen, in an arranged marriage. Both of them being dubious of the match, they each decide to view the other first without revealing themselves. They therefore change places with their own servants for the initial meeting, the lady with her maid and the gentleman with his valet. They fall madly in love. Their servants are also smitten with each other so that there are four people involved, two of whom think the people they love are beneath them in station and two who think the people they love are above them. It was a challenging play, for much of the humor depended upon the posturing and posing of the characters in their unaccustomed roles and the rapid-fire delivery of the dialogue.

Cyrene, cast as the lady opposite the governor as the gentleman, was not certain she was up to the part, though the marquis insisted she had just that combination of independence and spriteliness necessary. René was assigned the role of the valet, while the maid was played by Madame Pradel since Madame Vaudreuil could not be persuaded to tread the boards with them.

The governor's wife declared that she enjoyed a play as much as anyone and was delighted that La Pompadour had revived the pastime of amateur theatricals, but play she could not. To learn so much dialogue was simply beyond her, the marquise declared, though Cyrene thought privately that what the lady meant was that it was beneath her. Playacting had always enjoyed a rather risqué reputation, and the patronage of the king's mistress had done little to change that.

There was a great deal of practice necessary, for the governor, though not a perfectionist, required that the production have a certain polish. Everyone must be able to move with grace and style as well as declaim their lines with as few embarrassing mistakes as possible. He made his wishes clear, but it was, in fact, Madame Vaudreuil who saw that they were achieved. She took upon herself the job of stage director and sat in the back of the long room, where the performance would be held, calling out complaints and instructions. The marquis himself was unfailingly generous in his comments and tactful in his suggestions; still, Cyrene, remembering what Armand had said, began to watch the couple and to wonder if Madame la Marquise was not simply carrying out her husband's will.

For Cyrene, acting with him, playing scenes of a suggestive and amorous nature in such close proximity was a daunting experience, despite his charm and exquisite manners. Vaudreuil was somehow larger than life, with so high a polish on his person and his personality as to give an appearance of being mirror hard and bright. Moreover, there was a great deal of unconscious arrogance about him.

Nor did René help matters by the close watch he kept on her every movement, her every smile and gesture. It made her more nervous than she was already. Why he regarded her so closely, she could not imagine; she was not blind to the appreciation in the gaze the marquis turned on her, but there was no familiarity in the gentleman's manner and certainly none in hers.

The same could not be said for Madame Pradel, who missed no opportunity to place her hand on René's arm or to lean over him as they practiced their lines. It was a tasteless display, and quite distracting. Not that she was jealous, of course, or that she credited René with any such degree of concern over her. No, René's attitude toward her, she thought, was one of possessiveness, like a dog with a new bone. There was nothing in that to preen herself over and much to annoy her.

She particularly did not appreciate the way he came up behind her and stood listening as she sat having wine and cakes with the marquis when the rehearsal was over. They had been talking of this and that, with the governor, like some royal personage, asking questions or introducing topics and she merely responding. He asked if she had family and friends, indicating with a few words that he meant other than her mother and father, whom he knew were no longer living. She told of her grandfather in Le Havre and also of her estrangement from him.

"Ah, yes, I knew the gentleman in New France to the north, I believe."

"Did you really?" she asked, her eyes lighting with pleasure.

"It was some time ago, before I was appointed governor of Trois-Rivières. But I remember your grandfather striding around in a cloak of beaver fur so long it swept the ground. He always declared he would rather be warm than fashionable. It was a sentiment I thought quite practical at the time."

She laughed. "I daresay he is still the same; he was when last I saw him. And did you know my mother as a girl, perhaps?"

"Indeed, a most charming creature. You have a great look of her, as I remember. I'll never forget the despair among the beaus when she married. That was her first husband I speak of, naturally.''

"Her first husband? What can you mean? There was only one.''

"But I was sure . . . Your mother's name was Marie Claire? Marie Claire Le Blanc?''

"Yes, but I never heard that she had been married before. Who could he have been? And what became of him?''

The governor stared at her for long seconds, then it was as if a shutter closed somewhere behind his eyes. "Perhaps I was mistaken, mademoiselle. I must have been. Forgive me.''

"But you had the name correct,'' she protested in puzzlement.

"Correct name, perhaps, but most likely the wrong woman. My poor memory. In any case, the man I was thinking of died in the wilderness, as I recall. The lady married again soon after.''

"In New France?''

"So I believe.''

That was all right, then. Cyrene's own parents had met in New France but had been married at Le Havre.

It was then that René spoke from where he stood behind them. "If that is the end of the family history, Cyrene, *ma chérie*, shall we go now? Acting, I find, is most fatiguing. I long for my bed.''

Madame Pradel sauntered to René's side as Cyrene turned to look up inquiringly at him. The older woman gave a tinkling laugh of appreciation as she heard his comment. Her tone suggestive, she said, "Among other things, I don't doubt.''

René did not glance in her direction. He stepped around Cyrene's chair and offered his arm. Drawing her to her feet, entwining her arm in his so that she was held to his side, he looked down at her, the smile he gave her heated with promise as he agreed, "Among other things.''

Cyrene made no move to remonstrate him, either at the governor's house or on the short walk back to his lodgings.

When they were inside, however, and the door closed behind them, she drew away from him.

Over her shoulder she said, "Why did you do that?"

"Do what?"

"You know very well. Why did you sweep me from under the nose of the governor and all the others as if you could not wait to bed me?"

"Perhaps it was for that exact reason."

It was more than that, René knew. He resented the ease with which she seemed able to talk to Armand and even Vaudreuil while she had hardly a half-dozen words to say to him at any given time. Knowing the cause did not make it any easier to bear.

"Indeed?" she said, her voice chill. "What are you waiting for, then? If that is your pleasure, help me out of these clothes and let us retire to bed at once."

He heard the derision in her voice, saw the pain that fueled it. He was not unmoved by either; it was just that they did not count against his great need of her or his certain knowledge that there was communication of a vital kind between them as they lay in bed. Whether she knew it or not, or whether or not she willed it, there was also to be found surcease for his doubts and sanctuary, however temporary, from his fears.

"How can I resist so gracious an invitation?" he said, his eyes crystalline in their gray darkness. "By all means, what are we waiting for?"

Cyrene had quickly become used to having afternoon callers. Armand's visits became a routine affair. He often brought his friends with him, young men of his age and station who spent as much time laughing and joking among themselves as paying court to her. Not that she minded. It was almost like being with Gaston again, though, of course, Gaston never brought her tokens of candy or flowers with the dew still upon them, never wrote poems to the beauty of her wrists or the piquant arch of her brows.

Armand had asked if she meant to receive in the morning, to hold a levee, as so many ladies did, while she completed her toilette for the day. Cyrene had laughed aloud at the very idea. She had not yet gained the habit of lying in bed until the morning was half gone. She very much doubted that Armand and his friends would be up and dressed themselves in time to see her perform her sketchy toilette, and even if they were, the idea struck her as ridiculous. She was no queen whose every movement, from the time she opened her eyes in the morning until she closed them at night, must be attended with punctilio and a myriad of witnesses. It was bad enough to have René watching her every move without a gallery of other spectators as well.

She was growing used to René, however, used to looking up and finding his gray eyes upon her in speculation that was quickly hidden. She could not think why he kept her with him if he had such reservations, though sometimes she was forced to wonder if it was not his uncertainty about her that was her chief attraction.

She was sitting alone in the salon the next afternoon when Martha brought a visitor into the room. She had found him on the street outside as she was returning from the market, she said. He had been inquiring for Mademoiselle.

"Gaston!" Cyrene cried.

Her book went flying from her lap as she jumped up and ran to fling her arms around him. The younger Breton set his feet and took her onslaught, giving her a quick bear hug before he drew back to look at her.

"Now that's what I call a welcome," he said with a grin.

"Where did you come from? Why are you here? Is everything and everyone all right? Come and sit down and tell me." Her joy at seeing him was so great that she felt she was babbling, but she could not stop.

"Could I have something to drink? I came straight from the river and I have the devil of a thirst."

Cyrene looked around for Martha, but she was already disappearing toward the back of the house. The woman did not need to be told the needs of visitors, even those outfitted as Gaston was in a leather shirt and breeches. "You shall have it in a moment. Only tell me how M'sieur Pierre and M'sieur Jean are, and where you have left them."

"We were on our way to the Choctaw country when it came to us suddenly that we had only Lemonnier's word that you were safe and well. It was decided that one of us must come back and make sure of it. I was the one least likely to attract attention."

"That may be," she said with some severity, "but you are still in danger. You were seen at the warehouse. I can't believe you have been wandering the streets in clear daylight."

He shrugged. "I had to find you."

As much as Cyrene would like to keep him with her, it could not be done, for his sake. She summoned a smile. "Well, you have found me and as you can see, I do very well. You can go back and tell M'sieur Pierre and M'sieur Jean that, and tell them, too, that it will ease my mind if they stay away."

Gaston only watched her without comment, his expression reflective as he tugged at the gold ring in his ear. "You are looking very fine."

"I . . . thank you." For some reason, the richness of the silk dress she wore and the fineness of the lace on her coif made her as uncomfortable as when she had first donned them, though she was fast becoming used to such luxury.

"I heard a thing or two on the streets. It seems you're mighty thick now with the governor, playacting with him and everything. Maybe something could be arranged?"

Unhappiness rose in her eyes. "I don't think so. M'sieur le Marquis is an easy-going man, but he takes his position most seriously."

"The Grand Marquis, people are calling him. A grand hypocrite, I say, when everyone knows his wife—"

Cyrene reached out quickly to put her hand on his arm. "Not so loud. Someone will hear you."

"I don't care if they do," Gaston said, but he lowered his voice in deference to her request. "Anyway, if you're not as happy as a squirrel with a two-year supply of nuts, then I'm supposed to take you away with me to rejoin Papa and Uncle Pierre."

"You can't do that."

"No? Tell me why not? It should be as simple as a walk down to the river as dark begins to fall."

"I—I gave my word."

Gaston stared at her for a long moment, his gaze shrewd as he studied the color rising in her face. He slapped his hands down on his knees and clasped them there. "*Très bien.* If you stay, I stay."

"Impossible!"

Though there was exasperation in Cyrene's tone, there was a warm feeling inside her. She could say no more, however, for Martha returned then with glasses of wine and a plate of small cakes. By the time the woman finished setting them out, Armand arrived for his daily visit.

Cyrene presented the two young men to each other. There seemed nothing else to do, for to fail to identify Gaston in some manner would have merely made his presence all the more suspicious. It was always possible that Armand had not heard of him. She could only hope that it was so.

It was a futile hope. Armand looked at Gaston with the liveliest of interest. "Ah, yes," he said, "the smuggler."

Gaston flashed a grin as he executed a creditable bow. "I see my fame has gone before me."

"As to that, I don't know," Armand said gently, "but I have made it my business to discover what I may about Mademoiselle Cyrene."

"I begin to see." The younger Breton looked from Armand to Cyrene with lifted brows.

He only thought he did, Cyrene knew, but she made no protest. If he thought that Armand was a part of the reason she was staying on in New Orleans, then he might be encouraged to go before it was too late.

Armand, when he had taken a glass of the wine set out, presented Cyrene with his latest poetic effort. She thanked him with every show of appreciation and read parts of it aloud as a means of easing the situation. She expected afterward there would be an awkward pause, but somehow the conversation returned to the subject of smuggling and she was left to sit in a corner of the settee listening as the other two expounded on the deficiencies of the current trading system. Armand, it seemed, had thought before of trading in an illicit manner with the English, but his father would not hear of it. M'sieur Moulin preferred that his son take what fortune there was to be had from the land and forget such hazardous escapades.

Watching the acquaintance and respect between Gaston and Armand grow was entertaining but not particularly absorbing. It was a relief when Armand, true to his upbringing, rose at the end of the prescribed time for afternoon visits and took his leave. It could be seen that he did not like leaving Gaston on the field alone, particularly as the other young man showed him to the door with as much casual confidence as if he had been his host. But good manners were adamant. Go he must, and go he did.

Gaston closed the door behind Armand and came back to fling himself into a chair near Cyrene. Fixing her with a stern gaze, he demanded, "Does Moulin call often?"

"Yes, fairly."

"And what does Lemonnier think of it?"

"It's the custom and he accepts it as such."

"Does he, indeed? Well, I'll be damned if I would."

Cyrene frowned. "Then it's a good thing it doesn't concern you."

"I can't think what you get out of it, either, what with poems to the spots on your face."

"Spots! To a very small mole, a beauty mark!"

"To a spot."

She took a deep breath to calm her annoyance. "Many

ladies receive in the afternoon, and it's a mark of favor to have admirers write poetry about you.''

''I don't care what it is, I wouldn't want them cluttering up my house and I don't know why you do, unless it's to make René jealous.''

She denied the charge with indignation, but even as she spoke, she was not certain of the truth. She no longer knew what she felt for René. She had thought her love was gone, but what, then, was this joy she felt in his arms, the sweet thrill she found in his touch, the pleasure she had discovered in watching him, simply watching him, being near him, sharing his days and his nights? But it didn't make sense that she could still be in love with him. It made no sense at all.

Gaston was still at the lodgings when René returned as dusk began to fall. If he was surprised to see the younger man, he did not show it but rather invited him to dinner and inquired after Pierre and Jean. Cyrene, who had begun to take on some responsibility for the running of René's household, slipped away to confer with Martha over dinner, leaving the two alone. When she returned, René and Gaston appeared to be highly pleased with each other, with that purely masculine expansiveness of spirit that accompanies the reaching of an understanding.

So in charity were they with each other, in fact, that Cyrene expected René to invite Gaston to stay with them for the night. He did not, however. By the time dinner was over, it was well after nightfall. Gaston, persuaded by Cyrene to greater discretion than he had shown on his arrival, used the darkness for cover for his return to the flatboat.

Shortly after the younger man had gone, René took his place at his writing table. Cyrene was beginning to think that it was his way of avoiding the long hours between dinner and bedtime that must otherwise be filled with conversation. She realized that small talk was not her primary purpose in being with René; still, she found the way he was able to immerse himself in his box full of papers, ignoring her, to be vexing in the extreme.

She sat curled up on the settee before the fire with her new embroidered satin slippers kicked off and her feet tucked under her billowing skirts of silk in cream and gold-toned stripes. She had not powdered her hair since the great clouds of hair powder necessary for the task had a tendency to make her sneeze, but she had allowed Martha to dress it for her for the day in a chignon with waves and ringlets that fell to one shoulder. The weight of it after so many hours was causing the pins to dig into her scalp. Now she pulled them out one by one, releasing the long, dark gold skein and drawing it over her shoulder as she combed out the tangles with her fingers.

A pin she had missed slipped from the loosened tresses. It slid down the curve of her neck and over her shoulder into the deep décolletage of her gown. She gave a soft exclamation of annoyance as the cold pin settled. She leaned forward, inserting her fingers into the low bodice to retrieve the pin. When she settled back, she noticed that René had looked up from his writing table. He sat still, watching her.

She gave him a tentative smile. He returned it with warmth kindling in his eyes but resumed his work once more.

Cyrene sat suspended for long moments, watching the swift precision of his movements, the way the light of the flickering candles in his candelabra played over the planes and angles of his face and the contours of his lips, burnishing his skin, reflecting in the glossy black waves of his hair. The light shimmered on the plume he used and cast the shadow of his hard square fist, which moved endlessly across his page. She thought of that same hand upon her body and a faint shiver ran through her skin.

Cyrene moved her feet from under her skirts and stood up, stretching a little, then stepped to place her hairpins on a nearby table. She wandered to the fire and, taking the poker, prodded the flames to greater life. Returning the poker to its hook, she stood watching the blaze for long moments with her skirts gathered near her, well away from danger. Turning away as the heat became too intense, she wandered toward the writing table. She trailed her fingers along the smooth polish of its edge as she rounded it and touched René lightly on his shoulder as she leaned over him.

"What are you writing with such energy?" she asked in a pretense of lazy amusement. "It must be your memoirs at the very least."

"Something equally dull, letters to men of influence. Exiles cannot allow themselves to be forgotten, unless they wish to remain in exile."

"Would that be so terrible, to remain here?"

The salutation on the top of the page on which he was writing, she could see, was to Maurepas. The king's minister could certainly be said to be a man of influence, though she remembered that René had also claimed him for a friend.

René turned in his chair to face her. "Is that what you would like, for me to stay?"

"Take care!" she exclaimed. "You'll get ink on your sleeve." In turning, he had placed his velvet-clad forearm squarely on the paper on which he had written, a page not yet sanded. She reached out to catch his wrist to lift his arm, but he placed it back down firmly again.

"The sleeve doesn't matter, but the answer to my question does."

His gaze as he spoke was compelling. She met it, her own eyes filled with doubt. Did she wish him to stay? It was possible. She did not like to think of his going. But she could not concentrate on the answer, for instinct told her it was no accident that he had blotted his page with his sleeve. He did not want her to see what he was writing. That very suspicion made the sentence she had caught sight of stand out bright and sharp-edged in her mind: . . . *only one way to stop the forbidden trade known as smuggling, and that is by the vigorous prosecution of those caught in it so that they serve as an example* . . .

She must say something. "Are you sure you wish to go?"

He rose to his feet, his broad shoulders effectively blocking from view the litter of parchment sheets on his writing table. "Sometimes I think of France and long for her as an orphan does for its mother," he said, "and sometimes when I take you in my arms like this, I feel that wherever you are is home."

He was attempting to divert her attention, as he had before when she took an interest in his writing. Let him, then. Cyrene, moving into his arms, accepted his kiss. It made no difference, after all. She knew what he was and still could not escape her attraction to him, could not afford to defy him, to dare him to denounce the Bretons to the governor. His possession of her was inescapable, therefore she might as well take what enjoyment she could from it. It was little enough recompense.

Nevertheless, on the following morning, when René had left the house for the coffeehouse or to see the governor or to wherever it was that he disappeared of a morning, Cyrene went at once to the writing table in the salon. The polished surface was clear, without so much as a scrap of paper on it, though the inkstand with its plume on the rest stood ready. The lacquer box sat against one wall. Though Cyrene shook the lock and tugged it, and even delved into it none too gently with her hairpin, it remained securely fastened, holding its secrets.

On the evening of the Mardi Gras masquerade ball held by the governor and his wife, the official Government House was lighted from top to bottom. Torches flared beside the doorway, illuminating the avid faces of the crowd gathered in the muddy street to see the arriving guests who trailed behind servants or link boys carrying lanterns. It had rained during the day, and the night sky was dark with low-hanging clouds that threatened another deluge, but that did not deter the spectators. They jostled one another for the best positions, vying with vendors of hot rice cakes and meat cooked in pastry, of oranges and candied violets, and, at the same time, keeping a sharp eye out for pickpockets. Wide-eyed, they stared at the costumes the fortunate ones had either commissioned for the occasion or else gathered together from odds and ends unearthed in old trunks. The audience seemed to be divided equally between those who saw beauty in everything and those who searched out only the faults with comments more ribald and candid than prudent.

"What is he got up as, a tailor's dummy?"

"I think he is supposed to be the fat German king of England."

"Look at that. Anybody who would wear a cartwheel around her neck can't be bothered that her backside looks like the aft end of a whaling ship."

"She's despised Queen Maria Theresa, idiot!"

"And I'm the Queen of Sheba!"

"Ah, here is the good *père* in his robes."

"Yes, who looks like he should be defrocked."

"Only see the dainty shepherdess with her little crooked staff—"

"And unless I miss my guess, looking for another staff that's neither crooked nor little."

Due to the wet and muddy streets, René had hired a sedan chair to carry Cyrene to Government House. The vehicle with its four bearers was by no means luxurious; the leather seat was cracked and smelled of sweat, the stale perfume used to cover such odors, and the mildewed straw in the bottom that was caked with dried mud. René walked beside the chair with one hand on the door and the other on his sword hilt. The sword was not only a part of his costume as a musketeer, it was also a sensible precaution. Due to the throng in the streets, it was a night when the undesirables of the town could be expected to creep from their holes.

Cyrene and René had to wait in line before they could approach the door of Government House, so they had ample time to hear the various quips and jests flung at the guests. When it was their turn, René handed Cyrene down, then tossed a coin or two to the sedan-chair bearers, bidding them to have a drink while they waited until the ball was over. There was a murmur of disappointment over the cloaks she and René wore, which hid their costumes, but Cyrene deliberately closed her mind to it as she passed quickly into the building.

In an anteroom set aside for that purpose, René and Cyrene were relieved of their cloaks. Cyrene shook out the layered gauze in varying shades of green and gold that made up her costume of a wood nymph. At the same time, the mud was quickly brushed from René's boots by a servant stationed for that purpose. Their appearance attended to, they adjusted the ribbons that held in place their demimasks of cloth in the loose and fluttering fashion of the Venetian court, then allowed themselves to be led to the ballroom.

The assemblage of richly clad and jeweled people, chandeliers holding hundreds of candles like starbursts, elegant appointments in wall hangings and furniture, excellent music, food, and drink, and convivial company would have been outstanding in Paris itself. In this backwater post of New Orleans, it was brilliant. What was more, the guests were well aware that there had never been such a gathering in the short history of the town and suspected there might never be again. It gave an added zest to the excitement occasioned by the masquerade, a vivid, almost feverish pleasure that was the stuff of which legends are made. Never had the guests of the marquis smiled so much or laughed so shrilly, never had wine tasted so delicious or food been so ambrosial. The music caught their mood, enhancing it, singing in their blood. They danced as if their feet would not be still, until they were breathless and laughing with exhaustion, until the windows were thrown open to the coolness of the night to dissipate the heat and smell of so many warm, ripe, and liberally perfumed bodies.

Outside the rain began to fall again, the noise and cool wetness of it drifting into the room. No one paid any attention. What did the weather matter when there was pleasure to be had?

Cyrene danced a half-dozen times, once each with René and Armand, once with a harlequin, once with a grenadier, and twice with a saintly King Louis IX complete with a halo for a crown whom she was sure was the governor. Time ceased to have meaning. Secure behind her mask, there was, for the moment, nothing that could touch her, not even the sight of René in attendance to a lady dressed as an abbess who must be Madame Vaudreuil. She was supremely happy in the round of gaiety, with the beat of the music and the physical exertion of the dance throbbing in her veins and her mind. There was within her, she discovered, a capacity for pure enjoyment, an ability to forget problems and unpleasant situations and live only for the moment.

And then she saw Gaston.

It was him; she did not doubt it for an instant in spite of his mask. No one else had his combination of square build and hard-muscled shoulders or his cap of wild curls like the goat god Pan. No one else would dare to appear at the governor's masquerade dressed in the beaded leather and moccasins of a *voyageur*, a river rat who was only one step from being a convicted smuggler.

The music of a fast-paced *contredanse* was just ending. Cyrene sent her partner for a glass of wine, then made her way toward Gaston. She came up behind him where he stood near an open window.

"What do you think you are doing here?"

So annoyed was she, and so frightened for him and angry also over that fright, that her voice shook. He turned to face her, and through the slits of his mask his eyes were warm with understanding. "I had a visit from a gentleman of your acquaintance, *chère*. It was he who brought me."

"René," she said bitterly.

"Not at all. It was Moulin."

"Armand?"

"A fine friend, and a good man to have at your back."

"I'm glad you like each other," she said with deadly sarcasm, "but have you taken leave of your senses? What do you mean showing up here, dressed for all the world like an advertisement for your crimes?"

"No one has recognized me," he protested.

"A piece of luck you don't deserve. You must leave at once."

Irritation tightened his lips. "If you will stop making a fuss, there will be no need. You're the one likely to get me arrested."

"Don't be so unreasonable, Gaston. What can be the purpose of running into danger like this?"

"What danger, Cyrene? I understand that Lemonnier has arranged an alibi for us, Papa and Uncle Pierre and me. So far as anyone knows, we were never here on the night of the warehouse fire. I could ask what reward he had for his good work on our behalf, but that would be an unnecessary insult. It seems to me that you have paid for my safety; why should I not enjoy it?"

It was, of course, as he said. There had been time enough for the excuses made for the whereabouts of the Bretons to be accepted. Why, then, should Gaston not reappear? She abandoned that ground with mingled relief and chagrin, shifting for another attack.

"But to come here dressed as you are—it's like a slap in the face."

"A calculated gamble, it may be. Would a guilty man dare? No, therefore I must be innocent."

"Why gamble when you can be safe?"

He gave a slow smile. "Why should I be safe when with just a little courage I can be one of the favored ones, a guest of the governor instead of only a trader's son condemned to stand outside, like all those others out there, watching the high and mighty at their play?"

"It doesn't matter, not any of it, compared to being free," she said, her eyes dark as she glanced around her.

"So you say, but you are here and the others are still outside."

It was true, what she had said. None of it mattered, not the fancy gowns and fine surroundings, not her parade of admirers, not playing opposite the governor in the amateur theatricals or even being among the elect at the masquerade. She had wanted freedom and had traded the degree of it that she had for a prison of a different type, one made tenable by paint and gilding and the appeal of desire-drugged senses. It was no less a prison for all that. She had gone into it with her eyes open, however. There was no one who could rescue her from it except herself. The main thing that was required for that rescue was the will to effect it. All she had to do was find that will.

Beside her, Gaston interrupted her painful reverie with a harsh whisper. "Who is this coming?"

She looked up. Advancing toward them was a man in the costume that might have been that of a Roman general, consisting of a toga and breastplate worn, most incongruously, with a pair of breeches and a curled and powdered wig. He was burly and quick-moving. He scorned a mask so that the unpleasant expression on his face was pronounced in contrast with the blankness of those around him. Recognition was slow, but when it came, it rushed in upon her with sickening force.

"Dear God," she said under her breath.

"What is it?"

"The officer at the warehouse."

"Who?"

Gaston had not been there when the officer had caught and thrown her to the ground, mauling her as he made his capture, which had been rescinded only by René. Gaston did not know, nor was there time to explain. The lieutenant stopped before them and placed his hands on his hips.

"I'd know that hair anywhere," the man said, a sneer on his wet mouth as he surveyed the shining curtain that hung down Cyrene's back. "I had me a handful of it and of a soft tit. And I'll wager I have the same again, or else a nice conversation with the governor about you and about your friend here who looks mighty like a thief and a smuggler to me. What say you, my pretty? Will you play or pay?"

16

T HE LIEUTENANT WAS so sure of himself. In his crude
conceit, Cyrene saw, he thought he held the upper hand,
thought he could frighten her into submission. Fear was a
part of the emotion that leaped in her blood, but a greater
portion was sheer rage at being threatened once more. She
was grateful for her mask, which concealed both, however,
as she faced the officer in his ridiculous costume with her
head high and her shoulders squared.

"I don't believe, m'sieur," she said with deadly coldness,
"that I have your acquaintance."

She would have turned away then, back to Gaston who
stood frowning at the other man, but the lieutenant grabbed
her arm. "You know me, all right, and you're going to know
me a lot better. Don't go all high-and-mighty on me or I'll
have to take you down a peg or two right here."

Cyrene wrenched her arm from his damp and clumsy
grasp. "You forget yourself! I suggest that you have made a
mistake, m'sieur, one that can prove dangerous if you per-
sist."

He caught her elbow in a rough hold, dragging her off
balance so that she fell against him. "Oh, I'm going to per-
sist, all right. We'll see what kind of mistake there is and
who made it when I get through with you."

Gaston stepped forward, shoving the other man. "Let her
go, you nameless dog!"

"Keep out of this." The lieutenant threw the words at Gaston in growling menace. "Stay clear or I'll have you trussed up to the flogging post before you can spit."

"You're big on threats," Gaston snapped. "Let's step outside and see what else you can do."

"No, Gaston," Cyrene cried.

"I warned you, cockerel!"

"Have you," came a quiet drawl from behind them, "a warning for me also?"

Cyrene felt the officer stiffen. His hold on her elbow tightened. There was a movement too swift to follow, a sudden sharp blow, and the lieutenant's grasp was broken. Cyrene was drawn to stand in the curve of Governor Vaudreuil's arm.

She was unspeakably glad for the intervention, but at the same time she was embarrassed by it and thrown into a paralyzing dread that the reason for the necessity would be discovered.

The lieutenant seemed equally paralyzed. He gulped and began to stammer. "I—I beg pardon, Your Excellency. I didn't know—that is, I had no idea."

"You didn't know what?" the governor said, his voice cold.

"Nothing! Nothing at all." The lieutenant was pasty-white, his voice a croak. "Pray forgive—forgive me. I must have mistaken the lady for someone else."

"I feel sure of it. It is not a mistake you will make again, I trust."

"No, certainly not. No."

The marquis made a brief gesture. "We will forget the matter. You may leave us."

The lieutenant obeyed the command with all haste. Cyrene made an attempt to step away from the governor but found herself firmly held. She moistened her lips as she lifted her gaze to meet his. "You came most fortunately, sir. It was kind of you to rescue me; I am more grateful than I can say."

There was a soft footfall behind them and René spoke at her shoulder. "You may add my gratitude to Cyrene's. I saw the disturbance from across the room but was not able to arrive so timely.''

An expression of faint displeasure crossed the governor's face and he sighed. ''I might have known you would be close, Lemonnier. I suppose I must now relinquish Mademoiselle Cyrene to you for soothing.''

René inclined his dark head in a bow. ''That would be my preference, Your Excellency.''

''I somehow thought it might.''

A woman, obviously following in René's wake, joined them in a whispering rustle of taffeta petticoats. It was Madame Pradel, Cyrene thought, as her gaze rested on the expanse of bosom exposed by her Etruscan costume, which featured a full skirt, a copper corset constricting the lady's waist to amazingly tiny proportions, and a practically nonexistent bodice.

''*Lèse-majesté*, no less, René,'' the lady said. ''You should have proper respect for the rights of our reigning overlord to succor damsels in distress and offer consolation.''

''Our overlord, madame,'' the governor said austerely, ''is Louis of France.''

''So he is,'' she said in a pretense of surprise. ''I was forgetting, but then I'm sure Mademoiselle Cyrene was in danger of the same.''

''Not at all,'' Cyrene said, aware of the prick of the woman's sarcasm if not of the cause. Though, on consideration, the cause was not difficult to discover. Madame Pradel, having secured René's attention from the marquise, had not been pleased, perhaps, to have it diverted from her. There was time, however, for only the most fleeting recognition of this insight, for their group was enlarged by an abbess in a wimple and with a rosary banging her knees from the quickness of her stride.

The governor's wife, her tone stringent, said, ''What is the meaning of this public display? You will unhand Mademoiselle Nolté, Vaudreuil, before the clatter of tongues becomes deafening.''

The look Cyrene received from the governor's wife was chilling. More disturbing than that, however, was the intent look on the face of the man who sauntered after her to hover at the edge of their circle. Dressed in the gray-brown habit of a monk, with the hood standing like a collar around his scrawny neck and no mask to hide the cynical malignancy of his gaze, was Madame Vaudreuil's lackey, Touchet.

The Marquis de Vaudreuil gazed down his nose at his wife. "Mademoiselle Cyrene has had a shock. Scandalmongering being the natural pastime of the human animal, there is no need to abandon concern for a lady merely because of it."

"Please," Cyrene said, "I'm perfectly all right."

The governor removed his support of her, though without haste. René stepped to take the other man's place. He said in quiet tones, "The music is beginning. If you are truly without ill effects, shall we take the floor?"

"If you please," she answered, her voice low.

"An excellent idea," Madame Vaudreuil said sharply, her gimlet gaze moving from Cyrene to her husband. "Your arm for this minuet, Vaudreuil?"

"As you wish, *chère*."

The governor, his back stiff, bowed his lady from their circle. René followed with Cyrene's fingers upon his wrist. The dancers shifted to accommodate them. They joined the stately march of couples, bowing, bending, swinging in a sweep of petticoats and costume skirts, their feet lightly shuffling on the polished floor. The candlelight gleamed on silk and velvet, taffeta and satin, caught the lustrous sheen of pearls and glittered in the depths of multicolored jewels. It traced the edges of masks and flickered over the anonymous and lasciviously smiling mouths beneath the disguises. This was the Government House, and there was no license permitted, and yet a vague air of dissoluteness hung over the gathering, a reminder of the ancient bacchanalian festivals from which the tradition of Mardi Gras was derived.

Cyrene, circling behind René in the movements of the

dance, saw Gaston at the far end of the room serving as partner for Madame Pradel. The woman was gazing up at him as if he were some particularly appetizing sweet, while the younger Breton looked intrigued but also apprehensive.

René caught sight of her smile with its tinge of irony as she returned to his side and they began to promenade down the room, pointing their toes at each step. "Was it necessary," he said in goaded tones, "to make a public disturbance just now?"

There had been no opportunity for Cyrene to rid herself of her rage and chagrin, not only at being accosted by the lieutenant but also at the unwarranted censure of Madame Vaudreuil. It came boiling back now at his scathing comment.

"Why not?" she demanded. "There's nothing I like more than being pawed and fought over like some quai d'Orsay tart. Unless, of course, it's being condemned for a slut by a jealous wife!"

"You might have sat quietly somewhere without stirring up trouble."

"Indeed? Am I to understand that you think I enticed the lieutenant to remember me? Perhaps you are of the opinion that I flaunted myself before him?"

What René thought was that she was too beautiful, too memorable, for her own good or for his peace of mind. It was the irritation caused by his uncomfortable concern for her that had made him lash out at her. It would have suited him much better if she had been quiet and biddable and retiring. But then she would not have been Cyrene.

"Well?" she demanded.

"I am perfectly well aware that you did nothing to provoke the lieutenant except be yourself."

"Meaning what? That I should not have worn my hair unbound? That I should not have been grateful to the governor for his rescue? Perhaps you think that the best thing I could have done would have been to go with the lieutenant wherever he wished and allowed him to do with me what he would? That would have settled everything nicely, and without the least noise!"

He glanced around them, his expression harassed. "Will you lower your voice?"

"Oh, yes, tell me to mind my tongue, why don't you? It's the last refuge of a man who has started a quarrel he cannot finish."

"Very well," he said, his grip on her hand tight as he swung her about, ready to return down the length of the room, "what would you have me say? That I should have kept a better watch over you? That I should have been quicker to come to your aid? That I resent Vaudreuil for getting there first, and harbor murderous intentions toward the man who dared to touch you? That I am, in short, wildly jealous?"

She lifted her chin, her eyes blazing as she met his steely gaze. "Yes, why not?"

"Why not, indeed? It's perfectly true, all of it."

She stumbled, nearly tripping on the hem of her gown. When she looked back at him, he was staring straight ahead. For long moments her heart beat high in her throat, then as she watched the taut angles of his face, it subsided. So he had felt responsible for her, concerned for her, even jealous of her—what of it? To him she was no more than a possession, something to be guarded, protected against interlopers. It had nothing to do with her as a person, this jealousy, but rather with his disinclination to share her or to lose her so long as his interest held. His sense of responsibility, his concern, and most of all his jealousy would be gone the instant he grew tired of her.

"How very flattering," she said with brittle irony. "What can I have done to deserve it?"

René heard the disbelief in her voice and did not know whether to be enraged or relieved. To be both did not suit his idea of his own emotional stability; even less did it suit his cause.

The ball was over at midnight with a grand unmasking on the stroke of twelve. Lent began with the dying away of that final stroke, a stretch of forty endless days of fasting and austerity. The last bite of food was swallowed, the last drink hastily downed. The musicians put away their instruments. There was nothing to be done except to go home.

The guests departed, carrying by their strings the masks that now looked bedraggled and rather silly. They spoke smooth phrases of praise and appreciation for their night's entertainment to their host and hostess, called out farewells that echoed in the wet and empty streets, and scattered into the night.

A fine rain was still falling, dropping out of the black night sky with the relentless persistence that indicated it might not stop for days. The ditches along the street outside the Government House were running streams of water that reflected the flaring torches beside the door. The sedan chair René had commanded to wait was a welcome refuge, even for the relatively short walk to the lodging.

As Cyrene settled on the narrow seat of the chair and it was lifted on its poles, a linkboy came hurrying toward them with his lantern of pierced tin swinging on its bail. "Light the way, m'sieur? For you, very cheap!"

He was young and thin and soaked to the skin, but was gamely looking for custom on this dreary night. There were no few like him in New Orleans, orphans left to make their way, victims of the terrible death toll that had always plagued the colony. Most were cared for by the Ursuline nuns, but there were always those who preferred living in the streets to the discipline of the nuns.

René tossed the urchin a coin. The boy flashed a grin and set off down the street ahead of the chair. Government House was soon left behind. Around them was the dark, wet night, relieved only by the dancing yellow beacon of the linkboy's lantern.

The rain spattered on the small, square roof of the sedan chair. The leather curtains billowed inward to let in a fine mist. Now and then one of the chairmen slipped in the ankle-deep mud, causing the chair to lurch and tilt before it was righted. Cyrene braced her feet as best she could and held on to the loop set into the wall, but at one particularly violent jolt she threw out her hand to catch herself and bruised her wrist on the window frame.

She was nursing the aching arm when she heard a shout. The next thing she knew she was tumbling, sliding, first forward then backward, as the chair was thrown to the ground. Cyrene gave a startled cry. The chair teetered, rocking, before righting itself. She reached for the door and thrust it open.

"What is it? What's happening?"

Back the way they had come there sounded the thud and splatter of running feet. Cyrene turned her head sharply in that direction in time to see the chairmen in retreat with heads down and arms pumping. The linkboy was gone, but his lantern lay in the mud, its candle guttering, giving off a feeble light. There came the hiss of a sword blade being drawn. She swung in the other direction.

In that dim glow, René could be seen with his sword in his hand and the end of his long cape twisted about his wrist as he held off a pair of men. They were rough-looking, with battered and pockmarked faces that spoke of back streets and hidden deeds. One held a knife and was slashing the air with it so that the feeble lantern light gleamed along its edge and winked from its sharp tip. The other carried a weighted cudgel that he hefted while he breathed through his mouth, licking his lips with a wet, thick tongue.

What could be done? Possibilities slipped through Cyrene's mind like ghosts, but each was more unlikely to help than the last. She had never felt so useless in her life. She longed for her knife, left behind at the lodging. In agitation, she stepped from the chair into the street, her silk shoes sinking into the mud and water.

There was a soft sound behind her. Before she could turn, before she could move in the thick ooze that held her feet, a hard arm whipped across her throat. She gave a strangled cry, and the arm clamped tighter. She was pulled backward against a man's solid form, then forced step by staggering step toward the alleyway between the two nearest houses. An overpowering smell of woodsmoke, greasy leather, cheap liquor, and unwashed male struck her senses.

Cyrene tried to twist, to strike backward with her elbow. The arm pressed into her neck, cutting off the air. She coughed, gasping, as pain rose in a red mist behind her eyes. She could feel herself being half lifted, her heels dragging in the mud. Dimly she could see René as he flung a quick glance over his shoulder in her direction. He uttered a grating oath and redoubled his efforts, thrusting, feinting, his sword blade whining in the air.

She must do something. She must. Snatch at her abductor's hair, claw his eyes, something. Was it rational thought or instinct that guided her? She didn't know. The idea presented itself and she acted upon it. She let her muscles go suddenly limp, permitting her knees to buckle. Her teeth snapped together as her chin caught on the man's arm, but her assailant was pulled off balance. He let go of her as he threw out an arm to save himself. She pitched forward into the muck, her knees pressing into its softness through her skirts, her hands sinking past the wrists as she caught her weight.

The man muttered a savage obscenity and swung his fist. The blow caught the side of Cyrene's face. Pain exploded in her skull, but she used the momentum of the blow to dive away from him. As she scrambled in the clinging mud to put even more distance between them, she flung a glance over her shoulder.

The man was masked.

The surprise was so great that she faltered, going into a crouch, her eyes wide.

In that moment René's attackers broke and ran before his onslaught. One was howling with a sword slash down his arm, the other bent over a seeping hole in his chest so that he weaved as he lunged away into the night. René swung toward Cyrene, sending the blowing mist of rain wafting in her direction. The man in the mask looked up, saw René start forward, saw the glimmering light of the lantern shining wet and crimson on his sword.

The masked man thrust his hand into the pocket of his greatcoat and brought out a pistol. Cyrene cried out, launching herself toward him. He twisted away, aiming again. The hammer of the pistol clicked. There was a blue flash and a sputtering, fizzing sound.

The pistol had misfired in the damp. The man grunted, then, with vicious strength, threw the pistol at René and turned to run.

René saw the pistol coming almost before it was thrown. He flung up his arm and tried to dodge it, but his boots were held in the mud, preventing movement. He slipped, lurching to remain upright. The heavy butt of the weapon thudded into his temple. The pain was a bursting, numbing explosion behind his eyes. He dropped to one knee in the mud. Blood, hot and wet, welled and ran down his face. He could hear the thud of running footsteps as the man in the mask took to his heels, but could not move to go after him.

Cyrene struggled to her feet, staggering forward, then going to her knees once more beside René. Her hands were so muddy that she could not touch him, but she snatched up a handful of his cloak and rolled it into a pad, pressing it to the wound.

"I'm all right," he said. "It's of no moment."

His voice was gasping but vital and shaded with astringency. She believed him in spite of the blood trickling down his face. "Let's go home, then."

They rose, extracting themselves from the sticky mud, and turned toward their lodging. Before them, just at the edge of the lantern's light, there was a furtive movement. It was the linkboy trying to retrieve his lantern. René recognized him first. He took a step forward, his voice sharp as he called out.

"Hold there, you, boy! Come here."

The boy backed away, his eyes large in his narrow face. "I didn't know, m'sieur! I swear I didn't know!"

René started to call again, but Cyrene squeezed his arm.

She spoke in a quiet, calming tone. "What was it you didn't know? Tell us."

"I was just to light the way, that's all! That's all."

"We know, we paid you. What are you saying?"

"The other man, too. The one with the pistol. He showed you to me through the window. He said I was to light the way, give you a special price, even do it for free. I didn't know what he meant to do. I didn't know!"

"Did you know the man?" Cyrene asked. The street boys often knew many unusual things.

"No, mademoiselle. It was dark and he wore the mask."

Beside her, René reached into his purse and, squinting against the blood that still trickled into his eye, fished out a coin. He tossed it to the boy. "We believe you. Take your lantern and go."

The boy did not hesitate. He caught the spinning coin and snatched up his lantern almost in the same movement, then took to his heels as if there were demons behind him. Cyrene would have liked to do the same. It was pride and dignity and a stubborn reluctance to allow the man in the mask to put her to flight that prevented it. That and René's arm under her hand, increasing her courage, sharing her strength.

They did not realize how covered with bruises, blood, and mud they were until Martha opened the door of the lodging to them and they saw the horror on her dark brown face. Exclaiming, questioning, she hustled them inside and gingerly removed their cloaks, which had caught the worst of the dirt. She sat them down before the fire and slipped off their shoes, then hurried away to the kitchen where she put water on to heat for a bath and mixed hot rum toddies, which she insisted they drink.

Whether it was the potency of the rum or the effect of having something hot to warm her, the shivering deep inside Cyrene began to die away. The cut on René's temple had stopped bleeding, but it required tending. When Martha brought bandaging and a pan of hot water, Cyrene watched her attempts to tend her master, then rose and moved to stand at her shoulder.

"Permit me," she said, and took the wet cloth the woman was using to dab, more or less ineffectually, at the cut. "We've given you a fright, I think; why don't you have a toddy, too?"

"Mademoiselle is a lady of understanding," the woman said, relinquishing her place with transparent relief.

"There's no need for either of you to coddle me," René said, reaching up and attempting to take the cloth from Cyrene. "I can manage."

Cyrene fended him off. "You'll start it bleeding again. Lean back against the settee and hold still."

Wry amusement sprang into René's eyes at her scolding tone. There was something about injuries that turned women into martinets, he had discovered. He had taken care of himself for years, tying up much worse cuts and scrapes with rough-and-ready dispatch. However, it was not unpleasant to be coddled; he might as well enjoy it. René did as Cyrene bid him, folding his hands on his chest in all docility.

Cyrene eyed him with suspicion, but the look in his eyes was limpid, patient, in spite of the faint smile at the corners of his mouth. For an instant the trembling returned to her fingers and she felt awkward, unbearably clumsy. She dragged her gaze from his, concentrating fiercely on what she was doing, and slowly her deftness of touch, and her composure, returned.

The cut had bled copiously, as did all head injuries, and although deep at one end, it did not appear serious. Cyrene washed the area around it, washing away also the streaks of blood that had dried in his hair. Lacking any of the medicines with which her mother had once aided the healing of her own cuts and scrapes, she wrapped a strip of bandaging made from an old sheet around his head and hoped for the best.

The antagonism she had felt for René earlier in the evening was gone, she discovered, banished as much by their shared dishevelment as their shared danger. In its place was a kind of weary concern and a tight feeling that hurt her chest.

She said abruptly, "This attack on you, do you think it has anything to do with the other?"

"What do you mean?"

"The attempt on your life the night I took you from the river, of course. It appears to me that someone wants you dead."

He lifted a shoulder in a careless gesture. "More likely they wanted my money."

"They didn't take it before."

"An oversight. They didn't mean to kill me, and when they thought they had, they panicked."

"You don't believe that."

"Don't I?"

"There were two of them that night; I saw them toss you into the river. Tonight there were three, and one paid the linkboy to act as bell goat to lead you into their trap. It smacks of hired cutthroats to me."

"For what purpose?" He sat up, smiling a little, reaching to finger his bandaging, testing to be sure it was secure. "I'm practically a stranger here."

His casualness was incensing. "There must be something. Could you have been followed from France? Was there anything that happened there that might have made enemies for you, some connection, perhaps, with your reason for leaving?"

"Not that I'm aware. It was a coincidence brought about by greed and a rainy night. If you won't have that, then you might consider why one of these cutthroats, as you call them, was trying to kidnap you."

"That seems fairly obvious. I was a witness, and I don't doubt that had they been able to kill you I would have met the same fate."

"Too dramatic, I fear. It's more likely some man wanted you and took rather drastic means to appease his desires."

A laugh was surprised from her. "Don't be ridiculous."

"You doubt it? Think of your lieutenant. Desire and revenge make men do strange things."

"Speaking from experience, of course?"

"Oh, of course," he said, the look in his eyes suddenly desolate.

She stared at him for long moments with distress slowly creeping in upon her, bringing the rise of gooseflesh to her skin. To think that someone wished her harm, would plot to seize her, use her for their base desires and ends, was horrible. She turned sharply from him, flinging out her hands as if to ward off the suggestion. "No, it's impossible."

His voice soft, he said, "Is it?"

The fire crackled in the quiet room. Outside, the rain fell with a steady, endless pattering on the roof and heavier splattering as it poured from the eaves to the ground. Cyrene thought of the pent-up rage on the lieutenant's face when he had been prevented from harassing her. But that was not all. If one person could set out to hurt her, then why not others? Madame la Marquise, though she had no real reason, had looked at her for a brief instant this evening with virulent hatred in her eyes. And there was Touchet. She had humiliated the little man that evening on the beach, though she had not intended to. Such a one as he would not soon forgive the slight. Who else might there be? Armand, because she could not return his affection or respond to his vaunted adoration? The Bretons, for the threat she posed to them?

"No!" she cried, clasping her arms around her. "No, it wasn't me. It was you."

He rose, moving to put his hands on her shoulders. His voice quiet, he said, "Yes, I expect it was. Or else just robbery, with the two of us chosen at random."

His touch was soothing, his attempt to reassure her a kindly impulse. The only trouble was, she didn't believe him.

Their hot water was ready a short time later. Since the fire in the dressing room, lighted for their comfort as they dressed for the ball, had been allowed to go out, the porcelain hip bath was placed in the bedchamber. It sat with the water gently steaming, rapidly cooling. René remained in the salon, sipping the last of his toddy while Cyrene had first use of it. Martha bustled around, laying out toweling, testing the temperature, positioning the candles. Her fussy movements set Cyrene's teeth on edge. She permitted the woman to secure her hair on top of her head for her and to unbutton the back of her gown, then sent her, protesting, to bed.

She bathed quickly in order to leave a little heat in the water for René, though it was a great temptation to sit there soaking, letting the distress of the evening seep from her body. She was washing her face, wincing as she ran the cloth over her cheek where she had been struck, when René came into the room.

He closed the door behind him, his gaze moving to where Cyrene sat in the hip bath, her skin shimmering with wet and the blue and orange gleam of the fire behind her, the perfect curves of her body outlined in its glow, the oval of her face . . .

The warm appreciation rising in his eyes turned abruptly to concern. He came forward with quick strides and went to one knee beside her. "You were hurt; I should have known. What an idiot I am not to have seen."

She drew back as he reached out to touch her bruise. "It's nothing, really."

"Don't be so brave," he said shortly as he gripped her chin, tilting her cheek toward the light.

The bruise was livid, deep blue. It lay just under her cheekbone, however, in the concealing natural shadow. Though the skin was not broken, it would be some time before the discoloration faded. With gentle fingers, he probed the bone.

"Is your jaw sore?"

"A little."

"But you can move it?"

"Oh, yes," she said, "I have no trouble talking."

The look he gave her was unamused. "Are there any other injuries?"

She shook her head. He gave her a skeptical glance, then allowed his gaze to move slowly over her, inch by naked inch.

"All right, I bruised my arm on the door," she admitted with color rising in her face, "but that's all."

He took her wrist and turned it over. On the underside was a long scrape with bluish purple color beneath it. He sat for long moments, his lashes lowered, concealing his expression as his gaze rested on her arm. At last he bent his head and pressed his lips gently to the marred skin. His voice was soft, hardly more than a whisper, when he spoke. "I'm sorry."

His remorse, she thought, was for more than the events of the evening.

"Are you? For what?" she asked.

He lifted his head, meeting her gaze squarely. "For everything. I never meant—I didn't intend that you should be hurt."

She looked away, her voice quiet yet toneless as she spoke. "My bruises will heal. There has been no great harm done."

"Hasn't there? I would like to think so. For myself, I'm not so sure."

He rose in a single fluid movement, stepping away from the bath. Cyrene turned her head to look at him, but he kept his back to her. There seemed no answer to be made to what he had said, no consolation she had any right, or was to be given any encouragement, to offer. When he began to remove his shirt, stripping it off over his head, she rinsed her face and splashed water over her shoulders and breasts one last time before getting out to make way for him.

He was quick with his ablutions. By the time she had dried herself and put on his nightshirt, then brushed out the wild mass of tangles from her hair that were caused by wearing it loose, he was done. He came to her where she stood before the fire. He took the brush from her and laid it aside on the mantel, then closed his fingers in the soft, fire-warmed curtain of her tresses, wrapping his hands in the silken strands to draw her to him.

"Bright, courageous Cyrene. You deserve better, and I am a fool twice-damned, but I can't let you go."

He cupped her face, framing it in her hair, studying it minutely before he brushed her bruised cheek with his lips. He kissed her brow and her eyelids, the point of her chin and the delicate corners of her mouth before settling his lips with care upon hers. His movements gentle, infinitely tender, he sought her sweet flavor.

She should resist him, Cyrene knew, should deny his possession, but it was far too late to try. He had not meant to hurt her, he said; that was also futile. Still, in some strange way, it seemed that she might be healed by the same means that had brought her the most harm, by the ravishing tenderness of his kiss and the enclosing hold of his arms. To try was not, perhaps, the sensible course, but it was the compelling one. She was forced to it not only by his touch, but by some dimly sensed change in what lay between them. He was different. She could feel it, even if she could not grasp its cause, even if he did not recognize it himself.

She lifted her arms, sliding her hands over the hard-muscled planes of his chest and around his neck, clasping her hands in the luxuriant thickness of his hair. Her lips were pliant against his, soft and giving, heated with the desire that gathered inside her. A soft sigh left her and she moved closer still, until the curves of her body were fitted to his in a primitive and perfect interlocking.

After a moment he raised his head on a deep sigh. His eyes were silver with his need as he met her wide gaze, and his voice vibrated deep in his chest as he spoke. "It isn't fair that you should be so perfect, that everything good and fine should be so much a part of you."

"I'm not," she said with a troubled shake of her head. "It isn't."

A smile came and went across his lips. "No? Perhaps you're right. There is a wayward witch in you, too; one who has smuggled her way into my blood, casting spells so that

I think only of you, dream of you, long for you until I think I must be going mad. It wasn't supposed to be this way.''

She searched his face, seeing in its firm lines desire and what seemed to be respect mingled undeniably with regret. Her voice tight, hardly more than a whisper, she said, "How should it be?"

"Who can say? Perhaps it was meant, after all, as this must . . . surely . . . be.''

He lowered his lips to hers once more and, releasing her hair, bent to lift her in his arms. Cyrene felt the swooping swing as he turned toward the bed. A part of her wanted to demand that he explain what he had said, but there was an equally fervid part that did not want to know, was afraid to know. With tightly closed eyes, she warded off the doubts and fears, losing herself, deliberately, in the racing pleasure of the moment.

In this, also, he was different. His touch was always caring, but there was greater tenderness in it, an exquisite lingering care for her that was only partly due to her bruises. It was beguiling, bemusing; she was grateful for it and sought as best she could to return it.

It became a part of them and of this night, feeding, enhancing the thing they still required, were desperately in need of, the ultimate surcease. They sought it with a thousand small kisses and caresses, straining together with pounding hearts and tightly closed eyes, luxuriating, drowning, in purest sensation.

She felt the clamor of blood in her veins, its quick hot passage that radiated heat to her skin so that she stripped off her nightshirt and let it drift from her fingers and over the edge of the bed to the floor. Beneath her the linen sheets were smooth and cool, smelling of starch and freshness. Overhead the rain pattered down, a soothing sound of infinite release that mingled with the quickness of her breathing. The fire crackled softly, spreading its leaping yellow and orange pattern on the walls, making the darkness in the corners of the room seem deeper, turning the single burning candle into a fiery star.

By degrees awareness receded. The hardness of his body was a delight and an enticement. She explored it in unself-conscious wonder, spreading her fingers through the fine mat of hair on his chest, raking her nails gently along the flat expanse of his belly, rubbing her palms over the hair-roughened ridges of his thighs, circling, testing with sensitive fingertips the incredibly smooth and springing length of him. He encouraged her, incited her with the wet and tantalizing track of his tongue, tracing the hollows and tender mounds of her body in his turn, bringing her with deft and consummate care to readiness.

She trailed her nails over the rigid muscles of his broad back. They rippled under her touch, sending a shudder through him that was an indication of the constraint he held on himself. The knowledge filled her with boundless loving joy that fueled her own molten and liquid release. She gasped, pressing against him, then cried out as he grasped her waist, sliding his hand down to her hip to draw her against the unyielding rigidity of his body. She parted her thighs, taking him inside, accommodating his deep, thrusting entry.

He spoke her name, she thought; a hoarse plea as he raised himself above her. She moved against him, urging him deeper, trembling in her need for the surge of his strength. He gave it to her, unleashing the plunging urgency of his body's boundless, headlong drive toward fulfillment. She took him into her, encompassing, giving, rising to meet him, caught in the grace and power of life's most elemental and uncontrollable joy. Bodies entwined, close, so close, they strove and reached together that convulsing instant of exploding, unbearable beatitude.

And yet they were each trapped within themselves in their ravishing pleasure, separate though joined. They had removed their masks at the end of the masquerade and cast them aside, but, hidden inside themselves, they wore them still.

17

WHEN CYRENE WOKE, the morning light was still dim outside, dulled by the gray cloud cover of the continuing rain. She lay for long moments, aware of René's deep and even breathing beside her, of the firm warmth of his leg against her. There was no peace in her mind, however. The events of the night before had left a residue of disturbance. It was not just the fact that she and René had been attacked; there was something more hovering at the edges of her mind. It seemed to have come stealing out of her dreams as she slept, worrisome, haunting, a vision without substance.

Abruptly, she knew.

Gaston.

There was no one with so much reason to wish to destroy René, no one with more desire to take her from him, than the Bretons. Gaston's arrival back in the town coincided so nicely with the attack that it was difficult to believe it could be an accident.

The man who had tried to kidnap her had worn a mask. For most of the time, he had been behind her, out of her sight. Could it have been Gaston? Was it possible? She did not like to think so, but she could not be sure.

The other two men she had seen as well as anyone could wish. They were certainly not Pierre and Jean.

She did not think that the two older Bretons would lend

themselves to so base an attack, one that had been meant to end with bodily injury to René, if not death. Gaston, on the other hand, was young and hot-headed. He might accept René's hospitality and be able to laugh and talk with every show of the magnanimity of those who have lost in a sporting contest, but she thought that he still held a grudge for the loss they had suffered due to René's treachery and was resentful of the position in which Cyrene had been placed. It was not beyond him to have taken such means to be avenged, no matter how underhanded it might be. The possibility of securing her release would have been excuse enough.

And yet, could that be so? According to Gaston's view, she was no longer bound. After the passage of so many long days, René could not go to the governor to change his tale without appearing a dupe or else an unscrupulous conniver. He might profess not to care about the first, but he would not be human if it did not give him pause. As for the second, the governor had shown such partiality for Cyrene that he might well censure René without a hearing, taking her side for the sole purpose of setting her free. Particularly if she was allowed to talk to Vaudreuil, to explain.

The truth was, Cyrene had seen this weakness in René's control of her long before. She should have pressed it. She should have demanded that he let her go instead of weakly letting their arrangement continue, enjoying the social round, the *cachet* conferred upon her by his preference for her, delighting in her new finery even as she protested receiving it, reveling in his passion for her even as she scorned it. When had she become so supine? When had she become engrossed in the life he had made for her to the point that she had neglected to question who and what he was and what he had done to her?

"What are you thinking of?"

Cyrene turned her head sharply to find René awake beside her. He was watching her, his eyes filled with shadows as he lay on his side with his head resting on his bent arm.

"Nothing," she answered in haste. "Just . . . this and that."

She thought he was not going to speak again, that he might be drifting back to sleep, for his eyelids closed and his chest slowly lifted and fell. She was wrong.

His lashes swept upward, and he put his question quickly, as though he might not otherwise ask. "If I were to say, Come with me, return with me to France now, on the next ship, how would you answer?"

Her heart jarred inside her chest. The muscles in her stomach clenched. She thought of France as she had last seen it, a cool and gray-green country filled with bustle and noise, hauteur and irascibility, pastries and smiles. Dear France, bright, medieval, glorious France.

"I can't," she whispered.

"Why?"

What could she say? I hardly know you, and what I know I cannot trust? I don't belong in France anymore; I've outgrown its narrow ways? I would rather be a lady smuggler, unfettered, unconfined, than your precious, cosseted mistress? Here I have love and family of a sort, and there I could depend only on your uncertain desire?

"I just can't. How can you think that I could?"

He made a soft sound that might have been a laugh or a sigh. "I didn't think it; I only wondered."

She turned her head sharply. "Then you weren't asking?"

"Does it matter?" he said, reaching out to her, brushing the peak of her breast in a delicate caress that sent a frisson of delight along her nerves before drawing her toward him. "I have my answer, and it's enough."

Had she made a mistake? That question remained with her long after René had dressed and gone. Sometimes it seemed so, seemed that she was a fool to discard so easily the prospect offered her. To be the chosen woman of a man of wealth and position in Paris had its benefits, even a certain quasi-respectability. There would have been a town house and a carriage, the latest fashions, visits to the theater and to the

opera; a circle of friends of the same position, long hours of
René's company, his lovemaking, perhaps even his children.
Or if he preferred to return to his father's estate, there might
be a cottage in the country of her own not far away, a place
where she could read and sew and make a garden, a place of
beauty that he could share. Some such liaisons lasted for
years, even a lifetime.

And some lasted a few weeks or months before the man
grew tired and, if the woman was lucky, found her another
protector to take her off his hands.

René was not known for his constancy in affairs of the
heart. Rather the opposite, if anything.

She did not think she could bear being paid off, shuffled
away as an irksome responsibility. To live always with that
possibility over her would destroy some essential part of her,
making her like so many other women under such conditions, hard and suspicious and grasping.

Why did it have to be so difficult? Why could René not
have been more ordinary, more common? Or she herself less
so?

The street vendor came by at midafternoon, a stooped old
crone wrapped against the misting rain in an ancient velvet
cloak with tarnished gilt trim, shiny with wet and bare spots
where the nap had rubbed away. She cried of her scallions
and garlic in a quavering monotone, but her smile was cheery
and she smelled of fresh earth and pungent herbs.

It was Martha who called the woman in, being in need of
a handful of scallions to cast over the chicken she was cooking for dinner. She left the old vendor standing under the
protection of the gallery while she stepped into the salon to
speak to Cyrene. M'sieur usually gave her adequate money
to buy from such chance peddlers, she said, but had neglected to supply her of late. Did Mademoiselle have a livre
or two by her?

René had given Cyrene a purse with coins to use for the
little things she might require. So far there had been none,
and in any case the purse itself was an embarrassment to her,

too much the sign of the kept woman. She had tried to refuse it, but since he would not have it, she had stowed it away in the armoire. When she went to look for it there, she could not find it at first. It had been shuffled to the back, wedged in a corner on a lower shelf. As she searched it out, she had to push aside René's coats. There was a faint crackling sound as she touched one of them. She paid it scant attention but retrieved the purse and went out to Martha and the woman on the gallery to attend to the domestic crisis.

It was later that the memory of the odd rustling sound in René's coat returned to puzzle her. René was a meticulous man, more so than most, or that was her impression from her limited experience with her father and the Bretons. He seldom left his belongings scattered around, and unless the clothing he removed was in need of Martha's services, he always put it away. Martha washed and ironed his linen and, since he had no valet, cleaned and polished his boots; she brushed his coats and pressed the wrinkles from them. There had never been any need for Cyrene to rummage through his shelves in the armoire. If she had been asked, she would have said they held no secrets, for his shirts and coats and breeches, his cravats and his hats were stacked in neat piles and could be easily seen at a glance when the doors of the great armoire were thrown open. Nor were the shelves particularly crowded. Whatever he might have boasted in the way of a wardrobe in France, René had brought with him only a modest assortment of clothing for a gentleman: a half-dozen coats, a score or less pairs of breeches, and no more than three dozen each of shirts and cravats.

Cyrene approached the armoire with misgivings. Prying into other people's belongings, she had been taught as a child, was ill-bred, a sign of servants' manners. To ignore that teaching went against the grain to an amazing degree. Circumstances changed matters, she told herself. That did not keep her from feeling guilty and looking over her shoulder for Martha as she delved into the armoire, lifting René's shirts and pushing his cravats aside. When the dry crackling of paper she had heard came again, she practically snatched the coat from which it issued off the shelf. She thrust her hand into one pocket after the other. Nothing. She must have missed one, she thought, and searched them all again. They were empty.

She gave the coat, a *justaucorps* of peacock blue satin, a shake. The crackling came again. She traced it, grasping at the section of the coat skirt from which it came.

The paper was sewn into the lining. Cyrene stood still, hovering in indecision for the space of several heartbeats. It was not unknown for travelers to sew their valuables into the linings of their clothes, especially when venturing to distant lands over routes known to be dangerous. It could be, at times, a sensible precaution. Her own mother had told of how she had sewn her few jewels into the lining of an old fur robe on the voyage from New France to France as a young woman, and then had been horrified to find that her maid had used the robe to line a bed for her little lap dog.

Regardless, René did not strike Cyrene as the kind of man to depend on such a subterfuge to protect what he owned. There must be another explanation.

There was no such thing as a sewing basket in this bachelor household. Cyrene searched for something to slit the stitches with, at last finding a paper knife used to cut the bound pages of books. Sitting before the fire in the bedchamber, she began to open the seam of the coat lining. In a short time, she had a space large enough to insert three fingers. Gingerly, she slipped them into the lining, touching the small paper bundle she could feel through the cloth. She caught the bundle and drew it out.

Money. It was a thin sheaf of treasury notes. Crisp and new, their denominations were not large, but together they represented a substantial sum. She turned them this way and that, studying the engraving that marked them.

Various kinds of paper money, all of it much less valuable than the same amount in gold, were common tender in the colony. Hard gold or silver were, in fact, hardly ever seen, and when they were, they usually wound up in someone's stocking or mattress. The paper money, however, was usually crumpled, dirty, indelibly creased, and imbued with the smell of sweat. Crisp new notes were suspect. Too often they turned out to be counterfeit.

So it was with the ones Cyrene held in her hands. She had not seen a great deal of money in her life, more often bartering for her needs in the last few years or having them attended to by her parents and grandparents in the times before. Still, the few worthless notes she had seen had made a lasting impression; money was too scarce, too dear, for a person to be taken in by such a thing more than once. On these notes, the engraving was too fancy, yet not quite clear, the paper too flimsy. The notes were counterfeit. She would wager her life on it.

She had expected better of René. In spite of the way he had used her and the things he had done, she had somehow clung to the idea that there was something strong and fine in him. To discover that there was not was such a disappointment it made her feel physically ill. She drew back the hand that held the notes, aiming it toward the fire before her.

Slowly she lowered her hand once more to her lap. There would be no satisfaction in destroying the notes. Moreover, it would be a stupid gesture. What she held in her hand was not just pieces of counterfeit money; they were her passport to freedom. If there had been any doubt that she was able to leave René without repercussion, there was none now.

She gazed down at the notes, trying to think. She must send a message to Gaston, tell him that she was leaving, that he must make arrangements for them to journey into the wilderness to rejoin Pierre and Jean. She should get up and begin to gather her things, decide what she would take with her to wear among the finery that was all she had. It would be a kindness to say good-bye to Martha; she had become fond of the woman with her hard work and willingness to please. And she should compose some message for René.

There were things to be done. Still, she didn't move.

She sat turning the notes over, fighting a terrible urge to cry. She was an idiot. Somewhere inside herself, hidden, unacknowledged, there had been a lingering dream that René would realize how he had wronged her, would discover that his life would be barren without her at his side as his wife, the mother of his children. Foolish, foolish, foolish.

There came a quick, hard knock on the front door of the house. She jumped, startled, and panic ran in a swift current along her veins. She stuffed the notes back into the lining of the coat and began to fold it. The knock came again. Martha was in the kitchen and could not hear. Cyrene hurried to the armoire and slid the folded coat onto the shelf, then closed the doors on it. With one hand going to her hair to smooth any stray strands into her chignon under her lace coif, she picked up her skirts and went quickly into the salon.

It was only Armand at the door, come on his afternoon call. She railed silently at herself for being thrown into such disorder. Who had she expected? The authorities come to take her away for the crime of rifling through her lover's belongings? Hardly. René? He would not have knocked, and so she would have known if she had been in her right senses. It was too ridiculous.

She left Armand in the salon and went through to the pantry, calling down the stairs to Martha for chocolate for herself and wine for Armand. Returning to her guest, she took her place as hostess.

It felt strange, sitting making pleasant conversation when her mind was entirely elsewhere. She wished that she had never encouraged Armand or that he would have the sensitivity to sense he was not wanted and be gone. Instead he talked on and on of the ball, his inquisitive gaze upon her face.

At last he fell silent. He sipped his wine, watching her closely. She could think of nothing to say and so took refuge in her chocolate cup.

"Forgive me if I pry, *chère*," he said finally, "but you seem distraught. What can the trouble be?"

She had been wishing he would show more sensitivity. The moment he did so, she wished he were not nearly so observant of her state.

"Nothing at all," she said.

"It would relieve my mind considerably to believe it, but I have the evidence of my eyes. You are extremely pale, if you will permit me to say so, and on your cheek there is a bruise that—that sickens me to the soul. I have no right to ask, but I must. What has happened? Were you struck in the altercation with the lieutenant last night? Or can it be that Lemonnier became violent over the governor's attentions?"

"Oh!" she said, relief pouring over her in a wave. "You don't know."

His face lightened at her dazed exclamation. "No, but I'm endeavoring to find out."

"But of course," she said, and went on to tell him of the attack upon René and herself.

Armand clenched his hands on his wineglass, shaking his head as he stared down at it. "Useless, I have been so useless to you. First I was too far away to come to your aid when you were insulted by the pig of an officer, could only watch from afar as I tried to reach you. Now this. I long to be your protector, but I fail you in your need."

His regret was genuine, not the false lament of a mere social friend. There were others, perhaps, who had their dreams. She reached out to touch his hand. "Don't upset yourself. Your sympathy means much to me, more than your protection."

"Does it, really? How kind you are," he said, catching her fingers and raising them to his lips. "How very kind."

His grasp was a little tight, his gaze carried an intentness that indicated he might well say more unless prevented. She went on quickly. "I am also in grave need of your amusement just now to take my mind from things. Pray, have you no tidbits of scandal for me, no stories of clandestine escapades to divert me?"

He accepted the ploy with grace, settling back with his

wine and regaling her with a tale of how, at the masquerade, a gentleman known for his habit of spilling snuff down his cravat was seen coming from an empty card room with a lady who was brushing snuff from her bosom. From there, he went on to the antics of a pair of elderly roués who were trying to solicit the interest of a plump young widow who had inherited not only a plantation on Bayou St. John but also an indigo factory, a brick yard, and an operation for the making of candles from the wax berries of the local myrtle shrubs.

"And, of course," he went on, "Rouvilliere is still agitating about the activities of Madame Vaudreuil. He claims she dispenses drugs to the soldiers from her own house, with her own hands, when her steward is not available."

"What is Rouvilliere's purpose in all this? Does he hope to gain Vaudreuil's recall?"

Armand lifted a shoulder. "It may be simple revenge for all the clashes that he has not been able to win and especially the charges of malfeasance filed against him by Vaudreuil. It may also be an excess of duty. On the other hand, he may have his own candidate for the office of governor. But if his intention is merely to have the governor replaced, he may save himself the trouble. Vaudreuil is bound for New France and only awaits the appointment of his successor."

"It has been announced?"

"Not yet. My aunt in Paris—"

"Writes to say so, I suppose?" she finished for him, smiling. "The governor will be happy."

"As you say. It will be like going home for him—though I expect he prays nightly that his replacement reaches him before the Indians attack in force or the smuggling becomes a public outrage."

Cyrene ignored the last, seizing on the word that brought the race of alarm to her veins. "Indians?"

"I was forgetting you might not have heard. News came this morning of another trading party attacked. One man was killed, another injured."

"Their names?" Cyrene's stomach felt like a knotted fist as she thought of Pierre and Jean, out in the wilderness somewhere, searching out the English traders from the Carolinas and visiting the Indian villages with their goods.

"No one seems to know. I'm sorry." Armand knew enough of her story to realize the impact of his news. "The attack was only thirty or forty leagues upriver. Vaudreuil is said to be in a rage at the effrontery. He is preparing to send to our Choctaw allies a request for a meeting at Mobile for talks, a most precarious gamble as matters now stand."

"Precarious, for the governor?"

"Oh, he will be well protected by the king's soldiers, never fear. But in order for the Choctaw to take him at all seriously, he will be required to do more than exercise his charm and diplomacy. He will be required to hand out gifts on a sumptuous scale."

"Gifts he doesn't have," she said. She had seen the main warehouse. There had been nothing there to impress the poorest Indian, even before the fire.

"The governor gave out presents with a lavish hand this past November in Mobile, but more will be expected, of course, with the request for warriors to aid us."

"If he appeals to Maurepas, makes him see the seriousness of the situation, surely goods will be sent?"

"Possibly. We can only hope the merchandise will not be too shoddy. If France doesn't have a care, she will lose Louisiane for lack of a few beads and blankets."

"It does seem so," Cyrene said, lifting her hand to her head where a small ache was beginning to gather, an ache caused by the upsets of the morning.

"I am an imbecile to trouble you with all this when you don't feel well," Armand said, his dark eyes stricken. "Does your face hurt you? Would you not like a cool cloth to hold to it?"

"No, no," she assured him, lowering her hand and summoning a smile. "It's kind of you to worry, but I'm all right."

"Are you certain? To see you injured in that way cuts me

to the heart. It is none of my affair, but . . . it has been reported to the governor?''

''I assume René will tell him.''

''Good, good. Investigations will be made, then.''

''I suppose something may be discovered of the injured men, though odds are that we will learn they are scum who have now fled. As for the other, there is no way to identify him.''

''Perhaps not, and then again something may be done. I think I must make a few investigations of my own.''

''Not if it will be dangerous, as well it may.''

''You are not to worry. This is something I must do, something I wish to do for my own sake.''

She had no means of forcing him to desist. In any case, it seemed possible he might be able to discover something; he was such an excellent source of information. She permitted herself to be reassured.

They spoke of other things, with Armand stopping now and then to interject some exclamation of sympathy and self-blame as his gaze went to her face. At last, when Cyrene was beginning to think he would be with her still when dinnertime came, he took his leave, still lamenting that he had not been able to serve her.

Martha emerged from the kitchen almost immediately, where she must have been listening for Armand's departure, and began to clear away the clutter of wineglasses and chocolate cups and the remains of the tarts and cheese that had been provided. The woman had the chocolate pot in her hand when a knock sounded on the door once more, announcing another caller. With an expressive lift of her eyes in Cyrene's direction, Martha set down the pot, wiped her hands on her apron, and went to answer the door.

The man who stepped into the salon was Touchet. It had begun to rain outside once more, for the fresh, moist coolness of it came with him into the room, and his cape, which he stripped off, shone with wet. He removed his tricorne also and handed it with his cape and cane to Martha. Madame

Vaudreuil's man then sauntered toward Cyrene where she sat on the settee. He bowed over her hand in formal greeting, though without touching it to his lips, for which she was thankful. His gaze rested a moment on her bruised cheek, but he either saw nothing there to excite his interest or else thought it the better part of courtesy to pretend he did not.

It occurred to Cyrene as he came toward her with jaunty self-satisfaction in his step that he must have waited deliberately until Armand was gone. It made her feel uncomfortable to think of him loitering somewhere, watching the house, noting who arrived and left. She could not be surprised at it, however.

She depended on cool politeness to carry her over the first few moments of the visit, inviting Touchet to be seated, requesting that Martha bring wine once more, commenting on the wet weather and also on the magnificence of the entertainment that had been offered to them the evening before. At the same time, her mind was busy choosing and rejecting reasons why Madam Vaudreuil's lackey might have decided to pay her a call. It was a great relief when Touchet, after a glance around to be sure Martha was gone, came to the point.

"As much as I appreciate your charms, mademoiselle, this is not for me a visit of gallantry. I come as an emissary from one lady to another."

"From Madame Vaudreuil?"

"Just so, from the Marquise de Vaudreuil."

The insistence on the title was telling, meant undoubtedly to make her aware of the power and high standing of the woman of whom he spoke. It served merely to put Cyrene on her mettle. She felt the normal social need to come to his aid in some way when he paused, apparently at a loss. She ignored it. Let him flounder.

Touchet pursed his lips and a hard gleam came into his eyes. "The marquise is . . . concerned, concerned about you. She feels that Lemonnier may have taken advantage of you. She worries that you may not realize the hazardous path you are treading as his mistress."

"I am touched by her regard for my welfare," Cyrene said with a shading of irony.

"Yes. She does not have a great deal of time for such concerns, but as a great lady she takes her duty toward the people under her husband's jurisdiction seriously."

"I'm sure." Was there a veiled threat in that phrase, some hint that Cyrene was in the power of the marquis and therefore of his wife? It did not seem likely, but it was possible to read anything into Touchet's too-smooth tone.

"On the other hand, Madame la Marquise perceives in you a female above the ordinary, one of intelligence who cares for more than fine feathers and the pleasures of the moment. Because of this, she is prepared to invest in your future."

"My future?" Cyrene repeated. "I don't believe I understand."

He gave her a snide smile. "Let me make it clearer. She will pay you handsomely, enough to live on while you apprentice yourself to a milliner or dressmaker, or even set yourself up in a small pastry shop or some such, if you will agree to leave Louisiane for Paris to take advantage of this opportunity. The monies will be paid to you on the day you sail, when you are aboard the ship. *Le Parham* sails within the week."

"This—this is incredible!"

"I find it so myself, but that is the offer of the marquise."

It was, of course, a bribe; the fine phrases of concern were so much rhetoric. Madame Vaudreuil, it seemed, was afraid of her husband's attraction to Cyrene. It might also be that the woman expected the Bretons might follow her to Paris, thereby eliminating another of her problems. How very foolish. Madame greatly exaggerated her influence.

"You cannot be serious," she said.

"I assure you Madame la Marquise is very serious, indeed."

"I am not her responsibility. You must tell her for me that I am honored to think she has taken so much time and thought over my situation, but I must refuse. Louisiane is my home. I have no wish to leave it.''

Touchet frowned. "She won't be pleased."

"I regret that, but my answer remains the same."

"Is it, perhaps, affection that holds you? Or is it your prospects with Lemonnier? Or even young Moulin?"

She gave him a cold look. "That is none of your concern or Madame Vaudreuil's."

"You are making a mistake."

"Perhaps."

He leaned forward in his seat, his voice low. "Your position here could be made extremely unpleasant if you stay."

She got to her feet in a quick, smooth movement. "How kind of you to warn me. Now if you will forgive me for sending you away without refreshment, I believe I must ask you to leave me. I have a touch of the headache."

"Not yet," he said, rising slowly from his chair to face her. "We haven't come to an agreement."

"I fear we are as near as we can be." She refused to look away from his yellow-brown stare as she stood with lifted chin and clasped hands.

"I think not." His voice was soft with menace. "I feel sure there is something I can do that will persuade you to change your mind."

There came the sounds of a noisy approach from the rear of the house. For a moment, Cyrene thought it was Martha trying to make certain that she did not interrupt anything of importance as she brought the wine that was ordered. Then she heard Gaston's voice and turned with relief toward the dining room, from which it came.

It was both Gaston and Armand. One carried a tray with a bottle of sherry and a collection of tinkling glasses, the other a crystal compote piled high with small cakes and bonbons and also a stack of small plates. They jostled each other back and forth, laughing and protesting and uttering dire warnings. They made it safely to the table beside Cyrene with their burdens where they began to serve what they had brought with every show of skill in the art.

Gaston filled a glass, then turned with it to Touchet. "Wine, m'sieur?"

The presence of the two young men was not without purpose. It was plain from the look of frustrated rage on Touchet's face that he understood that fact as well as Cyrene. He made a curt bow in Gaston's direction, though his gaze did not leave her face. "Thank you, no, I cannot stay. I will convey your answer, mademoiselle, to the person concerned. It may be that we will have to discuss it further."

"For myself, I can assure you it will be of no avail whatever."

"We shall see," he said, and turned on his heel.

Armand moved quickly to gather Touchet's cape, tricorne, and cane, which had been left on a side table, then stepped to open the door. Touchet snatched his belongings from the younger man's hands and stalked from the room. His footsteps could be heard on the stairs for a moment, then were lost in the sound of the pouring rain.

Cyrene heaved a sigh of relief, then turned to face the two young men. She said with some asperity, "You may tell me now just what you two are doing here?"

Gaston and Armand had overheard enough to guess what had transpired, but they wanted the details. Cyrene related them as simply as possible, also expressing her profound relief at seeing them. Armand had noticed Touchet in a doorway as he had left a short while before. At first he had thought he was merely sheltering from the rain, then he had looked over his shoulder to see him making a dash for the house. He had been undecided about his course of action until he had caught sight of Gaston on his way to pay a visit. He had intercepted him, told him of Cyrene's visitor. They had decided it might be better to allow Touchet to have his say, whatever it might be, before they put in an appearance. Martha had seen them hanging about in the rain and her suspicions had been aroused until she recognized them. She had

practically hauled them into the kitchen. It had been an easy
matter then to eavesdrop, with their excuse for interruption
prepared if it was needed.

Both Armand and Gaston were incensed at what they insisted on calling the insult offered to her, though they could
not agree on what should be done about it. Armand thought
that Touchet should be called out, while Gaston seemed to
feel that the problem would be best handled between René
and the governor. They demolished the plate of cakes and
drank most of a bottle of wine while they argued about it,
but accomplished little more. By the time they finally left,
with many assurances of their support, Cyrene's headache
was full blown.

She had walked to the door with Armand and Gaston.
Beyond the gallery, the rain slanted down, dimpling the gray
lakes that had formed in the streets, falling from the eaves in
steady silver streams. Cyrene stepped back inside to take her
shawl from where it lay on the end of the settee and wrap it
around her, then moved back out onto the gallery once more.

There was something soothing in the steady fall of the
rain. She felt her headache recede and the tension begin to
drain from the back of her neck as she strolled along the
gallery. The wet dampness sweeping under the eaves in a
mist now and then was cool on her face. The street lay empty
before her. The houses sat huddled and wet on either side
with their shutters and doors tightly closed and small eddies
of smoke rising from their chimneys. She could smell the
faint aromas of baking bread and cooking onion and seafood
mixed with the tang of the smoke. She moved to lean her
back against the house wall, breathing deep, watching the
endless rain.

It was odd that both René and Madame Vaudreuil had
chosen today to suggest that she go to Paris. Their proposi-
tions were very different, of course, but she could not help
wondering if it were something less than accidental. She
could not picture René discussing his affair with her with the
governor's wife, telling her of when and how he had made

his suggestion. Still, it appeared that with him anything was possible.

She would not leave. She had not realized how attached she had become to this new land until two people had tried to persuade her to desert it. She loved its lush fecundity, the grand scale of its rivers and its wilderness, its dramatic changes of weather, even its rain. She had thought that she had been restricted in her movements by the Bretons, but that was as nothing to the restrictions she would face in France where her every movement and every word she spoke would be carefully watched; where women were expected to keep to their places, which were the kitchen and the bedroom and, one afternoon a week, perhaps, the salon.

Intolerable. Even if there were not the Bretons. How she missed them, gentle Pierre and irrepressible Jean. She prayed they were safe and well and had been as prosperous in their trading as they desired to be. She hoped they were not worrying too much about her, so much that they forgot to have a care for themselves.

What would they think of René if they knew of the counterfeit bills? They had gone from suspicion of him to qualified approval. Perhaps their first impression had been the right one. She should have paid more attention to them. But no, she had been too enthralled with the man she had saved.

She still did not believe what she had discovered, did not want to believe it. In spite of everything, she had thought there must be some explanation for what René had done in betraying the Bretons, some reason of loyalty to king and country or of respect for the integrity of the laws restricting trade that had overridden his obligation to them and to her. That there was not was a fact she could not bring herself to face.

Even now, she wondered if she could be wrong about the money, if it was real tender. Or if it was counterfeit, perhaps there was some reason for it being in his possession? Maybe he was holding it for someone or else did not realize that it was not genuine?

She was not so great a fool as to believe either could be possible, no matter how comforting it might be.

What, then, could she believe?

The notes were well made compared to most, very close to the real thing. It was likely, then, that they had come from France since the local facilities for such things were few. There was a printer but only for official announcements. All newsletters were imported from France; there was not enough considered to be of interest in the colony to warrant a local publication.

The only purpose in bringing the notes from France that made sense was to pass them off as real, exchanging them for necessary goods and services. There was no way of knowing how much René had already disposed of in that manner, how much damage he had done the economy of the colony. It was possible that he had intended to use some of the bills to engage in trade, passing them to the Rhode Islander, Captain Dodsworth, until he had met Touchet on the beach that day when she had seen them in close conversation. No doubt he had received a different proposition then.

The question that posed the most difficulty was the connection René had with the rash of counterfeit script that had been appearing in the town for the past year. It did not appear that he could have had any hand in that whatsoever. And yet, wasn't it too much of a coincidence that he should be involved in the same dirty game? Wasn't it possible that his involvement had been responsible for the attempt on his life the night she had saved him—and even the evening before?

The questions required answers. Too much that affected her personally depended on what those answers might be for her to ignore them. But how was she to find out what she needed to know?

She could ask René.

A shiver ran through her at the prospect. In order to carry it out, she would have to admit that she had pried into his belongings. She did not care to think what he would say or do if he learned of it.

The only other solution that presented itself was to find a way to look at the contents of the lacquer box that held the correspondence he worked on so assiduously, correspondence that might be connected with his activities in the colony. She would be willing to wager everything she owned or hoped to own that the answer was there. The only trouble was that it was locked and René kept the key with him at all times.

She had to have the key.

Naturally she could not leave the house or René until she had that key and the answers she sought.

18

RENÉ RETURNED AT dusk. By then Cyrene had not only had time to walk to the flatboat and bring back needle and thread to mend the opened seam of his coat but also to consider the problem that lay before her. The key she needed, René kept in his pocket. Since she had none of a pickpocket's training in removing a man's valuables, he must be induced to remove his clothes. There were, as far as she could see, three possible occasions when he might do so. The first was at bedtime, the second when he bathed, and the third was for the purpose of making love. When he took a bath or made himself ready for bed, he always put away his own clothing, leaving her no excuse for touching them, much less rummaging through them. That left only one possibility.

It did not necessarily follow that she would be given an opportunity to search, even if she did get him out of his coat and breeches; she was, in most cases of that nature, rather distracted herself. She would think of something. She must think of something.

Dinner was a quiet meal. René seemed preoccupied, his mind on other things though his gaze rested on Cyrene now and then, touching the bruise on her cheek until she was as conscious of it as of a brand. Her stomach was so tight with apprehension of what lay ahead that she could not eat, but sat dipping her spoon into her soup, tasting it now and then, or pushing her food from one side of her plate to the other.

They carried their claret, along with a tray of savories and nuts, into the salon before the fire. Cyrene was reminded of the fiasco of the afternoon, something that had almost slipped her mind in her concentration on the matter at hand. She told René of Touchet's visit and his offer, as much to fill the silence as anything else, though she was aware of a certain curiosity to hear what he would say about it.

"Why are you still here?" he asked, and sipped his wine.

Irritation stirred below her detachment. "I hardly know, to be sure. Having a price tag placed on myself is such an honor; it delights me beyond measure to have the marquise think that I can be bought!"

"I see. It's perversity that made you stay."

There was, perhaps, a certain amount of truth in that, though he could not know the other reasons that had urged her to go. She said in flat tones, "What else? Except, of course, the small matter of a threat."

He leaned his head back against his chair, watching her, swirling his wine. "And is that the only reason?"

To antagonize him was not going to help her cause. Besides, there was something vibrant in his low tone that caught at her heart, making it feel as if the space for it was too small. She forced a smile. "Certainly not. I also enjoy Martha's cooking and your ability to select wine, along with a few other attributes."

"Such as?"

"Let me see," she said with a frown. "Your choice in coats, not to mention jewels. The turn of your leg in your breeches. The benefits of your expertise in the pastime for which I am kept."

He set his wineglass down on the table beside him, saying abruptly, "Do you really think that's all I wanted of you?"

"Isn't it implied in the arrangement?"

"To hell with the arrangement."

"By all means. Do you wish to change it?"

She did not know where the challenge came from or why

she made it. There was no future for her with René; she knew that even if he did not.

"I wish . . ." he began, then stopped. After a moment, he sighed. "I suppose not."

She could not just sit there like a log and wait for his amorous impulse to create the situation she needed. Cyrene drained her wine and put her glass aside, then rose and went to René in his chair, kneeling at his feet with a billow of skirts. She put her hands on his thighs, feeling the muscles tense under her fingers as she spread her palms over the worsted of his breeches.

She looked up at him, her golden-brown eyes dark. "Tell me what you wish."

René reached out to trace the blue-shadowed injury to her face with his fingertips. Deep inside him, some sixth sense that he had developed over the past few years stirred. She was up to something, wanted something of him. He wondered what it was. It didn't matter; he would as soon she had it as to destroy this moment with questions.

"I wish," he said with measured slowness, "that we could start all over. I wish I had met you in France four years ago when we were both innocent—or, in my case, reasonably so. Failing that, I wish I could take you far away from here, to a place where there was no one except the two of us and no past."

There was such pain in his voice. It sent a tremor of foreboding through her. Then, as she heard the echo of his words, felt their meaning seep into her mind, it was as if she assimilated with them a sense of the same longing to start afresh, to meet on some neutral ground, to meet as a man and a woman without ties or mixed loyalties, without doubts.

"Very well," she said. "I will be anything and anyone you choose. A milkmaid? A merchant's daughter? A seller of sweets and candied violets? What would you have me?"

A smile curved the smooth contours of his mouth. "If you were the merchant's daughter, you would not be where you are now or doing what you are doing."

She was not sure he was taking notice of the delicate slide of her hands toward the apex of his legs. "You are still left with a choice."

"The seller of sweets would, I fear, have long ago lost her innocence in some back tenement."

She gave him a limpid look. "Then it's to be the milk-maid?"

He reached for her just as she reached her goal, drawing her up to sit on his lap and the hard length she had created there. "The idea of innocence has begun to pall after all. I think I will have you as you are, Cyrene, my siren, and where we are."

The play on her name pleased her fancy, even as she saw that her second attempt at seduction, like her first, was going to succeed, and she threw back her head to laugh with a curious triumphant joy tinged with the taste of tears. He bent his head to press his face into the soft curves of her bosom exposed by her gown, holding her tightly as if he meant never to let her go.

They undressed each other with deliberate care and soft wordless sounds of pleasure. Naked and languid with the engulfing arousal, they eased down from the discomfort of the chair to the hearth rug. At first Cyrene was aware, thinking of the weight of the key in René's coat pocket as the garment fell to the floor, hearing its dull clink. Then she ceased to reason or to plan. She joined René as together they cavorted in the fire's glow, letting it heat their blood to boiling as, mindless and uncaring, they found in each other the antidote to pain that rose always from its own source.

It was long moments before Cyrene, lying in the curve of René's body, with his arm over her waist, could bring herself to realize that what had just transpired was not her sole object. She swallowed, breathing deep, then jerked erect suddenly, holding her head as if listening.

"Martha," she whispered, "coming for the tray!"

She scrambled to her feet and dived for the heaped clothing around the chair. Scooping it up—petticoats, coat, bodice, breeches, shirt, and chemise—all in a wad, she made a dash for the bedchamber.

René was more alert and faster than she had expected. He was right behind her with their shoes and stockings in his arms. There would be no time to take the key from his pocket, though she could feel the shape of it under her hand. With a despairing mental curse, she flung the garments down on a chair, then arranged her face in an expression of impish glee, spun around, and caught René around the waist before going still. She pretended to listen. There was nothing, of course; there never had been.

She shrugged with a light laugh. "I must have been mistaken. But so long as we are here, and the bed is there . . ."

There was a glint of humor in his eyes. It disturbed her for an instant, making her feel transparent. He could not know, however. She held his gaze with her face lifted to his until he bent slowly to take her lips and turned with her toward the high mattress that awaited.

It was easier this time than the last to become lost in the vortex of desire, easier for her bodily responses to be tapped. And yet she could not quite reach the same degree of nothingness, the same careless splendor. The image of the coat and the key remained at the back of her mind, a taunt and a threat. It was a passionate relief when at last René subsided against her, when his soothing caresses of repletion and gratitude ceased and she heard his deep and even breathing.

There was a brief, uncomfortable feeling inside her as she considered her actions of the past few hours. She dismissed it. Some things were necessary; to be too nice in one's habits could be a weakness.

Still, she waited, staring up into the darkness and counting the slowly passing seconds off one by one. When a good half hour had passed, she eased away from René a few inches. He did not move. She waited again. She could hear her pulse like a soft, feathery drumbeat in her ears. The hard jar of her heart shook her left breast. She forced herself to breathe with a regular, even motion, in and out, again and again.

She shifted, easing over the mattress a few more inches. The filling of moss made a quiet snapping sound like a buried twig. A section of the bed ropes gave with a soft creak. She stopped once again.

She hated this creeping about, this need for subterfuge. It was foreign to her nature, abhorrent to everything she had ever been taught. She despised the circumstances that had brought her to it, the man who had caused them, and herself for instigating the entire chain of events in the first place. The only good thing she could see about what she was about to do was that it would end the entire degrading episode. It must, or she could not bear it.

What seemed like eons later, she pushed herself up on the mattress and swung her legs off, sliding slowly to the floor. The wood planking was cold to her bare feet, but she expected it and made no sound. Standing erect, she began to drift with infinite caution around the side of the bed that lay between her and the chair where the clothes were piled. She touched it lightly with her fingertips, barely grazing it, so that she would not bump into it in the dark.

"Where are you going?"

She gasped, her nerves leaping under the skin, as he spoke. Damn a man who slept so lightly! It was a moment before she could find her voice. "Nowhere. Go back to sleep."

"Were you looking for something?"

"No . . ." she began, then realized before the syllable was out that some explanation was required. Her mind raced, searching for the most plausible excuse, the one furthest from the truth. "No, not really, only Martha must have moved the chamber pot."

"Here on my side."

There was nothing else to be done. She found the pot. After a moment, she moved away again.

"Now what?"

"Nightshirt," she murmured.

"Never mind, I'll warm you."

She was only two steps from the chair. "Really, I—"

She was caught from behind and lifted in strong arms. René swung around with her. The bed ropes jounced as she landed on the mattress, then he was beside her, drawing her into the prison of his arms. The warmth of his body, the male smell of him, washed over her. She felt ill with the defeat and the thwarted rage it engendered. She wanted to lash out, to kick and scream.

None of that would help. She lay unmoving, but the effort to remain so sent a shudder through her.

"You really are cold," René said, and held her closer, drawing the bedclothes higher and tucking them around her shoulders.

What did he mean by that? Did he suspect? Had the things he had said and done been as much playacting as hers had been?

The possibility cooled her ire and left her staring morose and afraid into the dark.

René did not leave the house the next day. He worked at the table in the salon, covering sheet after sheet with his slashing script, the lacquer box sitting open at his feet. The sight of it lacerated Cyrene's sensibilities; it was a flagrant reminder of the events of the night before and the swift passage of time. The reason René was so intent on his task had nothing to do with the seemingly perpetual wet weather but was, she could guess without too much trouble, the proposed sailing of *Le Parham* on the following day.

Schemes for getting a look at the documents on the table, each wilder than the last, occupied Cyrene's mind. There was something in the way René watched her, something in his apparent consciousness at all times of where she was and what she was doing, that prevented her from putting them into action. She sat before the fire, pretending to write a letter in emulation of René's industry, even penning a few lines to one of the good sisters at the convent of Quimperle. She spent most of her time thinking, however, thinking until she began to fear she would go mad.

Then in late afternoon, as the gray light of dusk was gathering, the messenger came.

Cyrene answered the door to him. He was tall and vaguely military in bearing, though dressed in the striped jersey of a sailor and with a stocking cap on his head. From his shoulder swung a cloth bag from which he took a leather pouch. He had come for the dispatches, if M'sieur Lemonnier had them ready. The captain was making ready to weigh anchor at first light.

René nodded. "A moment only," he said, and continued writing.

She must do something. Now. At once. But what? Cyrene moved to the settee and picked up her letter and her pen from the nearby table, then put them down again. She looked at René at his writing table with its litter of papers, then glanced at the seaman.

The man was watching her as he stood with his hands behind his back, and a smile of appreciation hovered about his lips. As she caught his gaze, his smile widened and he narrowed one eye in the slightest suggestion of a wink.

The idea came full-blown, simple, but complete in detail. She caught her breath, wondering if she dared, knowing all the while that she had no choice. She returned the seaman's smile, then holding his gaze for an instant longer than necessary, she picked up her letter once more and turned and went from the room into her bedchamber.

When the door was closed behind her, she moved fast, striding to the armoire and jerking down her cloak. It whirled around her as she crossed the bedchamber and moved into the dressing room, then plunged through it and across the small dining room to the pantry. She hurried down the stairs, moving as silently as possible, folding her letter as she moved.

In the kitchen, Martha looked up. Cyrene clenched her teeth in grim exasperation; she had hoped the woman would be in her room.

"Mam'zelle Cyrene? What is it?"

Cyrene had no need to feign urgency. "Did you catch the spice man? I particularly wanted a bit of cinnamon to dust on my chocolate."

"I didn't hear him, mam'zelle. But cinnamon in chocolate? You must be *enceinte!*"

"No, no," she said over her shoulder with a forced laugh. "I'll see if I can catch him."

She was gone from the kitchen in an instant, closing the door softly behind her, then running from the rear garden and around the end wall of the house toward the street. The seaman would be returning to his ship in the direction of the river. She swung that way at once, keeping close to the house so that she could not be seen from the salon should anyone chance to look out the window. With her head down, she walked quickly away, hoping that René would write just a little longer, a few more sentences, that he would take his time sanding and sealing his pages.

At the first cross street, three houses down, she turned left. Her pace slowed at once. She stepped into the doorway of a milliner's shop that was closed for the day and, pretending to be searching for something in her pockets, prepared to wait.

It seemed that hours beyond counting passed before the seaman came along the street she had left, though it was only a matter of a few moments. She stood in the shadows, watching his quick, carefree stride. He passed the cross street with barely a glance, continuing on his way along the muddy planking that was laid in front of the houses. Cyrene counted his receding footsteps, letting him get well ahead of her. When he was half a block away, she emerged from the doorway, moving quickly back toward the main street.

The seaman was still in view. The only other people to be seen on such a damp and dreary evening were a laundress balancing a basket of freshly pressed shirts on her head and an elderly gentleman who leaned on his cane with every step. Cyrene picked up her skirts and began to run after the seaman.

''M'sieur!'' Her call was light, almost playful, certainly not loud. ''M'sieur, wait!''

The seaman swung around, alert, wary, his hand going to the cloth bag at his side. When he saw her, he relaxed and even came back a few steps.

''Well met, mademoiselle,'' he said, his teeth flashing in a smile.

''We are not met at all, as you well know,'' she said with exaggerated breathlessness. ''I have been chasing after you for miles.''

''What a pity! If I had known, I would have allowed you to catch me much sooner.''

She gave him as coquettish a smile as she could manage. ''What a rogue you are, to be sure, though a most handsome one! But I only wanted to give you my letter to be added to the others.'' She took the folded sheet from her cloak pocket as she spoke, holding it out to him.

''You have M'sieur Lemonnier's permission?''

''But of course.'' She smiled, a dulcet curving of the lips.

''I would think there isn't much he refuses you. Here, give it to me.''

Cyrene almost let him take it, then, as his fingers touched it, drew it back. ''Oh, but I forgot to seal it in my haste. How vexing! But I will just slip it inside my other letter, if you please. It will only take a moment.''

''Your other letter?''

''They are both to the nuns at Quimperle. Sister Mary will see that Sister Delores gets hers.''

''The letters I carry are communiqués of supreme importance; I really should not allow—''

''But you will, won't you? Oh, please, there will not be another ship for weeks and—and I am in need of the prayers of the good sisters.''

''Are you now? Lemonnier is your lover?''

She smiled, as if at pleasant memories of a kind she expected him to share, at least in part. ''Yes, he is.''

''And does M'sieur ever go away, ever leave you alone?''

"Sometimes. You would, perhaps, like to visit me when he goes?" How far would she go to gain what she wanted? She didn't know. That was the disturbing thing, more so than the fact that she was considering the possibility.

"I would like it very much."

"What a pity it is then that you must be leaving Louisiane . . ."

"Ah, but I will be returning."

"When will that be?" Smile, she must smile, even as she reached out for the bag of documents.

"A few months only, God willing."

"Yes, God willing. A sailor's life is a dangerous one, is it not? Such storms there were when I crossed from France. I spent the entire time on my knees."

"Praying or being sick?"

She gave a shudder, saying quite untruthfully, but because he seemed to expect it, "Oh, both! Are you never ill?"

She listened to him explain how fine a seaman he was and what he did to remain well even in the wildest storms while she delved into the bag at his side. She did not ask him to remove it from his shoulder, but searched as it hung, forcing him to raise his arm so that it acted as a shield for what she was doing. Her movements quick, she searched for one of the smaller missives that had simply been folded in thirds and sealed. There were a few, she knew; she had seen René include them in the box, though she thought they were most likely addressed to his family. Even as she found what she was seeking, she deftly extracted one of the official documents and thrust it under her cloak, clamping it to her body with her arm.

"Here we are," she said, and held up the smaller letter. Carefully pressing the sides of the stiff sheet so that the ends gaped open without breaking the wax seal, she slid her own folded sheet inside. She returned the letter to the bag and gave it a pat before smiling once more at the seaman. "Now I may be easy in my mind. I thank you with all my heart."

"It would be more satisfactory if it was with a kiss," he suggested, his dark eyes hopeful.

"Very well." She leaned forward to press her lips quickly to his. An odd disappointment flitted across her mind; it was just the pressure of one mouth against another, nothing more. She felt his arms begin to go around her, felt the document under her arm touch his chest. She whirled away from him with a quick laugh, retreating a few steps.

"Don't go," he said. "Come with me. I know a tavern where we can have a bottle of wine and a private room."

"Another time. Lemonnier is waiting for me!" She backed away.

"I will return!"

"I will pray that you do," she said, and meant it. She did not like to think of harm coming to him because of what she had done. Perhaps the document would not be missed, or if it was, not until it reached France and there had been many other opportunities for tampering with the bag. She liked him; it was not his fault that his kiss did not please her. Turning from him, she went quickly back toward the house.

Cyrene did not stop until she reached the back garden. Night was closing in, and a fine cool mist like fog floated in the air, threatening to become rain once more. A yellow shaft of wavering light fell from the window of the kitchen, coming from a lantern hanging from a beam. Cyrene paused to take out her prize, glancing quickly up at the house, wondering if she had been missed. She could, perhaps, risk a few short minutes more.

She broke the seal and unfolded the thick, heavy sheets. Holding them toward the window, she began to read.

The door from the kitchen swung open. Cyrene lifted her head to stare at René as he stepped outside but made no move to hide the papers she held. Shock possessed her along with an odd feeling of inevitability, so that it seemed not at all surprising that he should discover her there.

"I trust you find it interesting?" he said quietly.

"You're a spy." Her voice was blank.

"Not exactly. Shall we go inside to discuss it?"

He reached to take the document from her, then stood back for her to precede him. She moved in a daze into the kitchen and up the pantry stairs, hardly noticing Martha, who turned to watch them. She passed through the dining room and into the salon, then stood waiting in the middle of the floor. René stepped around her, going to the writing table where he dropped the letter onto its surface.

"The messenger was not to blame," Cyrene said in abrupt revival.

"I am aware. Except in that he was far too susceptible to your charm."

"He didn't know I took the letter. He will not be punished?"

"I see no point in it."

"The letter must be on the ship when it sails, of course."

"I will take it myself in a short while, as an afterthought."

She turned away from him, removing her cloak and draping it over the end of the settee. "That is very . . . generous."

"The fault is mine, for having you with me in the first place and for not being more vigilant in the second."

"Then I am relieved of responsibility, rather like a child who will get into trouble if it's permitted."

He smiled, a weary curving of his mouth. "More like a prisoner of war whose only duty is to escape."

"It didn't have to be that way. You might have . . . trusted me."

"That decision was not mine to make."

"No, you had to answer to your master," she said, her eyes dark with disdain. "To think, all that time you spent dancing attendance upon Madame Vaudreuil, all the time she doted on you, you were spying on the poor woman."

He did not appear at all upset by the charge. "It's a hazard of the king's service, one Madame Vaudreuil accepted when the marquis took the office of governor."

"I don't suppose it makes a great deal of difference whether you are a lackey to Madame Vaudreuil or to King Louis."

"It does to me," he said, his voice hardening. "Louis of France commands my loyalty as a Frenchman; he is my king. He is also a man mewed up in Versailles, eternally beset by people, each with a score to settle, a favor to beg, a place to request, or a wrong to be righted. He knows not who to believe, cannot tell who is friend or foe. This is particularly true of those involved in a regime in a place so far away as Louisiane. Serious charges have been made concerning the habits and behavior of the Marquis and Marquise de Vaudreuil and countercharges offered. They must be settled before the governor can be granted further promotion to what could well become a most sensitive area of the New World."

"I begin to see. You weren't exiled from France? There was no public disgrace, no quarrel with La Pompadour?"

"La Pompadour is the king's eyes and ears, an able lady, not too well versed in government but doing her best to help France without deserting her friends."

"Of whom you are one?"

"I have that honor."

Cyrene moved to the settee and dropped down upon it with the silken skirts of the gown she wore spreading around her. She watched René in fascination. It was almost as if she had never seen him before. There was new strength, new dignity in his bearing, as well as greater firmness in his features. It appeared that nothing about him was what it had seemed.

"This is the reason you came to Louisiane, on the service of the king?"

He inclined his head.

"No other reason?"

"If there is, it's personal."

To become rich through counterfeit notes could be personal, indeed. "I see. It concerns the Bretons, then?"

His gaze sharpened. "Why should you think so?"

"Why else would you betray them?"

René found himself admiring her, which was not at all the way it should be at this moment. Her swift recovery from what must have been a shock was remarkable; her impulse to protect the man who had aided her no less so. The interrogation she was conducting, almost as if he were on trial instead of the other way around, was as bemusing as it was irritating. Watching her, waiting to see what she would make of what she had discovered, was as marvelous as it was dangerous.

His answer did not come as swiftly as it might. "It was necessary to appear to have a care for Madame Vaudreuil's interests in order to encourage her confidence and that of her man, Touchet."

"That is the only reason?"

"Should there be another?"

She shook her head slowly as if in disbelief. "You tried to destroy us, and for so little purpose."

"It was the chance you took when you broke the law."

"Is that supposed to make it right, what you did, because we were breaking a stupid law that threatens to bring us to starvation and ruin?"

"I have no need to defend myself in this matter," he said, his voice soft.

"What of the matter of counterfeiting?"

He felt as if someone had struck him a solid blow to the midriff. He did not flinch but lifted a brow instead. "Counterfeiting?"

"I found the notes in your coat lining."

"My emergency funds?"

"If you think so, someone has taken you for a fool, and I don't think you are that." His lack of reaction was infuriating, but she had learned enough of him not to be misled by it. She rose to her feet in a single decisive movement. "There is no point in discussing any of this further. The only thing left is for me to go."

"Go?" he said as if he had never heard the word before.

She picked up her cloak and draped it over her arm, walking toward the door. "I would leave the things I have on with you, for your next woman, but you saw to it that I have nothing here to wear except what you gave me. I'll return them in the morning."

"I don't want them."

"Nor do I."

"You're forgetting something, aren't you?"

"Am I? Oh, you mean your hold over me? But your presence in Louisiane is clandestine, is it not? I'm sure you would not want Madame Vaudreuil, and even less the governor, to hear of your special attachment to Louis of France. Do you think my threat just might offset yours?"

He took a step after her, his bearing straight and tall. "What if I said I love you and don't want to lose you?"

"What if? Do you or do you not? I have no use for half measures. Not that it matters. I don't believe you love anything except your position, your power, your prestige. Your greatest concern at this moment, if the truth were known, is probably what you are going to say to the marquis about the loss of one of the players for his theatrical evening. What a pity. But don't worry, you'll think of something. Tell him I betrayed you both."

Cyrene moved to the door and pulled it open, then, once over the threshold, closed it firmly behind her.

The rain had stopped. The damp night air was cool on Cyrene's face, though the air was warmer. The chorus of peeper frogs and other small night creatures, silent for the few short weeks of the winter, had begun again. The noise was not loud, as it would be later, but it was a certain sign of the coming spring.

The walk back to the flatboat, which had seemed so long only the day before when she went for needle and thread, took no time at all. There was a glow of light in the window of the gently rocking craft and Gaston to greet her as she crossed the gangplank.

The two of them talked for long hours, then packed a couple of bundles and put them beside the door. The rest of the night for Cyrene was spent lying in her hammock, lulled by the slow swing of the boat on its mooring ropes, resting but not sleeping.

Daylight found Gaston and Cyrene in their pirogue, slicing through the fog that lay on the back bayous as they made their way around the rear of New Orleans. They were not heading north into the wilderness but only into Lake Pontchartrain. Pierre and Jean had gone no farther than Little Foot's village, which lay to the north of the lake. The reason for that was the Indian troubles, Gaston said, though he had given her a cheerful grin as he told the lie. She was the cause, Cyrene knew, and was comforted.

19

I T WAS GOOD to be doing something strenuous again. As the stiffness eased from her muscles so that they became pliant, moving freely to her command, the stiffness also left her mind.

She had a few regrets. She did not like the idea of allowing Madame Vaudreuil and Touchet to think that she had been frightened away. It was a small matter of pride, something that had always been a problem for her.

She wished that she had been able to say good-bye to Armand. She would not like him to think that she had forgotten him. He was a dear, and though his infatuation with her, if that was what his affection might best be called, would not last, she had no wish to cause him pain while it did.

And it had come to her in the night that she might have allowed René to speak more plainly about his supposed love for her. It would not have changed anything, but it might have made interesting hearing, a sop for her vanity that was undeniably injured by the way he had used her.

She thought of the way he had duped them all, pretending to be an outcast desperate to return to France and the good graces of his king. How easily they had all believed, perhaps because most of them felt the same.

How much else of what he had said was untrue? How much of the public image he had made for himself was a façade, a convenient screen for his real object?

A spy. Not against some enemy of his people but against his own kind, his own class; people who had taken him into their home, their lives. It could not be denied that the Vaudreuil regime was corrupt, but not, perhaps, more than any other. The governor was an impartial judge, a more than competent statesman with a special interest in the regulation of colonial governments since he had watched his own father govern New France. What did the rest amount to? Gossip and the machinations of a money-hungry wife?

But suppose there was truth in the rumors? Suppose René's pose was not as successful as it seemed. There was little that occurred at Versailles that was not noticed, discussed in whispers, carried on the wind to Paris and beyond. Was it possible that the attempts on René's life had something to do with his mission?

Cyrene's paddle missed a beat. If that was true, then he was still in danger.

Or was he? The ship for France, *Le Parham*, was sailing this morning with the dispatches in answer to the charges against the Vaudreuils on board. René must have completed what he had come here to do. There would be no point in injuring him now.

Except revenge.

But why would he remain in Louisiane for that possibility to catch up with him? Why had René not taken passage on the ship returning to France? It made no sense that he would stay. Regardless of the contents of the dispatches, the governor would not thank him for abusing his hospitality and his friendship in the way that he had, and he would certainly have René shown to the door when it was discovered. If it had not already been discovered.

Unless René did not realize his danger.

He was not stupid. None could know better than he what he risked.

It followed, then, that he remained because it was what he desired. And there were two possible reasons for that. Either he had not yet completed his inquiries into the activities of the governor and his wife or else he had some other purpose for staying. Some purpose that involved counterfeit notes.

Louisiane was corrupt, but so was Versailles. A man who would be a spy could not be entirely untouched by what was so prevalent. Could he?

The sun came up and there was warmth in its rays. It struck through the fog, turning it luminous, giving it an iridescent shimmer before it burned it away. They came at last to the lake, a vast open expanse like an inland sea. The water sparkled and danced, the surface breaking into a silent explosion of diamond gleams. The air was fresh and clean, moist and life-giving in the lungs. The cries of birds echoed from the tree-lined shore. It was going to be a fine day.

Free. She was free. The pleasure of it flowed like wine in Cyrene's veins, rising to her head to make her feel giddy with jubilation. Still, underneath were the dregs of a niggling despondency. That it was there was a great embarrassment to her. She would have thought she had more force of mind than to be morose over leaving a man of so little integrity. How could she miss him already? How could she mourn that she would never feel his touch or see his slow smile or sleep beside him again? She should not think of such things, should not want them, should not need them. But she did. Oh, she did.

They left the pirogue on the opposite side of the lake and followed the Indian trail to where the village of Little Foot lay. They saw nothing, heard nothing, but, in the way of the Indians, their presence was known. By the time they reached the village, Pierre and Jean were waiting for them.

It was a joyous reunion, with a great deal of hugging and backslapping and exclamations. Little Foot came forward and invited them all into her hut for food and drink, something that was welcome, indeed. They sat on the sleeping benches of the hut, talking, laughing, catching up on what had passed since they had last seen each other, while a small fire in the center sent smoke in a lazy, swirling column toward a hole in the ceiling.

Little Foot's daughter, Quick Squirrel, was not in evidence. Cyrene asked after her and learned that the girl had left her mother's hut for one of her own. The circumstances were not too clear, for at the same time Gaston and Jean began a loud altercation over gambling debts the younger man had managed to incur while on his own. The Indian woman fell silent as Gaston appealed to Cyrene for support of his claim that it had been necessary in order to gain entry into the right circle, which would allow him to keep an eye on her. His father made rude and hilarious comments about such logic. There was no heat in their argument, however. Gaston had watched over Cyrene and returned her to the older men, and they were satisfied with him.

It was later, over wooden cups of mulberry wine and a sweet cake made of nuts and honey, that they spoke of René. Cyrene told the Bretons exactly what had taken place; she was not in the habit of keeping things from them and saw no need for secrecy there in their circle. That she felt an obligation to protect René outside of it was due to a loyalty to her king and country not unlike his, nothing more. For the man himself she expressed only contempt.

"Come, *chère*, don't be hasty," Pierre said. "Things are not always what they seem."

"You would defend him after what he has done?" she asked in astonishment.

"I would not condemn him unheard. Not that I am his judge. It is not our place to judge others; we are none of us so free from stain. Besides, it isn't what people do that's important, rather it's the reason they do it."

"Yes, like greed!"

"And loyalty."

"Are you saying that because René has one admirable trait he must have good reason for the other things he has done?"

Pierre shook his head. "I'm saying give it time. Regret is a sad companion."

But there was no time left. One of the lookouts posted on the trail leading from the lake to the village came running with an alarm. Two Frenchmen were approaching and with them were a squad of soldiers.

They could have taken to the woods. Cyrene urged it, pleaded for it with the conviction that if she had not been with them, the Bretons would have been gone in an instant. It was their concern that held them, and that made her position intolerable, for she was also their greatest danger. That the men and their military escort had some connection with her presence she did not doubt. Their arrival on her and Gaston's heels was too apt. Moreover, she had felt somewhere inside, though she would not admit it, that her triumph over René had been too easy, that there was a price to be paid for her defiance.

Cyrene and the Bretons did not cower inside. They stood waiting before the door of Little Foot's hut, which was beside that of her father's Drowned Oak, chief of the village. The old warrior emerged also to stand with his trader's wool blanket in a deep burgundy red around him and his back straight. One by one, the other Indians ceased what they were doing and came forward, drawn by the sense that something momentous was about to happen. They stood with silent patience as the sun sank in blue and gold splendor tinged with melancholy behind the trees and the smoke-tainted evening air grew cooler.

The column of soldiers appeared among the trees. They marched with precision into the clearing of the village, their faded uniforms miraculously neat, their brass buttons gleaming and muskets ready. With the two men at the head of the column in plumed hats and velvet coats with gold braid, and with their swords at their sides, the detail was the very embodiment of the pomp and grandeur of France.

The column approached Drowned Oak in rigid and exemplary compliance with the rules of protocol. Neither René nor Touchet, who marched in the lead, indicated by so much as a glance that they were aware of the presence of anyone else. When the proper greetings had been exchanged, René took from under his arm a scroll hung with ribbons and seals and unrolled it, reading it to the old chief in a hard, clear voice.

Couched in the high-flown language of officialdom, it was an arrest order. The men known as Pierre, Jean, and Gaston Breton, along with the woman Cyrene Marie Estelle Nolté, were fugitives, accused of crimes against the king. They were to be placed in confinement and delivered to New Orleans, there to stand trial. The goods in their possession were to be confiscated as evidence against them. Any attempt to escape would be viewed as an admission of guilt and dealt with accordingly.

Cyrene was placed in wrist irons and guards were stationed on either side of her. The Bretons were subjected to full irons from neck to ankle and were also chained together. René took no part in the proceedings but remained some distance away, consulting with the young officer in charge of searching out the trade goods. Cyrene thought that he deliberately held himself aloof, distancing himself from them, though whether from tact or disdain she could not tell.

It was Touchet who saw them placed in bonds. There was gloating satisfaction in the man's narrow face as he checked the cuffs and tugged at the links, and the tone of his voice as he ordered them into the hut commandeered as their prison for the night, before the trip back to town in the morning, was an invitation to escape so that he could have the pleasure of shooting them down.

It was a pleasure they did not give him. Cyrene, watching the docility of the Bretons, the consciousness of defeat etched into their faces, knew with sick certainty that she had brought them to this. If she had never pulled René from the river, if she had never conceived of the crazy idea of using him to gain her independence, if she had never persuaded them to rob the king's warehouse, then they would not be here. It did not matter that their way of life ran counter to the good of France or that they had been involved in it for years before she came to them, she knew herself to blame.

There must be something she could do to help them, some

trick, some piece of information. The only trouble was that she could not think of what it might be. The order for their arrest was in the name of the king, not the governor. That the official edict had been in René's hands, that the soldiers seemed to be taking their orders from him made it appear that he had revealed himself as an agent of the crown. If he no longer feared that exposure, what defense was there against him?

The answer was none. None at all.

The return to New Orleans was without event. Cyrene was placed in a prison cell alone. It was a small room with a low and narrow bed covered by a thin blanket, a chamber pot, and a tiny high window. Through the window she could hear people coming and going outside in the Place Royale and the ringing of the bell from the church next door. Sometimes she thought she could hear the guards talking to the Bretons, but she was not allowed to speak to them, not allowed to send a message or to have visitors. For the most part, she was ignored. She soon realized that her position was a favored one, however. The food was palatable. In addition, her bonds were removed and the bundle of clothing she had carried to the Choctaw village had been dumped in her cell, and most mornings she was provided with a pan of cold water for her ablutions.

She had thought, even hoped, that René might come to her. He did not. Apparently, he had no need to explain himself, no inclination to savor the victory of his swift retaliation against her. She should have known he would not permit her to remain a threat to him. She might have if she had not been so disturbed over the discoveries she had made about him.

She mulled over the counterfeit notes in his possession again and again, wondering if her knowledge of them could even yet be used as a shield. One difficulty was that she had no idea what, if anything, he had done with them or about them. Another was that she could not use them if she could not see him to discuss it. But the strongest was that, given his credentials now, who would believe in the existence of the notes if he chose to deny any knowledge of them? Her claim would seem to be no more than the ravings of someone who already hears the whistle and crack of the whip.

The thought of the punishment that awaited her, the degradation of flogging and the branding iron, was a horror that she pushed to the back of her mind. Of much more concern was the fate of the others, particularly Pierre.

Again and again the wording of the arrest order came back to her. "The men known as Pierre, Jean, and Gaston Breton . . ." What did it mean? She had never known the Bretons by any other name, never heard even a whisper of anything else. It would not be surprising, given Pierre's escape from the galley, that he would take a cognomen, and yet the possibility had never occurred to her. She had always assumed that being so near the edge of the world here in Louisiane was enough, or at least that the Bretons had considered it so.

Pierre. It was not the whip that awaited him but hanging. It could not happen, not to gentle, wise Pierre. Her mind refused to accept that it was possible. She had come to rely on him, to feel that he would always be there, that among the shifting loyalties and changing alliances of the world, he would remain steadfast. No, it could not be.

But the memory of the words René had written, which she was not meant to see there, came back to her also. ". . . only one way to stop the forbidden trade known as smuggling, and that is by the vigorous prosecution of those caught in it so that they serve as an example . . ." They were, perhaps, to become that example.

Hour after hour, she sat staring at the wall, her body numb, her brain endlessly turning. And in the cell's dimness, the crystalline tracks of tears glistened as they crept down her face in her difficult and silent anguish.

On the afternoon of her third day of imprisonment, Cyrene was taken from her cell and marched under guard to the Government House. The crowd gathered outside buzzed with excitement as she appeared, much the same as they had on the night of the masquerade. This was no assemblage of the fashionable of the town, however. Inside the house, the large room where the guests of the marquis had gathered for their pleasure had become the official chamber for a meeting of the Superior Council. Their purpose was to ascertain the guilt or innocence of Cyrene and the Bretons. At the long table sat the appointed members of the council, including Intendant Commissary Rouvilliere, whose duty it was to preside over such meetings, a lawyer or two, the physician, and other men of standing. At the center of the table, in his capacity as head of His Majesty, King Louis's government in Louisiana, was the Marquis de Vaudreuil.

There was, however, a new prosecutor for the crown standing to one side leading and directing the tribunal. It was René Lemonnier.

The interrogation of the Bretons had already taken place. They stood alone and in chains before the judgment table, with no sign of legal representation, nothing other than their own words for their defense. To one side sat the evidence against them: their own goods in the containers clearly marked in English, still hung with the seals that had been put on them by the government clerks when they had been placed in the king's warehouse. At the near end of the table was the chair for witnesses, placed at a right angle to the council table so that the face of the person testifying could be seen by the accused, the prosecutor, and the council members alike. It was empty, however, as if the testimony against all of them had been completed. Standing to one side, as if he had just left the witness chair, was Touchet.

Cyrene was pushed into place beside the Bretons. She jostled against Pierre before she could regain her balance and he reached out awkwardly, his chains jangling, to steady her. She saw the rusty stains on his wrists and ankles, saw the concern in his eyes, and her heart thudded against her chest and the ache of tears rose once more behind her eyes. She gave the older man a quick, tremulous smile.

"I'm sorry, for everything," she whispered.

"Not I." The look in his eyes was rich and calm.

The intendant commissary rapped on the table. With a faintly acerbic edge in his voice, he said, "May we continue?"

Cyrene looked at the men before her. She had danced with many of them, laughed with them and their wives and daughters, broken bread with them at the governor's table. The governor himself had shown her a most decided partiality. Regardless, they stared back at her now as if she were a stranger. She felt herself diminished in a way she had not known in her prison cell. It was almost as if she had ceased to exist as a person, for these men, becoming instead a problem that must be solved with the least amount of trouble, the least unpleasantness.

It made her angry. The change felt good. She straightened her shoulders.

"This woman," René said, "is Cyrene Nolté. There is reason to believe that she is the leader of this organization of illicit trade. You have before you, gentlemen, account books with entries made out in her hand."

Pierre shuffled forward, his chains swinging. "This charge is ridiculous!"

René ignored him. "She was seen in active negotiation with Captain Dodsworth, the English commander of the vessel *Half Moon*, as we have heard from the witness Touchet. Moreover, the subterfuge that permitted the theft of the confiscated wares from the king's warehouse bears the marks of a feminine hand most likely to have been hers, and she was heard giving orders by the lieutenant who very nearly captured her that night. It is my contention that she is precisely what she has been called, a lady smuggler, and as such she should be punished to the fullest extent of the law, lest men conceive the idea that it is an easy way to a fortune."

What was René doing? Of all the men present, he had the best means of knowing exactly what her place was with the Bretons, exactly how successful she had been in her trading venture with the English captain. Had his pride been so damaged by the way she had left him that he required to see her dragged as low as possible for revenge? Or was he playing a deeper game?

"Cyrene has been with us only three years," Pierre said. "Our trading goes back much further."

René made a contemptuous gesture. "It may be true that you traded in a simple way. But deny if you can that you have made your greatest profit since she began to lead your expeditions."

"She went with us, yes, but she did not lead," Pierre said doggedly.

He was trying to protect her, Cyrene knew; the question of who led them had no importance to Pierre.

"Your profits have been greater these last few years, have they not? Answer, please, Jean Breton."

Jean looked miserable. At last he muttered, "Yes."

"Because this woman was with you?"

"It may have been a part of it, but—"

"Then I contend that she was the leader. That she has, in fact, been heard to call herself a lady smuggler."

"In jest only," Pierre insisted. "The responsibility was not hers!"

They were afraid for her, Pierre and Jean, afraid of how many more lashes of the whip she might receive, afraid she might be hanged. It was, she suspected as René continued to press the two men, exactly how he wanted them to feel. She had been brought before the court for that purpose and no other. She was sure of it when he put his next question.

"If she is not responsible for your recent prosperity, then how do you explain it? There is only one other way possible. Who is your backer?"

"There is no one," Pierre said.

"I think there is. I believe there is someone who has noticed your initiative, your modest gains, and sought to benefit. Tell us who that person is. Tell us who provided you with the funds for a larger operation, thereby assuring larger returns?"

They were pawns, the four of them—Pierre, Jean, Gaston, and herself. René obviously suspected that someone with high political connections, most likely Madame la Marquise or else the intendant commissary, was providing funds to the Bretons. He hoped to use their affection for Cyrene, if not fear for their own lives, to force the name of that person from them, thereby helping to prove or disprove the charges against the governor and his wife. In effect, it was not the Bretons and Cyrene who were on trial there at all, but the Marquis and Marquise de Vaudreuil.

Did the governor realize it? It was difficult to tell. Vaudreuil was a veteran of many political skirmishes. The blandly handsome façade of his face gave away nothing. Still, he knew who René was, must surely have seen his credentials as a special agent of the king. He was not a stupid man by any means, for all his smiling good grace.

But did it matter, any of it? There was no one behind the Bretons, Cyrene would wager her very life on it. If they could not provide René with the information he sought, what would there be left to do but to convict them of the charges against them and carry out the sentences that must and would be passed?

Pierre saw the implication of the questions directed at him also, for his voice was dull with despair as he repeated, "There was no one."

"I suggest that you lie," René said softly. "Think carefully before you suffer, and allow those you care for to suffer, for the sake of some high-born man who cares only for lining his pockets at the expense of your sweat and blood."

"There is no one, I swear this to you on the grave of my mother." Pierre's voice was so low that it could barely be heard.

"Why won't you believe us?" Jean cried.

Cyrene had heard enough.

She lifted her head, her eyes flashing. "He won't believe it because it isn't what he wants to hear. He speaks of others using our sweat and blood but is willing to do the same to get what he wants, what he needs for his greater glory!''

"Be silent!'' René snapped, his gaze hard as he willed her to obedience.

"Why should I, when it's our lives at stake?'' she shouted at him. "Who do you think you are to use us like this? Would you have us perjure ourselves to suit your ends? Do you know that here the punishment for perjury is death?''

"Silence,'' the intendant commissary said, but not loudly.

"We are damned if we say the truth and damned if we lie. It seems that what is required is a scapegoat. Very well! I will give you one.''

"Cyrene, no,'' Pierre said, his eyes coming alive with anguish as he turned to her. He swung back to the table. "You must listen to me, and me only. I am not just a smuggler. I am also—''

She could not let him speak. She raised her voice, infusing it with a cutting edge of sarcasm, her gaze blazing as she sought to hold their attention. "Hear me well! I am the leader of this desperate crew of smugglers! I, and no one else! There is no man behind us, high-born or not, and no other woman!''

There was the scrape of a chair and Intendant Commissary Rouvilliere got to his feet to lean across the table. "Woman? Who spoke of another woman? What do you know of such? You will tell us at once or be put to the test!''

Torture was not often used in the colony, at least officially, but the threat of it was always present in difficult cases. Cyrene heard Jean's groan of helplessness, could feel the color leave her face, but she refused to be cowed.

"There is no other woman, did you not hear me? I spoke of one because it is plain that—''

"Cyrene!''

It was the plea under the command in René's voice that made her pause. It was in his face also, along with rage and exasperation and something more she did not understand.

"It is plain,'' Rouvilliere said, "that the scandalous conduct of Madame Vaudreuil makes her immediately suspect.''

In the sudden quiet, the doors into the room swept open. There came the rustle of silk underskirts and the quick sharp tap of footsteps. Cyrene turned to see Madame Vaudreuil advancing into the chamber. The woman's head was held so high that the ribbons of her coif flew in the breeze of her passage, and her lips were a tight line in her pale face. She did not stop until she stood before the council table. It was, perhaps, an accident that she stood next to Cyrene, but it was one she did nothing to rectify.

"Madame," the governor said to his wife, "why come you here? It is not your place. You may leave us."

"I believe that my good name is being impugned in this council. I would defend it."

"That isn't necessary."

The marquise's eyes narrowed. "I will speak."

No one attempted to deny her further. Madame Vaudreuil watched the intendant commissary slowly ease back down into his seat, turned her head to look briefly, almost with approval, at Cyrene, then swung around to René.

"What this young woman says is true. I have never given money to her or her relatives for the purpose of trading with the enemies of France. I am a loyal subject of my king. The laws promulgated by his ministers in their wisdom concerning this colony may not be intelligent or to my liking, but it would be a matter of stupidity in me, the wife of the governor, to flout them. I am not a stupid woman."

Madame Vaudreuil stared around her as if waiting for a comment so that she might squash it. When none was forthcoming, she went on. "I have been accused of many things. I know this, but what do I care? Anyone who thinks that people of consequence accept the governing of distant colonies, living in squalor and ruling over thieves, exiles, and misfits merely for the glory is an imbecile. An office is like an estate. There are great expenses that must be met if it is to be properly managed. But like an estate, it should give a return to those who invest their time and energies in it. If this Louisiane does not return a reasonable revenue to my husband and myself, then we might as well have remained in Paris in comfort. This concept should be easily understood by anyone of sense.''

''Madame,'' René began.

''I am not finished! My husband is occupied at all times with the governing of this colony. It is not a sinecure, the office of governor, I assure you. It requires many long hours, much effort and patience, and the endless writing of reports for the lackwits in Paris who expect us to produce miracles. We are to enrich the coffers of the crown, keep the inhabitants of the colony safe and well and reasonably content, maintain peace and cooperation with the savages around us, prevent the incursions of the English to the east and the Spanish to the west, and all this with the outlay of a minimum from the king and with the constant meddling of men who have never set foot out of France and know nothing of conditions here. And who would not care if they did know! Since my husband concerns himself deeply with these affairs, it is left to me to see that we do not disperse our own fortune here with no return. This is my sole concern. My only connection with illicit trade was to invest in a venture or two before the late unpleasantness with England. Since then I have naturally abided by the conventions of war regarding such affairs. This is all I have to say on the matter.''

René gave the marquise a straight look. ''With all due respect, madame, what you have said cannot be so.''

Madame Vaudreuil drew herself up, her eyes icy with rage. ''Are you accusing me of being untruthful?''

''If I am wrong, I ask a thousand pardons, but I had the felicity of overhearing your agent Touchet engaging in criminal trade in your name with Captain Dodsworth aboard the *Half Moon*.''

''Never in my name!''

''I fear so, madame. Also for hashish and other such substances.''

Madame Vaudreuil turned slowly, her wide skirts swinging on their panniers in a majestic sweep as her gaze sought

and found Touchet. "You worm," she said, her voice virulent with scorn. "How dare you act without my orders? How
dare you?"

"But, madame," Touchet said, his thin face dissolving in
panic, "I thought . . . that is, you said . . . I understood any
profit would be welcome."

"Not that which harms my husband, dolt. Not that gained
in defiance of his most strict order. But where is this profit?
I have seen naught of it! If you carried out this trade, it was
on your own head, for your own gain. It was, in fact, a most
flagrant case of smuggling!"

"But, madame, please—"

"Smuggling," the marquise repeated to the room at large
as she turned away in a gesture of disdain, "is a crime for
which I suggest this man be bound over for trial."

Madame Vaudreuil was repudiating her henchman. Had
Touchet, in truth, overstepped the authority given him as she
claimed? Or was he being sacrificed, another scapegoat? Cyrene could not tell, though it seemed that the governor's wife,
having admitted so much concerning her pursuit of money,
had little reason to cavil at this one last detail. Or perhaps
that's what they were supposed to think? It might be that the
truth would be brought out when Touchet came to trial, if he
ever did. Again, it might be that they would never know.

Touchet did not seem hopeful of the outcome. He began
to curse and scream as the intendant commissary voiced the
reluctant order that sent the guards marching toward him.
The strident, panicked sound of his voice echoed in the
chamber as he was lifted and dragged away.

When the door had closed upon Touchet and it was quiet
once more, the governor's wife gave a curt nod, then swept
around and positioned herself to one side of the room. That
she did not intend to leave, and would deeply resent any
suggestion that she do so, was plain. A glance passed between husband and wife, and the governor inclined his head
in what might have been the smallest of bows to his lady.

"We must thank Madame Vaudreuil for her contribution

to these proceedings,'' René said, his tone courteous though a little dry, ''and for her condescension in giving them to us. I assume this issue is settled for the moment and we may now continue?''

The intendant commissary, at whom the last was directed, shifted uncomfortably in his seat, then nodded with only the briefest glance in René's direction.

''Thank you.'' René moved forward to stand between the council table and the prisoners. ''If I may have the indulgence of the gentlemen of the council, it is perhaps time that I became something of a witness as well as prosecutor in this most irregular affair. You will permit?''

''As you wish,'' the governor replied, and there was no demur from the other members. It was evident from the glances they exchanged that they were all aware of the special status René was able to claim and had no wish to have it recorded that they had obstructed him in the pursuit of his duty.

Cyrene, watching that byplay, felt a frisson of terror move through her. She had sensed before that René could be dangerous but never so strongly as at this moment. He was elegantly attired today in gray velvet with silver braiding. He also wore a wig, something that Cyrene had seen him without so often of late that in it he seemed a stranger. She thought fleetingly of the intimacies, the adventures, and the laughter she had shared with this man, and it was like a dream without substance, not quite real.

René clasped his hands behind his back and swept them all with an assessing glance. ''First of all, as you may all be aware, I was sent here to look into allegations of misconduct concerning the monies and management of this colony, with particular attention to the possibility of official participation in the trade with the English prohibited by the edict of the crown. When I arrived in New Orleans, the first step in my mission appeared to be to discover as much as possible about the smuggling that was so rife—how it was carried out, by whom, when, and where—before attempting to make a judgment of higher involvement. For this reason, I decided to set a watch for a time on the activities of some small trader suspected of smuggling. I singled out the prisoners as typical and began to monitor the flatboat where they lived and their comings and goings there. For the most part, I paid others to do the surveillance, though on occasion, over a period of nearly three months, I watched them myself in order to become thoroughly familiar with the situation.''

It was difficult to think of René at such a nefarious undertaking, which only went to show how credulous and lacking in judgment she was, Cyrene thought. Still, his explanation of how he had come to choose to watch the Bretons was too glib. Something about it nagged at her, though she could not quite grasp what it might be.

''One night while at this duty, I was attacked from behind, half stunned, then stabbed in the back. When I regained consciousness, I was in the river. I was rescued most fortuitously by Cyrene Nolté, not for any humane reasons, since she thought I was quite dead, but for the sake of the braiding on the coat I wore.''

A faint smile indented the corner of his mouth as he looked at Cyrene. She despised him for it and for so cleverly removing from himself any obligation to her for saving his life. He must not be thought ungrateful, heavens, no! But if he was willing to expose so much of the truth, what more would he tell? Would he, for instance, tell how he had come to join the Bretons?

''My position, as an injured man living on the flatboat, could not be bettered. My injuries were not major, but I exaggerated their effect in order to remain where I was. At the same time, I set myself to gain the confidence of the Bretons and Mademoiselle Nolté and succeeded to the point of being invited to join them in a trading venture.''

Once more his gaze sought hers, or so it seemed. Cyrene looked away, the tide of relief that rose inside her carrying a stain of color to her cheeks. It was a moment before she could attend again to what he was saying.

''The evidence against the Bretons was undeniable. They made little effort to hide their illegal trade. Added to this was certain other information that had been discovered in France concerning Pierre Breton that was damning, indeed. In fact, Breton is not his name at all. He, with his brother and his brother's son, are members of a most respectable, one might even say illustrious, family well known for their contribution to the establishment of France in the New World.''

Beside Cyrene, Pierre spoke out, his voice rough. ''If it please you, m'sieur, there is no need to go further. I freely confess to the crime of smuggling. I am ready to say whatever you will and accept the fullest penalty if you will allow me to speak to you in private.''

''You would perjure yourself? It isn't required,'' René said, and turned away to go on inexorably. ''Pierre Breton, as we know him, was from New France, where his family had been from the earliest days. He had a young wife with a rich father in the fur trade and an excellent knowledge of the wilderness. He also had a trapping concession that he shared with a friend, a man named Louis Nolté. One winter the two men went out to trap. They had a rich harvest of furs, beyond their dreams. There was a blizzard lasting four days, a whirlwind of snow and ice. Pierre came out of the wilderness alone, with the furs. He had been separated from Louis in the storm, he said. He had searched for him when it was over, but he was not to be found. For months there was no news of the fate of his friend. Then in the summer Nolté returned, as from the dead, and accused Pierre of theft and attempted murder.''

A murmur of comment went along the council table. The governor directed a fixed stare at Pierre, one that seemed to carry the light of recognition. It was, to Cyrene's knowledge, the first time the two men had come face-to-face in Louisiane. Pierre had always avoided the town and the kind of crowds that gathered around Vaudreuil. That the governor might remember him from New France was not surprising since he had remembered her grandfather and her mother.

At the same time, it was difficult to accept the events René described. Pierre and her father, friends all those years ago? There had never been a hint of it made to her. She could not believe it had been kept from her, could not think why that should be so. She turned her head to see Pierre staring straight ahead, his face as if carved from wax. As René began to speak again, she longed to scream at him demanding that he cease tormenting them, though at the same time she listened in tense concentration for what he would say next.

"Louis Nolté carried the scar of a wound in his breast. He also had Pierre's musket, which was engraved with his family insignia and known to be his greatest pride, and which he claimed Pierre had left behind in his flight. On Nolté's side, too, was the fact that Pierre had, without doubt, emerged from the blizzard with the furs. Pierre claimed that he had fired in self-defense, that Louis had attacked him. But what else could he be expected to say? He could give no reason for such an attack except the furs, and Nolté came from a family that was, if not as affluent as Pierre's, at least as respected. Pierre was convicted and sentenced to the galleys.

"But just as Pierre survived the blizzard, he survived this most punishing of punishments. After a few months, while off the coast of Saint-Domingue, his ship ran into a storm. It was blown onto a reef and sank with all hands. Except for Pierre. He swam ashore, leaving his identity behind on the bottom of the sea. He was reported dead. The news reached Paris at the same time that his young wife, supported by Louis Nolté, arrived there from the New World. The scandal in New France had made her father decide to give up his interests there and return to the mother country, carrying his daughter and Nolté with him. They went first to Paris; her father had, naturally, to show himself at Versailles to pay his court to the king, though he meant to establish himself as a merchant at Le Havre. Pierre's wife, supposing herself a widow, married Louis in a quiet ceremony. The couple decided to remain in Paris."

It fit. It fit all too well. The implications were almost too much to grasp, though Cyrene tried. There was no time for careful consideration, however.

René, pacing slowly between the council table and the prisoners, stopped in front of Jean. He watched him closely, though he spoke to the room at large. "Pierre managed in some way to get word to his brother Jean in New France. They arranged to meet in Louisiane. It was probably when they were re-united that Pierre learned of his wife's remarriage. He could not inform her that he was alive without risking a return to the galleys or even death for his escape. He may even have decided it would be best if he remained dead to her. He became Pierre Breton, a trader, and prospered after a fashion. The years passed. Then one day Louis Nolté, with his wife and daughter, walked off a ship from France. What happened then? How did it come about that the Nolté family, with both husband and wife ill with ship's fever, took up residence on the flatboat with the man who had tried to kill Louis and who had been married to Madame Nolté? What made it possible for them to do such a thing?"

Jean, returning René's hard stare with his own gaze clear and even a little amused, made no answer. It was as if he dared him to discover the truth. Beyond him, Gaston looked as stunned as Cyrene felt.

"Let us go back to France once again to see if the answer can be found. Louis Nolté was a man of means but not of wealth. He discovered in himself a passion for the amusements of Paris society: expensive parties, the theater and its actresses, and particularly the excitement of the gaming tables. His money did not last long, and he soon ran through his wife's marriage settlement and her inheritance from Pierre. He tried to borrow from his father-in-law, but he was a wily old man; he gave his daughter sufficient to keep her and his grandchild who had been born, but not a piastre to Louis. Nolté went to the moneylenders, always a mistake. In order to pay those debts, he began to be involved in certain unsavory schemes, among them the circulating of counterfeit notes. Over a period of time, he worked out various means of doing this, one of which involved gaining the trust of callow youths from the wealthy families of France and Europe who regularly made their way to Paris as to the center of the universe to gain experience and polish. One of these young men, when he realized how he had been duped, attempted suicide. His family investigated. Nolté's operation began to unravel. Fearing a scandal far worse than the one in New France, his wife's father used his influence and money to send Nolté to a form of exile in Louisiane. When his daughter insisted on accompanying her husband, he washed his hands of the entire family.

"By then, sixteen years had passed. Louisiane, once the privy of France, on the far edge of the world, indeed, had become more prominent with the appointment of the marquis as governor. Dispatches and letters passed back and forth as often as every six months. Perhaps Madame Nolté heard a rumor about a man who looked exactly like her dead husband. Perhaps Pierre could not bear not making himself known to her by some code, some form of communication. Possibly by this time the lady had begun to suspect that Nolté's version of the affair in New France lacked something of the truth, therefore neglected to mention the communication to her husband. Or there could have been a confrontation during which Madame Nolté learned Louis had tried to kill Pierre for her sake, for love of her and her money. Armed with this knowledge, did she then force her husband to go with her to Pierre when they arrived in Louisiane penniless and ill? No matter. Madame Nolté died of her fever in the arms of her first husband. Nearly three years went by, enough to allay suspicion, then Louis Nolté quietly disappeared one dark night, presumed drowned."

"Enough!" Pierre cried out, his voice strained, desperate. "Let Cyrene go, and also Gaston. Take me, but let them go!"

"Why should I do that?" René asked, his voice gentle.

"Because if you will, I will confess to the murder of Louis Nolté as well as to the charge of smuggling. I will admit it was I who knifed you and threw you into the river. I will tell you anything you want to know, this I swear! Only let the young ones go. They have no real part in this, particularly Cyrene. She came with us, yes, but there was nothing else for her to do. Let her go, I beg of you. Let them both go.''

20

T HE POWERS CONFERRED on René by the king were apparently without limit. No one attempted to gainsay him
as he accepted a part of Pierre's bargain, rejected part: Cyrene would be freed, Gaston would not. He directed that Jean
and Gaston be returned to the prison and Cyrene with them
so that she might collect her belongings. He effectively
brought the meeting of the Superior Council to an end by
dismissing the clerk who had been setting down the proceedings on paper and confiscating the records, declaring that for
all purposes the council had not, in fact, been in session. He
bid the council members a polite good day, then, with only
a single guard in attendance, took Pierre away to be closeted
with him.

His orders were carried out with dispatch. Before Cyrene
could collect her wits following Pierre's outburst, she had
been returned to the prison, then pushed out into the Place
Royale with her bundle of clothing in her arms.

She stood there in confusion, not sure where to go or what
to do. After a moment, she began to walk slowly in the
direction of the flatboat.

It was a lie; she knew it.

Pierre was not capable of killing. He might have injured
the man who was her father in self-defense, but he could not
have plotted as cold-bloodedly as René had suggested to
drown Louis Nolté. Nor could he have waited like some

assassin in the dark to catch René off guard, stab him in the back, and toss him into the river. It was simply not possible.

She knew it was not possible because she had seen René thrown into the river. It had not been the job of one man but of two. She remembered it plainly. The way the men had carried him, the way they had swung him between them, tossing him into the current like a piece of refuse. The way they had turned and hurried away. No, it was not Pierre.

Or was it?

Could it have been Pierre and Jean? There was something frighteningly familiar about the figures she remembered. And then on the flatboat when the two men had seen René, Jean had crossed himself as if he had need of protection from a ghost and Pierre had been less than pleased.

But no, she couldn't believe it, wouldn't believe it. If they had wanted René dead, what had there been to prevent them from finishing the job while he was injured? No.

As for her father, Pierre had often been short with him, exasperated that he had squandered the money he was given on drink and gaming and made no effort to contribute to his own maintenance, giving himself the airs of a gentleman while he lived off of Pierre's and Jean's labors. Why had Pierre let him stay? It must have been for her mother's sake at first. Later, it had perhaps been for hers, because she was her mother's daughter and he had grown fond of her. Because he had known that Louis Nolté would take her with him if he left and did not like to think of the kind of hand-to-mouth life she must lead with him.

Cyrene had been embarrassed by her father's lack of initiative, had tried so hard to make up for his shortcomings, for his sneers at the shelter over his head, at the menial tasks such as skinning animals and cleaning fish that were necessary to put food in his mouth. It was a sacrilege to speak or think ill of the dead, but if it had been her father who was supposed to have done Pierre an injury she would have sooner believed it. Certainly she had no trouble whatever featuring the man who had sired her as part of a counterfeiting scheme.

Counterfeiting. At least she had an inkling now of why René had used her so readily, so insistently. It had been revenge that drove him. He had not mentioned him by name or relationship, but the young man whom her father had driven to attempt suicide could only have been his brother. He must have enjoyed exacting reparation from her since he could not reach her father. No doubt the notes she had found in his coat had some connection with that affair. He may have thought to confront Louis Nolté with them, then use his power as the king's agent to bring him to justice. Balked of that, he had turned to her.

Her father and Pierre, both of them married to her mother. It seemed beyond belief that she had not known, that she had never heard so much as a whisper of that incredible tale.

But she had, of course, and recently. It was the governor who had spoken of her mother's first husband. He had not known the whole of the story. How confused he had been when she denied all knowledge. Why had her mother not told her as a child? Was she so ashamed? Was it because her mother had known Pierre was not dead and had thought to avoid any careless mention of him, which might set gossip and inquiries in motion? Or was it because she had not learned of it until she reached Louisiane? Later, on the flatboat, her mother had been so ill, had so quickly died. There had not, perhaps, been time to explain.

Pierre could have told her. The past was not much discussed in Louisiane in general, however. Moreover, from what she knew of Pierre, Cyrene suspected he had thought to spare her the knowledge that her mother was a bigamist in the eyes of the law and an adulteress in the eyes of God.

He was like that. His confession just now had been made, she was certain, to protect her and Gaston. He would have absolved Jean if he could, but it was not possible, so he had tried to save the young ones. In the same way, he had, she was sure, quietly permitted his wife to think him dead. It would have been an accident—the chance mention of some resemblance, an oblique reference to a man who had cheated the galleys—that had made her think he still lived. Further back, when Louis had tried to kill Pierre in New France during the blizzard, it had been that same instinct that had made him fail to tell exactly what had happened. Pierre had thought Louis dead at his hand, his body lost in the wilderness; he would have seen no reason to brand Louis an attempted murderer or become involved with the authorities over something that had been settled. It was a mistake for which he had paid dearly.

Granted, it was his nature to avoid hurting anyone unnecessarily, to sacrifice his own happiness, even his life, for those he cared for, but she did not think he would kill for those reasons. She did not believe he had tried to kill René, whatever the cause. It could not be denied, however, that someone had, not once but twice. It was possible that Pierre and Jean had been present at the first attempt, had been drawn into disposal of the body. It followed, then, that by admitting to the crime, Pierre was trying once more to protect someone else. But who?

Who?

She stopped suddenly on the gangplank to the flatboat so that it bounced, nearly catapulting her into the water. The answer was so plain that it was as if she had known it all the time but had refused to see. She examined it with frowning concentration, her chest filling with the hard, deep breath of growing rage.

Her face hardened, and she moved swiftly onto the flatboat. She flung her bundle down inside the cabin, tore it open, took out a few things, added others, including her knife in its sheath. In less than a half hour, she was stepping into the pirogue, which had been returned to the flatboat following their arrest. She picked up the paddle and sent the craft gliding out into the river.

Night came upon her miles away. She made shore and ate the cold *sagamite* she had brought, not daring to light a fire for fear of what, or who, it might draw to her. Rolling a bearskin around her, she curled up in the bottom of the boat and slept. When the gray and cloudy dawn came, she was on her way once more.

Little Foot met Cyrene at the door of her hut. The Indian woman's face was impassive as she watched Cyrene approach. She might have been expected to show surprise, even joy, at seeing her free. Instead, there was nothing except stoic acceptance.

They exchanged greetings. Cyrene forestalled an offer of hospitality by saying first, "Where is Quick Squirrel, your daughter?"

"Ah," Little Foot said, a quick exclamation that expressed anger and pain and disgust, "I knew it would come to this."

"Yes. Why did you agree?"

"It was the father of my son who asked."

Little Foot led Cyrene to her daughter's hut, called out for permission to enter, then left Cyrene there. Quick Squirrel came to the door and stood looking at Cyrene for long moments before she stepped back to permit her to move inside.

It was dim and smoky inside the hut, but it smelled of fresh-cut wood from its recent building. The furnishings were meager: a sleeping bench, a few pots and baskets, a bunch or two of dried herbs hanging from the roof poles. Food bubbled in a pot hanging over the center fire. On the sleeping bench lay Louis Nolté.

He was unshaven and pale, and there was a wild look in his red-rimmed eyes as he stared behind her as if he expected to see a troop of soldiers at her back. He sat bolt upright, clutching a bearskin coverlet to his chest.

"How did you find me?" he demanded, his voice no more than a croak.

"All I had to do was think of the kind of man you are."

He hardly blinked. "Who have you told? Who else is coming?"

"No one. They think you are dead."

"Good, good. You always were a good girl."

There was an ingratiating whine with an undertone of cunning in his voice that set Cyrene's teeth on edge. "Pierre is in trouble over you; he has been arrested. You must come and help him."

"Madness! What makes you think I could?"

"Because it's Lemonnier who is behind it, as I think you know."

He cursed in virulent phrases. "I thought you were keeping him occupied."

"Not enough so, apparently."

"I am the one who needs help, Cyrene, *ma chère*. The man is seeking to destroy me. He—he is a fiend, hounding me here, following me all this way from Paris. He wants to see me dead."

"And what of you, haven't you tried to kill him, too?"

The man on the bench sent a sharp look at Quick Squirrel, who had lifted her head to listen. He jerked his head at her, and the Indian girl rose and left the hut. He turned back to Cyrene.

"I had to stop Lemonnier, didn't I?"

"Why? You were supposed to have drowned."

"That was clever, wasn't it? But he wouldn't believe it. He wouldn't go away. He made me stay here with these savages, hiding like some animal in the woods. I couldn't see people, had no food worthy of the name, no drink, no amusements. It was intolerable."

No doubt it was, for him. Cyrene looked at the man who was supposed to be her father, and revulsion moved over her. He had aged considerably since she had last seen him. His face was shrunken and his hands palsied, and there was about him the unmistakable look of pox-ridden debauchery. She wondered that she had never seen it before.

"You were afraid of René," she said with what she recognized in herself as conscious cruelty.

"Yes, I was afraid! You don't know him. He was watching, always watching. He won't give up."

"So you stabbed him from behind, then ran away to Pierre and Jean for help in cleaning up the mess you had made."

''He was a danger to us all. If he had put me and Pierre and the others all in prison, what would have become of you?''

''The others are in prison now,'' she said, her voice cold.

He shrugged. ''It's not my affair.''

''You brought René Lemonnier down on them by destroying his brother.''

He shifted his eyes away from her clear gaze. ''He told you that? They were both too proud. His brother shouldn't have gambled if he couldn't afford to lose, shouldn't have been so trusting. Gullible idiots, all of them, not smart enough for me.''

''Not smart enough to recognize counterfeit when they saw it?''

''Except this René. When I heard he was in New Orleans, I knew why he had come. The notes. Should never have used the same ones. But I had a trunk half full, hidden away; a man can never tell what might be needed. Your mother didn't know. She wouldn't have come with me if she had known. She was like that.''

''René traced you to Louisiane by the notes you passed in town.''

''After three years, he tracked me down. He won't give up.''

Louis Nolté rambled on, repeating himself, damning himself. It had been Jean who had arranged for Louis to stay with Little Foot. He had been with her and her daughter on their journey to the gulf to meet with Pierre and Jean; that had been the reason why the Indian woman would not let Cyrene into her hut. Little Foot had been too knowing, too sharp of tongue for his liking. He had seduced her daughter Quick Squirrel with trinkets and fine words. That had amused him for a time, especially since it enraged Little Foot. But it had soon begun to pall. He had been elated when Cyrene became René's mistress. He had thought Lemonnier would be satisfied with that revenge and go away at last. But no, he had settled deeper into the society of the town and he still sent out his spies.

"So you hired thugs and attacked him again," Cyrene said, "as you hired the assassin to creep up on him while he lay injured on the flatboat."

"You ruined it for me. Why did you do that? I just wanted to get you out of the way so that the others could kill him."

Had he? She touched her fingers briefly to the bruise that still lay under her cheekbone. It was impossible to be sure, impossible to know what he might have done to her if she had obstructed his purpose. In any case, it no longer mattered.

"Listen to me. Pierre and Jean and Gaston are being held in prison, but it's really you that René wants. He has the authority to pardon them and it's possible he might do that if you will give yourself up to him."

"Give myself up!" He stared as if he thought her mad.

"You owe this to Pierre, to them all."

"I owe them nothing!"

"You wronged Pierre in New France all those years ago; you sent him to the galleys, took his furs, took his wife. Now René is after us all for what you did to his brother and Pierre is once more taking the blame for your crimes in order to protect me. If you are any kind of a man, you will do what is right."

"Do you take me for a simpleton? What do I care what happens to Pierre?"

"They know he escaped from the galleys. He'll hang! You will at least be returned to France for your trial for counterfeiting."

"Yes, and then be hanged or sent to the Bastille, which is a death sentence itself."

"You would let Pierre die in your place?"

"But of course!"

"I won't, not after all he has done. If you aren't willing to give yourself up, then I will have to tell René where he can find you."

"My own daughter?" he cried, his gaze wide, staring.

She stood looking into his watery eyes, and something she had begun to suspect as she listened to René's summation before the council became a certainty. "But that's just it," she said slowly, "I am not your daughter."

"What nonsense is this? Of course you are!"

"Legally, perhaps. But I have always known you were married to my mother a bare month before I was born. I thought it was a forced trip to the altar as with so many others, that I was the reason you and my mother weren't happy. But it wasn't that, was it? How long was it before she began to suspect what you had done?"

A smile twisted his face. "Not long, but she wasn't a fighter like you. She blamed herself, thought she must have done something to make me love her enough to try to kill Pierre."

"It was really my grandfather's money and the furs."

"How little you know of men, or love, if you think so—though they counted, oh, yes, they counted. But your mother is dead. And if Lemonnier doesn't go back to Paris soon, so will he be dead. Your grandfather, stingy old bastard that he is, can't live forever. I wonder what would happen then to his estate if you were to die in the wilderness, a victim of the savages and the recent unrest among the Choctaw? And if I was to wander into New Orleans from downriver, miraculously alive?"

He was not sane, perhaps the effects of the pox but probably a tendency of long-standing. It was so quiet Cyrene could hear the wind sighing through the branches of the trees outside, the murmur of voices from the next hut and the distant barking of dogs.

He was becoming restive. She must speak. "You would be the heir, I suppose, since everyone considers you my next of kin, but I am not going to die."

"Aren't you, *chère*? Aren't you? You are so headstrong and so foolhardy for venturing out here alone, and life is so uncertain."

She watched him bring the long knife out from under the bearskin, saw the blade of polished steel gleam in the dim light of the hut, and she felt no fear, no anger, no surprise, nothing except cold, exacting contempt. She reached for the knife in the sheath that hung from her waist, hidden among her skirts. The hilt was solid, giving the weapon a comforting weight in her hand as she brought it out and turned the winking tip toward Louis Nolté.

"You were right," she said, "I am a fighter."

He laughed as he came up off the bed wearing only a pair of breeches. "Maybe, but no match for a man."

"You think not?" She eased away from him to give herself room, her quick glance looking for obstacles that would have to be avoided, measuring the distance to the door as Gaston and Pierre had taught her in the lessons they had thought sufficient to discourage importunate suitors.

"I am taller, heavier, and have longer arms."

"You tried once to kill Pierre and three times to kill René, and they still live. I expect I will, too."

He lunged for her, his knife a silver arc cutting toward her belly. She leaped aside and felt the waft of air sliced by the blade. A fierce and fearful joy surged in her veins. He had none of Gaston's strength and agility and little of his watchful cunning.

"You're getting old," she taunted, "old and sick."

"I should have put you out of my way years ago." He feinted, then slashed at her in a backhand swing.

She whirled, putting the fire between them, giving him a mocking look across it. As he started around it toward her, she thrust her toe in its rough leather moccasin into the piled ashes and kicked upward, flinging bits of hot coals and roiling smoke into his face. He yelled, throwing up his free hand. She followed her advantage, thrusting toward his knife arm. He wrenched backward, but her knife tip sliced through flesh, leaving a welling red streak behind.

"You little bitch," he gasped, and plunged toward her, his eyes wild.

She could have finished him then. It was just a matter of
stepping to one side, ducking under his blade, and letting
him impale himself on her own. But she had been right; he
was crazed and ill. Whatever he might have done in the past,
whatever he might intend to do, she was not his executioner.

She sidestepped, diving away from him toward the sleeping bench and the bearskin that lay half on it, half on the
floor. She scooped it up in her left hand, whirling it over her
arm. This was the moment of her greatest danger, she realized, when she had lost her willingness to kill, when all she
wanted was to disarm the man before her and take him back
to explain to the governor and the council who he was and
what he had done.

Louis Nolté had thought to overpower her with strength
and speed. He could not do it. The pain she had inflicted
was so humiliating and her elusiveness such a frustration that
he dropped his cocky assurance to concentrate on showing
her she could be bested. He became crafty, and so more
deadly.

Cyrene retreated before him, her movements smooth, her
gaze intent. Twice she fended off his flashing blade with the
bearskin. Twice she avoided the traps he set: the corner of
the hut, the support arm for the pot over the fire. The weight
of the coverlet was tiring, making her shoulder ache. An end
slipped, drooping ' the packed earth floor. Her foot come
down on it. She stumbled.

Nolté leaped at her. In a flash, she swung the bearskin so
that it flared out like a thick net, enveloping his head and
arms in its folds. Bending swiftly, she shot out her left leg
and hooked her foot around his ankle. He plunged forward.
She twisted aside, trying to evade his fall. His flailing arm
caught her. She staggered headlong and was carried to the
hard earth floor with him.

Her breath was jarred from her in a soundless grunt as she
struck the packed dirt. Pain radiated through her shoulder
and hip and also in her knees where he landed on them. She
wrenched herself over, trying to get away from him. Gasping

curses, he grappled with her, then whipped the bearskin from his head. It landed in the fire. Breathing the acrid smell of burning fur, Cyrene wrestled with the man she had once thought of as her father. He raised his knife arm. She caught his wrist with her left hand. His teeth were bared in a grimace. Sweat beaded on his forehead, clinging to his brows. Her arm began to tremble with the effort to keep the knife from her.

Little Foot was outside somewhere beyond the hut. The Indian woman would come to her aid if she knew it was needed. Or would she? In any case, Cyrene had no breath, no time to call out.

She struggled back and forth, trying with desperation clouding her mind to roll Nolté from her, pushing with her feet for purchase. He could not be dislodged. Her foot touched the flaming bearskin. She hooked the toe of her moccasin under it and kicked, rolling once more and dragging it over them.

She felt the heat through her skirts, saw the flare as the material began to catch fire. Nolté's legs were bare to the knee. He gave a hoarse yell, jerking away from her as he kicked at the bearskin. Cyrene shoved him and scrambled away as he tumbled backward. She pushed to her feet, swaying, beating out the blue flames that licked at her skirt without taking her eyes from Nolté.

Nolté tried to get up, then collapsed on the dirt floor. He let his knife fall to the floor as he clutched his leg, gasping, "Cyrene . . . help. Help me."

She straightened a little, watching him carefully. Her grasp on her knife tightened. The bearskin lay in a smoldering heap beside him.

"There's a coal stuck to my leg." He was jerking in spasms. "Get it off, get it off!"

She moved a step closer.

"Hurry . . . please."

She didn't trust him, but that distrust was new and he had

been a part of her life for long years. She held her knife ready but stepped closer, dropping to one knee at his side.

His eyes narrowed. He let go of his leg, at the same time reaching like a striking snake for his knife. Beyond them the door of the hut opened, and in the light Cyrene saw the sheen run along his blade's edge as he turned it upward, ready to rend and eviscerate when he stabbed.

It was a trick. She was ready. She began her thrust, aiming for the heart with her shoulder muscles knotted and every ounce of her strength behind it.

"No!"

The agonized shout came from the doorway. There was a fluttering sound like the wings of pigeons, followed by a dull thud. Nolté fell back with a strangled cry, his arms outflung. A knife hilt quivered in his chest just under the breastbone.

Cyrene's blade met only air. She recovered, turning to stare.

It was the elder of the Bretons who crouched half in, half out of the low door. Behind him was René, and also Jean and Gaston.

"Pierre," she whispered, then added the word that rose unbidden in her mind. "Papa."

His face twisted. He moved forward into the hut a step, then another. He stopped. Cyrene rose to her feet. She moved toward him, then came to a halt, uncertain. She searched the face of the man who had fathered her and saw the slow rise of tears in his fine blue eyes.

"Papa," she said again.

He opened his arms. She ran to be caught in them, held close in their gentle solace, their tempered and solid belonging.

It was a week later, after Touchet had been sentenced to the galleys, when René came to propose.

He was most formally attired in wig and *justaucorps* of blue velvet. His silver shoe buckles gleamed and the tricorne tucked under his arm was trimmed with a white plume. He looked as out of place in the flatboat cabin as a diamond in a dung heap. Not that Cyrene considered the cabin a dung heap by any means, but his splendor seemed excessive, a pointed reminder of the inescapable differences between them.

She was cooking the evening meal, making biscuits to go with the squirrel stew that simmered over the fire. Pierre was out on the front deck, whittling wooden spoons. Jean and Gaston had gone to set out hooks for catfish to add to their provisions since it had been agreed that their days of smuggling were over, at least for some time.

Cyrene was standing at the worktable with flour to her wrists and biscuit dough in her hands as René came through the door. She stared at him until her eyes began to burn, then she lowered her head and went on with what she was doing, placing the raw biscuit she held in a greased Dutch oven, squeezing off another one from her bowl of dough.

"How are you, Cyrene?" he asked. She was thinner, her face more angular. He had done that to her, and the knowledge was an ache inside him.

"Well enough. Would you care for something to drink?"

"No, thank you."

Something in his voice made her hurry into speech. "I'm glad you came. I've been thinking of sending a note to tell you how grateful I am—we all are for the pardons."

"It was little enough. I trust there have been no repercussions among your father's friends?"

"No. I believe they consider that if the Bretons received their freedom for favors given, it was not Pierre who paid."

Her voice was carefully neutral, which was more telling, René thought, than the most bitter resentment. "I'm sorry."

She shrugged without looking at him.

"I've discovered that Pierre, wily old fox that he is, didn't tell me much that I couldn't have discovered for myself given time, except, of course, for where Nolté was hiding."

A smile flickered over her mouth. "I'm not surprised."

"No."

It made her uneasy, his standing there before her so formally. "There's a stool there by the fire if you care to sit down."

"Not while you stand."

"I don't mind, really."

He gave her a smile. "I do."

She finished the biscuits and cleaned her hands by rubbing them together until the dough rolled up and fell off, then rinsing them in a pan of water. Then she spooned a little melted lard over the tops of the biscuits to help them brown evenly, put the lid on the Dutch oven, and carried it to the fireplace. Raking aside the coals, she set the heavy oven on a bed of hot ash and ladled coals on top of it. She checked her stew, stirring the rich brown gravy with its aroma of onions, garlic, and peppers. It was doing well, the meat becoming nicely tender. She returned to the table, where she began to clear away the things she had been using.

"Could you leave that a moment?" René said. "I would like to talk to you."

"I thought that's what we were doing." She reached for a damp cloth and began to wipe up the dusting of spilled flour. She refused to look at René for fear of what she might see. What could he want? He sounded so serious and yet personal. If he had the effrontery to ask her to become his mistress again, she would not be responsible for what she did.

He drew a deep breath. "Very well. You know, don't you, that there was never any danger, to any of you, when you were brought before the council, that I could never, would never, harm you and yours?"

"I may know it now. I didn't then, none of us did."

"I am more sorry than I can say for having to put you through that, but I had a job to do. It was important to know what the Vaudreuils would do and say when confronted with Touchet's guilt."

"And now you are satisfied?"

"Reasonably so. There are undoubtedly abuses in this administration, but not to the point of treason, and there's nothing to say that a replacement would be any better. With Touchet behind a galley oar, there should be considerably fewer such abuses in the future.''

''Then I suppose your gambit was successful.''

''Not if I lose you by it.''

''You cannot lose me,'' she said evenly as her brown eyes clashed with his. ''In the sense that you mean, I was never yours.''

''That may be so; I won't quibble over it. I am only trying to say that I want you with me always. I want you to become my wife.''

''That is the most insulting—your what?''

He had roused her from her damnable calm, at any rate. It made him feel better for her to show at least a little disturbance since his own heart was pounding in his chest. ''I want you to become my wife. I have spoken to your father. He knows that I'm a second son with few prospects for some time beyond the income to a piece of land given me by my father, but I believe that the king will grant me a concession here in Louisiane in return for my services to him. I would like for you to share it with me, to help build something worth having here in the New World. It's what you spoke of once, to have a piece of land. Your father and the others would always be welcome there. If you will agree, I will spend my life making recompense—''

''No.''

''I know that you have no reason to trust me as a husband. It was the king's idea to give me a reputation as a womanizer, a ruse to make my supposed disgrace greater and my appeal to the governor's wife more certain. It also amused him, I think, to turn me into a libertine for the good of France when so many had accused him of the same to her ill. But I swear to you it isn't in my nature; I pledge that I will be faithful to you.''

She threw down the cloth she was holding and turned away from him. ''Your pledges, like your repute, are of no interest to me. I don't want recompense from you.''

"I know you have a right to be bitter, but I never meant to hurt you. I just want to take care of you. I want—"

"Please!" she said, her voice raw and her hands, hidden among her skirts, clenched into fists. "I can take care of myself. You owe me nothing. Whatever is done, is done. You did what you came here to do; your brother is avenged and your duty is completed. The best thing now would be for you to go back to France and forget about it."

"Is that what you intend to do? Forget?"

She turned to look at him, her eyes dark but unflinching. "As soon as I can."

He wanted to take her in his arms and shake her, or kiss her until she was weak and breathless, from lack of air if nothing else. The proud tilt of her head prevented it, that and his own guilt. He had done enough to injure the bright self-respect that was so much a part of her. Even if he could force her to capitulate, he would not do so. At least he would not use physical coercion unless it was absolutely imperative.

"Then," he said, inclining his head in a bow, "I will leave you to it."

Cyrenne did not watch him walk away. She could not, for the blur of tears in her eyes.

The Bretons and Cyrene were at the dinner table when the message came from the governor. The marquis requested the opportunity to speak to Mademoiselle Cyrene on a matter of importance. Would she do him the honor of a visit as soon as possible, preferably within the hour?

It was the equivalent of a command. She was not sure the governor would not send an armed escort for her if she did not arrive in a reasonable time. There was no question of not going, of course. She had been the instrument of considerable embarrassment for the marquis and his wife, and if she could make up for it in some way, she would, if only by swift compliance with his request.

The Marquis de Vaudreuil was in his study when Cyrene arrived. His wife was entertaining friends in the salon but came out to greet Cyrene with the utmost cordiality before

showing her to the room the governor used for his paper-
work.

"My husband wishes to speak to you alone, mademoiselle. I trust you will consider carefully what he asks." There
was speculation in the face of the governor's wife.

"Willingly, but may I know what it will be?"

"He will tell you himself, but believe me when I say he
does not take the matter lightly."

"Yes," Cyrene said, more mystified than ever and not
completely trustful of the smile the other woman gave her.
There was no time for more, however. Madame Vaudreuil
had reached the study door and turned the knob. She put
her head into the room, announced Cyrene, and, with a
quick, conspiratorial wink, went away back toward the salon.

Cyrene pushed open the door and stepped into the study.
The marquis put down a paper he was studying and came
forward to bow over her hand. A pair of *fauteuil* chairs sat
before a small fire, and he led her to one before spreading
the skirt of his coat and dropping gracefully into the other.
He took out a snuffbox, took a pinch, then snapped it shut
and had recourse to his handkerchief. He put the snuffbox
away in his waistcoat pocket.

"It was kind of you to come so promptly. I would not have
requested it on such short notice, but the matter is one of
some urgency."

"Please don't consider it. How may I be of service?

"Many ways, mademoiselle," he said, smiling, "many
ways. You will remember our play?"

"Yes, certainly."

"None can play the part of the lovelorn mistress so well
as you; you were preserved from prison and other harm for
this, I have no doubt. But rehearsals must recommence at
once if we are not to lose what we have gained."

This was the matter of such urgency? Cyrene hid her surprise as best she could, though there was still a touch of
asperity in her voice as she said, "Tonight?"

"Unfortunately not," the governor said, lowering his

lashes in a pensive expression. "You see, one of our principal players is packing to leave us."

She suspected the governor of levity at her expense. She was certain she had seen a flash of laughter, instantly suppressed, in his eyes. "Who might that be?"

"Lemonnier. For some reason he has taken a sudden dislike to our fair land of Louisiane. Word has come that *Le Parham* has been delayed at Belize for a few days for the replacement of a faulty mast that was only discovered on the way downriver. Fortunate, was it not, that they did not put out into the gulf before the defect was found? The outcome of it, however, is that Lemonnier intends to have himself conveyed to Belize to join the ship for the voyage to France. He must not be allowed to do this."

"For the sake of a play?"

"It's a most entertaining piece, you will agree? But no. We are in need of all the colonists we can acquire here. Until this afternoon, Lemonnier had great plans to become a landholder, to be an exporter of indigo and myrtle wax candles, to establish himself as a man of substance and responsibility who might be depended upon to contribute much to the good of the community. Now he goes. I ask myself why. I ask myself how he can be persuaded to stay. You, mademoiselle, are the answer."

"I? That's absurd."

"Is it? Can you deny that if you had agreed to marry him he would have remained here to do all that I said?"

"How did you—"

"Never concern yourself with how. Can you deny it?"

The marquis was, in his way, a formidable man. He hid it well behind his air of graceful assurance, but it was no less true. "No," she said shortly, "but he has no real wish either to make me his wife or to settle here."

"He asked you, did he not?"

"Well . . . yes."

"Why could you not agree?"

"Because he did not want—"

"Nonsense! It was because you did not feel worthy or rather was afraid he did not think you worthy but had asked in spite of it. In other words, it was pride."

"I did not care to be married out of duty or pity!"

"Few men feel it a duty to marry their mistresses. You should have fallen into his arms with glad cries and sweet kisses."

"Because he is a man of—of substance who does me the honor to correct the position in which he placed me by force? You have a very odd idea of what will make a happy marriage!"

He lifted a shoulder. "Ah, happiness, that is another matter. Marriage is an alliance, hopefully one that will do the most good for the greatest number, which may only incidentally be the husband and wife."

"I am to marry him, in your view, for the good of your play and the colony?"

He inclined his head graciously. "In a word, yes."

"You are wasting your time," she said with just an edge of triumph. "He won't ask me again."

"I fear you may be right. But I believe he might listen if you were to ask him."

Heat sprang into her face. She ignored it. "When he is even now packing to return to France? Why should he do that?"

"Because he loves you."

"Oh, please, that isn't a fair argument."

"It happens to be true. I have never seen a man so torn between the dictates of his heart and his duty to his king. It drove him to desperate means to find a quick solution to the problem of proving the loyalty of my wife and myself."

"You knew what he was doing?"

"I did not know. I suspected only."

"And you let him go on?"

He waved a hand. "I could not stop him. In any case, Lemonnier and I both know that these things are decided not on merit or lack of it, but on influence. It is a lamentable system, even a decadent one, but it works in its way. As a representative of France, I take pride in governing in the name of my king and using my abilities to their utmost. It's better than being a sycophant at court, fighting for the honor of holding the king's basin when he is ill.''

She returned abruptly to what he had said, able now to deal with it. ''It isn't love René feels for me. If anything, it's lust.''

''As strong an emotion as any.''

''But not one on which to base a marriage.''

''It can be a poor thing without it. But if you will not be married, I fear you must be ready to accept the consequences.''

''Consequences?'' Her voice was sharp, for she had the feeling they had come finally to the meat of what the governor meant to impart to her.

''Lemonnier, I fear, is a bit unscrupulous.''

''What do you mean?''

''When he left France, he had with him one or two blank *lettres de cachet* signed by the king in case of need. Very convenient instruments, these. They allow the bearer to remove the person whose name he places in the blank and to hold him, or her, in close confinement indefinitely.''

She stared at him, unable to believe what he seemed to be saying. ''You mean that René—''

''So I understand.''

''He can't!''

''He can. The king's signature makes it imperative for those in authority, myself included, to render him any aid necessary to secure the person he indicates.''

She looked at him for long seconds. ''Why are you telling me this? If it's true, why not just arrest me?''

The governor pursed his lips. ''Because you are a beautiful woman and I like you, but also because Lemonnier will use the *lettre de cachet* to take you away, and you are needed in Louisiane fully as much as he. It occurred to me that if you were to decide on marriage after all, if you were to go to him and say so, you both might stay.''

She got to her feet. ''I'll go to him, all right, and it's very likely he will stay in Louisiane, though not in the way you wish. When I am through, he may need a land concession in Louisiane, as a place to be buried!''

Cyrene's fuming thoughts kept pace with her quick footsteps as she made her way from the governor's house to René's lodgings. The perfidy of the man, to plan her removal from Louisiane in such a way! It was beyond belief, unforgivable. When did he mean to send the soldiers for her? In the middle of the night? More than likely, she would have been given no time to say good-bye, no time to pack; it would be just like him. And where would he take her? To his father's *château*? What then? Would she be a prisoner the rest of her life, kept under lock and key except for such times when it pleased him to permit her freedom? And would he visit her to take his pleasure or allow her to languish, forgotten and alone? She would die before she submitted to such a life.

No, she would kill him.

Martha let Cyrene in, then, with one look at her set and flushed face, the serving woman retreated to the kitchen regions. Cyrene advanced into the salon toward René, who stood before the fireplace with his hands behind him. A wary look hovered in his eyes as he watched her.

''I have just come from the governor,'' she said without preamble.

''I trust you found him well.''

''Oh, please, have done with the courtesies,'' she said in scathing tones. ''I have had an incredible tale from him and I want it explained.''

''A tale?''

''About a *lettre de cachet*.''

''Ah. What of it?''

Her eyes blazed as she came closer to him. ''Is it true?''

''If it is?''

"It will be," she said deliberately, "the most base and despicable trick I have ever heard of in my life."

"Because I want you with me?"

"You admit it!" she cried. "I couldn't believe it. I thought it must be a lie, some story to make me come here. I should have known it was just your style, just the sort of high-handed tactics you would take to get what you want! Dear God, is there nothing you won't do?"

"I asked you to marry me and you refused," he said, his face grim.

"That doesn't give you the right to take me against my will!"

"I don't need anything to give me the right. I have the power of the king."

"Which you have used for your own revenge!"

The flush of temper lay under the bronze of his skin. "Not yet, but press me and I well may!"

"Not yet, indeed! Why else would you make me your mistress?"

"Because I needed you more than I needed honor. Because I was afraid to let you out of my sight lest you do some wild thing that would force me to let you go to the flogging post though I would feel every lash on my own heart. Because I love you beyond thinking or telling; beyond duty or justice or pride of class; more than the service of my king, the towers of my father's house, or the cool and shining glories of France itself." His voice softened. "I am bound to you and you to me. Why else were we born? Why else did the fates send you here and deliver me to you? Why else did you save my life unless it was to let me love you?"

When he fell silent, she drew in her breath with a gasp, not knowing until then that she held it. She swallowed and licked her lips. Her voice low, she said, "I will not be taken to France by force."

Anger swept over him and with it despair. He could do no more, say no more. He had let her see his soul and to her it was as if he had not spoken. He swung away from her, striding to the writing table. He picked up a foolscap sheet that lay there and tore it across once, twice. Turning, he moved to her, took her hand, and slapped the pieces of torn paper into her palm.

He moved away from her as if he could not bear to be near, saying over his shoulder, "There is your *lettre de cachet*. You are free, free of me, free to remain here in this benighted wilderness if that is what you want. Go. Get out, now! Before I change my mind."

Free. She supposed she was, and yet she had never felt less so. There were ties of the heart stronger than any prohibition, any prison wall. Love and concern, that of Pierre and Jean and Gaston for her, kept her close to them now for fear of causing them worry. The days and the nights, the joys and the pain she had shared with René Lemonnier held her to him just as strongly, perhaps more surely.

It was odd. She had thought she could not depend on him, could not trust him, and yet she had depended on him to hold her, trusted him to use the *lettre de cachet* to keep her with him. It was only because she had been so certain he would that she had dared to goad him, dared to demand to know why he wanted her.

She had gone too far. She had become so used to pretending to doubt him that she had failed to accept his love when it was offered. She had wanted to hear more, to have some sort of proof so that she could find the words, and the right time, to tell him that she loved him, too.

The proof was in her hand. The time was now. Before it was too late.

She lifted her head. Her voice low, she said, "Stay with me."

He turned slowly. "What?"

"Stay with me," she repeated with tears shining like liquid gold in her eyes. "I love you. I will die if you go back to France without me. Don't go. Stay with me."

"Always. Before God, always, my Cyrene."

He was upon her in a single stride. He caught her in the

hard circle of his arms and swung her around so that her cloak whirled about her, sweeping over the writing table and sending papers fluttering, sliding from its surface. She clasped her arms around him, dropping the pieces of the letter she held. They showered to the floor like the petals of flowers, lying with the other sheets in a windblown drift.

On the pieces of the *lettre de cachet* Cyrene had dropped the line for the name was blank. There was another *lettre*, however, half hidden among the scattered sheets. On it in slashing black script was her name.

As he spun with Cyrene in his arms, René's booted foot caught the sheet, sending it flying toward the fire. In an instant it turned brown, burst into flames with a tiny, soft explosion, and was gone.

About the Author

Jennifer Blake was born near Goldonna, Louisiana, in her grand-parents' 120-year-old hand-built cottage. She grew up on an eighty-acre farm in the rolling hills of north Louisiana. While married and raising her children, she became a voracious reader. At last, she set out to write a book of her own. That first book was followed by thirty-six more, and today they have together reached over ten mil-lion copies in print, making Jennifer Blake one of the bestselling romance authors of our time. Her most recent novel is *Wildest Dreams*.

Jennifer and husband live near Quitman, Louisiana, in a house styled after Southern planters' cottages.

PRISONER OF DESIRE

To prevent the duel she was sure would kill her sister's fiancé, Anya Hamilton took as her prisoner the magnificently handsome Creole Ravel Duralde. But in a small, stark room on her lush Louisiana plantation, it was Anya who became Ravel's prisoner of passion and love.

ROYAL PASSION

Amid the color and music of a gypsy camp in the foothills of France, Mara Delacroix of Louisiana and Roderic, Prince of Ruthenia, met for the first time. Mara had to seduce Roderic, or her dear grandmother would suffer at the hands of the ruthless Nicholas de Landes. How could Mara know that passion would explode between them?

ROYAL SEDUCTION

Angeline was a beautiful, flame-haired innocent whose quiet life with her aunt was forever shattered when a prince came to town. A case of mistaken identity and a passionate interlude leaves Angeline a prisoner of desire, entangled in a prince's daring gamble.

SOUTHERN RAPTURE

Lettie Mason, a proper yet headstrong Boston schoolteacher, journeyed to a small Southern town to find and expose the wretched rogue—known as the Thorn—who'd killed her brother. The Thorn was a man with a reputation for both murder and mercy. How could Lettie reconcile these two different images of the same man and how could she accept the thrilling passion he aroused deep within her?

SURRENDER IN MOONLIGHT

From the moment they met and made love in a strange, deserted house, Lorna Forrester, a twenty-year-old New Orleans beauty, and Roman Cazenave, a daring blockade runner, were obsessed with each other. It was the beginning of an incredible adventure in danger and love ranging from the war-torn South to the lush Caribbean.

Contemporary romance from

JENNIFER BLAKE

JOY AND ANGER
Julie Bullard was one of Hollywood's rarest commodities—a female director. But could she shoot her newest movie with two different lovers on the set and someone threatening her life?

LOVE AND SMOKE
Poised and elegant, Riva Staulet's cool beauty still turns heads, but it had not always been that way. When Riva was Rebecca, the youngest of the poor but pretty Benson girls, she caught the eye of a charming young man of means. Now that man has his eye on the governor's mansion, and Riva will stop at nothing to avenge his cruel treatment of her years before—even if it means losing everything she has worked so hard for.